D1800066

JEREMIAH MAN

RUMOURS OF ANGELS

JEREMIAH MAN
RUMOURS OF ANGELS

STEPHEN NUTTALL

TATE PUBLISHING & *Enterprises*

TATE PUBLISHING
& Enterprises

Tate Publishing is committed to excellence in the publishing industry. Our staff of highly trained professionals, including editors, graphic designers, and marketing personnel, work together to produce the very finest books available. The company reflects the philosophy established by the founders, based on Psalms 68:11,

"THE LORD GAVE THE WORD AND GREAT WAS THE COMPANY OF THOSE WHO PUBLISHED IT."

If you would like further information, please contact us:
1.888.361.9473 | www.tatepublishing.com
TATE PUBLISHING & Enterprises, LLC | 127 E. Trade Center Terrace
Mustang, Oklahoma 73064 USA

Jeremiah Man: Rumours of Angels

Copyright © 2007 by Stephen Nuttall. All rights reserved.

No part of this publication may be reproduced, stored in a retrieval system or transmitted in any way by any means, electronic, mechanical, photocopy, recording or otherwise without the prior permission of the author except as provided by USA copyright law.

The opinions expressed by the author are not necessarily those of Tate Publishing, LLC.

This novel is a work of fiction. Names, descriptions, entitlies and incidents included in the story are products of the author's imagination. Any resemblance to actual persons, events and entities is entirely coincidental.

Book design copyright © 2007 by Tate Publishing, LLC. All rights reserved.
Cover design by Chris Webb
Interior design by Janae Glass

Published in the United States of America

ISBN: 978-1-5988691-6-3

06.12.20

CHAPTER ONE

It was a *dojo*. A place for training in martial arts. But the barefoot figure, dressed in black baggy trousers and a loose fitting tunic secured around the waist with a red cord, had no opponent.

Although it had assimilated techniques from the Japanese *judo* and *karate*, this Indian art of *thugee* could not be safely practiced with an *uke*, a partner. So it was done alone. And secretly. The moves were pure attack. Ruthless and deadly. Designed only for death. Sudden death by assassin.

The floor of the simple training hall was of aged oak, worn and polished to burnished smoothness by the relentless pounding feet of devotees down the years. The walls of bamboo, intertwined with fibre to keep out the elements of rain or scorching heat, completed the structure.

Hundreds of candles flickering against the backdrop of night provided the sole illumination, lighting up the massive stone effigy in the lotus position. Dominating the far wall, it stared down on the proceedings with sightless eyes. A terrifying looking woman. But more than just a woman. To her worshippers, she was a goddess. She was Kali.

And the practitioners of this shadowy cult were devoted to her, their goddess of death and destruction. For hundreds of years, in her name and as a holy ritual, they had practiced organised assassinations. Because she demanded blood and death.

Strangulation was the method, and they had claimed tens of thousands of victims over the three-hundred-year span of their existence. More ruthless and secret than even the legendary *Ninja*, they wormed their way into the confidence of their victims, infiltrating and gaining their trust. When a favourable opportunity occurred, they strangled them with their lethal killing cords.

Attempts were made to exterminate them, but they merely went underground and later their secrets were made available outside their birthplace to selected followers.

The *master* presently practising in the sacred hall was skilful beyond belief, his moves swift, powerful and lethal. Muscles rippling under his skin, he glided on bare feet in an intricate, elegant dance. Perfectly balanced, perfectly in control of body, mind and spirit. Dedicated to his art. Dedicated to his deity.

The *form* began with a crouching stance; then the cord around his waist was unleashed in a single fluid movement as though he were drawing a sword. A blur of motion, and in his hands it became a living thing. Flicking like a tongue of fire, it circled and spiralled before returning to his hand, the beauty and choreography of his movements belying the true purpose of the dance.

Having finished, he wiped the sweat from his face, bowed low before the deity and slipped silently out into the blackness of the night.

A few minutes passed before there was movement. Hiding in the shadows behind *her* statue had been a terrible risk. For to be discovered meant certain death.

But nevertheless the youngster had watched intently, determined to learn the art at all costs. A teenager, a *jakushou* with dark hair and wearing identical training clothes, the red cord around the slim waist identifying a fellow devotee.

Only after the *master* had left did the youngster take to the floor of that holy place and begin to emulate the moves observed and memorised in secret. At first slowly, then with ever increasing speed as the rhythm of the dance took over. That this *jakushou* was good, in fact more than that—exceptional—was not in doubt. In such young hands, the flowing of the red cord of mortality had a poignancy all of its own as it hummed in the air, flowing in the set *kata* moves of the dance. The dance of death.

CHAPTER TWO

CHRISTMAS EVE—TWENTY YEARS LATER

Shouting obscenities, the prisoner flung himself forward, grasping the policeman's throat in rage.

The response from police constable Jack Somerville was totally unexpected in its speed and ferocity. Executing a rough judo technique, he dropped below his assailant's centre of gravity, spinning him hard onto the stone floor of the charge room.

Unfortunately for the prisoner, the room had several metal pipes running along the wall. Perhaps more unfortunate was the fact that he was thrown face down onto them, his head driven forcibly by the full force of the officer's weight crushing onto him. With his fist a tight ball of calloused knuckle, he rained blow upon blow onto the head of the semi-conscious man, impervious to pain as his fist smashed into skull bone. A knuckle broke with an audible cracking sound.

There was shouting from somewhere. Somewhere outside his consciousness—muffled at first, then louder, followed by the sound of running feet. Unseen hands pulled him roughly away, forcing him out of the room. He struggled, his eyes bright with momentary madness, the veins on his forehead and neck standing out as adrenalin continued to pump. As far as he was concerned, it was not yet over.

Other officers were running to the prisoner who lay still, his body twisted in a heap on the floor. Unmoving.

Only when he had calmed, did he become aware of the pain. The broken knuckle had swollen to almost twice its normal size, and blood covered his blue shirt, his hand, his arm—and areas of the charge room wall.

Whether the blood was his or the prisoner's he didn't know. And he didn't particularly care. He was unaware. But the other officers saw it clearly. Something cold and detached and quite chilling.

Jack Somerville was smiling.

Despite the overhead florescent strip lights, an unnatural darkness had settled over the room like a mist. Seemingly unaffected by the oil-fired central heating pumping at full capacity, a cold chill swept in like an arctic breeze.

The boy's chest heaved painfully, his throat dry and harsh.

He was afraid. That in itself wasn't unusual. Because he'd spent most of his short life afraid. Afraid of many things. Of life. Of church. But above all, he was afraid of *him*.

Afraid of his demands. Burdens laid on him that were dark and evil. And the boy hated himself all over again as the thoughts clamoured in his troubled mind.

An expression of deep concentration came over his face as the constant babble of angry tongues tormented his mind as through an empty cavern of echoing sound. Hissing and urgent. Whispering and taunting.

It seemed that the voices had always been there, even in his dreams. Accusing, condemning, and shaming him with their accusations. But there was nowhere to hide from them. No escape from the cacophony that filled his mind, drawing him surely and relentlessly to the brink of madness.

He stood now on the very edge, staring into a chasm of blackness. He had been close before. But today was different from all other days.

Today, one voice spoke clearly and seductively in the labyrinths of his darkness. Soft, yet persuasive. Overwhelmingly irresistible. A voice that spoke above the wall of sound that filled his tormented mind.

He recognised that this was the time. This was the place. A phrase leapt into his mind.

"For such a time as this." He'd read it, or been told about it by someone. He couldn't remember where. But it didn't really matter. Nothing mattered now.

A low branch, sweeping gracefully down from an ancient oak, beckoned him, urging him forward. He climbed it easily, while demons of despair whispered into his ear their deceptive, evil words of hopelessness and utter loss.

Swiftly, with a sense of urgency lest his courage should fail him, he untied the rope from around his waist. Forming a loop at one end, he tied the other around the branch with sure knots. Leaning forward, he slipped his head into the noose, pulling it snugly around his neck.

The tongues inside the boy's anguished mind raved in a last frenzied babble of triumph as he pitched slowly forward into the silence he ached for.

Overhead, rain began to fall through the forest canopy in great tears of sorrow, releasing a dank smell of decayed leaves that wafted up from the sodden ground below.

She should have been asleep, but the four-year-old girl was finding it hard to settle. Especially when she could hear Christmas coming from the TV downstairs. It was Christmas Eve, and she was really excited.

As she snuggled into her teddy bear and tried to sleep, the radiance from the corner of the room found its way through her tightly shut eyelids, compelling her to open them. She stared, screwing up her eyes, because it was *very* bright. But she was not afraid.

She could hear the song filtering up from the lounge below her. It did sound beautiful. She could hear the words clearly, almost as if it was being sung especially for her.

"Glory be to God in the highest,
and on earth peace and goodwill to all men."

She stared at what seemed to be a man. But brighter. Different. He was dressed in a white robe with a golden belt looped around his waist, and she laughed when she saw that he was wearing sandals, and that his toenails were gold. As was his hair that hung down to the collar of his robe.

And he was so big! As he stood in the corner of her bedroom his head almost touched the ceiling.

She laughed shyly "You will have to bend down," she said, "or you will bump your head."

He smiled and reached out his hands to her. And she saw his eyes. The colour of the sky.

Climbing out of bed she ran towards him, feeling absolutely safe. He reached out a hand and touched her face. And when he spoke, his voice somehow reminded her of the sound a fast-flowing river made as it rushed and tumbled over rocks and stones.

She drew in her breath with a loud noise. "Are you Jesus?" she whispered sleepily.

He shook his head and smiled. And it was as if the sun had come out. "No. But I serve Him. When you grow older, do not forget."

Her childish mind couldn't understand at that moment, but deep in the secret place of her soul, a seed was planted.

"Good night," she whispered. "Happy Christmas." She clambered back into her bed. "Little Ted, can you see him? He is so *big*! Much bigger than daddy. And his eyes. Oh teddy, his eyes . . ."

The angel responded softly. "Be blessed, child of God. Remember, he is near to all who call on him."

Then the room reverberated with the sound of displaced air as two white wings unfurled from behind the angel and filled the room. Standing beside her as her eyelids fluttered in sleep, he spread them gently over her in a protective canopy.

Leaning close, he spoke beautiful words into her heart. Gentle, soothing, holy words from the father heart of God. And as he did so, the little girl fell into a deep, peaceful sleep.

The young child wouldn't remember much the next morning. As a dream that vanishes like vapour when the sleeper awakes, she soon forgot her encounter with the angel. As the years fled before her, and she grew into a young teenager, her life was full. Busy. Filled with the stuff of the world. So much in life to do. Vital things. So vital, so important, that soon the memory receded further and further into the deep recesses of her mind.

Until it was as if it had never been.

CHAPTER THREE

Detective Sergeant Jack Somerville lounged at his desk in the CID block on the top floor of Hartwood Police Station. He was reading the latest crime "stats," and they didn't make good reading.

He looked away for a moment, interlacing his fingers and stretching them palm outwards with a sigh. He wished he had something more inspiring to read. Like his Sherlock Holmes novels, ranged neatly in the bookcase under the window without a trace of irony alongside the dry legal textbooks of his profession. He was an avid Holmes fan. The difference between him and Holmes was that the great detective solved crimes. Mostly all Jack did was to record them. Detection was something that didn't happen that often. His title was Ds, Detective Sergeant. But he might just as well have been an administration clerk.

When he had first joined the "plain clothes" branch, he had yearned for the opportunity to investigate crimes of the type that the fictional detective came across every day. Cerebral crimes. But the reality was that nearly all was brutal, unthinking, on-the-spur-of-the-moment type stuff. Little planning went into the offences that he dealt with, and after thirty years he had yet to come up against a "Moriarty" type adversary.

He took a sip of unsweetened white coffee from a blue and orange "Simpsons" mug depicting Homer throttling Bart, and flicked to the page headed "Burglary." There was a definite trend in social nuisance crime. Criminal damage—especially broken windows and graffiti had doubled in just a couple of months. Drunkenness amongst young people was up by a third, and physical assaults classified as Actual Bodily Harm or ABH, had risen by a similar amount.

He laid down his pen and flexed his fingers again, painfully. He had a real problem with his knuckles; arthritis probably, and they played up on occasions. More so lately. He'd tried many remedies, even physiotherapy, but nothing seemed to make much difference. He was now resigned to it, a minor inconvenience admittedly.

From outside in the station yard came the sound of a car engine starting up, followed by the yelp of the siren. As it accelerated away on a response call, he reflected on new technology and the march of so-called progress. When he was a young Pc, they had called the sirens "blues and twos," but the two-tone horn with its familiar sound had now gone—replaced by the American style siren sound of "yelps," "howls" and "wails." Too much like *Hill Street Blues,* he thought sourly.

He cursed loudly as he caught himself doing exactly what he had promised he would never do. "Swinging the lamp," thinking back to the good old days, which had really never existed, except perhaps in his imagination. As a young Copper he had derided the old boys with their *Dixon of Dock Green* wistfulness and their tales of past glories, comparing the modern age very unflatteringly with how things were when they joined up.

The clock above his desk showed it was a little after 5:30pm on a typically wet, late December evening. The sun had long ago vanished over the horizon and other than the pollution from the epidemic of sodium street lights, darkness had fallen like a blanket over Hartwood.

He switched on the desk-top lamp, reading through the crime reports yet again. What was it that had caused Hartwood to change so much in such a relatively short space of time? What could account for the alarming rise in crime, anger and hate?

He stared at the calendar pinned to the wall above his desk. December 25th, Christmas Day, was ringed in red biro. It was just a few days off—the date of his retirement from the "Force" after thirty years of hard policing. And he was dreading it! The police was his life. But only because there was precious little outside for him.

From the décor of his office, no one would have guessed that it was Christmas. There was not a trace of festivity in his office. No cards adorned the walls. Or his desk. No cheerful streamers or tokens of the season hung from the ceiling.

Jack's office was always utilitarian. He didn't permit himself much in the way of gadgets, or "stuff" as he called it, cluttering up the place. But this time of all times, it seemed especially barren. Christmas had not touched his office. Which merely reflected the reality that Christmas had not touched Jack Somerville. His office was the outward and visible expression of the inward, although not entirely invisible, condition of his heart.

For him, it was a day like any other day. It would pass by unnoticed and unwanted, just as the last few Christmases had. He had worked through them, and he fully intended to work through this one too.

His colleagues didn't necessarily mean to be cruel, but they didn't understand his antipathy towards, what for them was a time of eating, drinking and being merry. Especially the drinking part. So they found it amusing to wish him "Merry Christmas" on as many occasions as they thought they could get away with. No-one was offered the season's greetings more than Jack was.

Initially it had provoked an angry response, but now he just accepted their tormenting with silent stoicism. It somewhat took the fun out of the game, but Jack's colleagues were nothing if not persistent.

He was an intelligent man, and widely read. So had he thought about it, which he didn't, he would have seen a parallel between himself and a Dickensian character with a similar disregard for festive cheer. But such analogous literary niceties were far from his thoughts.

He walked across the worn carpet to the window facing the street. It was a small office and it took him just six strides. Lifting the sash window he leaned out, oblivious to the icy wind that blasted in, lifting papers from his desk and scattering them untidily across the room.

That same disparaging wind brought further unwelcome reminders, as the teasing strains of a brass band crossed the mile or so of intervening space from the High Street and floated Christmas carols up to him in ironic spitefulness. He sighed. There was no escape from it, but he comforted himself with the thought that the madness would soon be over, and everyone would return to sanity. Until the next time.

Out of view, the streets heaved with the surging mass of humanity doing the last of its Christmas shopping. Coloured festive lights and gaudy tinsel, paid for by the traders in the hope of boosting their profits by the generation of sentimentalism were laced in the branches of the trees that lined the streets. Still more were draped in shop-front windows. All of them twinkling their promise of Christmas yet to come.

A commercial, spendthrift one undoubtedly. But that seemed to be what people wanted. Even an unashamedly money-driven celebration brought an anticipation of excitement and joy to most. An escape from the rat-race and the drudgery of a grey, totally predictable and dull life.

Fat plastic Santas sat alongside animated singing snowmen, elves, dwarves and fairies. A pantheon of mythical characters had replaced the baby in the manger. Peace on earth and goodwill to all mankind had been eclipsed by the marketing men and their relentless pressure on consumers to buy bigger and better presents than they had the year before. So it was the cash registers that rang joyously throughout the land, not the good news of the Christ child. The only heralding was that of another year of bumper profit. Absent were the tidings of great joy that the angels brought that very first Christmas Morning, the miracle of the baby in the manger all but forgotten.

But still the hearts of the recipients of lavish baubles would glow with happiness on Christmas morning. Because they knew no different.

There would be those who would pause sometime after lunch—just before vegetating in front of the TV for the afternoon—and wonder why they felt so let down. The so-called wonder of Christmas had yet again failed to materialise, and they were left bemused and disappointed that the event that had promised so much had in the end delivered so little. Wasn't there meant to be more than just eating and drinking? Wasn't there a story about angels and shepherds that used to play a part in the festivities? Sadly, most would not pursue the answer beyond the next glass of drink and mince pie, and an apathetic and anaesthetised world slowly and heedlessly descended into an eternity of separation from God.

With its restaurants and pubs replete with their *de rigueur* gaudy neon signs, Hartwood now was reminiscent of a brassy seafront promenade. That was part of the problem. Even three years ago the town had been a family place. Somewhere where you could take your children in the evening for chicken and chips without facing torrents of abuse. Or worse.

On the surface it was a pleasant place. Nice houses, good schools, plenty of shops. It was considered to be up-market, and people would travel in from the surrounding areas to take advantage of what it had to offer.

There had been a settlement there ever since Roman times and the River Marr which flowed through it had been instrumental in the town's prosperity, bringing trade and merchants from all over England.

It was just a shallow trickle now, compared to what it had been in its glory days, littered with broken metal trolleys from the nearby supermarket, dumped there by the youths when they had tired of playing around with them.

Unwise, some would say irresponsible, town planning had led to a rash of drinking and eating places that now smothered the community atmosphere. It had attracted a new breed of people with too much disposable income and too little sense of responsibility

Most evenings it would be buzzing from early evening. And then the fighting would start, followed by the attendant string of ambulances to pick up the pieces.

Before all this, Jack had regularly taken his two boys to the takeaway at Friday teatime. Clutching the hot delicious packages, they would go to the police station to eat them, and afterwards they would play snooker for a while. The boys loved the atmosphere, and most of the police officers knew them by name and enjoyed telling them hair raising stories of exciting chases and arrests that they had made. Jamie especially had loved that, and at nine-years-old, just a year older than his brother Andrew, he was already contemplating a life in the "Job."

Jack felt the familiar stab of grief, almost physical in its intensity, and groaned involuntarily as it scythed through him. His eyes became blurred; the street sounds faded into the background as the thoughts that haunted all his waking and most of his sleeping moments engulfed him in a tidal wave of despair.

A life in the police was not to be for Jamie. In fact there was to be no life. The car accident three years previously had seen to that when he had died alongside his brother, Andrew.

Jack too, had died that day. His joy had gone, sucked out in a moment of time, leaving nothing behind but a sterile vacuum. Now his life was arid and parched. As dry as the dust that blew through the wasteland of his heart.

He regularly told himself to get a grip, well aware of the emptiness of his existence. But so far he hadn't had much success and the hole in his life and in his heart remained a void that stubbornly refused to be filled.

Certainly not by the irritating jingle of Christmas songs, the twinkling of fairy lights and the laughter of excited children. The laughter of children especially. That was like a cheese-grater scraping across his hurting soul.

The boys had loved Christmas time. And Jack and his wife had even gone to church with them as a family on Christmas Day. Okay, it was a duty. He wasn't a believer. But somehow it was enjoyable. And the trudge back home afterwards for Christmas lunch was a highlight of the day. Not just because of the food that his wife Susan would prepare. But because they didn't open their presents until after lunch. It was a family tradition. And the excitement, from Jack as much as the boys, was almost irrepressible.

Their eyes bright with anticipation, they almost dragged him back home along the street from church. And he had teased them by going even slower than usual, until even he could bear it no longer, and they had run madly together the last few hundred yards, laughing and falling through the front door in their excitement.

He'd tried drink. Whisky for a while. Then wine, then beer. Copious amounts of it. But while drinking himself unconscious had helped at the time, afterwards the ache of emptiness and loss would still be with him.

He'd been no help to Susan, who'd been struggling with her own grief. He'd been too selfish to understand her needs. And he blamed her for the deaths, continually reminding her that she was at fault, because she had been driving the family car at the time.

She had been badly injured in the accident, and that had changed her. When she eventually came out of hospital she was a stranger. No longer the happy, bubbling extrovert woman he had married. She had become a sad, introverted invalid sitting around the house all day, refusing to go outside. She neglected the housework, did no cooking, and Jack had been forced to take on these responsibilities in addition to his demanding work. And he hated untidiness with a passion.

So the quarrelling and recriminations had festered and grown, fuelled by his condemnation and Susan's own self-loathing. Even when he didn't reproach her, the accusing look constantly in his eyes spoke eloquently enough.

She said she couldn't remember anything about the crash, although she often awoke in the night, screaming. She had visited psychiatrists on so many occasions, but they had all come to the same conclusion.

Dr. Iverson was the last of the doctors that Jack had spent a small fortune on. As far as he was concerned they had all been quacks. Part of him wasn't even sure if Susan really did suffer from amnesia. He wondered if she was deliberately hiding something. Dr. Iverson had said it was psychosomatic. Jack's opinion was that Dr. Iverson was psychosomatic.

"My dear," the learned man had said in that doctoral way, a mixture of contempt and aloofness, "the brain is a very delicate organ with areas about which we still know very little. Often when an individual experiences severe trauma as in your case, the mind just shuts down. The memories are so terrifying, so dreadful, that the mind refuses even to acknowledge them."

"Will I ever get my memory back?" she had asked.

"Can't say," was the doctor's response. "Sometimes one can go on for years. Then, suddenly, it all comes flooding back."

Things just got worse between them. Eventually they stopped speaking, and lived different lives. They became strangers and eventually the love that they had had for each other died. A slow, painful, wasting death.

Jack came home from work one day to find a note on the kitchen table. She had left him, leaving no forwarding address.

The drinking stopped some months later. He'd been unable to cope, not only with the headaches, but the fact that he was loosing his grip on reality. So now he spent his spare time, what little he had when he wasn't working, shut up in his flat. He'd sold up and moved out of the house after Susan had left.

He tried not to have too much time on his hands, and worked as much as he could. But inevitably he had to return to his lonely home. All he had now were cherished memories. Memories of a once happy and fulfilled life with a wonderful wife and two beautiful boys.

Time had moved on and he occasionally wondered what Susan was doing. There had been no contact since she had left. They had not divorced, and he had never thought to do so. He sighed deeply, and had a sudden overwhelming urge to be somewhere else. Somewhere with people. Somewhere where there were the smells, sights and sounds of everyday life. On impulse, he slammed the window down and headed for the canteen for another coffee, even though he didn't really need it.

His empty office inexplicably darkened as if heavy drapes had been pulled, cutting out the streetlight. In the stillness, Bart and Homer separated in mid-strangle, as the mug on his desk cracked into two separate halves, spilling dregs of cold coffee across the crime "stats."

Outside the window, a ball of intense white light played softly over the tops of the poplar trees that stretched from the traffic block to the community safety building.

CHAPTER FOUR

Laser beams in a myriad of colours played across the auditorium, illuminating the diffused interior and creating a frisson of excitement and anticipation. Over a thousand people were packed into the main body of the auditorium for the morning meeting, the more energetic worshippers having commandeered the top rows of the tiered seats running from ceiling to floor.

The place had the appearance and feel of opulence. Here, no expense was spared, as well-upholstered seats of maroon cloth vied with a mass of toning, thick piled carpet flowing in all directions from the centre of the hall.

Two huge Christmas trees planted in great ceramic pots stood grandly either side of a raised platform, their tips almost touching the ceiling fifty-feet above. Dressed with exact precision, immaculate in coloured lights, tinsel and assorted decorations they shimmered under the remorseless onslaught of the laser lighting.

A TV crew stood in readiness to record the proceedings for the next international religious TV slot. Cameramen methodically checked and focussed cameras. Light and sound professionals spoke urgently into headworn, cardioid condenser microphones as they went about their business.

Situated to the front above the raised platform, hung a huge screen. It was onto this that the image of Apostle Benedict Ademola would be projected during the meeting, ensuring that those seated at the rear would not miss the blessing.

Enthusiastic young men scurried to and fro with clipboards tucked under their arms and headphones settled comfortably around their necks. Lengths of electrical cable trailed and plug-in jacks swung from their ends. The air of busyness and expectation was tangible.

A fifty-strong choir grouped in a half circle and dressed in deep red robes sang swaying to the music. Silver amulets hung around their necks on red silk bands oscillated in time to their movement.

Bass and tenor male voices first took up the chorus, then the female altos and trebles soaring above them, culminating with an interweaving of their voices in a complex musical arrangement.

Their voices rose to a crescendo as they neared the end of a song of exhortation, and as they faded, the lights were suddenly and dramatically extinguished in the auditorium. A spotlight illuminated the stage, weaving figures of eight, and the crowd began to clap. Faster and faster danced the light in a frenzy of rhythm that was echoed by the devotees now clapping in time as they rose spontaneously to their feet. Then just as the noise and light reached an almost unbearable pitch, the music ceased and the spotlight was extinguished simultaneously.

For a long moment there was total darkness. Total silence.

High up in the roof it seemed, a solitary horn began to sound; a second took up the call, then a third and yet still others echoing and reverberating around the hall. Heralding the imminent presence of greatness.

The crowd stood in silence, as a moment of fearful reverence fell upon them. And then something touched them. Perhaps it was just a feeling, but something other-worldly, something that they could not easily describe draped itself around them like a cloak. Undetected by most in that place, unwholesomeness came near.

A single pool of light from a spotlight positioned on a metal gantry, hit the stage. The heavy drapes were hoisted upwards and away. And the man that they were waiting for, Apostle Benedict Ademola stepped onto the platform and into the spotlight.

Hartwood Community Church, situated prominently on a corner plot in the centre of the town of Hartwood had been there for nearly fifty years. It had started with a membership of just twenty committed souls, and had grown progressively over the years to its present two hundred members. Most were in their twenties to fifties, but there was a sizeable children's presence and a handful of faithful old saints in their eighties and nineties.

The building was quite plain, the interior walls painted in a cream wash. There were no altars, no statues of saints and no stained glass. In fact there were no trappings of religion at all. The only items that identified this place as a meeting hall for the church were the two embroidered banners hanging on the wall behind the lectern positioned on a low platform at the front.

One proclaimed, "If I speak in the tongues of men and of angels, but have not love, I am only a resounding gong or a clanging cymbal. If I have the gift of prophecy and can fathom all mysteries and all knowledge, and if I have a faith that can move mountains, but have not love, I am nothing."

The other was an embroidery of the Lord Jesus with the words underneath, "And they sang a new song: You are worthy to take the scroll and to open its seals, because you were slain, and with your blood you purchased men for God from every tribe and language and people and nation."

A beige ribbed carpet that had been in place for as long as most could remember, covered the floor. It was old but spotlessly clean.

It was Sunday morning, and the hall was filled with light and colour. A Christmas tree, decked in coloured lights and decorations, filled a corner at the front. Strategically arrayed candles flickered invitingly as a CD player delivered gentle carols to the half-empty church.

It was 10:20am and the service was due to begin in ten minutes time. But Pastor Marcus Bentley was not perturbed by the empty spaces. Every since he and his wife Lissette had been called to this place by God some ten years previously, he had grown accustomed to what was known as "Hartwood Time."

"Hartwood Time," was peculiar to this church family. If a meeting was scheduled for half-past, then the church would assemble at that time and not a moment before. Every Sunday it was the same—right up to the last moment—a cause of alarm to visiting speakers, but at the appointed time every seat would be taken.

For some reason today, they were more than usually overcrowded with new faces. Marcus was slightly worried by that. If the influx of people continued, there would be standing room only by the time the service started.

He was a conservative minister. He liked to be thought of as a "plain old-fashioned" type of preacher. He loved God to the best that he was able, he loved the Bible, which he believed was God's Word for today, and he taught the truth of that Word as best he could. He sometimes wished that he could hear God more. To receive guidance. To know what to do in difficult circumstances. But he knew that God didn't act like that anymore.

In Bible times, the people heard God speak in many different ways. He spoke through dreams, in an audible voice, through prophets and angels as well as through scripture.

But God didn't speak to his people today. After he gave the Bible he stopped communicating. True, he still spoke through the scriptures—on rare occasions amazingly so, and Marcus cherished the times that he had experienced this. But he increasingly felt that something was missing in his life.

He often watched the faces of his flock as they filed in on Sunday mornings, wondering what direction the church was heading in. What were the plans that God had for their lives? Was there a direction anyway? He used to think that there was a purpose, but latterly he wasn't sure where he was heading himself, let alone where he was meant to be leading the church.

His wife, usually referred to as Lissie, was sitting at the front engaged in conversation with one of the young mothers. She stopped for a moment as she caught his eye and smiled, before returning to where she had left off. Despite the smile, the hint of anguish in her eyes would have revealed to the discerning observer that there were unresolved issues in their lives.

She was an attractive, brown haired woman in her late twenties, this morning dressed in dark blue trousers and a matching loose fitting jumper. A keep-fit adherent alternating between the gym and serious walking, the years of conscious good living showed in her easy movement and healthy complexion.

He was slim, in fact probably too slim. A bit more fat wouldn't have hurt him. His dark hair was cropped close, and he wore wire framed spectacles low on his nose. He was dressed in a dark suit as was his habit when preaching on Sunday morning, believing that he owed a duty to his flock to make an effort when at the front.

Looking out, he saw that three of his four elders were in their usual places. There was Michael Reed, the oldest at sixty-five. He had been retired from his accountancy practice for some years now. He was a quiet, softly spoken man with grey hair, most of which he had managed to retain. Although he would never set the place alight spiritually, he had a wealth of wisdom that had many times been a blessing to the church. He sat next to Grace, his wife of almost forty-five years. She was his exact opposite in almost every way. He was grey; she still had dark brown hair. He was quiet and reserved, she was excitable and vocal. He was conservative, she was charismatic. He dressed in a smart grey suit that added the right tone of gravitas to his slim five foot ten inch frame. She dressed casually in trousers and a loose cotton top.

Michael had problems with the changes that had been happening in the church, but Grace couldn't wait for the new things that she believed God was bringing in.

At the back of the church sat Phil Sellars. At forty, he was the youngest of the elders. He was a short man who struggled constantly to keep his weight under control. He had tried nearly every diet known to man in an attempt to recapture the physique he had had as a twenty-something. Currently he was doing "Atkins," which caused Jenny his wife alarm and despondency.

She was a nurse, and she couldn't see that eating sausages and bacon every morning could possibly be good for him. She was trim and blond, ate fruit at nearly every meal time, and drank copious amounts of water instead of tea.

On the left of the aisle sat Steve Coleman. He worked at the Home Office, but he never talked much about his job. Everyone assumed that the reason was because it was either very secret, or very boring. He was in his early forties, and was a widower, his wife having died suddenly from a short illness some three years earlier.

He had a good-looking young daughter in her teens who had infrequently attended church in the past when Janet was alive. She never attended now, and that was no surprise to anyone who knew her father. With Steve devoid of any Christian joy and dead as a dried up stick, what would she ever see in his life that would attract her to the church?

He never talked about his daughter, and it was common knowledge that she wasn't living a good life. In a rare unguarded moment, he had confessed that they rarely spoke to each other, something that caused him much pain.

He had never been the life-and-soul-of-the-party type, having a propensity to dourness. But since the death of his wife, who had meant everything to him, he had become insufferable. He attended church on Sunday and met with the other elders each week, but he was a more of a hindrance than a help.

He had become an irritant in the side, to put it mildly. Marcus had once said that he should start a branch of the "Seek it and Stop it" club, because whatever the other elders proposed, Steve would be totally against it. He was the professional adversary. Anti change, anti anything new.

Just the previous week, elders Phil, Michael, Billy Southgate and Marcus had met privately to discuss the situation about him. They felt guilty meeting behind his back, but the situation would have been impossible with him present.

It was time for him to step down, but they knew they would have a battle on their hands. He had become a champion for the handful of embittered church members who found change distasteful. In Steve they had a kindred spirit, and supported him whenever there was a church forum. Removing him from eldership would be an unpleasant and potentially divisive task.

Quite a few other people were standing and talking; half-a-dozen young children ran around, laughing and chasing each other and an excited hubbub of chattering voices filled the hall.

Henry Carson, an elderly man in his mid-eighties, was smiling and chatting. He had been an elder in his previous church, but the congregation had dwindled to such a small number that it had no longer been financially viable to keep going. Reluctantly the handful of members had dispersed, and the building sold off. Henry had transferred to Hartwood because it was near to where he lived. It was a nice block of flats directly opposite, which was a real godsend as Henry's health was becoming increasingly problematic and he was starting to feel his age. He now walked with difficulty using a stick.

His wife, Ruby, had died a few years previously. They had been married for sixty years and he still missed her terribly. He had been broken-hearted, and had never really recovered from the loss. But that didn't stop his godly nature from shining through and he was dearly loved by the church.

Then there was Marie Barrington. Aged sixty, she carried herself well, dressed smartly, and could have passed for at least ten years younger. She was a feisty, capable woman who didn't suffer fools gladly. She had lived alone since her husband, a doctor, had left her for a younger woman some twenty years previously. But she certainly wasn't one to sit around and waste time moping.

One of her passions was the Law. She was a local Magistrate with a reputation for being firm In fact the local criminally inclined would say that that was something of an understatement. They knew her to be absolutely ruthless in passing sentence, and they both disliked her and respected her with equal intensity.

Her other passion was God. She loved Him with all her heart, and devoured his Word ravenously. She loved the way that God spoke to her from the Bible. The Word seemed to have an answer for every problem of life. She carried it with her everywhere, even into the courtroom. To prevent awkward questions, she had taken the covering off of another book and slipped her Bible inside. The new cover was a strong, dark blue one. Gold lettering tooled on the spine proclaimed it to be *Stones Justice's Manual*. So no one queried the fact that she consulted it quite a lot!

Although it was not unusual to see new faces, because God was blessing that little church and had been adding to its number for some years, today was different. Today there were not just a couple of visiting people, or a new family of mum, dad and children. Today for some reason a large group of men women and children had appeared.

Marcus caught the eye of Billy Southgate who had just wandered in. A balding, slim man in his early fifties with spectacles, Billy quietly joined him in the milling area outside the hall. With his slight build, the pastor seemed diminutive standing alongside him. He gave Billy a hug, from which he recoiled slightly. He wasn't much of a touchy feely kind of guy.

"Happy Christmas," said the pastor.

"Same to you, Marcus."

"Where on earth have all the new people come from this morning, Billy?" He quickly got to the point. The elder could be a bit garrulous and there wasn't time for much extensive talk that morning.

Billy was concerned, a frown furrowing his forehead. "Not sure, but it's a good problem to have more people. I think they're from the place up the road. You know, Benedict Ademola's church. I have heard that there have been difficulties and some families have been chucked out."

He seemed to be on the verge of saying more, so Marcus quickly moved on as diplomatically as he could. "I don't like this at all. There have been rumblings from the leaders of the other churches about the 'difficulties' as you call them, for some time."

"Do you want me to speak to the new people?"

"Okay, if you don't mind, after the service. Keep it low-key though. We don't want to make too much of it at the moment. Just welcome them—you know what to do."

"Do you think you should go to see Benedict? I could come with you as a bit of support . . . ?"

Marcus acted like he hadn't heard the offer. Billy could be a bit quick tempered, something that he desperately tried to control, and God had been working on him. But he was the last person needed when visiting Ademola.

"Believe it or not the, 'First Church of God' is about to become 'Benedict Ademola Ministries,'" continued Billy. "Seems he can't resist seeing his name splashed all over the place."

Marcus stopped, surprised. "Really? Benedict Ademola Ministries?" He laughed.

"Be careful," said Billy. "I've heard bad things about him. He's ruthless and horrible things happen to those who fall out with him."

Marcus shrugged it off and clapped his friend on the back, before stepping inside the meeting hall. He half-turned. "Don't you worry my friend. It's time we got the service underway." Then he was gone, swallowed up by the assembly of worshippers. Billy stood staring after him for a moment, and the frown across his forehead deepened noticeably.

"Billy?"

He looked up, startled. "Marie—sorry, I was thinking."

She smiled. "That's okay." She sounded a little embarrassed, which was most unlike her.

He raised his eyebrows. "What can I do for you?"

"I feel a bit awkward. I've not done this before." She handed him a folded piece of paper. "I know we don't do this in church usually, and I know that Marcus frowns on it. But would you read this? I think it's a word from God."

He was surprised. "I'm not sure if I'm the right person for this?"

"God said it was for you."

Billy took it reluctantly. He hated it when people used the term "God said." It was spiritual blackmail. Because he knew that God didn't speak. "Uhm, thanks . . ." he said.

As Marie hurried away, Billy unfolded it with one hand and glanced sceptically down. It confirmed his view. It was a bit of pointless nonsense that made absolutely no sense. Scrawled on the paper was a scripture reference, not a familiar one. He thought he might look it up at some time, but not right then. Shaking his head sadly, he stuffed it into his top pocket as music began to issue from inside the hall. A Word from God? Hah!

At10:30, right on time, the church was full. In fact it was over-full as Marcus had feared, and a dozen or so people had to stand with their backs against the rear wall of the hall, whilst a handful loitered in the corridor, peering quizzically through the double doors.

The music group, who had been outside praying before the service, returned. James Caruthers, the worship leader, caught the eye of young Richard on the sound desk and made the motion which meant, "Is my mike on?"

Having received an affirmative, he scratched his beard before leaning into the microphone, strumming gently on his guitar.

"We extend a really warm welcome to you all this morning, in this week leading up to Christmas. If you are a visitor, then you are especially welcome, and we hope that you enjoy your time with us. We are here, to praise Jesus, to bring our worship to Him who alone is worthy of all our praise. To look forward to Christmas Day when we celebrate his birth."

James was a large, solidly built man with a stature that belied his sensitive nature. As he scanned the expectant faces in front of him, he whispered a silent prayer in his heart. "Father, send your Spirit. Touch the lives of your people in this place. Be especially close to those who desperately need to feel your touch at this time. Help those of us who lead, to minister your love and grace to those who are hurting, to those who are desperate for truth and meaning in life. Turn your people once again to you. As the hearts and minds of many look across the world at this time to that small town of Bethlehem, help them, as wise men did so long ago, to search and to find you."

The flute, the piano, the bass guitar and the drums joined in as James began to play his guitar and sing, the congregation joining in as the words flashed up on the white screen at the front. It was just a simple, well-known carol. But somehow that morning, it took on a new meaning, a significance and a power that touched the hearts of worshippers hungry for God.

O little town of Bethlehem
How still we see thee lie
Above thy deep and dreamless sleep
The silent stars go by.
Yet in thy dark streets shineth
The everlasting light
The hope and fears of all the years
Are met in thee tonight

All James could see was a sea of faces before him, upturned in adoration; hearts full of praise for the Lord that they loved. There were some that morning who had never experienced such unpretentious, heartfelt worship. And the Holy Spirit was touching them, just as James had prayed that he would. The new people had known large choirs, professional slickness and huge congregations. But this was the first time that they had had a real encounter with God. A God of love and grace; a God of compassion. A God of freedom.

Many eyes were damp, and tears of joy rolled unashamedly down their cheeks. There was a reality, a life in that place that so many in the world yearned for but tragically so few found.

So that morning, in that simple church in the midst of worship, the people brought their fears and their uncertainties, their sadness, their pain and their hope, and committed it all to the one who came to earth as a helpless baby in a stable, but who grew up to change the world and draw all mankind to himself.

CHAPTER FIVE

The woman was dreaming. A vivid dream. There was a wood. All that she could see were trees. Trees that surrounded her on all sides with wet, clinging tendrils reaching down, clutching at her hair and face in a clammy embrace.

For some reason she felt afraid. A fear that cut deep into her bones, chilling her and triggering her instinct to run. To flee. To get away. But where to? Because the trees were everywhere, stretching into the distance on all sides.

And then there was the noise. At first just a whisper. But gradually the volume grew and the sound intensified until she realised with rising panic that she was hearing laughter. But not like any laughter she had ever heard before. This laughter was totally humourless. Demonic. Evil.

It was the *sound* of depravity. Growing louder all the time.

She realised with a churning in the pit of her stomach what this meant. Whatever this corruption was, it was coming closer . . .

Apostle Dr. Benedict Ademola raised a hand, the one holding the black leather King James Bible, in acknowledgement of the rapturous applause he was receiving from his people. In the process, his jacket sleeve rode up his outstretched arm exposing his gold Rolex watch. On his finger a ring of gold set with a black stone motif sparkled under the lights.

He walked lightly forward, surprisingly so for such a large man, the spotlight following like a dog on a leash. A light tan, tailor-made suit had a remarkably slimming effect, but even the best tailor was unable to disguise the fact that here was a corpulent man, a man used to the best things in life. It was fine food, and not exercise or restraint that had moulded this man. He was well over six-foot and even without the razzmatazz of lights and trumpet calls, he would be an imposing sight. But the most striking thing about him was his eyes. His face smiled a lot—at least his lips adopted the smiling position and his face and eyes crinkled as they fell into a semblance of geniality. But there was no vestige of warmth there.

It was his eyes that betrayed him. If the eyes are the windows of the soul, then the Lord help him. Because his were grey, cold, and lifeless.

He spoke in a deliberate and measured voice, wasting no time with preliminaries.

"I am saddened to have to bring you this news. I desire to bring you blessings, but the Lord is leading me to speak words of rebuke at this time." He paused for effect. "There are those in our fellowship who are divisive. There are those who have fallen away and are no longer in the truth."

There was a murmur from the masses gathered before him as he brought his right hand up to his chest to cover his heart, sighing loudly.

"As much as it pains me, we have no choice but to disfellowship them, lest they taint all of us." Gazing out at his captive audience, his face reflected both compassion and a resigned acceptance of the frailty of men. "I am hurting," he uttered. "This betrayal strikes at our heart. But how can two walk together unless they are in agreement?"

There was a rustle of agreement from the audience.

Taking a sheet of folded paper from the top pocket of his jacket, he opened it and read out a list of some thirty names, pausing now and then as a particularly well-known one was announced. "Many of you have called these people your friends. You have fellowshipped with them and your children have attended school with their children. Many of you were in business with them." He deliberately spoke in the past tense as he made these observations and nods of assent and collective "yeses" were heard.

He glided to the front of the platform, his cold eyes roving across the auditorium. The silence was total. "Have I the need to explain what we must do?" The camera zoomed in, highlighting the action on the screen. "They are the tares amongst the wheat. The only way to deal with tares is to rip them out before they contaminate the whole crop."

Here the camera closed in until only his face was visible and the pain in his eyes could be clearly seen. His voice quavered with emotion. "What hurts us the most is the sense of loss." The camera panned out to a full length shot once again. "Sheep that we nurtured, sheep that we took to our hearts and loved—all gone."

His voice strengthened. "But we will deal immediately and decisively with this issue. You will find it beneficial to cease all friendships and business relationships at once with those that I have disfellowshipped. Your children must cease amity with the children of the tares."

Benedict paused and his eyes bored into the congregation. "I have already made the necessary arrangements to have them removed from amongst us." He paused a moment, and brushed dust from the sleeve of his jacket. "They have lied. They have made false accusations against me. But you, beloved, know the truth. I am loved around the world by millions. I have an international ministry!"

Opening his Bible, he quoted: "Wherefore come out from among them, and be ye separate, saith the Lord, and touch not the unclean thing; and I will receive you."

He laid the Bible aside. "Come out my friends, whether it is business or friendship. Separate ye from the tares. What doth darkness have to do with light?"

He sounded angry. "They said that we held them captive. But we never tried to keep them by force!" he shouted. "If they had come to us we would have let them go with our blessing. But they have gone behind our backs. They have gone to tiny, so-called churches. Churches that are *nothing* in this town."

The lights in the auditorium brightened, the camera zoomed in for a close up shot of the apostle. He lifted a hand to his forehead as he listened for God's voice. "Enough! Let us now look to the Lord, asking him to confirm his presence by the working of miracles, signs and wonders. This morning, you will see what God can do for you."

As stewards began to move amongst the assembly, the choir moved back on stage and began singing softly—a song about the miracle of healing.

"There is someone here this morning who has been in a wheelchair for many years. God is saying that he wants to restore them." A handful of people in wheelchairs scattered throughout the auditorium appeared hopeful for a moment, only to have those hopes dashed, as Benedict Ademola pointed to a middle-aged woman near to the front in a battery operated wheelchair. "Stewards, bring that person to me."

The worship had drawn to a close and Marcus Bentley was at the lectern. "Before I speak this morning my friends, bow your heads with me and let's pray together." He closed his eyes and the congregation followed suit.

"Father, the Psalmist says,
'You have searched me
and you know me.
You know when I sit and when I rise;
you perceive my thoughts from afar.
You discern my going out and my lying down;
you are familiar with all my ways.'"

He paused a moment, before continuing. "This morning Father," he said, "you know how hard I find it to speak about your Glory. I guess I feel much the same as Simon Peter did that day when he saw you on the shores of the Sea of Galilee and cried out, 'Go away from me, Lord; I am a sinful man.'"

Marcus could not look at his congregation and kept his eyes fixed firmly on the floor. His heart was heavy with the burden of the sin he was carrying. "I know that I am inadequate," he prayed. "My words are insufficient. But I thank you that your word does not leave your mouth empty. It *always* accomplishes that which you desire. You work despite our efforts, not because of them, and as you take the darkest night and turn it into glorious day so you take drab, clumsy and graceless words and give them brilliance, colour and life."

He lifted his head. "Father, take the plain, ordinary caterpillar that is my life, and turn it into a beautiful butterfly. This morning, you know that I all I have to offer are plain words. But the prayer of my heart is that you would take them and turn them into something beautiful for you. Amen."

He preached that morning on the Birth of Jesus. The ancient story of the shepherds in the field, who were filled with dread as they heard the angels singing. And of the wise men who had journeyed so far in search of a King.

"Two thousand years ago," he said, "wise men came in search of a King. Not just any King, but the one who was born to be the saviour of the world." He lifted his eyes to look at his flock. "Today, wise men and women still search for that same King . . ."

As he preached, a warmth filled the place where the church was gathered together. A radiance of something quite tangible reached out to God's people as they listened. The pastor was quite right. His words were ordinary. He would never win the prize for oratory.

He was right on another point too. God could take plain and simple words and turn them into something beautiful. God could use anyone to speak his Word, no matter how sinful they were. As Marcus preached, unheard and unseen by the saints gathered below, a solitary angel began to sing, "Holy, Holy, Holy to God in the highest, and peace to men on earth." As the beautiful, pure angelic voice rang out, a second took up the refrain, and then another and another, until the heavens rang with the sound of angels praising God and singing.

The clouds parted, and a shaft of light shone through, bathing that small church in a holy embrace and lighting up the faces of the people within. As the pastor gazed fondly out at his sun-kissed flock, he spoke the words of scripture that God himself had given to Moses so many centuries past:

"The Lord bless you
and keep you;
the Lord make his face shine upon you
and be gracious to you;
the Lord turn his face toward you
and give you peace."

The wheelchair, complete with its occupant, had been manhandled onto the platform and Benedict was standing centre stage, a roving microphone in his hand.

He spoke to the crowd, for the time being ignoring the disabled woman who shared the platform with him.

"God is going to perform a miracle here today; thank you ah-Jesus!" His congregation responded with a round of applause. Whether it was directed at God or whether Benedict was the recipient of the accolade was unclear.

"Thank you ah-Jesus, thank you ah-Jesus," he intoned again in a breathy voice. He drew out the "e" vowels as he pronounced the name of Jesus, in almost a hiss. "Jesus wants to heal several people today, but he is looking for faith! Do you ah-have the faith?" he shouted.

There was a shouted response, but not as exuberant as the apostle required. "Do you have the faith?" he shouted again, and this time there was an edge to his voice. The response on this occasion was more to his liking as a loud chorus of "yeses" came back to him.

Benedict was satisfied. "Thank you ah-Jesus."

The steward crouching down talking to the woman in the wheelchair was taking notes. When he was done, he approached Benedict hovering a few feet away, respectfully waiting. Finally the apostle glanced across—an invitation to speak.

"This woman, Apostle Ademola, has been in a wheelchair for twelve years following an accident."

There was a sigh from the crowd.

"She has been unable to walk in all that time and requires constant assistance in her everyday life. The woman believes that you can heal her."

The steward turned back towards the fortunate lady whose name had either not been obtained or was considered too unimportant to impart.

Benedict focussed his eyes on her for the first time. "Do you ah-have the faith to be healed?" he asked.

She responded by waving both arms in the air, trying her best to show the kind of faith that would be required both for her healing and to please him. Evidently she had done the correct thing, because he was at her side in half-a-dozen quick strides. He placed a hand on her head, whilst speaking into the microphone.

"Ah-thank you Jesus. Ah-thank you Jesus."

The camera zoomed in, and his face filled the screen, showing his eyes closed, his face portraying a pious expression. "In the name of Jesus, in the name of Jesus," he said.

The camera panned back, showing a view of the woman in the wheelchair as the apostle passed the microphone to the aide. Then he quickly bent down, grasped the woman by her wrists, and pulled her to her feet. A gasp went up from the congregation and the camera pulled back further, showing her now on her feet, supported by him.

The aide leant forward, pointing the microphone in the vicinity of Benedict's face as he hollered, "In the name of Jesus, *heal this woman now!*" For a moment her legs sagged at the knees, and a look of worry passed over her face. Benedict tightened his grip on her wrists. She cried a small cry of pain, which fortunately the microphone being held by the aide was unable to pick up.

"Now walk," he commanded moving backwards, maintaining his hold on her.

All eyes were now on the platform. Music began to play quietly. "Ah-thank you Jesus, ah-thank you Jesus." He released his grip, and the woman took a couple of faltering steps. The congregation came to their feet, shouting out encouragement as the woman slowly began to stagger forward.

He took up a position several metres from her, holding out his arms as she began to lurch towards him. She moved hesitantly, and stumbled, tears streaming down her face. The music played louder, filling the auditorium with sound.

He caught hold of her before she fell, and the camera panned all the way out showing healer and healed locked in an embrace. It did not pick up the cold, dead look in his eyes. It did not pick out the shadows that had descended and which now began to fill the auditorium. The TV lights still blazed, but with a strangely subdued illumination.

Oddly, no-one seemed to notice.

CHAPTER SIX

It was 6AM Monday morning, and Jack Somerville flipped the wall switch in order to supplement the meagre light from his desk lamp. His office seemed to be increasingly gloomy nowadays.

Settling in his chair, he flicked through the stack of crime reports that filled his tray, each one charting the theft of yet another motor vehicle in what had become a local epidemic. He wasn't sure what had started the chain of association, but somehow his mind had gone off at a tangent from car thefts, more specifically joyriding which was known as "TWOC" an abbreviation of "taking without consent," to "RTA"—"road traffic accident."

He didn't want to think about car accidents. The one that had taken his young sons' lives, that senseless crash that had prematurely taken two precious souls—three if he counted his wife—was still too fresh in his mind.

But he forced his mind to go there. He had a job to do and it was possible that there was a link between stolen cars and non-stop RTA's. It was a wild chance, but he hadn't anything else to go on at present.

He examined the five buff files he had specially requested from CID Admin, now neatly stacked on his desk. Each one of them represented at least one life snuffed out in a car accident within the past three years. He viewed them dispassionately as they sat arranged in alphabetical order. Cameron through to Williams. Somewhere between "C" and "W" was "S" for Somerville. If the girl in Admin had thought about it she would have kept that one back. But staff changed so often and it *had* been three years—a lifetime. She was probably totally unaware of the connection.

And he didn't *have* to read that particular file. In fact he had no intention of doing so.

He methodically tidied his desk, although it didn't need it. A delaying tactic to avoid having to face what he knew he had to do. He picked up a couple of law books and opened the large bottom drawer in which to dump them. In the bottom lay the broken Simpson's mug that he had washed and carefully put away. He deposited the books, next to it, and slamming the drawer shut, took a deep breath. Then he sat silently for a while, summoning the strength of mind that he needed. Until he felt he could to do it.

The first wallet-style folder bore a white sticky label with the name "Cameron. P." Underneath were other neatly typed details. Jack shook his head. Only forty-four years old; still a young man. He slipped out the "Fatal RTA" report, a file of police statements held together with a paper-clip, a form setting out details of the deceased's driving licence and car insurance, and a detailed sketch-plan of the scene. There were a dozen photographs in colour taken by the Scenes of Crime photographer just after the crash, an autopsy report from the coroner showing time of death as 11:55pm, and various print-outs from the police computer. These showed the time the call was received, the units responding and their time of arrival. There were also some details of enquiries made.

He arranged the photographs in a neat row on his desk, placing the sketch plan alongside them. The statements and printouts he spread out underneath. The accident had occurred at night, and the photos showed a short section of country road illuminated by high-powered lamps, along with a heap of twisted, mangled red scrap-metal that was an unidentifiable motor vehicle. It was wrapped around the trunk of a large tree at the side of the road. Close by, lying on its side and half in the ditch, was a blue Ford, its rear sticking into the air with both front doors hanging open. He glanced briefly at the usual measurements of skid marks, debris etc, and a short note as to the condition of the road, road-signs and other street furniture.

The accident report set out the details that had been pieced together by the AI, the Accident Investigator, and Jack scan read it quickly. The conclusion was that the red vehicle being driven by Mr. Cameron had swerved to avoid being hit head-on by the blue vehicle driven by the unknown driver. Cameron had then skidded, hit the tree and died instantly. The driver and passenger of the blue Ford had been injured as evidenced by blood on the windscreen and passenger seat, but they had extricated themselves and made good their escape. The vehicle had been reported stolen two days earlier in Kent. So that was that. There had been no witnesses; the road was a quiet one without any nearby habitation. Case closed. That was not what the file actually said. The official police line in matters involving a death was that the case was never closed. The reality was that nothing could be done, unless at some time in the future a DNA sample from a totally unassociated crime was found that matched the blood the thieves had left behind. That's if the bleeding hearts who opposed samples from all arrested persons didn't get their way.

He sighed and dropped the file into his "out" tray where it would be cleared by one of the girls and filed, and reached for the next one. His hands were shaking and beads of perspiration formed on his forehead. He felt angry with himself. Angry that three years on, he was still having problems. He picked up the file with a sweaty hand and turned it over slowly, reading the label, "Gardner. C."

He startled as a female voice sounded close behind. Usually, he could at least be guaranteed an hour or two of solitude at that time in the morning. Before the nine to five's arrived. Only admin types worked those hours. Real coppers like him worked far longer and more unsocial hours.

"Jack, meet our latest CID transfer, Dc Peter Lewis," said Detective Chief Inspector Michelle Radigan in clipped tones. Michelle was in her mid-forties, with the look one would associate with an aggressive rights campaigner. Her face was scrubbed scrupulously clean, and not a vestige of make up or face powder adorned her features. In all the years Jack had known her, he had never seen her made up. He knew that she had never married. He had never seen her with a man, and she had never mentioned one. Jack had always presumed that she either had no social life, and therefore made no effort, or was a lesbian and was therefore supposed to look that way. Her strangely styled, unnatural looking blonde hair helped to confirm that impression in his mind anyway. She was of medium height and slim, but with a certain wiry toughness that gave a clear signal that she was not to be messed with.

Jack twisted in his chair. He indicated the files on his desk. "I'm looking for a lead on one or two of the TWOC's."

DCI Radigan nodded, barely glancing at the folders laid out on the desk. She clearly wasn't interested in such trivia. "Great. Look Jack, I'll be brief as Peter and I have a meeting with the Divisional Management Team in five minutes." Anticipating the question she added, "It's an early morning raid we are monitoring. You don't need to be involved Jack, its being run by HQ."

Almost as an afterthought and before Jack could reply and express his annoyance at not being kept in the loop, she nodded in the direction of the huge man standing next to her. "He'll be working with us from tomorrow. And by *us*, read *you*. He's fresh off Regional Crime Squad, so he knows a lot that can benefit us. Lewis, meet Jack Somerville, our Ds."

"Christ, it's about time you lot did some proper work," said Jack sourly. "At least we're not getting a 'top' to help us out this time."

He didn't value his uniformed colleagues and goaded them by referring derogatorily to them as "woodentops," more usually abbreviated to "tops," on account of the helmets that they wore. Uniformed officers who expressed an interest in CID often worked as an "aide" so that they could gain experience and have their potential analysed. Jack thought most of them were rubbish.

Dc Lewis gave him an odd look as though he was about to say something, then reached out a hand instead. Jack noted the black leather gloves he was wearing and the tacky gold cuff-links with the police crest on them. Pretty naff, he thought as he shook the hand which totally engulfed his. He could at least have removed his glove before shaking hands. That was just common courtesy.

He came to an instant decision. He didn't like Peter Lewis and instinctively mistrusted him. He was a big man, well over six-foot tall and built like a bear. He wouldn't have appeared out of place playing in the England rugby side. But it was his face that was the most startling.

His nose had obviously been broken badly and was horribly misshapen. Little piggy eyes stared intently from under sunken brows. The skin was badly scared, seemingly stretched taut across his face and he had a cruel, thin, almost bloodless mouth. He must have had some serious surgery at some stage. It was a wonder he wasn't pensioned off, thought Jack, on account of the risk of him frightening innocent children. The impression given as a whole was of an extremely ugly, aggressive man, and Jack wondered briefly what cruel accident had conspired to mould such a face.

Lewis glanced down at the folders, picking the next one off of the pile. He read aloud from the neat white label, "Somerville A, and Somerville J." He flipped it open and glanced inside, riffling through the documents before Jack snatched it angrily from him.

"Let me know if I can be of help," the big man said, in a surprisingly soft baritone voice, and followed the DCI out of the office.

"You could have let me know about the raid, Michelle," shouted Jack at the retreating DCI, "you know, protocol and all that!" As there was no reply, he muttered the rest of what he was thinking to himself. And it wasn't complimentary about Crime Squad, DCI's in particular and women in general.

There was something different about Lewis, but he wasn't sure what it was. And that worried him. He liked to compartmentalise people. To put them in a category—put them in a box that he could label. And he was having trouble doing that with Lewis. He shrugged, which was his standard response to things he didn't quite understand, and decided that he didn't like him. That was a start. Life was getting far too complicated, that was for sure.

It was actually far more complicated than he knew. And he would have been shaken had he been aware of the darkness that had hovered continually in his office for the past three years. Darkness in the form of Isagoge, a shapeless demon of self-pity. Jack didn't believe in the forces of evil, or even the forces of good for that matter. He sided with Nietzsche. God was dead and with him had gone the power for both good and evil. So he would have been traumatized to the depths of his soul, could he have seen Isagoge leave suddenly. In fact he did not just leave; he was forcibly and violently expelled against his will.

So Jack methodically straightened his desk yet again, oblivious to what was happening around him, just so long as his desk was tidy and the leather bound law-books and his Conan Doyle's were sitting in straight rows in their bookcase. Then he tucked the waste-paper bin under his desk and switched off the desk lamp that suddenly seemed unnecessary in the unusual brightness that filled his office.

Somewhere in the heavenlies, far above the reach of mortal eyes and ears, a trumpet sounded.

Just a single note, long and clear, pure and loud. And as he addressed the legions of angels under his command, a mighty warrior spoke just three words.

"So it begins," he said.

Nick Tait worked as a consultant at a firm of mortgage brokers. The name "Consultant," looked grand on his business cards, but he was in reality a low-paid clerk who just did paperwork. He'd been working there for the last fifteen years since leaving school, and frankly, he was bored. Mind numbingly, soporifically, brain decaying bored.

He sometimes wondered what had happened to his life. Where was the excitement that it had once promised? Now it seemed that all he had to look forward to day after day was the relentless grind of paper and form-filling. Discount mortgages, buy-to-let mortgages, stepped mortgages, fixed mortgages—hardly the stuff of his dreams.

But for his growing interest in metaphysics, he really felt he would have gone totally nuts. The new stuff he was being taught gave him an outlet for the dryness in his life and in his soul. An excitement to counter the drudgery of living day to day in a glass box, drowning under a mound of paper.

Startled out of the depths of his musing, he became aware that Lorna Brooks from Administration was hurrying towards him with a stack of paperwork. He quite liked her, although she was a bit of an airhead. But she did brighten his day.

She teetered unsteadily along, the pile of papers threatening to fall at any moment. She was in her mid-thirties and had been working for the Company for just under three months.

"Merry Christmas, Nick," she said breathily in that seductive manner she had, "I've got something for you."

He met her eyes and scowled, and she laughed, dropping the pile of papers onto his desk.

"Lighten up dear, it might never happen."

Nick smiled, showing his perfect white teeth, but there wasn't much humour. "Yeah, happy Christmas to you too. What have you brought me this time?" They went through this same routine almost every day.

She pulled a face as she responded. "The usual mortgage applications, mostly buy-to-let. Seems that the property investors are still on a roll. One or two looking for equity release in their homes. Oh, and your expenses claims form."

Nick seemed disappointed. "Huh, nothing changes does it?" He appraised Lorna's slim, toned figure appreciatively. She was looking particularly good today. Her blonde hair was carefully cut into a bob, and she wore only a trace of makeup. She could have passed for a twenty something, and she obviously went to great pains to look after herself. Probably a jogger, he thought.

Lorna turned to go, and as she did so spotted the paperback on his desk. He had been reading it earlier during a particularly boring period when he should have been working. A broad smile lit up her face and she picked it up, reading the title aloud. "*Deity Uncovered*, by Dr. Benedict Ademola."

Nick removed the book from her hand. "Probably not your sort of thing."

"I've read it."

Nick gazed at her thoughtfully. "I didn't realise you were interested in . . ." he paused as he struggled to think of the correct word. "Religion," he finished lamely, and Lorna smiled at his embarrassment.

"Well I am interested in 'religion' as you put it. I've been a spiritual seeker for some time. I started with Yoga, went on to Transcendental Meditation, then Buddhism, then Angels, then New Age . . ."

Nick let out his breath in a slow whistle. "Sounds like you've explored everything," he said with evident admiration. "You're a real spiritual Magellan. I feel I'm just a beginner compared to you."

She shook her head in denial.

"So in all your searching, what conclusions have you come to?" he asked.

"I'm still looking for my personal deity. I've tried all the meditation, chanting—you know. I guess you have to try all paths and find out what suits you best, right?"

Tait nodded. "I believe one has to keep an open mind on these things. It doesn't pay to be narrow minded because then you can miss the truth."

"Ah," she said then, with a little squeal of excitement, "but what is truth? If you've read the book you will see that Dr. Ademola denies it even exists. He says there are no absolutes."

He stared at her as if seeing her for the first time. "All the time you've worked here, I've had you figured wrong," he admitted apologetically. "I took you for more of a conventional thinker."

"You mean a shallow, bigoted thinker Nick?"

He blushed. He'd actually been thinking that she was a bit dense. Having blonde moments and such. But her evaluation of the situation would do as well.

"Sorry. But okay, if there is no truth, how can we ever find our personal deity?"

She retrieved the book from Tait and flicked it open until she found what she was looking for. She read aloud.

"The evolution of our consciousness is inexorable. With this development comes different ways of experiencing reality or truth. Everything changes. All religions are naïve and will not endure. It is inevitable that an acute paradigm shift in our consciousness will take place. But only in those who have the courage to grasp the truth, to be ready to accept the mantle of change. We are the vanguard my friends, the people who walk in the light.

What do I mean by grasping the truth? What is the reality to which I refer? The higher adepts will recognise at once the validity of what I am saying. My fellow seekers—there is no truth!

And if there is no truth, there is correspondingly no reality. God
is whoever you perceive him or her to be."

"So there is no absolute God," he queried, testing her.

She laughed, a clear tinkling sound. "If that is your truth. If it is true
for you, then so be it. But my truth is different. It says that there are no
absolutes. That doesn't invalidate what anyone else believes. There is no
right or wrong. Just difference."

"But if as Dr. Ademola says, there is no truth, how can you ever
believe in anything, no matter how liberal your view?"

"Wow, this is getting deep." Lorna paused for a moment, gathering
her thoughts. It had been some time since she'd had to justify her beliefs,
and she found it quite stimulating. "It depends on how you define truth.
If you define it in a narrow, naïve way as a belief that is accepted as an
eternal verity, then you are missing the point. There are no eternal veri-
ties, everything changes." She placed the book gently on his desk, and
turned to leave.

Tait sat open mouthed. How on earth did a scatter-brain like Lorna
understand the most profound philosophy of Benedict Ademola?

"Wait!" Tait was intrigued. He had spoken to this girl almost every
day since she had started, and although she was pretty, he had figured
her as just another blonde.

Lorna stopped in the doorway and turned towards him. There was a
long pause, and she raised her eyebrows enquiringly.

He came straight to the point. "What about continuing this discussion with some like-minded people?"

She hesitated. "I'm not sure if that would be right . . . ?"

"Dr. Ademola will be there."

"You're kidding?"

Tait smiled smugly.

"Okay, it'll be better than sitting in with just the cat for company. But
if you are having me on . . ."

"Wednesday?"

"That'll be fine, my place or yours?" She laughed at the corniness of
the remark.

He tore a yellow "post-it" note from the block on his desk and scribbled an address. "Meet me here at 7pm," he said.

Lorna glanced at it, folded it in half and tucked it into her pocket. "Perhaps," she replied, and swept out of the office with a grin.

Tait picked up the telephone and dialled, drumming his fingers on the desk. "Do what thou wilt shall be the whole of the law," he said as a voice answered at the other end.

"So mote it be," came the response.

"Master, I've found someone who could be useful," Tait said.

He paused. "No, a female, Lorna Brooks." He listened attentively for a few moments. "No she's fine. Been working here for a few months." He paused to listen. "Yes, I told her to meet us at your house on Wednesday." He listened for a few moments more, and then replaced the receiver.

CHAPTER SEVEN

The Hartwood Gazette was the first newspaper to report it. "GREAT BALLS OF FIRE!" the bold headline shouted; underneath was the photograph of an elderly lady.

Local Hartwood resident Mrs. Doris Turvey has reported seeing balls of light, floating in the sky above the woods. They apparently hung in the air for nearly an hour, before streaking off into the night sky. Many other local people also rang The Gazette with similar stories. The source of the light remains unexplained so far.

The Gazette spoke to local community police constable Jeff Harding who said, "We don't want people to get worried about this. There is obviously a rational explanation and I'm sure we will find out what it is in due course. It could well be a weather balloon, because that's what most sightings of this sort tend to be. But if anyone does feel nervous or concerned, then by all means call me at the local police station."

The dream had ended, but the terror had not left. Still it was with her, hanging in the air like wisps of morning mist. As did the memory of trees. The smell of trees. And something else; dankness and the odour of wet earth. Or the stench and the sound of something evil coming close?

She cried then. Because she felt alone and helpless. Powerless in the face of something she did not understand. But knowing the meaning of fear well enough.

When she could bear it no longer, she screamed herself awake.

_____

The police officer firmly shut the office door at the police station, ensuring that no-one was able to overhear, picked up the telephone and dialled.

"Do what thou wilt shall be the whole of the law."

"So mote it be," responded the terse voice.

"I have information. Not much. But HQ have called in an undercover operative."

"I need more."

"That's it. Such things are tightly controlled on a 'need to know basis.'"

"It's not good enough."

"I'm sorry master, but that's all I have."

"Then find out."

"But I . . ." The voice trembled slightly. It could have been anger. Or fear.

The master cut in. "Do it." And the line went dead.

_____

The church building was dim, the sole illumination coming from the street lights that had yet to switch off on their time-controlled cycle. The Christmas tree, now that its lights were off, was sad and forlorn—almost undressed. The place had a melancholy air, perfectly matching the mood of its solitary occupant slumped on a blue cushioned straight-backed chair. Humanly speaking, Marcus sat alone. His head was bowed, and his shoulders shook as great sobs spilt out of him. His face was streaked with tears, his hair dishevelled. So different from the man who had preached on the glory of God in that very same place the previous day. His voice trembled as he prayed.

"Forgive me Lord," he whispered. "I don't even know what to pray. I feel like rubbish. I know I am weak and useless. Help me please, not to fall again. I need your strength now." He sat in silence, soaking up the atmosphere that lingered from the worship of the saints down the years.

He was unaware of the figure alongside him. Tall and majestic, his blond hair falling about his broad shoulders, stood Aanfial, a captain in the army of God.

He wore a short plain tunic that fell to just above his knees, and as he moved it whipped around his muscular legs displaying an ugly scar that ran the length of his outside right thigh. A scabbard containing his sword was slung across his back, held by a band of thick leather. His physique was huge, his chest massive, and his finely honed body rippled as he moved.

Now his sky-blue eyes gazed with compassion at the broken man praying at his side. Placing a hand gently onto the head of the frail, weeping man, he knelt beside him on the floor, his face upturned to the heavens.

"Mighty God," he prayed, and his words had a power and a resonance that filled the room. "Have mercy on your faithful servant. You know the plans you have for him, plans to prosper him and not to harm him. Plans to give him a hope and a future."

The angelic being paused and his piercing eyes stared at the dark shadows in the corner of the hall. "Dark powers are gathering in this place. Mighty God, protect your people here from the evil one," he pleaded. "Surround them with your shield of love."

He paused for a moment, wondering if the prayer cover was sufficient for him to intervene. Then he shook his head. "Hartwood, you need to get your prayer warriors into action. There is a distinct lack of prayer that is permitting the forces of darkness to take territory in this town." He surveyed the sobbing Pastor with sorrow.

"You need to undergo this trial," he said. "I pray that the Lord will see you through."

As he stood his mighty wings unfurled—a terrible and awesome sight. Then he unsheathed his sword, and it shimmered as burnished gold; a blaze of incandescent light filled the place and his once plain garments shone burning white. And as the light flared, so the shadows that had been pressing forward drew back with a sound like the howling of the wind.

"Light has come into the world," intoned the angel, "and the darkness has not overcome it." Then he strode from the room without so much as a backwards glance.

Marcus sighed deep and long as he made his way to his office across the corridor. For just a moment he had felt he could win his latest battle. He didn't know why, but a new strength had surged through him as he prayed. But that had passed and he knew that he had lost the fight yet again.

For a long time he sat looking at the locked drawer, a desperate struggle going on in his mind. Finally, he fumbled for the key with a shaking hand.

It was some time later that Lissette found him slumped over his desk. Clutched in his hand was an empty bottle of spirits. In the corner, invisible to human eyes, crouched something dark. And totally evil.

Shaun O'Connor sat in his garden chair on the decking at the rear of his house in the late evening. On the table by his side was a bottle of whisky, and in his hand was a half-full glass of the amber liquid. He didn't sleep well nowadays, usually waking before dawn, and he found it more relaxing to sit outside rather than fret inside where he felt trapped and isolated. Provided it wasn't raining, he would sit and have a drink or two.

He was well wrapped up in a thick coat, woollen hat and gloves against the chill of the heavy frost that had settled like a blanket across his back garden so that it appeared almost respectable under its covering, the discarded bottles and unkempt grass transformed from ugliness to beauty for a short time.

He ran a gloved hand through his thinning mousey hair and took another sip of his drink. Staring up into the dark sky, he wondered at the blazing trail of light that was speeding across the heavens, falling swiftly like a stone as it passed over the Hartwood. It was followed by a second, and then a third, until the sky was lit up like fireworks night.

A comet? He wasn't sure, but in that moment as the light passed over him, bathing him in a pale moon-like glow, something touched him. In a deep place that he had long forgotten, something stirred. In his minds eye he could see the old days in Ireland when he had been with his wife Rosaleen. She had loved him. But that was before she'd found him with another woman.

His eyes misted as he remembered the lost opportunities. The lost childhood of his daughter. The loss of family. He hoped she was managing. He really did. He'd had no contact for over five years. Not with Rosaleen, nor with Colleen. She would be well grown up by now.

At that thought, his heart ached with the misery and hurt of the empty years that lay behind, and the desolate ones that lay ahead. Why had he been so stupid? Why had he so carelessly thrown away the best thing that he had ever had? He had some idea. He guessed that his self-ishness was at the heart of it.

When he first heard the voice singing, he dismissed it because he was often delusional. He knew that. It wouldn't be the first time, and probably not the last. That was the problem with drinking too much, too often and for too long.

But the singing didn't go away. He could still hear it clearly inside his head. Like nothing he had ever heard before in all his life, and his home country was no stranger to beautiful music. Whether it was male or female he couldn't tell. But it had a purity and a timbre—almost a holiness about it that stirred his heart in a strange way. A haunting refrain that seemed to enter his mind not from outside in but from inside out. Almost as if it had bypassed his normal auditory system. Even his befuddled mind recognised that it didn't make any sense.

Slowly the words of the simple song became clear, ringing out as crisp and fresh as the frosty night air that surrounded him.

Holy, Holy, Holy Lord,
God of power and might.
All creation proclaims your glory.

Shaun sat captivated, long after the voice had faded away and the lights
had gone. Ridiculous, he thought, to feel the sudden sense of loss that he
then experienced. Why was he getting so maudlin over a shooting star
and someone singing?

He remembered that it was almost Christmas. Not that that particular time of year meant much to him now. It hadn't for some time. It was
a family thing after all, and he was alone.

It was then that the insane desire first began to rise up in him. He
knew then beyond doubt that he *was* getting delusional. Because he had
a strange urge to wish his ex-wife and daughter a happy Christmas, and
that stirred up emotions that he would rather not face.

He got up angrily. What the hell was all this about? He took a large
gulp of whisky on his way indoors, but it didn't seem to help any.

James Caruthers was praying. He'd had a powerful conviction that
somewhere there was danger. He had absolutely no idea what it was, but
God wanted urgent prayer.

He was working late at his office at IT Sites, a web design company.
At present he was building a web-site for "Manjaro.co.uk," a Christian
fair-trade business that imported hand-made artefacts from Kenya.

Technical books were piled on his desk spilling out from a central
stack and threatening to slide onto the floor at any moment. A pile of
unopened Christmas cards lay on his desk, waiting for him to get round
to them. Some had been there for nearly two weeks, so it didn't look too
promising that they would be viewed this side of Christmas. Propped
up next to a half-eaten sandwich and a polystyrene cup was a popular
"Dummies" textbook. He was not the tidiest of workers, and even he
admitted that his admin was sloppy, but he was always in demand for
his skills.

He'd been on the phone to a client, his mind full of formulas, graphics and codes. The next moment a voice had "gone off" in his head. Not audibly. Not a voice at all in as much as he didn't hear it with his ears. He "heard" it with his mind. He was uncomfortably aware that he wasn't making much sense. It was difficult to describe and he found himself floundering. It was one of those "you had to be there" experiences, or in this case a "had to have heard it" experience.

When he thought about it later, the closest he came to describing it was that it was an invasive thought, an alien thought. Something from outside his own senses. So compelling that it cut straight through the maths that up to that moment had filled his mind, so that he had had no choice but to stop what he was doing.

There was a sense of urgency. He had to pray immediately.

Making a quick apology, he slammed down the phone.

This was an unusual experience for him and he felt a bit stupid. What if someone were to come in and see him? Nevertheless the compulsion on him was too great, and falling reluctantly to his knees at the side of his desk he began to pray obediently about the unknown danger that God had placed on his heart.

"Father, I ask for your protection right now on those that you have commanded me to pray for. Surround your people with your love and power like an impenetrable hedge that no danger can pass through." He continued to pray in the Spirit for some time, interceding faithfully as God lead him.

Similarly all over Hartwood, Christian men and women were also falling to their knees to pray, compelled by the Spirit of God. They had no idea for whom or even why they were being called to pray. But God was calling his people to rise up and take the land that he had given to them. And they obeyed.

Benedict was sitting in the brown leather upholstered chair in his office, his feet propped up on the desk, calmly surveying the two men sitting on the opposite side. He was in his shirtsleeves, methodically clicking the top of a ballpoint pen as he spoke.

"Bren, would you mind leaving us alone for a while?"

Brenda Marney, sitting at her desk in the corner picked up her notepad and pen and left the room, glancing across at the two men and nodding as she did so. She was Benedict's personal assistant and some would say, confidant. She was extremely efficient and knew more about his church business than anyone other than Benedict himself. No one was closer to the apostle than she was. He was a man who trusted no-one, rarely let his guard down and permitted no-one into his inner circle. With the exception of Brenda. But even with her, there was a line to be drawn.

Removing the glass stopper from the decanter on his desk, he poured three glasses of port. "Not too early for you?" he enquired, as without waiting for a response he set two of them down in reach of Cooper and Riley. Riley immediately reached for his and downed it in a single gulp, much to the distaste of Benedict.

"Happy Christmas," he said, taking a delicate sip from his glass. "Gentlemen, I asked you here because we have a problem. A problem with those who have left the church. If this encourages others to follow suit, we could have a situation. I want to make it clear that I will not tolerate this for much longer." He paused, looking enquiringly at Nelson Riley and Darrell Cooper for a response.

Cooper sipped his port and spoke first. He was dressed in dark blue trousers and a light blue short sleeved shirt. A logo on the breast said, "Ecoguard Security." On the floor at his side was his black leather briefcase.

He was exhausted, and it showed. He owned a small security company, but had lost several of his biggest contracts over time and had struggled to find new ones. He had insisted on running his company pretty much along the same lines as when he had started it in the "80's." Ironically, considering his use of sophisticated equipment for blackmailing purposes, he'd never seen the point of spending money on new technology or equipment and had fallen behind the competition. Clients were looking for high-tech solutions more often than the standard manned guarding that he provided. Things had got so bad that he had taken to covering some of the contracts himself in an attempt to keep costs down. He worked the office during the day, and drove the van at night.

"We shouldn't get too worried by a handful of people. If what you say about them is true, then they won't be much of a loss."

Benedict didn't seem too pleased by Cooper's assessment of the situation.

"You have heard the saying, 'how do you eat an elephant'?"

Cooper stared. What on earth was he going on about? "Umh, I'm not sure what you mean."

"It's quite straightforward if you have the wit to think about it. How do you eat an elephant?" Benedict repeated the question wearily, staring at Riley as he did so.

Riley, dressed in his usual green sports jacket and wearing a blue tie, was equally nonplussed. He was far from comfortable in the presence of Benedict. He shook his head.

Benedict stood up. "Doesn't anyone here have any sense?" he thundered. "The answer is, 'piece by piece. Piece by piece!'" He paused to let the information sink in. "You fools. It might be a handful now, but it is the slow drip that can destroy all I have built over the years. No one handed me this church on a plate. I built it myself. It is now the largest church in the area dwarfing all other pitiful, small ministries. Tell me," he demanded, jabbing a finger at them both, "what has anyone else built in this town?"

There wasn't any prudent response to that, and so neither man deigned to answer the question.

"We lost fifty last fortnight Mr. Benedict," said Riley, thinking that was the safest course of action, "and another thirty-seven this week. That is a significant loss of funds. Eighty-seven people consisting of twenty-five families." He scribbled some figures on a scrap of paper. "That equates to seven thousand pounds a month in tithes!" He kept his eyes lowered for fear of betraying his emotions.

He was in fact far more concerned than he showed, because he had been helping himself to tithes for the past year. Now he was concerned that with a loss of members and subsequent income, there was every possibility that Benedict would be checking the books, and every chance that he would be found out. He consoled himself with the thought that he would soon be far away, where even the apostle would be unable to find him.

"It's still miniscule by my standards," said Benedict. "In a church this size no-one will miss them. But it is the principle. These people are bringing my reputation into question. I won't let it go on." His voice was low and menacing, and both Cooper and Riley shrank back. "It could cause panic among the flock. We don't want a mass exodus from the church because of some half-witted tares."

For Benedict's benefit, because he really couldn't care less, Cooper asked the question. "Do we know where they have moved on to? Are they in other churches? We need to get in first before people start listening to what they are saying."

Benedict starred hard at Cooper. "Before they start listening to what?"

Cooper was taken aback. "I wasn't saying they had anything to tell . . ."

Benedict got really angry then, and shouted. "There is nothing done here in darkness. We are in the light, and the people that follow me remain in the light. It is outside our church that there is deception and lies. If people leave, they walk in darkness!"

"There is talk," said Riley, immediately wishing that he kept his mouth shut.

An invisible, but evil mess of blackness named Bune stirred from his position at the right-hand of the apostle. His red eyes glared malevolently. "Dangerous," he hissed in Benedict's ear. "Dangerous."

"Talk? What talk? There is no talk!" Benedict frowned, leaning forward in his chair and fixating Riley with an ugly stare.

Summoning up all his courage, Riley turned to Benedict, studiously avoiding his eyes. He focussed on a point just to the left of him. "Mr. Benedict, I . . . I want out. This has gone too far for me," he stammered nervously. "Everything is starting to fall apart and I don't want to be around when it finally does happen."

"Fall apart?" hissed the apostle. "You have no idea what you are saying. Just answer the question!" His voice was a snarl of impatience. "What talk?"

"I met up with some ex-members the other day. They are attending a little church just off the town centre. Hartwood Community Church, I think it's called."

Cooper interrupted. "It's just a small church. Around two hundred people. I haven't heard them doing much . . ." He trailed off as Benedict directed his gaze at him.

Riley shifted uncomfortably in his chair, wishing that there was another glass of port handy. "There are around forty of our people there. The pastor has taken them in and by all accounts they are enjoying it." He looked at the ceiling for inspiration, wondering how he could tell Benedict.

Cooper interrupted. "I wouldn't worry. The pastor there is rumoured to be deep in sin. A bit like Riley here," he smirked.

The apostle stood up, and walked slowly over to Riley. When he spoke, his words were filled with menace. "I will ask you just once more. What talk?"

"There is talk of tapes—and CD recordings," he said fearfully.

A shadow passed across the apostle's face, and for a moment, Riley thought he saw fear. But it was gone as quickly as it had appeared, and he knew he was mistaken. Benedict Ademola didn't feel fear. He just imparted it to others.

"Recordings of private conversations between church members and you, Apostle Benedict. And recordings of your preaching," continued Riley. He sat back nervously wondering what the reaction would be.

The demon Bune was so tightly fused to Ademola that had he been visible to human eyes, it would not have been possible to see where one began and the other ended. Around his neck he wore a chain of silver. Numerous rings of sparkling red, blue and yellow precious stones adorned his fingers. His enormous black bulk smothered the desk area where his human sat. His malevolent eyes surveyed the two men sitting opposite as dark clouds swirled in the room.

He began to speak through his puppet, the human that he owned body and soul. Although spoken quietly, his voice carried an authority that could not be resisted.

"Riley, if you leave you're on your own. Only I can protect you. By leaving, you're saying that you can manage without the covering that I alone provide. And you haven't done well so far, have you? In fact, if there was a prize for stupidity, you would win it! But remember one thing. Keep your mouth shut. If you betray me . . ." He left the sentence unfinished, but they knew exactly what he meant.

"And you Cooper. I know that what you crave is money. But there is far more at stake than mere financial gain. There are things here beyond price. Eternal things that I wouldn't expect you to understand. I'm speaking here of power, real power without limit."

His voice had a soothing, hypnotic effect on them, and Riley and Cooper sat strangely quiet, as his will became their desire. "I suggest you both get out of here and apply yourselves to the things of importance, the work of the church." He gazed intently into their faces, wondering for just a moment whether either of them were the infiltrators that his source had warned him of. He dismissed that quickly. They had been with him a long time. Long enough to ensure that their spirits had been sufficiently crushed. They were his.

Both tamely nodded assent and stood up, relieved to be escaping his cloying presence.

"By the way Riley . . ." Benedict called after the departing figure, causing the object of his address to become hot and bothered all over again. "Don't forget that the church accounts are due. They are late once again. Have them on my desk by tomorrow evening, would you?"

As the two subdued men left his presence, Amduscias, demon of betrayal clung to Darrell Cooper. Abraxas, demon of lust dug ever deeper into to Nelson Riley's thigh.

Bune spoke ever so gently into the mind of his creature. Velvet soft speech that flowed along the long-surrendered auditory system with a viscous, relentless power and authority. "We need to find out about those recordings. As for those two, they have become a liability. Riley is stealing from us, and Cooper is exploiting him. Both are now a danger. We need to watch them closely."

CHAPTER EIGHT

Sixteen-year-old Emily Bowman was about to be thrust into a situation that would shake her to the very depths of her being.

It was Ashley Coleman who had put the pressure on her. Smart, blue-eyed, beautiful, confident, popular Ashley. She usually had the best looking boys chasing after her; always did well in exams; and in sport. Everyone wanted to be friends with her. In fact, it seemed there was nothing at which she didn't excel.

Ashley had always been aggressive towards her, insulting her at every opportunity. It was bullying. Mental bullying. But Emily lacked the strength to do anything about it. She just did her best to keep out of the way of Coleman and her hangers-on.

She had tried to fit in, tried to be casual. She'd started swearing and drinking excessively for a while so as to gain some street credibility, seeking out the girls who were recognised as fashionably rebellious. But she would only go so far, and so that hadn't worked. Mainly because they didn't want her. Or at least Ashley didn't. And that meant of course that no-one did.

On this Monday morning she found herself cornered outside the school gates. Then Ashley had tossed her blonde hair and laughed that derisive laugh of hers because she had found out that Emily was still a virgin. "Are you frigid or something?" she had sniggered, "or are you gay?"

Emily's friend Sophie Cooper had tried to defend her, but as the other girls gathered around burst into laughter, Sophie found herself going quite red and retreated under the enormous peer pressure.

Everyone knew that Ashley slept with all her boyfriends, and she had the reputation of being a very glamorous and sophisticated woman of the world. She was definitely cool.

Emily tried to sound firm. "It isn't the right time for me," she retorted, "and anyway, it's meant to be special, not something that you just throw away with the first hormonal boy you meet."

She had attended Hartwood Community Church with her parents Joan and Bob some years back, although very infrequently. They still attended, although she found it hard to think why that was. Her mum she could just about understand, but her dad! He was the archetypal hypocrite that every non-believer associated church goers with. If it was true that many people didn't go to church because they saw the faces of those coming out, then her dad was that man. One look at his unsmiling, hard face was enough to put people off for life.

The Bowmans had found the behaviour of the "religious maniacs" in their once traditional church difficult to cope with. Everyone was so embarrassing, so lively, so happy-clappy. Why couldn't they just quieten down a bit and sing a few of the old hymns? All this new, noisy singing and all the talk about Jesus, sin and hell. And redemption! Whatever that was.

It was the new pastor that had started it. Before *he* came it had been nice and undemanding, just the way things should be. The new man was too confrontational. He even called them sinners! So much for God being love. And all the talk about people who didn't know Jesus being "lost" was too much to take. They all knew folk who belonged to other religions. And some who didn't believe in God at all. And that didn't make them bad people, did it?

Emily had very soon stopped attending and her parents had never bothered her about it. But all the same, some of the teaching had stuck with her. And her reply only served to make the other girls laugh louder. "Ooh, it's not the right time," they mocked in unison, before walking away and leaving Emily alone at the school gate. They had no time for a "kid," someone who wasn't as mature as they were. They didn't want to spend time with a loser.

That's why Emily, despite Sophie begging her not to, had readily agreed to meet up with Brandon Riley when he had asked her out. That in itself had been a surprise because he'd never shown any interest in her before and he was after all, drop dead gorgeous. Chestnut hair, dark brown eyes, good build. A bit spotty perhaps, but at eighteen she supposed that was to be expected.

She wore a new dress that made her look a couple of years older than she really was, and it fitted in all the right places. Even her mum, usually too preoccupied with her self to notice anything that Emily did, passed comment.

"Boyfriend?" she had asked, tearing her eyes away from the soap which flickered on the outsized television dominating the living room. She sucked on her cigarette, blowing a lungful of blue smoke into the air. "Don't make a noise when you get back, that's all, your dad's on earlies tomorrow." She turned back to the soap; a violent story about a dysfunctional family's feuding. She was ironically unaware that her own life surpassed the fiction on almost every level.

Emily, not even bothering to reply, went out by the front door, slamming it noisily behind her.

Joan sat for a moment, her mind unusually disturbed. This wasn't the way that she had planned to spend her life. This wasn't the way things were meant to be. When she had married Bob, he'd been such fun. He'd been ambitious and had worked so hard it seemed inevitable he would be promoted. He was one of the best workers at the paper mill. That was obvious to everyone. He was sure to be made foreman when the present man retired. Emily had been just six-weeks-old then, and the future seemed so good for them all.

"With my extra money, we can easily afford the baby, and perhaps a decent holiday," he had cheerfully announced.

Only something had gone wrong, and he hadn't got the job. He'd been called before the general manager on a Monday morning, and his heart had sunk as he was given the news. A new, younger man half his age had been given it, and from that day Bob had changed.

"These naff kids coming in and taking over," he had moaned to Joan. "I've forgotten more about the paper process than they'll ever know." In his anger and jealousy, his enthusiasm for the job began to dwindle. Although he worked hard enough to avoid dismissal, he only scraped through his annual appraisals and was out of the promotion race for ever as far as his line manager was concerned.

So Bob Bowman just lived for his days off, enduring the mind numbing routine of the Mill from Monday to Friday each week, waiting for his life to be given back to him at the weekend. He started drinking as a way of forgetting all that could have been, and gradually his hopes and dreams died, as did many of his brain cells from acute alcoholism. And as these things died, so did his love for Joan and Emily.

Joan turned her attention back to the soap. "Blast!" She had missed the end. Now she would never know whether Jim Tarling had buried his ex-wife under the patio, or whether it had been his gay lover that had done it. She continued to stare mindlessly at the screen for some time after the programme had ended. Because it meant she didn't have to think about reality.

Henry Carson was praying. With his Bible open in front of him, he was reading the book of Ephesians. Placing his finger on a passage he read, "Be strong with the Lord's mighty power. Put on all of God's armour so that you will be able to stand firm against all strategies and tricks of the Devil." He pulled a face. "Spiritual warfare," he muttered aloud, "that's what's needed in this place."

As he read about the powers of this dark world, some thoughts began to fall into place. And some curious instances began to make sense.

The church had been going through a difficult time recently. There had been many blessings, but on the other hand quite a few people had also fallen ill, some with serious, life-threatening illnesses. There had been some schisms in the congregation, and quite a few members had still not resolved their differences. And then there was Marcus. Henry was worried about him. He didn't look too good, and his preaching was definitely getting a bit tired. New families were still coming in, but several had left, disillusioned, and there were things going on that just didn't make sense. Long-time friends had fallen out with each other. People who were usually calm and controlled were loosing their tempers at the slightest provocation.

He made a quick decision. Taking hold of his stick, he began to make his way from his flat to the church across the road. It was a short distance, but it took him some time. His walking was definitely getting slower.

It was a grey day, and clouds covered the sky with the threat of rain. He didn't usually venture out if there was the risk of bad weather. But he knew that God was speaking to him, and he trusted that he was well able to protect him until he had accomplished the task he had been called to do. Whatever that was!

He sensed that something was up even as he entered the church building. There was danger there. Perhaps an intruder? He looked around cautiously, and his heart beat just a little faster at the prospect. Twenty years ago he would have relished a tussle. But now he was old, and not very strong. In fact he was quite feeble physically. But not mentally. His mind had been honed spiritually by years of studying the Word of God. And as unlikely as it appeared outwardly, he was a formidable spiritual foe.

He discerned a heaviness there that was quite tangible. And an awful smell like rotten eggs that seemed to be coming from Marcus's office.

A verse of scripture from the book of Ephesians that he had been studying earlier leapt into his mind. "Our struggle is not against flesh and blood, but against the rulers, against the authorities, against the powers of this dark world and against the spiritual powers of evil in the heavenly realms."

Henry began to pray in tongues as he saw in an instant of clarity that the danger was not physical, but something far worse. There was evil in the place that stuck right to the soul, sucking the life out.

"The sword of the spirit," he said grimly, for he knew now for certain that the battle was against darkness and evil from the spiritual realm. The fight was against someone with an implacable hatred. An entity of ruthless power whose sole mission was the destruction of those made in the image of God.

He grasped his walking stick firmly in his hand and taking a deep breath threw open the door to the pastor's office and hobbled in, brandishing the stick above his head like an Old Testament prophet on the warpath.

Lissette stared across the desk at her young husband with sadness in her eyes. "Marky," she said, using her pet name for him, "you have got to see somebody about this problem. Look at the time. I was so worried about you when you didn't come home."

"No!" He was rougher than he had intended to be, and Lissette flinched and sat back, a look of hurt on her pretty face. Marcus reached across the desk towards her. "Sorry," he apologised, "but how can I pastor the church if it becomes common knowledge? And you know I will be okay, you don't have to be concerned about me." He sighed and buried his head in his hands. "I will just have to work it out."

"How can I not be worried when I have to come and look for you because you haven't come home? You didn't call me. Anything might have happened." She paused thoughtfully. "Or is it me?"

Marcus was astonished. "Is it you? I don't know what you mean."

Lissette put her hand on his. "You've been unhappy for so long now. Is it because I haven't been able to have children since, you know, since that time?"

He shook his head. It was true that he dearly wanted a child. A son, a daughter, it didn't really matter which. And the fact that Lissette had been unable to conceive since that awful time two years ago had been a cause of deep sadness for both of them. There was something missing in their lives.

"You know I desperately want to have children—we both do. But it's not that Lissie. And I have never blamed you."

She stood up and walked over to where her husband was sitting.

"I know you haven't." She ran a hand tiredly through her hair. "It's such a struggle. I don't know why you drink so much. But you won't discuss it. You won't open up to me, so I don't know anymore what to say or do. You can't keep it hidden for ever. You need at least to speak to the elders of the church. You don't give people enough credit," she said. "They, the church, love you Marcus and I know that if you were to go to them—"

He cut her off with another emphatic *"No!"* this time making no attempt to apologise for the harshness in his voice. "Just leave it Lissie, just leave it."

She drew back from him then, her face pale and drawn. "Darling . . ." She struggled to get the words out. "Marcus, I'm sorry . . ." She stared at him for some sign that he was listening to her, but he remained silent with his head bowed. "I can't take any more. I'm tired of covering up for you, tired of making excuses to our friends. I'll be at home if you want me. But you need to sort this out—and soon."

She ran out of the room then, hot tears spilling down her cheeks.

How long he sat, he had no idea. Time seemed irrelevant, just like everything else. Even his calling. At one time he had cherished his work and had been filled with joy working for the Lord. He had loved his church and his faithful flock. Deep inside he still did, but somehow the fire had gone out. The embers had grown cold and were threatening to die out altogether. He'd been living a lie for so long now that he struggled to discern what was true and what wasn't.

So far, his sermons had still been lucid and relevant, and no-one seemed to notice that they had gradually got shorter and shorter. God was still blessing, still serving up butterflies. But Marcus was running on empty, and he knew it. He was in grave danger of serving up to his flock not caterpillars, but maggots.

Sadly, everyone, paid workers and volunteers alike were so busy themselves that the lack of joy and spiritual fervour in their pastor hadn't registered. It had slipped by unnoticed in the whirlwind activities of church life.

He could remember when his problem had started. Working particularly hard, often staying late at the church preparing sermons, counselling the sick and the struggling, attending meetings, thinking up strategies and a hundred and one other things, a drink had, at first, been a real boost, relaxing his mind and helping his day along.

As he sat and mused, in the corner, unknown and unseen, the darkness stirred. Not physical darkness, but a spiritual darkness. And it was growing in size. But Marcus was totally unaware. He was too preoccupied with himself. His problems had filled his mind, leaving no room for anything or indeed anyone, else.

Were it not for that depressed spiritual state, he may have heard the prompting of God. But he was oblivious, and he did not hear the still, small voice that was simply urging him to pray. To speak the words of scripture that are powerful in tearing down spiritual strongholds.

Hours had passed by, as outside, afternoon sounds filtered in through the window—the excited sound of children on their way home from school, the bellow of the tradesmen as they went about their work; vehicles coming and going, and the occasional ambulance or police siren screaming off into the distance. The usual noises of the world going about its business. But he heard none of it.

He sat staring straight ahead, his face wooden and expressionless. What was it that he was meant to be doing? He couldn't think—his mind was a blank. Everything seemed such an effort, his whole body felt so heavy. So hard to move. So difficult to think. Like wading through mud.

So he didn't move or think. He gave up and just sat.

Which is what he was doing when the door was flung energetically open and Henry Carson burst in, his stick in one hand, an open Bible in the other.

Marcus came back to awareness with a feeling of panic. He was vaguely aware that time had passed, but he couldn't remember what he had been doing. For a brief moment, he didn't even recognise where he was. What on earth had happened to him? He tried to clear a head that felt thick and pounding, and the world gradually came back into focus. He was in his office. But what was Henry doing brandishing a stick? And why was it so dark?

He was unaware that the darkness was attributable to a demon named Abigar. Small and black with scaled, reptilian skin, he crouched in the corner where he had taken up residence some months previously. At that precise moment his bright little eyes were focussed on Henry. His lips curled back in what passed for a grin as he began to slither forward. The raised stick bothered him not the slightest. For he was spirit, and the things of the world could not touch him.

As Jack sat at his desk, a wave of depression washed over him. After thirty years in the Force he prided himself on his pragmatic approach. He believed that he had experienced most things that life could throw at him, and he'd never yet seen or heard anything that had made him change his point of view. And that point of view, his outlook on life, was simple. You are born and you die. In between is emptiness and heart-ache interspersed with rare bouts of happiness. That was it. There was nothing else.

He would have agreed with Joan Bowman whom he had never met, that all known life is concentrated on a lump of rock called the Earth that revolves in a cold empty nothingness called the universe, pitted with other equally cold long-dead rocks called planets. Stars were just pin-prick holes in a soulless universe giving an enticing illusion of life when in reality there was nothing. There was no design, no order. The dead hand of evolution was all there was. No heart, no feeling, no plan. Only randomness and emptiness.

Just like his life.

He despised himself for his momentary weakness and self-pity and forced himself to concentrate on his work. Already, he'd taken hours to do what should have taken him minutes. Thefts and road accidents! Hardly the most scintillating matters. What were the facts? There weren't any really. He shook his head sadly as the question slipped into his mind. Whatever was he still doing in this job?

The answer was unwelcome. *Hiding!* That was what he was doing. But from who or what? He didn't have those answers. He didn't even want to think about the consequences of finding them. What he wanted was peace. In his mind and in his life. But as long as he lived, he would not find that. Not now. Not after what had happened. That's what he believed.

He returned reluctantly to the files. There was a certain solace in paperwork. He hated it, but the sheer mind-numbing routine of it closed off his mind from things he would rather not dwell on. He could switch off and let the dullness take the pain away for a time.

There were three files left, all buff coloured and containing the details of the RTA's he'd not managed to go through the previous evening. He had done Cameron and Gardner. He was left with Somerville, Mahoney and Williams. He had intended to take them home, but knowing that the file on his boys was one of them, he hadn't been able to do it. He didn't want it in his flat. It was too much like bringing the tragedy back with him.

Not that he didn't carry the memories around with him. He did. In his head—they never left—but he had so far managed to keep any tangible reminders out.

Because his flat contained nothing that he'd shared with Susan and the boys. No memories. No keepsakes. Absolutely nothing. When he moved out he'd given everything to a charity. All the furniture, every stick of it. Every cup and plate, every piece of bedding—literally the entire contents.

The charity people had been amazed at such generosity. The men who came with the removal van assumed that it was an acrimonious divorce.

"I 'eard of a bloke once that packed up work after his wife divorced him, so that he didn't have to give 'er any maintenance," said the driver. "He gave the car away and burnt all the furniture. Then he hired a mechanical digger and drove it at the house. The local council had to demolish it after 'cause it wasn't safe." The man had smirked then, expressing what he thought was solidarity with an ill-used husband. "Good for 'im, eh? Women seem to get it all their own way."

Jack hadn't said anything. Nothing much mattered any more, and he couldn't be bothered to correct the false assumption that would become a story to be shared over a pint of beer.

He'd kept a photo of his boys in his wallet, and the Simpsons mug that the boys had given to him. And he had kept his wedding ring. For reasons that not even he understood, he still wore it.

Bringing himself back to the job in hand, he picked up a folder. The white label, neatly typed like all the others read, "Williams. J born 03.03.52." He examined the contents of the wallet. It was the standard documents.

He picked up the last file and flipped it open. He saw straightaway that someone had made a mistake in filing it. The label said "N. Mahoney. Born 26.07.77." But it wasn't an RTA. It was a sudden death. A suicide in fact. The suicide of a teenaged boy over a decade previously.

Jack couldn't face that. He shoved his chair back and left the office. "I'm off down the road for a few hours!" he shouted to the control room staff, "I'm on the radio if you want me."

CHAPTER NINE

Nelson Riley was feeling frustrated. His computer in the church office was freezing up again and he didn't know what to do about it. He was not particularly competent in IT. He could use a computer okay, but if something went wrong—well that was it. It wasn't as if he had a lot of time either. As treasurer, the accounts which were his responsibility were late and Benedict had been getting increasingly irritated. He was deeply afraid of the apostle's fits of temper. In all his life he'd never witnessed such anger as he could display, and he had come across some mean people in his time.

As he had been given an ultimatum, he was working late into the evening, desperate to get them sorted out before Benedict totally lost patience with him.

He moved out of his office to Brenda Marney's and slid behind her desk. Firing up her computer he slipped off his green sports jacket, flinging it carelessly across the back of her chair, aware that the armpits of his shirt were damp with sweat. He slid the disc into the "A" drive and wiped his hand across his forehead that was beaded with moisture. Why did he always feel so blasted hot in this office? He was irritated by the knowledge that it was probably more fear than heat that was causing the excess moisture.

He was startled as Brenda came in. She was equally surprised to see him in her office. "Working late?" she asked, although the answer was pretty obvious.

"Hope you don't mind. My computer's crashed and I have to do the accounts, Bren. They are a bit late, and you know how the boss is. I've got to have them with him by tomorrow evening."

Brenda nodded, knowing only too well. She stood behind him,

eyeing the information on the computer screen. Finally she said, "You sound tired."

He nodded. "Too much pressure at the office. And now all this. I don't have time for a life."

She pointed at the screen, and as she did do an expensive looking gold bangle slipped down her wrist. "I can tell you now that the information there is wrong."

Riley peered closer. How did she keep all this knowledge in her mind he wondered?

"Here, let me." She leant across and he could smell the faint whiff of Chanel perfume as she moved. Approaching fifty years of age, she remained elegant and desirable. Dressed in a maroon matching skirt and jacket, she looked every inch the power executive. But she was really just Benedict's woman.

She made some adjustment with a dozen clicks of the mouse. "There, that'll stop you getting into trouble."

Riley nodded his thanks gratefully. "I'd better get back home. My son should be back soon and he'll expect his dinner."

For a moment, pain showed in her deep brown eyes. "It's Brandon, isn't it?"

Despite his awareness of her retentive memory, he was still taken aback by her knowledge.

"Yeah, he's seventeen, going on thirty!" There was awe in his voice as he spoke. "Is there anything you don't know about this church and its people?"

"How to forget," she said bleakly.

"What?"

"Nothing. You'd better get on."

He stood, just as Benedict walked into the room.

The apostle ignored Riley initially, and spoke straight at Brenda, who seemed somewhat uneasy at his presence. He in turn seemed surprised to see her.

"Bren, whatever are you still doing here?" He didn't even pause for a reply. "Never mind, I'm glad you are. There are some urgent problems that I need to deal with. Curse those evangelicals criticising again. Seems there is some stuff that I said last week that they want to use against me. Can you fetch the master CD of last Sunday's sermon for me to go through and edit before it is copied and distributed?"

She nodded acquiescently and left the office quickly.

Then he turned, and focussed on Riley.

Riley didn't believe in the power of evil, not really. He didn't believe in God, so believing in an opposite and negative power gave him some difficulty. Yin and yang. Good and bad. Positive and negative. Black and white. You couldn't have one without the other. So he chose to believe in neither.

Some may have thought that strange, seeing as he was a member of the First Church of God, latterly Benedict Ademola Ministries. But Riley knew what he was doing. He didn't worship God, he worshipped power and money and if that meant going though the motions every Sunday, with an occasional mid-week meeting thrown in—well that was all right by him. He didn't feel too guilty in this particular church because he'd always known that Benedict was a charlatan. But a charlatan to be feared nonetheless. There was something about him, something that rang warning bells whenever one was in close proximity with him. He exercised a control over people's lives; that was for sure.

And for all his talk about Jesus, he'd never displayed anything in his life that was even remotely Christ-like. He held his church together by sheer force of control and fear. People stayed not because they loved him as he so often claimed, but because they feared him. He'd brainwashed them until they didn't know what else or who else to follow, leading them by devious mind games down a series of mental mazes. It wasn't until he had blocked their every escape route that they finally realised they were prisoners. It was Benedict or nothing. After years of mental conditioning, "nothing" was too hard to contemplate, so they reluctantly chose slavery of mind and spirit over the random emptiness of the world.

It was a gradual, insidious process. He didn't reveal his strategy all at once. When people first joined the church they were delighted at the warmth and friendship experienced. "Love Bombing," he called it. The choir sounded great. There was a certain comfort in belonging, and the security of rules and assurance. Benedict's rules and Benedict's assurances of course, but in a world devoid of absolutes, any certainty was fine.

Gradually he would move in on the new attendees, subtly influencing them until they found themselves totally reliant on the church. And that meant being totally reliant on Benedict. Because he *was* the church.

Contact with outside friends and family would slowly but certainly be cut off as "dangerous influences." Later it would be made clear that the "truth" lay only with him and his church. All else was false and would lead to hellfire and damnation. Safety lay exclusively in Benedict Ademola and in him alone. One of his favourite scripture quotes was, "If two are not in agreement, how can they walk together?" He had twisted this in his usual manipulative way to his own advantage, to reinforce his control over the people's lives. His interpretation of the scripture was that those in his church had no business with anyone outside. So they became increasingly isolated. Increasingly afraid and uncertain. Increasingly *his*.

Later, the children would be enrolled into the church school, members would be encouraged to work only with and for each other so far as was possible, and the bondage would be complete. To leave the church meant leaving ones friends, losing one's job and leaving the children without a school. Not surprisingly most took the line of least resistance, the easy option and chose to stay, even when things got difficult and questions began to be asked.

And it was dangerous to ask too many questions. His eyes and ears were everywhere. People were only too willing to pass information onto him, to sell out even a family member in the hope of currying favour. If he was busy bullying someone else, then they at least would be left alone.

Those who transgressed his rules would be openly named and shamed from the front of the church during the Sunday morning service, and threatened with expulsion with all the social and economic deprivation that that would mean.

One word that was never mentioned in that place was "love." There was plenty of teaching on God's anger and retribution. A veritable barrage of Benedict's opinions and rantings about "those outside." But love was never heard. Love was neither given nor received. For how can anyone give that which they have not got themselves? And at least one young man from the church had killed himself in despair, although it had all been hushed up and made to go away by judicious use of people in the right places.

Now, he didn't say a word. He merely walked up to Riley, staring silently at him with a strange look in his eyes, all the while rhythmically clicking the ball-point pen that he carelessly toyed with in his hand.

Riley found that more unnerving than the usual display of raw anger.

"I'm working late—on the accounts Mr. Benedict. To get them up-to-date."

Click went the pen.

"They should be done tomorrow—by the end of the day," he said, trying to sound normal but failing totally.

Benedict continued to stare coldly at him, as if probing his mind. Riley hated that remorseless stare; he found it impossible to tear his gaze away from it and was compelled to return the gaze of those cold grey eyes. Eyes that were as mirrors. And in those merciless, implacable reflectors, Nelson Riley's past life was displayed openly and obscenely before him.

Click.

He could see evil things, depraved things. Things in his past life that he feared. Things that he had pushed into his subconscious mind. Things that he didn't want to remember.

Riley trembled as he fought to hold back memories that threatened to engulf him. Thoughts that he had long ago relegated to the deepest recesses of his mind.

Click.

Areas that he had thought inviolate and secure were suddenly displayed, his very soul prised open. His life and thoughts were laid bare, as feelings of self revulsion welled up within. His ears began to pound, and darkness like an engulfing fog enveloped his brain. And something—*someone*—foul and evil began to stir inside him.

CLICK!

CHAPTER TEN

It was a crisp, cold day and the citizens of Hartwood and the surrounding environs were well wrapped up against the biting northerly wind. Scarves and sensible boots were in evidence, even amongst the younger element to whom such practical things were usually anathema. The sky was pretty much grey, and the weather forecasters were having their usual discussions as to whether or not it would snow. It hadn't done so at Christmas time for as long as Jack could remember, so it seemed facile even to discuss it.

He could understand children wanting snow. It transformed the boring old town into a wonderland. But it was an absolute pain to anyone else.

Another thing he never understood was why shoppers left it so late to buy their Christmas gifts and stock up on food and wine. It seemed that the world and his uncle were pouring unchecked into every shop. People staggered along, weighed down by parcels and bags crammed with every conceivable product. And to judge from the groaning shopping trolleys being steered erratically across the supermarket car park, it appeared that the holiday period would be at least a month's duration. However did they get through all that food and drink and other stuff?

There were the usual arguments between couples. Women shouting, exasperated by their male companions. Children, who should have been in bed dragged along mournfully at the rear, aggrieved at their parents. Occasionally one of them would dart an angry glance back at their offspring, and shout a few choice curse words to move them along. This encouragement had little or no effect on the children at all. They were used to it. And the parents were too weary to offer more than token threats in response to their rebellion. It was a game in which parents, offspring and society in general were ultimately the losers. The parents shouted. The youngsters ignored them.

Christmas brought out the worst in so many families. Perhaps they weren't used to being together, and the unaccustomed closeness showed up the fault lines in their relationships. So much for goodwill towards all men! Jack was suddenly glad that he didn't have to pretend. He didn't like Christmas and he didn't like people. And he wasn't afraid to show it. Much better than all that sham that went on in the name of the season of goodwill to all mankind.

He hadn't bought presents. Not this year. Not for the past three years. He didn't have anyone to buy for anyway, even if he'd had the inclination. Which he didn't.

Suddenly aware that his mind wasn't on his work, he made himself focus less on what people were buying, and more on what they were doing. What they looked like. Who they were. This season was a time when street crime soared. Pickpockets were out in force, and unguarded wallets and purses in open coats and shopping bags were fair game. Unlocked cars also provided an Aladdin's cave of opportunity for sharp eyed thieves. And there were plenty of those around.

There was also the problem of binge drinking. Office parties offered an excuse for getting bladdered. Not that one was needed. But that wasn't Jack's responsibility. He was crime. He was always very clear on that. Drunks and fights, unless they were good ones, were down to the uniformed "tops."

He wandered down a side alley leading to a small shopping mall. Beggars had started to use it as a resting place, annoying shoppers with insistent demands for money. If they were refused, they could get quite violent. Some of them had dogs with them. Skinny mongrels with tempers as short as those of their owners.

Today it was clear, so Jack took a short cut through one of the stores and exited back onto the High Street where the incessant jangle of carols and Christmas songs from the seventies assaulted his ears. Didn't anyone ever write any new ones? He wondered how the shop assistants managed. The hundredth rendering of "Jingle Bells," and "They Said There'd Be Snow at Christmas," must be absolute purgatory.

His maudlin train of thought was interrupted by the police radio in his pocket coming to life.

"Go ahead, bravo foxtrot three," said the control room operator. Then came the frustrating "pips" as BF3 spoke his message, heard only by the operator. Jack always thought it a nonsense that only one side of the conversation could be heard, unless the operator switched on the "talk-through" facility. In this case, the operator obviously didn't think it expedient.

"All received BF3. Standby one." Then the "pips" continued.

Jack felt mildly irritated. BF3 was a local foot patrol officer named Simon Green. He was a young officer, still in his probationary period. If there was any decent crime going on that he had fallen over, then Jack wanted to know about it ASAP. But then, the control room had long been taken over by civvies, and the police who used to run them had been distributed across the county to goodness knows where. All in the name of efficiency. But it was really cost-cutting, and the civvies, try as they might, didn't have the same experience or understanding that the police had. For a start, they had never been at the sharp end. They had never fought with a violent man in a lonely side-street, struggling to subdue him whilst calling up frantically for help. And then to experience that moment of utter relief when the sound of police sirens could be heard making their way to the scene.

The radio came back to life. "Any unit in the vicinity of Hartwood High Street? Slight disturbance at the back of the shopping mall."

Jack responded, speaking into his set as he walked quickly back the way he had come. "CM3 on my way. Just a short distance away."

"All received charlie mike three," responded the operator. "No other units required at this time."

Jack smiled. At the hint of a fight, every punchy police officer within a five-mile radius would be itching to get in on the action. They had just been pre-empted from volunteering by the operator, who had clearly dealt with the Hartwood contingency before.

Entering the store that he had exited from just a few minutes previously, he attracted some mild curiosity as he hurried across the shop floor, manoeuvring his way around customers oblivious to what was going on.

"Sorry," he apologised, as he collided with a middle-aged woman examining a rack of clothing. "Excuse me." He pivoted around a huddle of elderly ladies, negotiated a free-standing display of perfume that wobbled alarmingly, and raced for the exit.

Pc Green was standing talking to a group of six youths not much younger than he was himself. Two of them were sitting on a low brick wall, drinking from cans of lager. The other four had surrounded the officer, and were laughing derisively.

"Look lads, you've had a bit of drink, now get on your way and don't be stupid."

The youths on the wall joined in the general laughter and lifted their cans in mock salute. One of those standing, a solid looking youth wearing a blue jean jacket, spat heavily onto the pavement.

"Don't you have better 'fings to do?" he asked, to the accompaniment of further disrespectful laughter.

A skinny teenager of around seventeen or eighteen years-of-age dragged a packet of cigarettes from his pocket, shook one loose, and lit up. Drawing deeply, he blew a cloud of smoke towards the officer.

It was at that moment that Jack arrived. The young officer greeted him with some relief. "Hi sarge."

"Problem?" growled Jack.

The smoking youth sniggered. "Problem?" he parroted, and the others fell about laughing at the wit of their contemporary.

Jack hadn't seen any of them before, and he knew most of the local oiks. "Do you know any of these pieces of crap?" he asked the young bobby, who seemed astonished at Jack's turn of phrase. He hadn't been told about this type of policing from his tutor constable.

"No . . . I don't think so."

The Ds rounded on them. "Right, I'll say this just the once. Clear off out of the town. We've got enough to do without you causing trouble." He glared at the one smoking. "Put that cigarette out." Turning to the youth holding the can of drink, he stretched out his hand. "This is a prohibited area. Under the licensing law, drinking of alcohol in the street is prohibited. Give me that."

The youth stood up, slightly unsteady on his feet, waving the can in

Jack's face. "Who are you calling crap?" he said belligerently. "We know our rights, and you can't talk to us like that. I want your name and number, 'cos I'm going to report you." There was a corresponding rumbling of dissent from the others.

"Why don't you—" began the youth with the can. But he got no further. Jack's right hand snaked out, knocking the can to the ground where the contents ran out in an ever widening puddle across the footpath. Continuing the momentum of the movement, he slapped him hard across the face with his outstretched palm. The force of the blow caused him to topple backwards over the wall.

Without pausing, he snatched the cigarette from the mouth of the other startled youngster who had only just sat down on the wall, placed his foot in the centre of his chest and pushed. It was enough to cause him to join his friend in an undignified heap on the ground.

The others had backed off, and had gone quiet. "Don't mess with us," snarled Jack, the adrenalin flowing in his veins, "Or you will get something you won't like. Now get out of here. If I see you around again I *will* arrest you."

The chastened youths walked off, mumbling between themselves, glancing back only when they were a safe distance away.

The Ds turned to the officer. "Let me give you a bit of advice son. We might live in a politically correct age where you are expected to be a bloody social worker rather than a police officer. But if you have no pride in that uniform, some of us still have."

"But sarge, I—"

What the young officer was thinking Jack didn't hear, because he wasn't interested. "Listen. If you let the scroats walk all over you, you will never be an effective police officer. Remember, you are our visible representation. It's up to you. Wear that uniform with pride. If they think they can get away with insulting the cloth, what chance does the public stand? All these brain-dead prats understand is straightforward policing, alright? No chat. Just do it." Then he turned and walked away, leaving the officer confused and angry. His tutor constable had told him how to deal with this kind of situation. And it hadn't entailed any form of violence.

It was Brenda that saved him. As she returned to the office, Benedict instinctively glanced towards her, breaking eye contact with Riley who mumbled something about not feeling well, before rushing towards the door.

"Wait!"

He froze, almost loosing control of his bladder so fragile was his emotional state.

Brenda walked quickly towards him holding his jacket. "You almost forgot this," she said. She glanced quizzically at him, noting his pale face and the sweat that beaded on his brow.

Riley nodded, grabbed it and fled from the office. He headed straight for the toilets, where he was immediately and violently sick. Wiping his mouth with his handkerchief, he found that his hands were still trembling, and it was with a pounding heart and unsteady legs that he walked the short distance back to the small flat he rented off the High Street. He was still full of the unwholesome images that Benedict had stirred up in his mind. Images that refused to go away. He felt nauseated and deeply afraid.

He made a cup of tea in his tiny kitchen, pouring in a liberal dose of whisky before collapsing on the sofa. He remained there long enough for the alcohol to do its job, and he began to calm down.

When the phone rang it caused a resurgence of panic. So he sat rigid for a time, unable to react. He had no idea who it could be. He didn't have any friends and had broken contact with his relatives a long time ago. That was in part due to Benedict's teaching on those not in agreement being unable to walk together. And Riley wasn't in agreement with many people. And so he walked alone. The fact that just one solitary Christmas card adorned his sideboard was a testimony to that loneliness and isolation.

There was only his son, Brandon, and although they shared the flat, their relationship was not good. Not since the "incident" at the church some years back. It had been covered up pretty well. Not for his sake. He wasn't fool enough to believe that his skin was worth anything. But Benedict's was. And *his* church, of course, needed protecting.

But his wife somehow suspected, and she left him in disgust when she inevitably found out.

The phone continued to ring insistently, until finally he reluctantly picked it up. Holding the receiver nervously away from his ear, as if the distance would create a safe barrier, he spoke timidly.

"Yes?"

The voice was muffled and unusually deep. "Listen. If you value your life, get rid of what's in your jacket pocket. Destroy it—quickly!" There was a note of urgency in the message.

"What is all this . . ."

Nothing further was said and his question was cut off in mid-sentence as the telephone at the other end was replaced.

The demon Isagoge was satisfied. As long as he could maintain Jack's anger, he would control him. And it was necessary that he did just that. He'd had him for many years now, and it had become easy. He didn't even have to work at it much anymore. An occasional word whispered into his ear was all that was required. Maintenance. That's what was needed. Spiritual maintenance.

He fluttered off to seek his comrades for some gossip and a time of unholy sharing. He could afford to leave Jack alone for a while. There was no danger of him turning over a new leaf. Isagoge laughed loudly at the very thought. He was justifiably proud at what he had achieved.

Jack was back at Hartwood police station, where he seemed to spend most of his life. So far, it had been a bad day, but not the worst he had had. The incident in the High Street had bucked him up a bit. Confrontation and the resulting adrenalin flow had that effect on him. Nevertheless, for the first time in many, many months he contemplated a stiff drink. Somehow he managed to resist, absolutely determined not to let his life fall apart again.

He laid the Mahoney file to one side. He wasn't really interested in suicides. They had no bearing on the "TWOC's" that he was looking at. But that left just the Somerville file. And he was sure he wasn't going to read that one. He shouldn't even have it, he knew. It was sheer lunacy. He was finding life difficult enough without dragging everything up again—.

Andrew and Jamie Somerville. He sat looking at the file, placing a hand on it as if somehow he could touch something of what they had once been.

But this was all there was, he thought bitterly. All that remained of two precious lives. All that was left of his two boys, *his* family. A family that had lived and laughed and cried together. Just a buff file, a wad of documents and their names, neatly typed on a white piece of sticky-backed paper.

He wished that he could cry, but his tear ducts were as dry as his heart was barren. He was dead inside, unable to respond with any emotion other than that of anger. And sometimes fear.

Outside the office, the two angels on guard duty prevented the demon from entering. Isagoge was furious. Having left, as he thought, his victim safely occupied with despair, he was angry and not a little frightened at finding his way back barred. "You have no right," he said. "He's mine. I've controlled him for years."

The larger of the two angels drew himself up to his full height. "Begone little imp, or it will be bad for you."

"The Lord has his hand on this one, he is no longer yours," said the other.

"This town is ours," wailed Isagoge, "you have no prayer warriors, you have no strength. We can, we *will* keep what is lawfully ours."

The big angel took a pace forward threateningly, half drawing his sword. A shaft of light from the blade lit up the face of the demon, and he stumbled back in pain, shielding his eyes.

"You dare to speak to me about the law?" he said, his tone low and menacing.

The demon stepped rapidly backwards out of range.

"You may have him for now," said Isagoge grudgingly, not wanting to loose too much face, "But I will be back with others, and then you will not be so bold."

Both warriors darted forward, and Isagoge leapt into the air on his short stumpy wings, fluttering a like a bat on a summer evening. He headed back to Hartwood cursing the fact that he'd left Jack alone. He consoled himself with the fact that soon he would have reinforcements, and the two brash angels would regret their boldness.

The big angel was sombre. "I guess he'll be back."

The other nodded. "Yes, and unfortunately he's right. We don't have much prayer cover. We are not strong and cannot win a fight with any significant numbers of the enemy."

His companion sighed. "The Spirit is working my friend. He is drawing his people together."

"Well, we must pray that they respond quickly. We don't have much time."

Shaun O'Connor was thinking. Usually his alcohol induced musings faded over the course of time. But his time it was different. The thoughts refused to leave his mind. They sat there, nagging at him in a way that he didn't understand. Or particularly like.

He had long ago lost Rosaleen and his daughter Colleen. Not intentionally. Not straight away. Slowly and imperceptibly their love for him had eroded. Selfishly, ignorantly, he had let them go. Because he hadn't even thought about what he had, until he no longer had it.

The place in his heart that he should have kept pure for his wife and daughter he had given away cheaply. To women, mostly, but drink had played its part. He'd thought he was smart. A man of the world, able to balance commitment to marriage with the occasional straying into the arms of another. And a good social life. That had been important. And a good social life meant a good drinking life with his cronies.

"You damn fool," he shouted aloud in his pain. Knowing, too late, that he had given up the best thing that had ever happened to him in his crummy life. He'd exchanged everything for nothing. Lost all, for nights of loveless passion with women whose names he couldn't even remember.

He sipped his drink, but it tasted as bitter as wormwood in his mouth and he spat it out distastefully, a feeling of panic beginning to rise in him.

Whiskey was all he had. If he didn't have that, he had nothing. He didn't know it then. But that was the last time in his life that alcohol would touch his lips.

Riley scrabbled in the pocket of the jacket flung carelessly on the settee. There was nothing. He checked the other pocket and his fingers closed over something flat. Pulling it out, he recognised the distinctive plastic case containing a CD.

He'd never seen it before and it was more than a bit odd that it should be there. But it was obviously important enough for someone to want him to dump it. His mind was still brittle following his earlier encounter with Benedict, and he had to exert himself to think clearly. It was all a bit surreal. But the warning had been clear and it convinced him that he needed to do something. And if nothing else, the fear that he felt was real enough . . .

He considered just dumping it and getting out of the place. He'd been thinking of doing that for a while, but he hadn't planned for it to happen just yet. He didn't have the money for one thing. And was it possible for him to start again somewhere?

Where would he go? What would he do? He realised with a terrible feeling of emptiness that there was no-one, and nowhere for him to go to.

On impulse he inserted the disk into his computer's CD drive. If there was danger, he had a right at least to see what it was all about.

The programme opened automatically and displayed the contents. A set of accounts in spreadsheet format. It wasn't a set that he was familiar with. He clicked on the appropriate button, magnifying the page so that it filled the screen, and then whistled a long, drawn out note of surprise.

It was clear that what he had in front of him was a record of the church accounts. A private record. Because it didn't show money flowing in as one would expect. Quite the reverse. It showed money flowing out. Large sums of money!

Row after row of figures going back many years showed varying amounts being transferred to half-a-dozen accounts in several countries. The largest was to a bank account in the Caribbean named, "Awakening!"

As he paged down, he was stunned. As treasurer he was aware that the church pulled in large sums of money from its gullible disciples, but even he was astonished by the figures that he could see displayed in front of him. None of the church members ever saw the accounts. Benedict simply didn't publish them. It wasn't their business after all. They just tithed the money in, and how and where it was spent was not their problem.

A quick scrutiny revealed that huge sums, several millions of pounds, had been diverted from the church into the secret accounts.

There were entries showing the purchase and the revenue from land, buildings and other business dealings both in the UK and abroad. It was obvious that this was an enormously profitable, if illegal business that the Inland Revenue and probably the fraud squad would be most interested in.

Riley didn't possess many skills, but he knew accounting, and it was plain that someone, and that someone had to be Benedict, was keeping two sets of books. One for the Tax Man—and another for himself. In order to milk such large sums, members must have been handing over incredible sums of money.

His first feeling was one of smugness. Benedict had been caught with his hand in the till. But that feeling quickly turned to panic as he realised that the apostle would inevitably find out that he had the information. He had just witnessed the apostle's power. No secret was hidden for long from his gaze. He sat back and tried to think clearly. Which wasn't easy after what he had been through.

Bren! The thought exploded into his brain. It was Brenda who had handed him his jacket. She was the only person who could have had access to the disk, and she had handed him his jacket as he was leaving her office. She must have slipped it into the pocket. Not that that made a lot of sense. Why would she do it? It was totally illogical, but it was the only explanation that seemed to fit, even though she was Benedict's confident, his closest and most loyal follower. None of it made sense. But he knew that he had to get it rid of it, and fast.

He shuddered at the thought of Benedict finding out, because if—when he did—he knew that his mind, if not his very life, would be in jeopardy.

A thought struck him. And made him want to retch. But though afraid, his natural greed gave him courage. After all, he owed him after what he had done to his mind.

Riley was a poor man. The wage that he was paid for working in the Insurance office was gone as soon as he received it. Because it went to Cooper. He felt his anger stir up against his blackmailer. Perhaps this was his way out? With money he could get away. He could start a new life where no-one knew him.

There and then he decided that he *would* go away. Not just now. He needed time to arrange things. But he would go as soon as he could, and the information on the disk was his ticket to freedom.

So he did it. Surprising himself at his own audacity. He burnt off a copy on a rewriteable DVD disc.

Then it was done. But where to put it? Looking around his flat, he considered places where he could hide it. It needed to be absolutely safe where no-one would ever find it, but where it would be easily accessible when he needed it.

He smiled cunningly. He knew just the place. A place where Benedict certainly would never look. He spent the next fifteen minutes preparing the hiding place until finally he was satisfied.

Afterwards, he telephoned the local police station asking to be put through to the senior officer on duty. He spent quite some time talking when he was finally connected. "I understand," he said at last, his voice reedy and nervous, "but can't you come any earlier? Okay, okay. 5:30pm will have to do then. I'll wait here for you. But please, Mr. Benedict's a dangerous man. Don't come in a marked police car or anything like that will you?"

He replaced the receiver and sat back to while away the time until they arrived. He wondered briefly why it was that he paid his taxes. When you couldn't get the police round without having to wait hours, something was definitely wrong with the country. But he felt some consolation. Despite his fear, he couldn't suppress a satisfied feeling. Soon, he would be out of the country. And Benedict would be history!

CHAPTER ELEVEN

For Emily, the evening had been fun at first. Brandon had shown her every consideration, a real gentleman, insisting on paying for all the drinks. And as it was the festive season she had accepted, permitting herself to drink more than she usually did. Not that she was drunk, but she felt mellow and relaxed.

The bar that they had gone to was packed with people having their office celebrations. It was festooned with streamers. Seasonal pop hits played incessantly and roasted chestnuts crackled on a shovel over a coal fire. Somehow the warmth of the fire and thoughts of an impending Christmas stirred up faded childhood memories. Not that her childhood had been that great. But it could have been worse.

She looked across at Brandon and laughed with pleasure, basking in the reflected glow of other people's celebrations, and the attention that he was lavishing upon her.

It was when he suggested giving her a lift home that the problems started. She'd giggled a bit, and although it was a first date she'd agreed because he had been fun and had done nothing that alarmed her. He had an old Vauxhall car that was a bit ropey, but in the dark it was cool, and she felt quite proud being driven through the High Street. She hoped that she would spot some of the girls that she knew—perhaps even Ashley. How she would love to rub her nose in it.

The first inkling that something was wrong came when instead of taking the route to her home he took a side road that led away from town towards the countryside. She made a joke of it at first. "Hey, do you want some help with the navigation, 'cos my house is back in that direction?" He responded by driving faster.

She became alarmed then. "Look, this isn't funny Brandon. You take me home now or I'll jump!" She reached for the door handle, but he only laughed as it flopped uselessly in her hand.

"I've gotta get that fixed," he grinned, and a shudder went through her as she realised she was trapped.

She tried desperately to think. At school there had been a lesson from the local police officer on personal safety, but just when she could do with some answers, she couldn't remember a thing. Probably because she hadn't paid any attention at the time.

The youth turned into a dirt track by the side of a field, braking hard and bringing the car to a skidding halt in a flurry of gravel and dirt. Despite her seatbelt, Emily was flung forward as the car slid violently sideways.

She acted instinctively when he leant over, forcing his mouth against hers, his hands pawing at her clothing. She bit down on his bottom lip. Hard! His response was fast and savage. He swung back a fist, and punched her straight in the face.

Emily screamed as she felt her nose break, her blood spattering the new dress and tasting oddly metallic as it ran into her mouth. He hit her again, and she felt her lips split. She tried to fight back, but she was defenceless against the maddened youth.

Taking a handful of her hair, hair that she had carefully arranged so as to look her best for him, he began to drag her towards his side of the car. It was only her seat belt, still buckled around her that prevented her being pulled bodily from the seat. He had a savage look on his face. "A virgin eh?" he rasped. "Too good for anyone are you?" His hand grabbed a handful of her dress, ripping it open with a powerful wrench. "Well, we'll soon see about that."

It was only then that naïve Emily realised the whole evening had been a set up. It was a put-up job, arranged to humiliate her. Ashley of course was behind it. Why else had someone like Brandon asked her out?

Her swollen face was hurting badly, but still she continued to struggle fiercely. There was no-one around to help her, even if she did scream. And she desperately didn't want to be hit again.

"Help me," she pleaded in a whisper. Tears streamed down her face. "Help me someone."

Aanfial gazed down from his vantage point on the roof of the factory on the outskirts of Hartwood. Although the streets were dark, his piercing eyes missed nothing. Beside him was Talial and Auriel, both warriors in God's army. Aanfial was their captain, their commanding officer.

They were watching the group of demons dressed in their black shapeless smocks, shouting and laughing harshly as they clambered over the Vauxhall car, peering in at the windows. As they were spirit, they could not be seen by the occupants of the car.

With one exception, they were obviously minor entities, wearing none of the badges or the jewels of office of the higher demon. They were very sure of themselves, which was to be expected as they had taken more and more of Hartwood in succeeding years with little challenge from the church.

They were presently enjoying the spectacle of a young teenage girl and her tormentor huddled in a car just outside the residential area. One demon stood out from the others. Not only was he was far bigger, with an air of importance, but he also wore the white jewels of a senior demon. His smock with the two diamonds affixed to the collar along with the diamond rings on his left hand denoted that he was a regional leader.

Earlier in town Aanfial had seen numerous demons. Some had been unattached, but most were fixed firmly to humans. Humans totally oblivious to their perilous state. A high percentage of the attached demons were clinging to youths; they were the ones who were swearing loudly, sicking up onto the pavement the alcohol that they had been filling themselves with all evening. Other entities were on the wing, flying along the streets of the town in pursuit of any mischief that they could make.

Many unruly youths were out that evening, and soon there was the tinkling sound of breaking glass along with shrill laughter and raucous swearing.

"Urban art!" shouted a staggering youth with spiked hair, as he raked a key along the entire length of an expensive saloon car, provoking gales of alcoholic laughter from those with him. Several were emptying their bladders in shop doorways. It would be very late the next day before they eventually crawled out of their beds with the realisation that they had drunk away their whole week's money.

Under railway arches, in parked cars and in a sprawl of housing across the area, drugs were being smoked and injected. With their proliferation, there had been the corresponding huge increase in dealers who were only too willing to provide. At a cost of course.

The cost was hard cash, but as dependency and frequency of use went up, money was quickly depleted. Soon, burglaries, thefts and street robberies soared as desperate addicts sought to fund their increasingly demanding lifestyle.

Later still, the next "fix" became all-consuming. Now nothing mattered. Eating, hygiene, friendships—none of these things were of concern. Only the next drug-induced "rush."

Young people sold whatever they could lay their hands on in a desperate attempt to hang onto the "good times." Soon, all they had left were their bodies, which they sold for a paltry handful of cash, until they were so ruined that even that avenue was closed to them. Gaunt and hollow eyed, old beyond their years and covered in skin rashes and rancid with sexually transmitted disease, they were on the scrapheap before they had even begun to live.

What was surprising to some social commentators was that even ordinarily well-mannered, law-abiding youngsters were adopting the same lifestyles. Crime and hatred in Hartwood was no longer the exclusive domain of the feckless, criminally minded layabout.

So the streets became more or less deserted of ordinary folk, who had learned the hard way that they were not safe anymore. Despite the insistent claims of the police that the fear of crime was worse than the reality, residents had faced the threats and torrent of abuse too often to venture outdoors after dark when the crazies took over.

Numerous parents living on good class estates wondered where they had gone wrong as they retrieved their wayward youngsters once again from the police station.

Had they seen the demonic control that existed in their town, they would have understood.

Unfortunately the only hope of fighting such evil, the church, had mostly fallen into decay along with the truth. The weapons of spiritual warfare had gone rusty with disuse. God had been relegated to the realm of superstition. The intellectuals who ran many of the churches denied the reality of evil, and substituted a social gospel for the power of the Word of God and his Christ. Sitting at the feet of liberal theology, the people of God slept. And whilst they did, darkness was falling across the world.

"Barbas," shrieked the small lust-demon, "get out of the way and let me get on with my job." He pushed against the large demon angrily. "I have to maintain control, or I'll loose him."

Barbas, a cruelty-demon and leader of the region turned, giving the smaller demon a resounding cuff as he did so, causing him to tumble backwards several feet.

"You forget yourself Ronwe," he hissed, "watch your mouth before I cut you." He put a hand menacingly on the hilt of his short sword.

Zaebos and Cunali laughed loudly. "Ronwe's so small, it looks like someone has already cut him. In half!" cackled Cunali.

"We'd better look after him," spluttered Zaebos, "because people his size are in short supply!" He fell about in mirth at his own wit, with Cunali joining in enthusiastically.

Ronwe gave them a sour look, as he glanced towards the boy and girl in the car. With rising panic, he could see that Brandon was already beginning to break free.

He stood rubbing himself where he hurt. "You think you're so smart, but you Zaebos, if you're that clever, why are you only a lowly demon of shame? And Cunali, you are even pettier with your ministry of low self-esteem. Neither of you can do your work until I have finished doing mine!"

"You talk big," shouted Zaebos, drawing his sword and advancing forward. Cunali likewise began circling from behind.

It was only the intervention of Barbas that saved him. "Enough!"

The roar caused all three feuding demons to freeze in their tracks. A sulphur-like yellow glow filled the air as Barbas drew his sword. "You have work to do, in case you've forgotten. Or do you want to argue with my sword? Even better, why not try explaining to Master Bune why you thought your petty quarrel was more pressing then his orders?"

At the mention of the dreaded Bune, master of the region, all three demons went deathly quiet and a dreadful fear fell upon them.

Ronwe, looking smug, resumed his position by the car and continued to whisper seductive evil into the mind of Brandon.

Jack was not in the best of moods when Lewis walked in. "What do you want?" he asked curtly, avoiding looking directly at the Dc so that he would not see the unconsummated grief that still haunted his eyes.

"I thought you wanted to speak with me?" Lewis sat down opposite, noting the buff "Somerville" folder on the desk. His eyes seemed incapable of registering anything as he stretched out a giant hand and picked it up. Jack noted sourly that he was still wearing gloves. Didn't he ever take the damn things off?

"Sarge, you don't want to be doing this," he said.

At any other time Jack would have been furious with anyone who had the nerve to interfere with his business. But he was feeling vulnerable and angry with himself. He didn't trust himself to argue, not now. The worst possible thing that could happen would be for him to show weakness in front of someone like Lewis. In no time at all it would be all round the canteen and his reputation would be finished.

He couldn't allow that to happen. He had survived almost thirty years with his reputation as a hard-hitting, no nonsense policeman intact, and with just a week to go he was adamant he was not going to loose the only things he had managed to hang onto. His self-respect and his reputation. He guarded both with equal jealousy. He had lost his sons, lost his wife, lost everything that really mattered. He was one hundred percent sure that respect and reputation he *would* keep.

"Just take it Lewis. I was looking for any possible link between the rise in TWOC's and non-stop RTA's. When you've finished, file it in admin." He got up and headed out of the door.

The big Dc emptied the contents of the file onto Jack's desk. There were the usual photographs, sketch plan, and other paperwork such as statements. The photographs showed a Ford estate, lying on its roof in the road. Portable spotlights lit up the area, showing the wet road surface where the fire brigade had hosed down the burning wreck. Scattered debris could clearly be seen, caused when the car had struck the bridge. He turned to the investigating officer's report.

> The circumstances of this accident are that at 10:45 pm on 12th June, a red Ford motor vehicle being driven by Mrs. Susan Somerville skidded on the wet road surface in Back Lane, Hartwood and collided with the iron bridge. The car appears to have immediately burst into flames. Mrs. Somerville survived, but the two children, Andrew aged eight years and Jamie aged nine years were trapped and subsequently sustained fatal injuries. The road is in a quiet, rural location and there were no witnesses to the accident. There are no signs of any other vehicles being involved. The circumstances suggest the deceased lost control on the damp road surface and collided with the bridge. Speed must have been a factor, but there would be nothing to gain by prosecuting the unfortunate mother, who I would suggest has suffered enough. I request that this be filed and no further action taken.

The senior officer had concurred. The report was stamped in red ink. *Case Closed.*

There was nothing in the file to suggest the remotest connection with any stolen vehicles, so he carefully returned all the documents to the folder.

He stood up to leave, and as he did so he spotted another, similar buff folder with the name "Mahoney" neatly typed on it. Almost as an afterthought he picked it up and read the name aloud, pronouncing so that it rhymed with "baloney."

It was a suicide, and the investigator had been Detective Sergeant

Michelle Radigan. That was before she had been promoted to her current position.

It was a sad case, and against his better judgement he found himself being drawn into it as he read the statements.

Nathan Mahoney was a sixteen-year-old boy. He was well thought of by his peers and school teachers and by all accounts he was bright, and had been predicted to do well in his GCSE "A" levels. He was a churchgoer and attended a place called The First Church of God. He was a likeable boy and kept himself out of trouble. He was unremarkable in all respects. Just a normal, healthy teenager.

At least on the surface. Because on Christmas Eve twelve-years previously he had gone to a lonely wood and hung himself.

Lewis turned the page. The poor lad. He wondered what it was that had tortured him so much that the only release he could find was in death. He knew from past experience that suicide could be a tempting way out of a painful existence. He'd contemplated it himself when he'd had his accident. But a young man with no obvious problems? That was incomprehensible.

He began to slip the documents back inside the wallet. As he did so, a half-page of white paper fluttered out. It had been attached to another document at some time, because it still bore the impressed outline of a wire paperclip.

It was a transcript of a telephone call made to HQ information room on the day that Nathan Mahoney had killed himself. All calls were automatically recorded, and showed the whole conversation from start to finish. The conversation considered important had been highlighted. The call was from a Mr. Mahoney—Nathan's father, and it showed a telephone number and an address.

The call was brief and to the point. Mr. Mahoney was worried about his son Nathan. He hadn't come home from school and he wanted to know whether there had been any accidents. The police operator had told him that she wasn't aware of any, but advised him to enquire at the local hospital. She ended by saying that if he hadn't returned in the next couple of hours, to call back.

Lewis knew that that call *would* have been made. Because Nathan never did return.

CHAPTER TWELVE

Auriel was furious, and his golden eyes flashed with fire as he watched Brandon attack Emily.

"My captain," he pleaded, "am I just to sit here and watch?"

He reached across his shoulder, his hand grasping the hilt of the huge sword sheathed in a scabbard strapped across his back, and his fury was terrible. "I am in a mood to cleave some demons for the Lord." He stood, and his great wings unfurled like a canopy above him. Few angels had the wingspan that he did, and fewer still could beat him for sheer speed and agility in the sky.

Aanfial placed a powerful hand on the young angel, gently preventing him from drawing his sword. He smoothed the ruffled feathers of his wings. "You will need your courage soon enough my young warrior," he said, "but not quite yet. Not by power, or by might but by my Spirit says the Lord." The captain quoted the Scripture quietly, and the youthful angel bowed his head as the mildly rebuking word was spoken.

"Trust the Spirit, young Auriel," said Talial. "Be strong. He who searches all things, even the mind of God, knows what he is doing." The angel spoke without ever taking his eyes off of the four demons arguing below.

"Talial," said the captain, "the Spirit is working in this town but the prayers of the saints are still weak; we are not yet strong enough to take on this motley lot in an open fight. But maybe we can make an opportunity to help young Emily."

"Yes, captain," was the only response. Talial was an angel of few words. He preferred that his actions did the talking for him.

Auriel agreed. "The minute the saints begin to pray in earnest . . ." he muttered. The look on his face showed quite plainly what he would do.

"Talial—you surely must be itching to despatch a few unholy monsters yourself?"

Auriel had heard of the legendary fighting exploits of this giant with the bow and arrows of gold, one of the mightiest of the angel warriors. He had reputedly fought in the great battle at the beginning, when Lucifer himself had been cast down from heaven. It was said that Talial had fought unceasingly for seven days and seven nights against the renegade angels that had sided with Lucifer's bid to ascend to the Throne of Almighty God. Countless numbers of these dark angels had perished at his hand.

And such was Talial's reputation that an intermediary from Lucifer himself had offered untold worlds and power to him if he would but worship the dark lord and betray Adonai.

His answer had been to prostrate himself before the throne of God, and swear afresh his eternal loyalty to the Lord of Lords and King of Kings.

But he never commented on these matters, and had maintained his silence down the aeons of time.

Now he nodded in agreement, and touched the great bow that lay at his side. It was twice the size of an ordinary bow, and only he had the strength to draw it.

"Captain," he responded in his deep voice, "you let me know when we have sufficient prayer cover. I've an arrow or two that wants to find a home in a demon." Then he went back to his intense surveillance of the depraved drama continuing below.

"Be patient my friends," said Aanfial. "We have to be very careful here. The Spirit has indicated that Emily Bowman is of paramount significance in God's plans."

"An opportunity," interjected Auriel. "Captain, you said just now that we might make an opportunity . . . ?"

Aanfial had a serious expression on his face as he half drew his sword from its scabbard. It glowed with white light. "People are praying, and praying in the Spirit," he exclaimed with satisfaction. He rammed the sword home and beckoned both angels to his side. "This is what we'll do," he explained.

"Do what thou wilt shall be the whole of the law," said the police officer, speaking breathlessly into the telephone.

"So mote it be."

"Riley has made contact."

"And?" The voice was abrupt.

"He knows."

"He knows what?"

"The Awakening!"

There was a pause at the other end. Then, "How have you come by this?"

"He rang the station. Fortunately I was passed the call."

"Who else knows?"

"Nobody. He's scared."

"What did you tell him?"

"That I would send a police officer."

"Very good. You will obviously go yourself." The instructions that followed were clear and simple. Then the telephone receiver was replaced.

For a moment the four demons believed that finally the end had come! Zaebos, Cunali and Ronwe were cowering as a flash of light lit up the night sky above them, before spiralling away like a comet to the South. Even Barbas was stunned for just a moment before he realised.

"It's one of the enemy," he shouted, looking across to his cowering underlings, convinced that the abyss was about to open under their feet. Barbas snarled at their feebleness. "You three get yourselves sorted, *now!*" he shouted, drawing his short sword, causing a haze of yellow fog to cascade around him as he did so. "Cunali—left side, Zaebos—right side," he ordered, pointing with his sword towards the wooded area in front of them.

"We obey," they cried in unison, running to carry out their leader's command, drawing their swords as they did so; Dark, sulphurous clad figures scurrying to their respective posts, their eyes searching the sky in the direction the enemy had gone.

"Ronwe, keep your eyes on the boy. You were boasting just a moment ago about your superior art. Now make sure you use it, and quickly."

Barbas was too experienced to let the sudden disturbance throw his plans into disarray for long, and already his mind was working. There had been no trouble with the enemy in a long, long time. In fact they hadn't so much as sighted an angel for many months. He moved into the shadows, his unblinking red eyes scanning the southerly heavens. There was nothing to be seen. The darkness was absolute.

He cursed as he realised that there were just the four of them if an attack came. The rest of his command had seen the chance for some fun and were now streaming after the enemy in an undisciplined flapping cloud of evil. He was aware of his own capabilities, but he had no confidence at all in the fighting prowess of his three underlings. They were good for tormenting helpless humans. But that was all.

Aanfial, flying low, checked back over his shoulder with satisfaction as he saw the demons take up the chase. He slowed subtly. He didn't want them giving up in discouragement too early.

It was up to Auriel and Talial now to carry out the rescue of Emily. He went into an acrobatic spin, sending a shower of silver-speckled light over the sleeping town of Hartwood, before heading upwards into the star-studded heavens.

Cunali, crouching in the dense undergrowth gripped his sword tightly. He was frightened. He hadn't had much experience of the enemy, and the few skirmishes that he had been involved in had been confined to areas where the prayer cover had been either weak or non-existent. Therefore the enemy had been weak. He startled as a shout came from somewhere ahead.

"Cunali, report!" demanded Barbas.

Cunali instinctively straightened from his crouching position in order to respond. "Clear, nothing to report," he responded, aware that his voice was quavering.

Those quavering words were the last that he spoke before being despatched to the abyss. Talial had been waiting patiently for a target to show itself, and even in near total darkness all he had needed was that one moment of carelessness. From the impossible distance of the factory rooftop, he drew his powerful bow, unleashing a golden arrow. It flew from the bowstring with a soft twang, the feathered fletchings spinning the shaft as it sped silently, straight and true to its target; Cunali's cowardly heart. There was a silent implosion of darkness, and all that remained to show that the demon of low self-esteem had ever existed was a black scorch-mark on the grass.

"Zaebos, report in," called Barbas. There was no reply. He cursed the incompetence of the demons he had been saddled with and called again. His voice rasped with anger. "Zaebos!" But there was no response.

Barbas moved silently back towards the car where he had sent Ronwe, ensuring he remained under cover of the trees. Had he gone forward, he would have seen a second blackened patch of ground where once Zaebos had stood.

On the roof of the factory, Talial laid down his bow.

Emily had no strength left. She had fought Brandon with all her might, but he was so strong. Like a man possessed. Her face was hurting badly and had swollen considerably, causing her right eye to close and her head also ached where a large clump of hair had been torn out. The rest of her hair now hung in a straggled mess around her. Blood soaked the front of her torn dress, and her face was streaked with tears.

She tried again to reason with him, although she didn't think it would make much difference. He seemed beyond hearing. Beyond reason.

"Brandon, why are you doing this?" Her voice trembled, and the desperation and hurt in her voice was evident. She retreated as far as she could to her side of the car, pressing up against the passenger door.

If she could have seen Ronwe, then it would have been evident. But even Brandon was unaware of the whispered seduction of the demon of lust.

"She wants you," whispered Ronwe seductively, "she came with you of her own free will, and so you have a right," he suggested, exhaling yellow vapour into the youth's face as he spoke. He continued to whisper other thoughts, evil thoughts, thoughts straight from the pit of hell as he brought Brandon deeper and deeper under his control.

This was a job that Ronwe excelled at. It was also a job that he enjoyed mightily. Lust. That was not only what he did, it was also what he was.

"Brandon!" She shouted at him. His face was blank, his eyes dead—almost as if he was in some kind of trance, and for the first time Emily wondered not whether she would avoid rape, but whether she would get out alive.

Ronwe was agitated by the shouting from Barbas and Cunali. In his irritation he lost some control over the boy.

He was unaware of Auriel crouching on the far side of the car out of sight, his robes subdued and grey. The angel took the opportunity provided by the demon's preoccupation and laid his hand on Brandon's head, speaking quietly into his ear. Speaking into Brandon's soul; speaking God's words of peace, of love and purity.

The youth let out a deep sigh. His spirit was being touched by a new authority. A mighty force. An irresistible power. Somewhere deep inside him, a part that he himself had no knowledge of, a battle had begun. Two opposite forces were fighting for the victory. The Spirit of God against the power of evil and the depravity that it carried in its train.

It was no contest. The light of God flooded into his soul, piercing the darkness as with a sword, and the shadows fled before it.

Brandon cringed back in his seat as far away from Emily as he could, a look of sheer horror on his face as he saw as if for the first time, what he had done. The deadness in his eyes faded as the words of holiness that Auriel had planted displaced the evil that Ronwe had sown.

Ronwe, steeped as he was in darkness and evil, was nonetheless a cunning adversary. And although afraid and distracted, still he smelt the sweet fragrance of the Christ's Holy Spirit as he came and touched Brandon's soul. And it made him want to retch. And run. And hide. Because it was the smell of the enemy. To him it was not the sweet fragrance of the Lord. It was the smell of death!

It was in that same instant that he became aware of the presence of Auriel on the far side of the car. He saw the angel's hand resting on Brandon's head.

Looking wildly around, his eyes were wide with fear. But there were no other angels that he could see. This must be the only one. He fervently hoped it was. Mustering his limited supply of courage, he drew his sword. His diminutive size was now to his advantage as he dived underneath the car, his short sword held out straight in front of him.

The fierce attack of the little demon caught the angel unawares, and the sword pierced his right leg as the lust-demon shot past him in triumph.

"Little rat," he said contemptuously, "do you think you can overcome me with such a pinprick?" Nevertheless his leg ached sorely from the poisonous demonic blade.

Ronwe prepared to launch himself again, his red eyes flashing in anticipation of victory. "You are helpless, angel. Your so-called saints give you no prayer cover at all."

Auriel responded by drawing himself up to his full height, and he was an imposing sight. As he spread his wings and filled the air above him, the demon fell back in spite of his bluster.

He would have been slain that very instant but for the intervention of Barbas whose sword now cut the angelic warrior deeply in a typically cowardly attack from behind. Part of his right wing sagged uselessly from the slashing blow, and he fell forward onto his knees in the dust.

Despite the agony, he twisted agilely to face the new danger, seeing the leering face of the chief demon standing over him. This new fiend was three or four times the size of Ronwe and altogether a far more ferocious attacker. Auriel knew that with lack of serious prayer cover and the injuries he had sustained, he was far too weak to defeat this huge demon. But he would certainly try.

First he had to deal with Ronwe, who was now stabbing at the air with his weapon and making boastful threats. The angel rolled sideways, at the same instant unsheathing his golden sword in a blur of motion. Then his drab grey robe glorified, shining with a light so intense that it blinded Ronwe and split the night apart around the three combatants. His voice shook the very air as he leapt forward with the cry, "To

Him who sits upon the Throne and to the Lamb," and his sword flashed before him.

The speed at which he left the ground had caught Ronwe off guard; he feinted with a low attack and as the demon clumsily brought his sword down to cover himself, he changed direction lightening-fast. The demon's eyes flickered momentarily in terror. Then he went into the abyss with a piercing shriek as Auriel's blade cleaved through his body from the top of his left shoulder down to his waist.

Without pause, he went into a sideways roll, anticipating the rear attack from Barbas. But too late! Barbas had not been standing idly by whilst Ronwe was being despatched, and the larger demon's steel caught the wounded angel another blow, slicing deeply into his shoulder. He fell heavily, his sword falling from his hand and disappearing into the undergrowth.

"Precious angel," mocked Barbas, "you are so far out of your league." The point of his sword jabbed hard into the warrior's throat. "Where is your Lord now, when you need him most?

The angel did not answer, gazing steadily at the strutting demon with the white jewelled collar. Then he looked away, a gesture that Barbas took for defeat. But the angel was searching urgently for his weapon. He couldn't see it, the grass and bushes obscuring its location. He mentally calculated the possibility of finding it before Barbas managed to finish him off, and decided that it was zero.

Barbas laughed, suddenly realising his error. This angel didn't know he had lost. He stepped back a pace. "Bring it on," he mocked, "if you are fast enough."

Still, Auriel did not reply, his golden eyes implacable.

Then came the rustling of many wings and dozens of demons landed, hot and angry after a fruitless chase through the skies after Aanfial. They drew their swords excitedly as they saw the wounded angel, rushing towards him with shrill cries of fury.

Barbas strode forward slashing and stabbing with his sword, demons falling to his right and his left under the savage onslaught. They swiftly fell back, astounded and afraid as the cries of their wounded comrades filled the air.

"He is mine, and you will not touch him unless I say."

Recognising a demon standing at the front of the disorganised huddle, he beckoned him over. "Oni," he commanded, "take three of your demons with you and scout the area thoroughly. Leave the rest with me in case—"

Oni interrupted. "Sir," he whined, "we have been chasing all over the sky after the enemy. We are tired—"

Barbas stepped forward, and his voice was soft. "I understand," he said quietly, "you need rest?"

Oni grinned, and nodded. "Thank you sir," he began, "once we have all rested . . ."

He said no more, as Barbas stabbed forward with his blade, running him through the chest with such violence that the weapon penetrated the front and exited out of his back. "Then rest for eternity," he said.

The fatally injured demon barely registered a look of disbelief, dispatched before he even had time to scream.

Barbas surveyed the remaining demons, his eyes red orbs of anger, his sword held menacingly in front of him. "Anyone else tired," he asked?

There was a flurry of "No sir," and "we're ready sir," from the frightened remnant, several at the rear falling in the crush as those at the front moved rapidly backwards out of the path of the raging demon.

Barbas called another forward. "Name?" he demanded curtly.

"Mush, my lord," came the quavering response.

Although not entitled, Barbas liked being called "lord." It suited his opinion of his worth. This little demon obviously recognised greatness when in its presence. "You heard my order to Oni. Are you capable of carrying it out?"

Mush nodded nervously. "At once," he stuttered, turning to the cowering demons behind him. "You, you and you, come with me. The rest of you stay with my Lord Barbas as he commands."

Then there was a burst of activity as the three took to the air behind their new leader, each of them grateful to be out of the sight and reach of such an unpredictable and ruthless demon.

CHAPTER Thirteen

Benedict eased back into his chair, fiddling with the ball-point pen in his hand. He wasn't totally relaxed. Things hadn't gone too well lately. He'd played it down and his official line was that it didn't matter, but undeniably the loss of a large number of people from the church was serious. It could well be the crack that caused a haemorrhage of members if he didn't handle this carefully. He glanced at the clock. It was almost 6:45pm.

Picking up the desk telephone, he placed a white linen handkerchief across the mouthpiece and dialled. "Mr. Cooper, please," he said softly.

Cooper's wife answered, slightly hesitantly. "Sorry, he's not home just yet. Can I take a message?"

"Very good. Please ask him come to his office at 8pm tonight to meet Nelson Riley. He'll know what it's about. Something very important with Mr. Benedict."

Replacing the phone briefly, he then dialled another number and waited patiently for it to be answered.

"Do what thou wilt shall be the whole of the law."

"So mote it be. I have need of the *jakushou*."

After a short conversation, he placed the telephone carefully back in its cradle.

"Come and look at this, Jenny!" Phil Sellars was collapsed on the sofa in front of the TV set watching the evening news. His wife joined him from the kitchen where she had been preparing dinner, wiping her hands on her apron.

"What's up?"

"It's the local news. People have reported seeing bright lights in the sky over Hartwood—hold on, they're interviewing someone now."

Jenny sat alongside, putting her legs up so that her feet rested in his lap.

The newscaster, a young woman in a smart grey suit, was talking to a middle-aged man in Wellington boots, brown cord trousers and a tweed jacket. They were stood in a field at the edge of the woods. She held a microphone in her right hand, whilst with her left she tried to hold back the long brown hair that was flying about her face in the strong wind.

The camera cut to the man. "I was hoping to get some photos of badgers," he said, holding up a digital camera, "and so I was standing just about here waiting for some kind of movement." He pointed to a spot a few feet in front of him.

The camera cut back. "You didn't see badgers did you?" asked the interviewer helpfully, thrusting the microphone towards him. "What *did* you see Mr. Jarrold?"

"Lights, bright lights up over there" he said, indicating towards the dark sky. "I've never seen anything like it. It was like firework night!" The camera focussed, panning across the heavens before picking up the interviewer once again.

She brought the microphone back towards herself and asked, "Perhaps it *was* fireworks?"

"I thought that, at first. But then a strange thing happened. After speeding off towards town, they then seemed to sort of, loop the loop, and back they came towards where I was standing!"

"What do you think? You've lived here a long time."

"Christmas angels!"

"Christmas angels?" She committed the cardinal sin and pulled a face of obvious disbelief, quickly correcting herself as she realised what she was doing.

"You know. Like in the Bible. At the birth of Jesus." Mr. Jarrold screwed up in his face in concentration. "I can't remember it very well," he explained apologetically, "I haven't really read it since I was at school." He scratched his head, looking embarrassed. "Didn't the shepherds hear the angels sing or something?"

The interviewer was better informed, but didn't want to be drawn into a religious discussion. "They sang 'Glory to God in the highest and peace to men on earth,'" she said, in a voice that made it plain that she didn't believe any of it. "Did you hear them sing?"

Mr. Jarrold indicated that he hadn't actually heard any singing.

"Did you manage to take any photos?" the interviewer asked hopefully, indicating the digital camera slung over his shoulder.

The TV camera zoomed in close, registering the disappointment on his face. "I tried, but nothing came out, nothing at all," he said. "The camera's blank."

He paused then, and his eyes opened wide in amazement. "But something even stranger has happened." He took several deep breaths, like a man preparing to dive into water.

The microphone was thrust back towards him as he stuttered, a look of awe and disbelief on his face. "I've just realised. My asthma. It's gone! He stared up at the skies in wonder, before looking straight at the interviewer. "What does it mean?" he asked. "I've suffered all my life with breathing trouble, but suddenly—it's gone! What can this be . . . ?" He seemed as though he was about to burst into tears, and the interviewer quickly retrieved the microphone.

The camera cut back to her, still struggling with her hair. "Strange goings on in Hartwood at Christmas," she said, "and rumours of angels being seen abroad." The camera pulled back slightly, to a head and shoulders shot. "This is Carol Prestwick in Hartwood for Newsnight."

Phil turned quizzically towards his wife. "What do you make of that?"

Jenny was quiet for a moment. "I think that God is on the move," she said, and went back to the kitchen.

Darrell Cooper was checking his briefcase carefully. His wife had passed on the message about meeting Riley. He was surprised that he had rung his home. He'd never done that before. He was also surprised at another meeting quiet so soon and at such a late hour. He'd been about to sit down to dinner with his wife and daughter, Sophie. But then Benedict always did please himself.

So Cooper was carefully checking the covert recording device hidden in his innocuous black leather briefcase. He ensured that the pinhole camera was properly connected, its battery was fully charged and that the lens aligned accurately with the minute hole in the side of the case. He checked the voice activated recording device, tested the operation of the on/off switch concealed under the handle before closing it and scrambling the digital lock. Because he believed in covering his back at all times. And in making opportunities.

That's why he'd been blackmailing Nelson Riley for many years. He'd used the very same technique, and what a profitable source of income that was. He smiled at his own cleverness. What a dork Riley was. And how he'd raged when confronted with the evidence of his sexual indiscretions with one of the young boys at church.

At least he'd raged at first. Then he'd squirmed. And finally he'd sobbed as he viewed the filmed evidence complete with sound track.

He'd gone to Riley's flat one morning, and presented him with the CD.

"What is this?" Nelson had demanded suspiciously. He'd never liked Cooper and made no attempt to hide his irritation at the unwelcome visit.

"Stick it in the computer and you'll see."

"Don't waste my time. Why should I be interested in anything you've got?"

Cooper had shrugged then. "Up to you. I can give you a hint."

He'd got exasperated then. "Get out of my home. I assure you that nothing you have is of interest to me."

"It might be to the police."

The mention of the police caused him to pause. He looked uncomfortable. "The police? What on earth . . ."

He'd reluctantly taken hold of the CD and inserted it into the disc drive of his computer. When the disgusting images first appeared, he'd thrown himself at Cooper wrestling him to the ground and punching him around the head in uncontrolled fury.

Cooper, momentarily taken aback by the sudden, unexpected violence had enabled the other to gain the upper hand. But the moment of surprise passed, and being a much stronger man he'd thrown Riley off, kicking his prostrate body vigorously until his will to fight had evaporated.

Riley, injured and bleeding but not quite finished had then launched himself desperately at the computer, seizing the incriminating evidence and smashing it to fragments under his foot.

Cooper had laughed mockingly then. "Please," he said, "do you think I am stupid enough to bring you the only copy? What planet do you live on?"

It was then that Riley had begun to sob as the shame and fear washed over him. "What do you want, you animal?"

"Animal? That's rich! You've seen yourself. I'll send you another and you can have a look at the section two minutes from the start again. You're the filthy animal and I can smell you from here!" He'd laughed again, good humouredly, knowing he had the upper hand. He sat down in Nelson's chair, winked conspiratorially at his trembling victim, and outlined his demands.

And Nelson had paid. He'd had no choice otherwise he would have lost his job, his wife and his freedom. As it was, his wife found out and left him anyway.

Cooper, feeling smug, left Kate and Sophie to sort dinner. "I'm just going to the office to drop something off. I'll be back in less than ten minutes. Don't start without me!"

He was as good as his word, and as he sat down to the last ever dinner of his life, he glanced at his watch. He had just enough time before he had to return for the meeting. "Pass the potatoes," he said.

Talial silently approached the car. The hysterical demons were too busy to think of anything other than the cruel sport they were having with the angel. He glanced miserably towards his fallen comrade, but his duty was to Emily and his loyalty to his Lord was total. As a servant of God

Most High, he was sworn to obey; indeed it was his joy and the purpose of his life. And the Spirit had clearly instructed him to rescue Emily. He knew that there was no other choice.

She was leaning against the passenger door shivering in fright as he slid the tip of his golden blade down between the side of the passenger window and the car door, causing the glass to drop down with a crash. The window was wide open.

She stared at the escape route for a moment, hardly daring to believe that there was a way out of the car that had become a prison to her.

The angel placed his hand on her head. "You can easily fit through," he whispered, gently, guiding her with a tender hand.

That is how Emily inexplicably found herself outside, looking in at Brandon in the car, his head against the steering wheel as he sobbed.

Talial took a last look at Auriel, and as he did so felt a strange wetness on his cheek. Hurriedly, he grasped Emily by the arm and moved silently into the night, guiding her to safety.

Barbas prodded Auriel harder with his sword. "Lost your tongue, pathetic creature of God?" He smirked broadly at the lack of response. "I should cut you to ribbons where you stand."

He was suddenly interrupted by a shout from behind him.

"My lord," shrieked one of the smaller demons suddenly, "look!"

Barbas glared impatiently, and with a flush of rage saw that Emily was gone.

Then, before the stunned demons realised what was happening, the car engine burst into life with a sudden harsh roar as Brandon floored the accelerator, driving wildly away in a cloud of dust and grit.

The demon turned to Auriel, his face distorted with hatred. His eyes, always red, now flushed the colour of stale blood as he spat out his words. "I *will* make an example of you," he said slowly and menacingly, "an example that will be remembered by your worthless kind for all time. You have been tested, and found wanting. Do you really believe that you can win against my lord?"

He gestured to the demons holding the weakened angel, who grimaced in pain as the wounds across his back gaped open. But still he stolidly said nothing, his eyes impassive. He wondered what had happened to his captain and Talial, but praised God that Emily had escaped.

Barbas addressed the grinning demons. "You Mantus, and you Barqu and Cresil. See if you can't soften him up a bit," he commanded. "Show him the meaning of pain."

They were only too pleased to comply, and for the next few minutes blows rained down on the captive servant of God. One slashed at his face with his talons, opening a huge diagonal wound. When he got tired, another demon gleefully took his place.

Mantus, a grotesquely ugly demon, gloried in the brutality. His deep set eyes glowed with satisfaction at the damage he was inflicting on the semi-conscious messenger of God. He pounded a huge, misshapen fist into Auriel's chest, sending both him and the three demons holding him crashing to the ground. Drawing his sword, he made several cuts to the limp body before Barbas stopped him.

"Time enough for killing later, Mantus," he said.

Mantus withdrew, but the brutality continued unabated until Barbas decided that the angel was sufficiently softened.

"Enough!" He kicked out with a rock-hard foot, sending demons sprawling. He pressed his face close to the barely conscious angel, his breath reeking of the foulness of hell. With a scabrous, taloned hand he grabbed hold of one of his wings, pulling at it roughly so that it projected outwards from his body.

"I have a puzzle for you," he whispered. "When is an angel not an angel?" He didn't wait for a response, judging that none would be forthcoming. "I'll tell you," he exclaimed with a roar. "It's when he's had his wings clipped . . ."

There was a bellow of approval from the assembled demons, and Auriel realised with a shudder what Barbas planned to do.

"You have already lost, Barbas. It doesn't matter what you do to me, or to any of the servants of God. You know the scriptures. It is written: 'For your sake we face death all day long; we are considered as sheep to be slaughtered.'"

"Then sheep, prepare for that slaughter!" laughed Barbas. He raised his sword high above his head as Auriel's eyes bored defiantly into his; purest gold versus bloody red.

The angel lifted his head to the heavens and cried loudly into the black sky. But it was not the sound of pain or fear that Barbas had expected. It was not a cry for mercy. It was a shout of defiance! "To the Lamb and Him who sits upon the throne!" roared the angel, and the air around him clashed with power.

Then Barbas brought his blade down with sickening force. Again and again and again . . .

CHAPTER FOURTEEN

Benedict walked unhurriedly to the far side of Cooper's office and picked up the tray on which the bottle of port was sitting, re-positioning it on the desk. He moved several items out of the way to make room. Pouring a quantity of the heavy ruby liquid into a glass, he took a sip and glanced at the clock.

He wiped the bottle and other things he had moved on the desk, paying particular attention to a shiny black briefcase. Satisfied with what he had done, he settled back in Cooper's chair to wait.

Riley was ready when the bell rang. He opened the door cautiously, keeping the security chain in place until a police warrant card was thrust through the gap. Grasping it with a shaking hand, he scrutinised it carefully, comparing the photographic image on it with the officer standing outside, before slipping off the chain and opening the door.

He checked both ways along the dark, empty street. "Are you sure no-one saw you?" The officer nodded affirmatively. "Never fear Mr. Riley. We will look after you."

He squinted, unable to see anyone else. "We?"

"The police."

"Of course. Do you want to talk here?"

"I think that's wise."

"Don't you have safe houses or something?"

"That's only in books Mr. Riley. It's either your flat or at the station." The officer's eyes glinted. "Come on, we're talking fraud here. Hardly the crime of the century."

Riley hesitated and the officer grew impatient.

"Look, you called me, I didn't call you. Do you want help or not?"

He flung the door wide open. "Okay, okay, but I just don't know who to trust anymore. You don't know what he's capable of." He held the CD up. "Do you want to look at it?"

"Of course," said the officer.

The frightened man went down the hallway, heading for his computer. As if from afar, he heard the front-door slam shut behind him.

The demon Abigar was in a state of shock. He had dominated the pastor very easily, and had expected little resistance from the old man carrying a stick. So he slithered confidently towards him as he entered the office. Only to find himself contorted with pain as he was suddenly thrown violently backwards with sickening power.

"I come against you, demon!" Henry cried, his voice shaking slightly but resolute nevertheless, "in the name of Jesus."

The demon's bright little eyes opened wider in disbelief as the old man stared directly at him. And Henry's eyes betrayed no fear. He knew. The old man knew!

At the mention of the "Name," Abigar felt as if a hand had tightened around his throat, and he gasped loudly as a further bolt of pain shot through him.

Henry continued speaking words of power. "I proclaim the name of Jesus in this place," thundered the old man, "that at his name every knee shall bow, in heaven and on earth and under the earth. And every tongue shall confess that Jesus Christ is Lord, to the glory of God the Father."

Abigar felt the strength draining from his body. This one was strong in the Enemy. He had never had such a power encounter before. And he was suddenly afraid.

"Henry," the voice was weak, "what on earth is happening? What is all this talk of demons?"

"Hang on a moment, there's some serious spiritual warfare I'm engaged in here." He turned back to the demon, whilst Marcus watched in disbelief as he addressed an empty space in the corner of his office, fearing that the old man had lost his mind.

"Lord Jesus," He prayed, "would you surround us with your Holy Spirit? I pray a hedge around us, impenetrable to the powers of darkness. I plead the blood of Your Son Jesus, shed for us at Calvary." And as he spoke, God answered his prayer. The power of the Holy Spirit filled the room, and the darkness fled before Him.

"Through the power of the Holy Spirit and the blood of Jesus," continued the old man, and he began to sing a song of praise to the Lord in an unknown tongue.

The demon doubled up in pain and screamed as the name of Jesus was again uttered; pain like red-hot coals racked his body. He felt the shackles begin to tighten around him, and he was flung outside and into the night. He was thrown, helpless, through the air for some considerable time, before crashing heavily to the ground. When he was able, he fluttered off weakly into the night in search of Barbas. Something was happening in this town. Something he had never encountered before. The enemy was beginning to fight back.

Henry turned, a look of satisfaction on his face. "We need to pray," he said, "and then we need to talk."

Marcus nodded, confused and just a little afraid as to what he had been hearing. But he was quite happy to take any suggestion after what he had been through. He was totally bemused and totally crushed.

"Henry, what was that? I felt the most awful presence of evil . . ."

The old man nodded, clearly shaken by his encounter with Abigar. "It was a demon all right. But it's obvious that you've never been baptised in the Spirit."

"Show me," said Marcus, surprising himself at his boldness.

"I am going to ask God to fill you now."

"Wait, I'm not sure . . ."

But Henry wasn't going to be dissuaded. He knelt painfully by the side of the pastor's desk, easing himself down inch by inch on his aching joints. He held his stick in front of him, leaning on it with the air of a patriarch of old. He motioned to Marcus to kneel beside him.

"Father," he began, "in the name of Jesus I stand against Satan and his demons, and over thrones and powers and principalities. As your body on earth and in your name, dear Lord, I come against the powers of evil that may be here. I proclaim your Lordship and majesty. May your rule and reign be established in this place, this town and over all the earth." His simple prayer, prayed in power, had a dramatic effect that was unseen by human eyes.

Several black forms inside the church building cried out, and leapt away into the air, angry at being unseated from places that they had held securely for many years. All over Hartwood, demons in the very act of mischief stopped as shudders of fear washed over them. In strongholds above and below Hartwood, evil apparitions found their swords falling from their hands with a clatter onto the ground. They knew. And they were afraid. Someone was praying in the power of the Holy Spirit. Someone was waging spiritual warfare.

Henry continued to pray. "Thank you Father for your love. That in you we are eternally secure." He raised a hand to the heavens. "I praise you Lord for the cross, for your blood, for your sacrifice. That in you is hope and new life." He placed a hand on Marcus's head. "I ask you now, as you did on the day of Pentecost, to send your Holy Spirit on this man of God, our pastor. Would you baptise him in your Spirit? Send the fire Lord, and fill him to overflowing."

Then he spoke again in the unknown language, a tongue which Marcus had never heard before. Every now and then he heard the name "Adonai," which he knew meant "Lord" in Hebrew, but that was all he understood.

But although he did not understand, the power was undeniable. He realised with dismay that there was a lot that he hadn't understood, much that he had denied during his ministry. Then a warmth and gentleness filled the place where the two saints prayed, and the darkness for this moment at least, was banished. And Marcus, for the first time felt the overwhelming power of the Holy Spirit within him. He leaned forward, placing his forehead against the carpeted floor of the office, and wept. Great shudders convulsed his body as he cried out his sorrow and love to Almighty God. A paradoxical mixture of bitterness and sweetness. A recognition of his sin in the eyes of a Holy God, and an acceptance of the forgiveness extended to those who truly repent. Wave after wave of love, joy and peace washed over him, until he was caught up in the most intense worship of Jesus that he had ever known. He had been baptised in the power of the Holy Spirit!

Henry knelt silently beside him, praying silently in the spiritual language given by God. The old man's heart was full, and as he prayed it overflowed into rivers of praise that ascended to the very throne room of the Lord himself.

Bune whispered soothingly into Benedict's ear, his heavily jewelled hand gently stroking his captive human's head. "It is time to deal with both of them. They must not be permitted to ruin the master's plan. It is too important. *They* are not important, neither are *you* important. Only the plan and its implementation is important." Then he whispered instructions into a passive, compliant mind.

It was 6:50pm. Benedict finished his drink and went into the small kitchen situated next to the office. He washed the glass thoroughly, then dried it carefully ensuring that his hands didn't come into contact with the glass.

Holding it through the tea-towel, he set the glass down on the desk, then thoroughly wiped the silver tray and the port decanter. Not until he was satisfied did he set them back down on the tray, again holding each object through the tea-towel. Then he set the tray with the two glasses on it down on a small table in front of the desk, placing a chair either side of it. He glanced around the office, ensuring that all was in order, before sitting back down again to wait.

He didn't have long. At 7.30pm precisely, the door opened and Riley, holding a bloody handkerchief to his head, was pushed roughly into the room.

Marcus and the old man were sitting in the office drinking tea. The prayer session had flown by. Marcus couldn't remember the last time he had prayed for so long, and with such passion. He'd cleared a lot of rubbish from his life in those two hours. Most importantly he'd been delivered from the demon of alcohol that had been sucking the life out of him for so long. He had done business with God. And now he not only felt free, he *was* free. Wonderfully released and full of praise to the God who loved him. He was so full of the Spirit that he positively bubbled, causing Henry to give a word of caution.

"Now, don't you go frightening the flock," he admonished with a gleam in his eye, "they won't be used to a lively Marcus Bentley. You'll have to break them in gently!"

"I feel cheated. My theological training didn't prepare me for any of this. We discussed it of course—"

Henry finished his sentence for him. "But the gifts are not for today, right?" He smiled. "Have you ever wondered what happened to the 'Gifts of the Spirit,' the prophecies, the voice of God, the healing of the sick, and spiritual warfare?" he paused to take a sip from his cup, gauging Marcus's response.

"Whoa, slow down. I'm still trying to come to terms with what has just happened to me. I've never felt like this before. I'm a real mix of emotions. I've read about this in the book of Acts, especially when the Spirit came and touched the disciples at Pentecost. But I never expected it to happen today. Not to me! I don't know whether to praise God in joy, or fall down and weep."

"It might take some time for you to get used to, but in the meantime, you could try both!"

"It can take as long as it needs. I spent three years at theological college learning that God doesn't speak today, and that demons don't exist. If it takes another three to get used to the fact that He does and they do, then that won't be time wasted!"

Marcus got to his feet and walked to the window, staring out at the dark and empty street thoughtfully. "I have always believed that although God spoke in years gone by, today he is dumb. I have spent my entire ministry believing that the gifts of the spirit died out after scripture was complete. Of course I believed he still spoke through the Bible, but that's it. There are no such things as demons today, no power of the Spirit, no healings—well, nothing very much really," he finished lamely.

The old man smiled. "I was in the same boat once, so don't be too hard on yourself. I believe that many theological schools teach a similar liberal view. Fortunately I didn't go to college so I never knew any better. I just read the Bible and trusted that God would do the things that he says in it. And he did!"

"I've always believed that my job was to live a normal Christian life," responded Marcus, "and to help others to do the same. That meant reading God's Word, praying and sharing my faith when the opportunity was there. I emphasised the importance of right doctrine and living a life of holiness and discipline."

"But without the power to make it possible!"

"So it seems."

"Remember I've been in this church for some years. I've witnessed the problems."

"I realise now what I was doing," explained Marcus. "I was reading the Bible and interpreting it by my experience, rather than through the experience of the people who actually lived in Biblical times. People who saw, who actually witnessed these things."

"Don't dismiss everything that you've done over the years. And don't beat yourself up too much. Your preaching has always been inspired, and God has used it many times to speak to us. Only yesterday you were speaking about caterpillars and butterflies." He couldn't resist a gentle dig. "I bet you didn't expect to make the change from the chrysalis quite so soon!"

Marcus laughed wryly. "True. But what do I do now? Everything has changed, and I can't go on preaching in quite the same way. I want everyone to experience what I have."

"You won't have to say much. Why, people have only got to look at your face to see that something amazing has happened! I would think—"

Marcus interrupted. "—Wait a minute! How is it that you've been coming to this church all the years that I've been pastoring, and yet you and I have never had this conversation before?"

Henry sighed. "You wouldn't listen. Don't you remember me submitting a paper to the elders some years back, asking that we have some teaching on these things?"

Marcus flushed guiltily. He did remember. "I think we put it in the 'too difficult to handle' drawer," he confessed.

Henry shrugged. "Well, I tried several times afterwards, but there wasn't any encouragement. In the end, God just told me to pray for you and the elders, and that's what I've been doing. I've waited ten years for this moment," he said quietly.

"Thank you for your faithfulness," said Marcus. "Things will be different now, I promise."

"Don't underestimate the difficulties. There are still many people who will oppose change." He couldn't resist adding, "They had a good teacher in you!"

He continued quickly, before Marcus could reply. "The presence of this demon is quite worrying. Where there is one, there are usually more. They are like flies, swarming together. I really believe that God is calling the church family together to pray about this." He joined the pastor at the window, walking stiffly with the aid of his stick.

"You are right," said Marcus, looking round at the old man. He shook his head, still amazed at the strange things that had happened. "Get them to pray urgently now, right where they are. There's no time to waste. But I also want everyone that can, to come to a prayer meeting Wednesday evening. Unfortunately that the earliest I can do it."

Henry smiled for the umpteenth time that evening. "I'm sure God knows that! I'll make a start on ringing round. Even if we do have to wait until the day after tomorrow, we'll give the devil something to think about. We've been too quiet for too long."

"Amen to that!" said Marcus emphatically.

Henry spent the next hour poring over the church contact book, making telephone calls and inviting everyone that could, to come to a prayer meeting the day after the next.

The phone rang several times before James managed to get to it. Somehow it had got buried under a pile of books and papers. Scooping it up, he jammed it between ear and shoulder so that he could carry on working.

"Lo, you're through to James."

There was a stunned silence as Henry gave him a brief précis of the evening's events.

"James . . . are you there?"

"You're kidding me, right?" He tugged at a corner of his beard with his free hand, a habit he resorted to when thinking.

Henry sighed. "James, are you listening to me?"

"Erm, yes, but I—"

"Forgive me for being blunt, but we haven't time to pussy foot about. I have never been more serious in all my life."

"I'm not sure about this demon stuff . . ."

"Neither was Marcus, but I think you'll find he's changed his mind a bit since his encounter with one!"

James glanced at his wristwatch. "Does the prayer meeting have to be Wednesday? It's my night out with the boys."

The old man confirmed that it was so.

"Right," said James resignedly, "I'll start praying right now. But I could do with some answers. It's just too . . . too unusual. Do you know what I mean?"

"James, this is pretty unusual for all of us. But the Lord is obviously doing something here and we must respond urgently to his call."

"I hope that it's not just you, me, and the pastor that turn up. You know how difficult it is to get people to a prayer meeting at the best of times. Even when you give them tea and scones we only get a handful. It's so bad you could hold it in a telephone kiosk and still have room! And now, asking people out during a week-day evening . . ." He trailed off doubtfully.

"This is the Lord's work James. He'll bring in those that he wants."

"There is one thing . . ." He twisted his beard so hard that it hurt.

"Yes, James?"

"Well, it's the weirdest thing, but a couple of hours ago I had the most overwhelming conviction that I should pray for someone or something. I haven't the foggiest idea what it was about—perhaps it was for you guys? But it wasn't about demons," he said defensively. "Definitely nothing to do with demons."

Henry smiled at the other end of the phone. "See you Wednesday."

"Okay," James said hesitantly, aware that he was coming across as a bit flaky. "I don't mean to prevaricate. I'll be at the meeting to hear what this is all about."

"Thank you. Remember, people will be arriving from around 5pm. Oh, and one last thing; Ephesians 6:12."

James hung up and was shocked to find that his hands were shaking. Feeling the leading of God to pray is one thing, he thought. The power of the Holy Spirit was also acceptable. But demons in the 21st Century?

He reached for his Bible and read aloud the verse that Henry had quoted to him. "For we are not fighting against people made of flesh and blood, but against the evil rulers and authorities of the unseen world, against those mighty powers of darkness who rule this world, and against the wicked spirits in the heavenly realms."

He started to pray silently, feeling unsettled in his spirit.

CHAPTER FIFTEEN

Joan Bowman was starting to get worried. Emily wasn't usually so late and she had school the next morning. She'd tried ringing her on her mobile, but all she got was her voicemail. She hurriedly left a message for Emily to call her immediately she picked it up. Bob would be in from his late shift any minute, and he would expect his dinner to be on the table, so she had to get on. She would find the right time to voice her concerns about Emily after he had eaten. If she jumped on him too quickly when he came in, there would be trouble. Violent trouble. She headed for the kitchen to see how the meal was doing.

Brandon Riley drove along the arterial road like a maniac, his accelerator foot flat to the floor. He had no idea where he was going, or what he would do when he got there. He leaned closer towards the windscreen in order to see the road more clearly in the headlights, because his vision was blinded by the tears that streamed down his face.

The wind howled in through the open passenger window, causing discarded fast-food paper wrappings to fly up off the floor and flap frenetically around the interior. But the terrified youth was not about to stop. He was fleeing as far as he could from the scene while he could. Anyway, the window winder, like the door opener was bust, so he just had to put up with it.

Emily had run off. He had no idea where she was, and he hadn't stopped to look for her. She certainly couldn't come to any worse harm than she had at his hand. He laughed hysterically at his stupidity. Who could she be in danger from? A rapist? A thug? Someone like him?

In his own eyes, he'd become the spectre of fear that haunted girls' minds when they were out alone. The unspoken dread that lurked just beyond their consciousness. He'd often warned *his* girlfriends about the dangers, insisting that he drop them off at their home instead of letting them walk alone. And now? Now what?

He thought too much. Not clearly, but distractedly. His mind wasn't on his driving, but on terrible scenes that replayed over and over in his mind as if they'd been recorded in a never ending loop.

Several times his inattention caused him to swerve out of control and cross the centre line, careering along crazily on the wrong side. An oncoming lorry angrily sounding its horn and flashing its headlights, pierced the fog that enveloped his brain in its numbing embrace. He swerved back in panic, fighting to maintain control on the sharp right-hand bend that loomed ahead—over steered, and caused the front near-side to strike a lamppost a glancing blow. There came the scream of tortured metal as the wing was torn away like a piece of tin foil and flung into the night, followed immediately by the car tilting alarmingly onto one side as it reacted to the action of centrifugal force.

Brandon gripped the wheel tightly and slammed on the brakes in desperation; he had insufficient experience to know that was totally the wrong thing to do, and it caused the rear of the car to break away as it lost adhesion on the road. Turning in a half-circle, amazingly staying upright on the tarmac, it somehow slid around the bend sideways before the youth managed to bring it back under control.

But his fear of being caught was greater than his fear of totalling the car, so he continued to press the accelerator, undaunted by his brush with disaster. His mind was racing almost as fast as the car. In a state of numb terror, he still had no idea what to do, or where to go. He drove blindly and hopelessly, alone and desperately afraid.

He despaired at what he had become. Of what he was. Had he actually *wanted* to rape Emily? He knew he had done some serious damage when he'd punched her.

He formed a fist with the evil hand, and smashed it against the dashboard over and over, oblivious to the pain and the breaking of the scaphoid bone in his wrist. Strangely, it was a form of release, bringing some clarity of mind in the intensity of the hurting.

She had no doubt gone to the police—and he didn't blame her. He could imagine her arriving at the station distressed and injured, her clothing torn and disarrayed. And then the adrenalin rush of police officers to their cars to begin the manhunt. He guessed that they wouldn't be treating him too well when they found him.

But such was his self-pity that even now his thoughts were not totally for the girl. They were for himself. For Brandon Riley.

The thought that he would go to prison was not pleasant. Even the idea caused a sweat to break out across his forehead. He'd heard how sex offenders were treated in prison. "Nonces," they were known as. And the other prisoners made their lives a living hell.

Not that he had an inkling what hell was like.

Sadly, he was soon to find out . . .

———————

Emily was running for her life. A mixture of fear and fatigue causing her heart to pound in her chest with desperate intensity at the mixture of fear and unaccustomed exertion.

Stumbling blindly through the woods on the outskirts of Hartwood in the pitch black of night, she was oblivious to the branches whipping into her face. The pain was minimal compared to what Brandon had inflicted on her. Anyway, this new pain was welcome. Healing, clean and cathartic. Because she was in control again. Able to make her own decisions after being a prisoner for what had seemed an eternity. Exiting the woods, she struggled along the deserted streets feeling terribly vulnerable and alone.

She may have felt alone, but she wasn't. She was being held by the sure hand of God ministering to her through an angel. At her side was Aanfial, guiding her with a light touch on her shoulder every now and again ensuring that she moved in the right direction. Because he knew where she had to be taken. Why, he had no idea. But the Spirit had commanded him.

The exhausted young woman stopped for a moment, undecided what to do next, as a group of drunken men headed noisily towards her. Feeling vulnerable and dangerously conspicuous in the illumination of the sodium street-lighting, she looked around for a place to hide, not wanting them to see her in her distressed condition. She wasn't sure whether it was just her pride, or the danger the bellicose men represented, but she was desperate not to be seen.

But there was nowhere to go. No side alleyways, no doorways to duck into, no parked cars to hide behind. She was totally exposed in full view on the footpath.

The large angel standing in front of her, quietly quoted a word of sacred scripture. "For in the day of trouble he will keep me safe in his dwelling; he will hide me in the shelter of his tabernacle."

And although she shrank back from the approaching group, an amazing thing happened. Although the shouting, cursing group passed within feet of her, they ignored her as though she didn't exist. She could have reached out a hand and touched the leather jacket of the nearest man. Indeed at one stage he appeared to look straight at her, but there was no flicker of acknowledgement in his bloodshot eyes that he had seen her.

Then they had passed, and she ran on, seeing the building just ahead of her the moment she rounded the corner. It looked warm and inviting, as she forced herself across the small car park to the glazed double doors at the front. Here was an oasis, a sanctuary emanating an almost tangible promise of peace and rest to her hurting body and soul.

She hysterically hammered on the door with such force that it seemed the toughened glass was in danger of shattering. Her fear now erupted uncontrollably. She fell to the ground, broken both in body and in spirit as she sobbed from the depths of her heart, calling for help from whoever would respond.

And that is how she was found, in a pathetic weeping heap outside the church.

"It's Emily Bowman," said Marcus.

A half-pack of lagers rolling in the passenger foot-well was the main object of Brandon's attention. A drink would help to dull the pain.

Unless he interrupted the pictures constantly looping in his mind, he feared he would go mad.

Flicking his eyes off the road, he was sure he could get hold of one of the plastic carrier-rings without having to stop the car. He put out his hand, his fingers reaching. Abruptly he was forced to correct his steering yet again, and the lager pack rolled maddeningly out of reach.

Angrily, he swerved the vehicle violently from side, agitating the cans until they started to roll. Closer they came until a last stretch, a bit more, then reaching with his fingers fully extended . . .

Closing his hand around them, he dragged them onto his lap. Feverishly yanking one free, holding it gripped between his knees, he pulled clumsily at the ring opener.

Then the beer that had been rolling freely on the floor moments earlier, spurted out under pressure, spraying over the dashboard and windscreen before soaking into his trousers.

At any other time he would have been furious. Now all he wanted was the drink, and he greedily sucked what remained of it down his throat. Wiping the windscreen with his open hand, he tried desperately to clear the liquid from it. But it just smeared across in an opaque film of alcohol and blood that flowed from his injured hand, making his view of the unlit road ahead even more hazardous.

Undaunted, he downed the remaining cans in quick succession. Things did seem better then. At least his brain no longer screamed at him, and he felt relaxed as the strong alcohol began its work, absorbing into his bloodstream and depressing the central cortex of his brain.

That, combined with the coating on the windscreen is why he didn't see the bend until the last moment, and he didn't stand a chance. The combination of the drink and the trauma of his mind had combined into a lethal cocktail.

He hit the barrier head-on. This time he was not so lucky, and he never regained control. The car rolled over twice before careering into the path of a vehicle on the opposite side of the road. Both burst into incandescent balls of fire on impact, and he and the solitary driver of the other car died instantly.

The demon of betrayal clung to Riley's back, his talons digging deep into his captive's brain. He bowed his head deferentially to Master Bune as he entered, a gesture that Bune pointedly ignored. Abraxas was too lowly to be noticed.

Riley moaned and tried to move, but the disposable plastic handcuffs that secured him to the upright chair in the centre of the room held him fast. Opening his eyes slowly, he winced as the light hit them and wondered what had happened. His head was throbbing, and he could see dried blood, his blood, on the front of his shirt.

There was a familiar sound. "Click," it went.

The throbbing of his head became a violent ache, as flashes of light seared across his brain. And as he gradually became aware of his surroundings, he realised with bewilderment that he was in Cooper's office.

"Click."

He tried focusing his blurred vision and despite the lights that blazed and seared his tender eyes, he wondered at the darkness that paradoxically seemed to hover around him like a dirty cloud. In a daze, he saw Benedict seated in front of him, idly toying with his pen. Then he remembered. Then he knew fear.

"I don't understand," he said. But even in his stupefied state he recognised betrayal. This police officer belonged to Benedict just like everyone else. He should have known better than to try a double-cross.

"Just shut up, and listen to the master," the guardian of the law said brutally from behind him.

So Riley sat and said nothing. He had little or no choice. The darkness that was the demon Abraxas began to expand and grow, until it had enveloped Riley like a viscous oil slick. Reaching his chest, it sent out a feeler, a tentacle of evil that slid like a surgical scalpel into the cavity of his heart until he was totally wrapped in its cold embrace. The room grew darker still until all that was visible to the helpless man were the merciless eyes of Apostle Benedict Ademola. Curiously they had changed from their usual cold slate colour, and had taken on the quality of burning embers.

The demon Bune now possessing him totally, spoke as he acknowledged Riley for the first time. He laid his pen down on the desk. "Please listen to us carefully," he said. It was clearly a command and not a question of politeness. His voice had a deep hypnotic quality that would brook no refusal.

The captive sat unmoving, no longer struggling against his bonds, resigned to the control of the apostle.

With gloved hands, the police officer poured two glassfuls of Port from a bottle. One was proffered for Riley to drink. The other was passed respectfully to Benedict. Riley shook his head violently. But the officer refused to take no for an answer, and forced the glass to his lips, tipping it roughly backwards. Riley swallowed involuntarily against his will, much of it spilling onto his shirt and mixing with the dried blood that had soaked into it.

"Down to business," decided Benedict, sitting on the edge of the desk. He took a sip of his drink before throwing a key to the officer, who quietly locked the door. "We don't want to be disturbed," he said softly.

"Please . . ." said Riley, "don't hurt me Mr. Benedict."

"Mr. Riley," said Bune, although it was the body and voice of Benedict that formed the words, "This is the situation as I see it."

The lust-demon began to tighten his grip on Riley's brain.

"You recently professed concern about the numbers of people leaving the church, did you not?"

"I . . . I did," he stammered. "Look, about the disk. I won't say anything, Mr. Benedict. I swear. I'll go away somewhere. You'll never hear from me again."

Bune ignored him and continued. "If we remember rightly, you were concerned about the tithes?"

Riley felt his face going pale. "Well, I did say that there would be a loss, that's to say quite a few people no longer giving to the work . . ." He knew he was spluttering in fear, but couldn't stop himself.

Bune nodded soothingly. He lifted a large sheaf of papers off of the desk. "Remind us, you gave a figure I believe for the amount of income that we would loose?"

Riley licked his dry lips nervously. He didn't like the look of the paperwork that he was holding. "Yeah, I think I did."

"And?"

"About seven-thousand a month."

"Seven-thousand a month?" said Bune. "I hate to contradict—it's nearer nine, but what's a couple of thousand pounds here or there?"

Riley definitely didn't like the way the conversation was moving. He shuddered and a bead of sweat ran down his face, but he was helpless to do anything about it. "I suppose—"

Bune smiled. "Just like you Mr. Riley, to suppose. Let's do that shall we? Let us suppose." He riffled through the papers until he found what he was looking for. "Ah, here we are." He walked over and showed it to him, watching him curiously as he did so. "Perhaps you could tell us what the items highlighted in red refer to?"

He examined the paper with a sinking feeling in the pit of his stomach, running an eye over the highlighted items. It was a list of tithes that had never been paid into the church account. They had never been paid in for the simple reason that he, Nelson Riley, had helped himself to them. But that didn't worry him nearly as much as the disk did. He could see it clearly on the desk in front of him.

"Let us suppose that you have helped yourself Mr. Riley? Let us further suppose that your greed became too much for you and you betrayed our trust?"

He squirmed and avoided Benedict's eyes. "All right Mr. Benedict, I put my hands up to it." He risked a glance upwards, and wished he hadn't. Because his eyes met Benedict's eyes and they were incandescent orbs of blood. He found himself stuttering again, and despised himself for his weakness. "Look," he said desperately, "can't we work something out? I can pay it back."

Bune hissed angrily.

Riley tried again, desperately this time. "Look, I've been blackmailed by that creep Cooper for years. How do you think I've been paying him? I had no choice. He's bled me dry."

Bune silenced him with a wave of his hand, and moved closer to the hapless man who cringed backwards as he approached. It was only the presence of the silent guardian of the law standing behind that prevented his chair from toppling backwards.

"Mr. Riley, of course we can sort this out," he said soothingly, "there is always a way to sort out our problems."

Riley let out his pent-up breath with a gasp, the relief showing on his face. "Mr. Benedict, you won't regret this."

"Of course not." He turned to walk away, and then almost as an after-thought said, "You mentioned the disk, Mr. Riley?"

He nodded vigorously. "I gave it to the officer here."

"Who else did you talk to about it? Who else knows?"

"Honest, Mr. Benedict. No-one. I swear on my life. No-one! It was in my pocket, that's all I know."

"In your pocket, Mr. Riley? It got there of its own volition of course?"

Riley was desperate. "No, you don't understand—"

The apostle nodded, and Bune stroked his head, his jewels glinting in the overhead light. Abraxas disengaged himself and scurried to the window-ledge out of the way, his yellow pin-prick eyes greedily drinking in the events.

Something thrown from behind Riley fell to the floor to his left; then to his right. Then in front of him, and finally over his head and body. A shower, a cascade of tiny white particles. He saw them, but his brain struggled to understand. Words were being spoken. Strange words. Harsh words. Ritualistic words.

He licked his lips nervously. And tasted sugar.

Then the *jakushou* moved rapidly. Riley had no chance to cry out but the once. Just one, high-pitched cry before the red cord flew through the air in a graceful parabola of movement. It looped over his head in a beautiful, fast-flowing movement before tightening in a silent and deadly strangle. Riley would never scream again.

He felt his eyes forcing their way from their sockets as the cruel ligature tightened relentlessly around his throat, cutting deep into the skin and subcutaneous tissue of his neck. He tried vainly, but no sound emanated from his constricted windpipe.

With a Herculean effort he toppled the chair forward, falling onto his side. Looking up, silently pleading with his eyes for his life. Vainly begging, even as he flailed his body from side to side in a useless attempt to escape the inexorable tightening of the cord that was taking his life.

There was not a vestige of pride in the man. The front of his trousers was wet where he had lost control of his bladder, but he didn't notice or care. All he wanted was to live.

But it was not to be. The last thing he saw before his eyes clouded over forever were the blood red eyes of Bune piercing his very soul. Then he took on a vacant stare. As if he were far away.

CHAPTER Sixteen

Darrell Cooper arrived back at his office at precisely 8pm. The stairs were in darkness as usual. Since his business had gone to the dogs, he'd had to move out of his former plush office and he now rented something sub-standard. The landlord didn't bother with minor things like health and safety. As long as he got his rent, that was all he was concerned about. But at least the rent was reasonable in an area where office space realised extortionate prices. Prices that he could no longer afford. And as his clients didn't visit him, it didn't really matter.

He groped his way up the stairs and cursed loudly because the lights were off in the office too. He was sure he'd left them on earlier because he knew he'd be returning in the dark, and the glass panel at the top of the door would let sufficient light through to illuminate the hallway. A sort of homing beacon. It was probably the fuses again. Everything in the god-forsaken building only worked intermittently.

He fiddled clumsily with the key before he managed to open the door. He hoped that Benedict and Riley would be on time. He wanted to get this over with and get back home. His searching hand found the light switch and he flicked it up and down several times just to make sure, before cursing aloud. It wasn't just the stairway. All the lights had fused.

He made his way gingerly towards the kitchen where he kept a torch. His eyes were not yet accustomed to the darkness, and he stumbled over something on the floor. He flailed his arms wildly to keep his balance, and it was that sudden movement that caused the blow from behind to strike him across the shoulders rather than the head. He staggered, expelling his breath in a loud gasp of surprise and pain, but stubbornly remained on his feet.

Cooper was no fighter, and he was well out of shape. Whatever muscle he may have had in an earlier life was now covered by a substantial layer of fat. But he had spent many years in the security industry, and had had more than his share of scraps, especially when doing door work earlier on in his career. And so when the blow came, his reaction wasn't quite what was expected.

Instead of tamely falling down, he lashed out with his fist, imparting a substantial blow to his attacker's facial region. There was a grunt of pain, but that was as far as he got. A second blow, more accurate this time, caught him squarely across the back of the head and this time he dropped heavily to the floor in an unconscious heap.

Which is where the armed-response police officers found him fifteen minutes later.

Jack had just sat down in his lounge to watch the local evening news. There was a piece about angels and a couple of gullible people were telling about strange lights they had seen in the sky over Hartwood. The camera cut to a representative from a local UFO society, a slight, excited man wearing an army camouflage jacket and a pair of binoculars around his neck. The interviewer asked him his view, and whether he thought it could be visitors from another planet. Jack never got to know his answer, because at that moment the telephone rang.

It was FIR, the force information room at police headquarters.

"What is it this time?" he said.

He sighed as he put down the receiver. It was a pain being on call, but nevertheless he welcomed the chance to get out of the flat. Anything rather than watch the trash that was on TV.

The job sounded interesting anyway. A body had been found, and a suspect was in custody. So there was at least the chance of solving it this time. Detection rates hadn't been very good lately, so a chance to improve the figures would be welcome.

He made up a flask of coffee and threw some food into a bag. If other incidents he'd dealt with were anything to go by, he would be out a long time. And getting food to officers on the ground wasn't always a priority with the hierarchy.

He drove to the station to collect the things he required for the investigation, and to arrange a briefing with the specialists and detectives he would need to involve.

Emily mechanically sipped the hot, sweet tea that Marcus had provided, clutching tightly at the blanket wrapped around her. The pastor had cleaned her face up as best he could with a damp tissue, but was afraid to do too much because her injuries appeared quite serious. There was still a trickle of blood from her nose, and he was careful not to disturb the clots that had formed in the nostrils, for fear of starting more heavy bleeding.

"It's just as well that we were here," said Marcus. He tried to sound light-hearted to reassure her, but Emily showed no signs of even hearing him.

"Lean forwards a bit, it will help," he asserted tenderly, then moved her gently forward when she didn't respond. "Hang on just a minute." Hurrying out of the office he returned with a large white handkerchief dipped in cold water. "Put this lightly on your nose, it will help the swelling a bit."

Untrained as he was, even he could see that the young girl's nose was probably broken and that she had clearly been through a terrible ordeal.

She had been in his office for almost fifteen minutes, but had not yet spoken a word. Her eyes were wide open in fear, her pupils were dilated and she was shaking uncontrollably.

Henry came back into the office. He'd been trying to telephone the Bowman home, but there was no response. They were probably out looking for Emily he thought, and most likely out of their minds with worry.

"Emily, have you any idea where your parents are?" said Marcus.

The girl shrugged. She was breathing heavily through her mouth, a natural consequence of her nose being totally blocked by blood clots.

Marcus sat in the chair opposite, trying to keep as still as possible, because every time he moved, she twitched alarmingly.

Henry spoke quietly. "Emily, we have to call an ambulance. We have to get you examined properly."

She did not answer, but pulled the blanket tighter around her.

"I think we have to call the police as well." Marcus said it as gently as he knew how. Although Emily hadn't spoken a word, one look at the torn dress that was only just hanging together was a strong clue as to the probable turn of events.

Marcus stood up, and the girl shrank back, her wide eyes full of fear.

"It's okay," he said reassuringly, "but I have to make this call."

Marcus looked enquiringly at the old man. It was quite clear. He didn't know what to make of the situation either.

The pastor went into the office next door to his, dialled "999," relayed what had happened and put down the phone.

"On their way," he said. "Perhaps you would let us pray for you in the meantime?"

She did not answer, and continued to stare straight ahead.

Marcus took the silence as implicit assent and began to pray.

"Lord, I have no idea what has happened to this young girl, but you know, and have brought her to us for a purpose. And you love her. Would you be a refuge to her, a shelter from the storm. Touch her with the power of Your Holy Spirit. Send your healing. And your forgiveness. In the name of Jesus, Amen."

They had grown so accustomed to her silence that they were startled when she spoke.

"God can't forgive me. No-one can. And everyone will hate me when they find out what has happened." Her voice was dry and factual. "And I hate *her*. I hate her so much."

"Don't you believe it," said Henry. "There's no pit so deep that Jesus can't reach down. You must have been through a terrible time, but hatred will only destroy you." He glanced at Marcus.

"God does love you," he said.

Emily's head was bowed, but she glanced fleetingly up at Henry and made eye contact for a moment before hanging her head once more. "How could God love someone like me?" she mumbled through swollen lips.

Henry smiled gently. "Why would he love any of us? Because he *is* love that's why. He really loves you! And God understands what you've been through."

Emily shook her head. "No-one can understand what I've been through," she whispered through dry lips, "look at the state of me."

"You're wrong there," said the old saint. "When I was out in Jerusalem some years ago, I saw the bones of a young man that had been dug up on an historical dig. He'd been crucified and a nail was still in place piercing through both his ankles. Both his legs had been broken and there was damage to his wrist bones where nails had been driven through them too."

Emily didn't look up. "What has that to do with anything?" she mumbled.

"Everything. It was a painful way to die. In fact the Romans stopped using it precisely because it was so cruel." Henry leant forward on his stick and stared straight into Emily's eyes. "Jesus went through that for you. So he knows pain and humiliation. He knows."

"Do you believe in God?" Marcus asked.

She shrugged. "I used to come to this church with my mum and dad once." She paused. "When I was with . . . with him, with Brandon, I . . . I was so afraid. I thought I was going to die. I feel so dirty, so . . . violated! And look at my face. I am so messed up, so ugly." She looked down to the floor once again, hiding her face.

Henry hobbled to her side, wrapped his arms around her and hugged her tightly.

Then, slowly and haltingly, Emily recounted what had happened, beginning with her being taunted by the girls at school, and ending with her escape and flight through the woods.

"I just ran and ran," exclaimed Emily. "I didn't know if he was chasing me or what. I was so scared . . ."

As Emily falteringly gave her story, Henry's heart went out to the young, vulnerable child, for that was all she was. "Emily, look at me. This wasn't your fault. Do you understand? It's not your fault."

Emily nodded miserably. "I guess so."

He cradled the frightened girl's hands in his, noting how cold they were. "Listen to me," he insisted.

She observed him cautiously through half-closed, puffy eyes. The swelling and bruising from the fractured nose had spread rapidly causing bruising around her eyes. One side of her face was turning an ugly blue-black colour.

The old man's eyes bored into hers. Although well past their youth, they were still bright with passion, strong and commanding. His voice was soft and quite deliberate. "It wasn't your fault!"

Emily stared at him, her eyes searching his face questioningly. Then a single tear welled up in her eye, rolling slowly down her cheek and marking a furrow through the dirt and grime. As if a barrier had been lifted inside her, she threw her arms around the old man's neck and sobbed uncontrollably.

Henry said nothing but held the girl tightly in his arms, praying softly to the God who loved her. And his eyes were sparkling too.

The wailing of the emergency services could be heard coming closer, and Marcus went outside to meet them. The driver killed the sirens as he pulled into the car park, stopping outside the front doors, the blue lights rhythmically flashing in the darkness and lighting up the surrounding area in an eerie disco pattern.

"She's in here," said Marcus, holding the doors open. "The police are on their way too. The poor girl's been attacked."

The attendant, a strong looking woman in her thirties, nodded. "Is she conscious? Can she walk?"

"Well, she managed to run here, but that was probably adrenalin fuelled. And yes, she is sitting and talking to Henry, one of our church members at the moment."

The attendant swiftly pulled a collapsible wheelchair from the rear of the ambulance, grabbed a box of equipment and walked briskly inside.

The driver came round from the far side, a clip board in his hand. "Any idea of her details, who she is?"

"Yes, her parents sometimes attend the church." He gave what information he had.

"Bowman, did you say Bowman?" queried the driver.

"B-O-W-M-A-N." Marcus spelt out the name.

"It's just that we were called to a serious road accident earlier on involving a man of the same name. Might be a coincidence. What did you say the address was?"

He repeated it. "It's just off the High Street, behind the library."

The driver thumbed back through the papers on his clipboard to the earlier call, and shook his head slowly in disbelief.

"I don't know what this is all about. But the police will be very interested. It's the same address. Poor kid."

Marcus felt a chill touch his heart. "What happened . . . ?"

"It was a young drunk that the police were after. A head-on. That's all I know."

"What sort of . . . I mean the injuries, are they serious?"

"Can't get much more serious I'm afraid. Everyone's dead!"

The driver headed inside to assist with Emily, leaving Marcus standing silently in the foyer of the church.

He sighed deeply. What on earth was going on in Hartwood? He called after the driver. "Just one thing."

He paused and looked back. "Sure."

"Don't tell her about the car accident will you? She's been through quite a lot. I'm trying to get hold of her mum."

"Of course, we wouldn't do that anyway." He went inside shaking his head. "What a rancid world we live in," he said.

Joan Bowman had never known her husband to be late. He was a man of utmost punctuality—in fact there was a clockwork precision about the way that he did things. So when he didn't come home on time as usual, she was immediately worried. And what with Emily still being out as well.

Bob's dinner had gone cold, and was congealing on the dining table.

The customary beer that she had poured for him was now flat and warm. He wouldn't have liked that.

Not knowing what to do, she sat, staring silently at nothing in particular, her hands nervously twisting the hem of her faded blue-checked apron.

She couldn't pretend that he'd had been a great husband over the past few years. In fact he'd been a bit of a brute. He would often hit her when he got angry, which was most days. Joan wouldn't have been capable of articulating it, even if she had thought about it, but she instinctively knew that there had been a rhythm to their lives, an acceptance of the order of things that brought her certainty if nothing else.

Her life was like a play that she performed over and over. The same monotonous existence day after day. She knew it by heart. But it was just an act, devoid of any reality. But she'd had no-where else to go; long ago she had lost touch with her family, mainly because Bob had been so obnoxious that he had driven a wedge between them. She didn't really have any friends to speak of, just one or two acquaintances from the church, but they weren't her sort. They were religious people.

Bob was a creature of ingrained habit, obsessively so. He always left for work at the same time and got home at the same time. He never called her during his working hours, and his conversation when he was home was sparse. He would eat his dinner, drink his beer, and then head off to watch the television.

Sometimes he vented his frustration on her and slapped her before going off to bed. They had slept in separate rooms for many years, so his snoring didn't cause her any anguish. She'd grown used to the way things were.

Bob went to Hartwood Church with her every Sunday morning where they sat right at the back, with him glaring most of the time. She never could work out why he insisted on attending. She felt really uncomfortable going, and would have stopped if she could. But he insisted, so that was that.

The pastor, Marcus Bentley, had called them to the office one day and asked whether they would be happier in another church. But truly, Bob wouldn't have been happy anywhere, and he refused to leave on a "point of principle." So he continued to sit at the back and complain, deriding the service. Loathing what he referred to as 'over emotional singing,' and despising the worshippers with raised hands who took part.

She could vaguely remember that sometime in the distant past things had been better, but that was before Bob had been turned down for promotion at work. Before the bitterness that had slowly but relentlessly destroyed them, had set in.

If Joan had been asked whether she was happy, the truth would have been that she wasn't. But then she believed that happiness was wishful thinking. She supposed that very few people found happiness in life. If, on the other hand she'd been asked if she was content, she would have said that she was.

Contentment was acceptable. Happiness wasn't something she even considered. She recognised her lot in life, just as she recognised the relentless certainty of her mundane and largely useless existence.

The only time she felt a pang somewhere deep inside, was when she remembered how things once were. Before they were married. Rare times when her mind recaptured a sense not only of what was, but also what could have been.

The title of the song "The Way We Were," came to mind; that had been their song when they had first met. But that was another time, another play that she'd taken part in a long time ago, now just a half-remembered vestige of another life. Another existence where there had been hope and laughter. And joy.

She stopped herself sharply, before the thoughts and images that she had carefully stored away in the recesses of her mind like fragile ornaments wrapped in tissue should start to unpack themselves. Because there was no going back.

She jumped up, dabbing at her eyes with her apron as she heard the heavy knock at the front door. Bob? But he never knocked. He had his key. She opened it with growing trepidation, confronted by the sight of a uniformed police officer.

"Mrs. Bowman?"

She nodded, unable to find words, her heart pounding. The moment seemed strangely familiar, experienced somewhere, sometime before.

Time seemed to stretch out in an agonising clarity of slow motion, in that peculiar feeling people called déjà vu.

"May I come in? I have some bad news for you I'm afraid." It had been raining, and she could smell the dampness; see the beads of water rolling gently off his dark-blue waterproof coat. He removed his cap, mechanically shaking the wetness from it as he stepped into the small, half-papered hallway, wiping his shoes on the coconut "welcome" mat.

She heard his words, but they didn't register. He was saying that Bob had been killed in a car accident. But that wasn't right. That couldn't be true. She stared at the officer uncomprehendingly.

"He'll be home any moment now for dinner," she said finally. She gestured towards the table and the dinner that she had prepared, the dinner that he would never eat. Her voice was strained and fragile. "He's as regular as clockwork. He always comes home on time. I expect . . ." Her voice trailed off as she once again dabbed at her eyes.

The policeman understood. He'd done this many times before. "I'm sorry," he said, "do you want someone to come over, someone to stay with you for a while? A friend, a relative perhaps?"

Joan shook her head. "Thank you," she whispered as she closed the door behind him, "but there's no-one really."

She sat on the straight-backed kitchen chair staring at the meal she'd made. For a long time she sat, still and unmoving. Then, as the crushing enormity of what had happened began to filter in, as the reality hit home, so the tears began to fall.

She cried for Bob. And she cried for herself. She cried out of the depths of her loneliness and grief for a wasted life, and for the happiness that had once in a distant time been theirs. Now all was gone. Life was grey and bland and hopeless. The final curtain had fallen, and she was alone on the stage of a cold unfeeling universe of barren floating rocks and long-dead stars.

Somewhere a telephone was ringing emptily in the air, but the sound failed to elicit any response in the vacuum of Joan Bowman's mind.

The being clothed in white wept alongside her. The angel of the Lord kept watch. Kneeling at her side, he prayed passionately to God that his mercy and compassion would fall upon her. That she would know that God was with her, and that he loved her so.

CHAPTER SEVENTEEN

Jack was annoyed, and he didn't bother trying to conceal the fact.

"Look Michelle, I'm the bloody Ds at this station, and I'm not used to having Dc's that I don't know, have never worked with and what's more, don't like, being foisted on me."

DCI Radigan remained unperturbed. She'd grown used to his outbursts when things weren't going right. She jabbed a finger in his direction. "There's no-one else," she said tartly, "so it's him or no one. And before you choose 'no one', remember how much paperwork is involved, how many enquiries, interviews, exhibits, statements—"

"Okay, okay, I get the picture. But I still think it's a liberty to team me up with Peter bloody Lewis of all people."

"It's your call, Jack."

"I *said* okay. I'll work with him if I have to, but he'd better keep his distance, that's all!" He was about to go, when something about her struck him. Something unusual.

"There's something different about you tonight." It came as a bit of a shock when he realised what it was. "It's not my business of course, but I can't help noticing that you're wearing make up. That's unusual for you. Off somewhere special?"

She involuntarily put a hand to her right cheek. "I don't have to discuss my private life with you," she responded furiously, surprising Jack by the anger in her voice. "I consider your remark to be sexist in the extreme. I don't make comments about your hair or your aftershave. Now are you going to discuss my face, or are you going to get on with what you are paid for?"

"Oops, on my way," he replied, realising that he had overstepped the mark. He stalked off, still muttering about Lewis.

"Lewis is already at the scene," she shouted in the direction of his retreating back, "and don't forget the murder incident box."

The murder box contained everything that might be needed at a crime scene, from disposable gloves and statement forms to barrier tape and torches. One never knew what might be needed, so it was best to take every conceivable aid. It was stacked in a store cupboard at present—on the top shelf.

"Typical," complained Jack, "some people just didn't think. Storing it in such a stupid place." He reached up, but even stretching as far as he could his fingers only just touched the wooden box. He cursed and went to get a chair to stand on.

That was almost a disaster. Unprepared for how heavy the box was as he slid it from the shelf, the weight caught him of balance, causing the chair on which he stood to totter alarmingly.

He regained his balance with an effort, as a helping hand was extended. He was surprised to see Michelle standing next to him. She grabbed hold of one end of the box and swung it to the ground.

"I can't leave you alone for a moment can I, Jack?" she said condescendingly, and walked back to her office.

Muttering threats, Jack dragged the box into the corridor. Seizing the only remaining set of car keys from the hook on the CID office wall, his face registered disbelief. "Michelle," he shouted aloud, "I don't believe it; he's taken the only decent car we've got." Heaving the box into the car with an effort, he drove to the scene of the crime, a block of offices on the east side of town, in a Ford Focus and a foul mood.

Parking opposite the building, he sat in the front seat to change into a paper Scenes of Crime coverall that would protect the scene and ensure that he didn't contaminate any potential DNA evidence. He waved his warrant card at the "top" who guarded the entrance. "There's the murder box in the car. Bring it up will you?"

He trudged up the uncarpeted concrete stairs. The stairwell was dark, and Jack swore as his arthritic hand made heavy contact with the banister. As he ascended further upwards, diffused light struggling through a filthy pane of glass above an office door made it slightly easier to see where he was going.

A cheap plastic sign announced that the office was that of Ecoguard, and Peter Lewis was sifting papers when he walked in. He was dressed in an identical paper suit that only just fitted him, looking far too tight as it stretched protestingly over his bulky outline. He looked quite ludicrous, thought Jack, especially with his trade-mark black gloves still in evidence under the rubber ones.

"Evening sarge," he said, "Are you all right? Sorry that you've been called out, but you were the next one on the rota." He proffered his hand. "We don't know each other very well. Not yet, anyway, but I'm sure we're going to get on just fine."

"Am I all right?" responded Jack sourly. "What are you, my doctor or something? Of course I'm all right." He took one look at the scarred face with its piggy eyes and tight mouth, and decided that it would never happen. They would *never* get on.

"Perhaps I should be asking you if you are all right," he responded acidly, ignoring the extended hand, and pointing to a darkening bruise on Lewis's right cheek. He had shaken hands with him when they had first met, and that was more than enough.

Lewis was embarrassed. "That's the problem with being this size," he said, "doorways are always too low or too narrow, especially in the dark."

The Ds flopped in the chair behind the leather topped desk. He sat quietly for a moment, taking in the scene.

In front of him in an untidy heap, was a male body dressed in a green sports jacket and casual trousers. It seemed as though he had ended his life on his knees.

Jack was no stranger to death, and yet he had never got used to the strange phenomenon. No matter how many bodies he saw, they always exerted a peculiar fascination for him. Death was, in his eyes, a strange state. It wasn't so much the absence of life. It was the destruction of everything that a person had been. Memories, skills, friends, joys, dislikes—a lifetime wiped out. All that a person had been, now irrevocably lost. The death of others reminded Jack of his own mortality.

Here was a man who had probably got up that morning, had his breakfast, said goodbye to his family and gone off to work. He would have expected his day to be the usual routine and that he'd be home once his work was done. But his family would never see him again. Ever.

It appeared uncannily as if he had only a moment or so ago lost his balance and toppled forward, coming to rest with the side of his head against the carpet. It was the lifeless eyes looking endlessly upwards, and the dark stain spread out over the carpet in the region of his head that refuted that illusion, proclaiming the reality that violent death had come.

Jack stepped over the blue plastic barrier tape with the words "Police—Do Not Cross" written repetitively along it, that segregated the body and the immediate murder scene from the rest of the office. Leaning closer he could see a length of red cord, knotted at both ends and twisted around the man's neck. It was so deeply embedded in the tissue that only the ends of the cord were clearly visible, trailing down either side of the head, providing a conduit along which the blood had run. From here it had dripped onto the carpet, forming a crust that had not yet dried out completely.

Something caught Jack's attention. Something tied into one of the knots at the end of the cord. "Lewis, look at this," he said.

The Dc came across hurriedly. "Looks like a coin. Why on earth would anyone do that?"

"Why would anyone kill another?" replied the Ds. "Make sure that we check it out once SOCO is finished."

Turning his back abruptly on Lewis, Jack examined the floor carefully. The first thing he noticed was that the office carpet was poor quality. Under the desk it was showing signs of serious wear. And the second thing was the crunching under his feet. He knelt down to examine it. White crystals!

"What have we here?" asked Jack, leaning in order to see better.

The Dc observed the figure of his sergeant with his face hovering just above the floor. He joined him in a similar crouching position. "Sugar?"

"They must have had one heck of a tea party then, there's so much of the stuff everywhere."

"Well, Riley wasn't the cleanest of people. He probably hasn't vacuumed since he started renting the place. It could have lain around for weeks. Months even."

Jack replied scathingly to the Dc. "If you were to observe," he said, the condescension heavy in his voice, "rather than just see, you might detect something that makes that observation rather facile."

Lewis snorted something that sounded suspiciously like "Sherlock."

"Something to say, Lewis?"

"Sugar," replied Lewis hastily. "It must have occurred during the struggle." He could see that the crystals were on the body as well as the carpet.

Jack didn't pursue the perceived insult, but continued his sweeping observation, his eyes searching. "Have you seen a sugar bowl?"

He shook his head. "No, I haven't." He went into the kitchen and returned in triumph with a glass bowl. "Voila!" He looked into the bowl, then at the copious spillage on the floor. "Can't be from here, sarge, this bowl's almost full."

"Get soco to bag a sample of the stuff on the floor. We need to be absolutely sure what it is."

Jack stood up and stepped back several feet until he was the other side of the barrier tape. Even at a cursory glance the office was shabby, the walls badly painted in a cream matt paint that failed to hide the fact that there was patterned wallpaper underneath. Overhead, a single, unshaded light bulb hanging in the centre of the room was the sole source of illumination.

Two doors led off from the main office in which he now stood, both of which were standing open revealing a small kitchen on one side and a toilet on the other. In front of the desk, placed eight feet or so away, was a single straight backed chair. A small table lay on its side next to the chair; a drinking glass, and fragments of what appeared to be a similar glass lay scattered on the carpet. A silver tray and a glass decanter lay alongside, and there was a strong smell of drink in the air. Jack sniffed the air deeply. Probably Port or Sherry, he thought.

Jack pointed at the overturned table. "Looks like someone had a drink before Cooper was killed."

Lewis made a note to have the glasses checked for prints, although he knew the soco boys would do that as a matter of course.

He was interrupted by two uniformed officers lugging the box up the stairs and into the office.

"There will do." Jack indicated a place near the door as he sat back once again, surveying the scene from a different angle; breathing in the atmosphere of violence and death as the uniformed officers left, wiping their brows.

"Right, update me with what you've got," he said at last.

Lewis took out his pocket book, flipped it open and began to read his notes. "HQIR received a call around 8:10pm this evening. Caller was female—local accent. She reported that there was a serious disturbance in one of the offices in Garland Street. Lots of shouting and screaming."

Jack interrupted. "Do we know where she was calling from?"

"Yeah, a local TK."

"There are quite a few telephone kiosks she could have used. Do we have a precise location?"

He checked his notes. "Yup, the one 'round the corner from here, in the High Street."

Jack didn't answer, so after a pause Lewis carried on reading. "When the local armed-response bobbies arrived, they saw lights on in a fourth floor office. That's the one we're in now," he explained helpfully.

"Who were the officers?"

"Rob Whitehead and Del Grover, both experienced guys."

"Statements?"

"They're back at the station doing them now."

"Right, but I want to read them before they go off duty."

Lewis made a note to call the station, and carried on reading. "They came up the stairs and saw lights through the window above the office door—that door," he explained, pointing to the one Jack had just entered by. "They came in and found the prisoner unconscious across the desk. He'd obviously been in a fight because he had blood all over him. On his face, head and clothing."

"Who's the prisoner?"

"He's not known to us locally. Bloke by the name of Darrell Cooper. He owns Ecoguard, a small security firm that he runs from these offices."

"Form?"

"Only some petty thefts when he was a young man. Other than that he's clean."

"And the deceased?"

"Nelson Riley. He works, or at least used to work, for a local insurance company."

"How did we ID him?"

"From his driving licence."

"And the fact that he's in insurance?"

"Payslip in his wallet with the name of the company on it."

"Go on."

"Pc Whitehead dealt with Cooper, while Pc Grover checked the body. He didn't mess around with it too much. It was pretty obvious that the guy was dead, so he did the right thing and got straight on the radio to call out the circus."

"Have you spoken to Whitehead and the other bobby personally?"

"Pc Grover."

"Eh?"

"The other Pc, his name is Grover."

"I don't care what his bloody name is. I want to know what Cooper said. Did he give any explanation for what had happened?"

"After he was cautioned he said he couldn't remember anything. Says the last thing he remembers was looking for a torch."

Jack stood up and examined the bulb dangling overhead before wandering around the office as carefully as he could without interfering with the scene. He noted the double glazed windows that looked out onto a rear yard. It was small and unkempt, and housed two "wheelie" waste disposal bins that were overflowing with rubbish.

Walking over to the door, he checked the lock.

"Is there a key to this door?"

"Don't know. I'll get it checked."

"Okay, let me know as soon as you find out. When was death certified?"

The notebook was flipped open again. "The police surgeon Dr Ackley certified death at 9pm."

"soco?"

"Scenes of Crime have been called and should be here at any time now."

"Incident Office?"

"Being set up first thing in the morning—in the assembly room at the nick the last I heard. HQ Press Office is preparing a Press Release—I've told them to check it with you before anything goes out."

Jack grunted half-heartedly. It seemed as if all the early preliminaries had been covered. "What do you think?"

Lewis seemed surprised at being asked for an opinion. "Robbery?" He indicated the untidy search that had been made. "Was Riley a burglar caught in the act? A fight ensued and Cooper kills him."

"One should always look for a possible alternative. That's a prime rule in criminal investigation. And before you can make any snide comments, yes. It's a Sherlock Holmes quote."

Lewis had the sense to keep quiet.

Jack opened the desk drawer, looking carefully inside before removing some letters and other personal items. "You're the exhibit officer. Bag up these things for me, and give them a reference number. "I also want every file, every piece of paper, cassette tapes, CDs—anything for that matter, bagged and taken back to the nick. Oh, and take this." Sitting to one side of the desk was a black leather briefcase which he handed to Lewis, holding it by the edges. "We might get some 'prints' off of it. When SOCO have done their job and the mortuary have taken the body, meet me back at the station. And don't forget to be careful with all this. I don't want your hands all over it before the experts get a chance to examine it."

"What's your guess?" asked Lewis.

"I never guess." Jack flipped the Focus car keys onto the desk. "Your car's parked outside. Let me have my keys."

The Dc handed over the Audi keys, and smiled understandingly. "All yours, boss," he said.

There was something not quite right about the way his mouth moved when he smiled thought Jack. It was almost as though it were made of moulded plastic.

"There's some help on the way. A couple of Dc's. Oh, and the DCI will probably pay a visit." He walked to the car, peeling off the paper coverall as he did so, his mind buzzing.

CHAPTER Eighteen

It was morning, the day after the murder and Jack was examining several objects laid out in front of him. Of immediate interest was a mobile phone SOCO had found on Riley's body, and the one he had retrieved from Cooper's property bag at the nick. They were covered in white powder where SOCO had "printed" them. He picked up his desk phone.

"Yeah, it's Jack. How you doing?"

"Alright until you rang!" Geoff Stanton was one of the whiz-kids at HQ. What he couldn't find out about a person wasn't worth knowing.

Jack totally ignored the rebuff. "Great—look I need someone to analyse a couple of mobile phones for me urgently. How soon can you do it?"

"Depends on what you've got."

"It's a murder enquiry. Radigan is driving everyone nuts here. We need to get this done soon."

"I might have known. That puts it towards, if not at the top of the pile. Can you get them over to me now?"

"First thing. I'll get one of the 'tops' to drop the package in to you."

"Still as complimentary as ever. Let's hope you don't need a favour from them one day!"

"Yeah, when hell freezes over I will. Thanks Geoff. Speak later." He threw down the phone and settled back in his chair to think.

There were things about the crime that didn't make sense. He dialled through to Michelle. Her answer-phone cut in, and he suppressed a swear word.

"Boss, I need to run a few things past you about the enquiry. It's a bit fishy if you ask me. Give me a call when you get back." He slammed down the phone for the second time.

"Morning coffee, Jack?"

The smell of fresh brewed coffee wafted from behind. It was Peter Lewis.

"Yeah, why not," he said grudgingly, accepting the proffered mug, not really wanting the company but knowing that he had to speak to Lewis sooner or later.

Lewis sat down on the opposite side of the desk, nursing his coffee, the mug barely visible in his oversized gloved hand.

Jack wanted to ask him why he wore gloves all the time, but instead he asked, "What have you got then?"

The big Dc set down his mug and opening his pocket book, flipped through several pages until he came to the right section.

"There's a couple of things sarge." He cleared his throat. "The cord that was used to strangle Riley?" He rummaged in the A3 envelope he was carrying and threw an exhibit bag onto the desk. "This is it. It's about eighteen-inches in length and made of natural fibre. It's also hand-dyed." He threw another bag onto the table next to it. "This is what was tied into the end."

Jack picked up the bag containing the red cord first and examined it carefully through the plastic. Then he picked up the second bag. "It's a coin." He smeared the bag tight against it, trying to make out what it was. "Blimey, it's an Indian Rupee!"

Lewis moved on. It wasn't often that he had managed to startle Jack, and he was enjoying the precious moment. "You asked about a key to the office door?" He reached into the envelope and brought out a rim-lock key. "I found this on the floor behind the door. I guess it must have been dropped during the fight."

"Let's see it."

Lewis handed over the single brass key.

"Anything strange, Lewis?"

Lewis smiled. "It's not on a key ring."

Jack sniffed bad temperedly. He didn't much like others doing the sleuthing for him.

"Okay," he responded begrudgingly, "you're right. I don't know many people who keep their office keys—or any keys for that matter—without having a key ring."

"Perhaps it's a spare?"

"Could be anything. But why would Cooper use a spare?"

"Perhaps Riley used it to get in before Cooper arrived?"

"There's too much 'perhaps' in this investigation Lewis. I want some proper answers here."

"Right, got it sarge." Lewis took a sip from his cup before continuing. "The white crystals? As we thought, it's sugar."

"Hmm, that doesn't help us much, does it?"

"I guess not at the moment. I haven't a clue what that's all about."

"Anything else?"

"Yeah. The drinks glasses and the tray that were on the floor." He looked up, expecting a response. There was none, so he continued. "One glass, the shattered one, had Riley's fingerprints on it, and the Post Mortem showed he'd been drinking Port just before his death."

There was along pause, finally broken by Jack. "And?"

"That's it. The other glass was clean and so was the tray. As was the desk, the telephone, the briefcase and both the mobile phones."

"Sounds like he did have a housekeeper after all," intoned the Ds sarcastically.

"Which makes it seem more and more likely that this isn't a straightforward killing at all. It has all the hallmarks of Riley being set up."

"Or Cooper being set up. Or both. Anything else?"

"No. That's about it for now."

Jack started to get up. "I've got to brief Radigan on some of this stuff."

"Before you go sarge." Lewis took another gulp of coffee. "Look, I know it's none of my business but I know about your tragedy. The car accident? If I can be of any help . . ."

Jack cut him off abruptly. "Dead right, it's not your business. Confine your thinking if you can manage it, to the investigation."

"I know how hard it must be—"

Lewis had said totally the wrong thing, and now Jack was incensed.

"Constable, you don't have a bloody clue how hard it must be. All right?" His voice was flat with menace.

"Okay, okay. I'm sorry. It was a stupid thing to say. I just wanted to help."

But Jack had been wound up, and there was no going back. "What gives you the right to intrude into my private life? If you can bring my kids back from the dead and sort out my wife's damn mental problems, then you can help. Otherwise butt out before I put you through the nearest window."

He stood up threateningly, but the look in Lewis' eyes caused him to stop short of violence. He was inches from the big man as he spoke through clenched teeth, looking angrily up into the scarred face looming over him.

"You want to know how I am? Okay, you asked for it so I'll tell you how I am. Then perhaps you'll leave me alone!" He sounded as though he had gravel in his throat.

"There isn't a day goes by without my thinking of my boys. All I have left is a memory—a photograph that I look at every morning before I come to work, and every night before I go to bed. I don't sleep much. When I do I have nightmares. The same one every night. I see the accident—the car's ablaze. I'm running towards it, but my blasted legs won't move fast enough. It's like I'm running through waist-high mud. By the time I do get to it, it's too late. I can't get past the flames, it's too hot. I try again and again, but each time I'm driven back, my hands and face on fire. I can hear my boys screaming, holding out their arms to me. But I can't do a thing." His voice was cracked and broken. "Then I wake up, and I realise that it's me that has been screaming," he whispered, "and I can feel the white burning heat of the furnace in my face."

He fumbled in his jacket, and taking out his wallet, removed a dog-eared photograph which he flung down on the desk. "There they are. Jamie and Andrew—my boys."

The photograph showed two smiling boys in pyjamas. A Christmas tree stood in the background, and underneath a pile of brightly wrapped gifts. "When they died, I died. I have no life worth talking about now. I live each day hoping that it'll be my last. If there was a God, I'd ask him to take me. But if he did exist, he'd probably be so malicious that he'd refuse."

He placed the photograph carefully back in its place in his wallet, his eyes as dry as dust. "It's all I can do to get out of bed every morning." He jabbed a finger towards Lewis's chest, and said quietly. "Don't pity me. Save your platitudes for someone who cares. And if you ever mention this to me again, I won't be responsible for my actions!" He slammed his mug down on the table causing hot coffee to slop over the side, and stormed out.

Lewis mopped the wet puddle on the desk with a paper tissue, before allowing a long breath to escape from between his pursed lips.

He checked the number on the door and knocked. It was opened by a tubby, red-faced man with thinning grey hair. From his dishevelled, bleary eyed appearance it was apparent that Lewis had got him out of bed.

"If you are selling stuff, I'm not interested," he said, looking suspiciously at the large man with the disturbing features. He went to close the door.

Lewis wrapped a leather gloved hand around the side of the door, preventing it from closing and showed his warrant card. "Dc Lewis from Hartwood police station."

The man stepped backwards, and opened the door wide. "Sorry. But we get so many hawkers around here," he said lamely. He paused, curious. "What can I do for you?"

"Mr. Mahoney?" asked Lewis.

Mahoney grimaced and sighed. "Yeah, that's me. Call me Ben."

Lewis thrust his hands into his overcoat pockets. "I'd like to talk to you about Nathan," he said.

Once inside, he sat awkwardly on the settee in the tiny sitting room, filling it with his immense bulk. He glanced around, noting the frayed curtains and the layer of dust that was everywhere. The room was sparsely furnished too. A low, glass-topped coffee table with its tray of cups and a tea pot, an old model TV set and video, a settee and another chair completed the inventory. A single closed door led off, presumably to the kitchen.

"I am sorry to raise this after so many years Mr. Mahoney." He checked himself. "Sorry, Ben, but it is important."

Ben grimaced for the second time. "So important that you want to cause me grief all over again?"

"Sorry, but it's vital."

"Pity that your lot didn't think that way when it happened is all I can say."

Lewis was surprised. "Excuse me?" he responded.

"When Nat killed himself. Your lot did nothing. I gave a statement and that was it. Oh, there was a coroners hearing, but they just said that he took his own life while the balance of his mind was disturbed."

Ben Mahoney brushed a tear from his eye. "He was a sixteen-year-old boy for God's sake. He had everything to live for. Until he fell into the clutches of Riley and Benedict that is."

Lewis was surprised. "What was so bad that Nathan killed himself over it?"

"It's too late now. Nothing good can come of going over it again." Ben stood up. "I think you had better leave now. I'm through talking. He's gone and that's that."

"You're right." Lewis stood up. "There's no point in worrying about the truth, is there Mr. Mahoney?"

Mahoney was furious. "Don't you dare get condescending with me! What right have you to talk about truth? Truth wasn't on the agenda when my son was killed. All you lot wanted was to get it over and done with, and the least embarrassment the better."

"I don't understand."

"Do I have to spell it out? My son's life was less important than the reputation of certain prominent members of society. So a whitewash was done, and everything was neatly filed away with a minimum of fuss."

"Are you saying that a proper investigation wasn't done?"

Mahoney snorted derisively. "Proper investigation? There wasn't an investigation at all!"

"But I've seen the report."

"Detective, it isn't my place to tell you how to conduct your business. But if you believe that because something is written in an official record it means that it is true, then you might just be in the wrong job."

"So why don't you tell me what this is all about?"

For the first time, Ben seemed scared. "There's no use in opening up a can of worms after all this time." He stood up. "Now I'm through."

"Please, you have to give me something. How can you tell me that your son died in circumstances that were not properly investigated. In fact, from what you are saying, were actually covered up, and let me walk away with nothing?"

Mahoney cut him short. "I said I'm through. Goodbye," he said firmly, opening the front door wide.

Lewis left, but not before a last request. "If you change your mind, give me a call." He handed over his card with contact details. "You can get me at any time on one of the numbers."

Mahoney accepted it reluctantly as Lewis walked down the pathway from the house.

"One last thing."

He looked back at the sad figure framed in the doorway. "Yes?"

"I know you mean well. But please drop it Mr. Lewis. No good can come of dragging this up now." He turned and slammed the door shut.

Lewis stood outside for several minutes after the door had been closed, looking up and down the street. Then he slipped silently through the side gate, and disappeared around to the rear of the house.

Emily opened her eyes, and for a moment had no idea where she was. She was in bed. That much she knew. But the ceiling and walls of the room were cream painted—far too bright for her bedroom, the walls of which were papered anyway. It was several seconds before realisation came flooding back in a rush, as her eyes focussed on a nurse standing at her side. Her nose felt totally blocked, forcing her to breathe through her mouth. And her head ached excruciatingly.

"No, don't touch your face love." The nurse gently stopped her as she put up a hand to explore her face which felt strangely tight. "Doctor's set your nose and bandaged it up, so it's best to leave it be for a few days."

The young girl lay back on the pile of pillows behind her, and closed her eyes. "Is my mum here?" she asked.

"She's outside. She's been waiting for you to come round from the operation. I'll bring her in now that you're back with us." The young nurse smiled, and tidied the bed before going off in search of Mrs. Bowman.

"Emily!" Joan Bowman rushed into the hospital room, and stopped short when she saw the face of her daughter. She sat down heavily in the chair by the side of the bed, taking her daughter's hand gently.

Emily pulled it away from her, and tucked it under the sheets. "I want to go home," she said sullenly.

Joan removed her hand from off of the bed and fiddled with her coat to cover up her sense of rejection. "Please, Emily. Be patient for now." She rubbed her eyes wearily. Since the news of her husband's accident she had been in such a state that she was absolutely exhausted. How she was keeping herself together she just didn't know.

She knew that quite some time had passed since the news had been broken to her, although she couldn't remember much. Had it not been for the police banging at her front door yet again, she would probably have sat in her kitchen for ever.

As it was, the shock of hearing about Emily had galvanised her brain into action and she had rushed to the hospital. The police had been very good, and a kindly officer had given her a lift in his police car.

"Shouldn't really," he'd said, "but you've been through quite enough without having to find a taxi at this time of night." He'd taken her arm and helped her through the automatic doors of casualty. "Will you be okay now?"

She'd nodded and walked unsteadily inside.

Now Emily kept her eyes firmly closed. "You aren't usually interested in me, so why bother now?" She was hurting inside, and her mother was the only one she felt able to express her emotions to. In the way that people so often do, instead of being able to articulate her feelings, she went on the attack as her suppressed anger surfaced.

She sat up, grimacing in pain. "That horrible Coleman girl. How I hate her. I would like to put my hands round her throat and squeeze the life out of her." Her eyes filled with rage at the prospect of revenge on the person who had ruined her life.

It was all too much. Joan took out a handkerchief and wiped her eyes. "Emily . . ." She struggled to find the right words. "You've all I've got."

Something in her mother's voice made Emily take notice. "You've got dad," she said, but even as she said it she knew that something was wrong.

"Emily, I know you and your dad weren't close . . ."

"Not close?" Emily would have leapt from the bed had she been able to. "He hated me. He never spoke to me except to criticise and complain. I never knew him. He was just a photograph that sat on the mantelpiece. That's all he was to me!"

Joan sat silently, wringing her small white handkerchief in her hands.

"What is it? Has something happened? Is he ill?"

"Worse than that." There was a long silence as Joan struggled to find the appropriate words. But there was no easy way of saying what she had to. There simply was no right thing to say at such a time. "Oh Emily, he's dead. There's been an awful accident and your dad's dead!" Then she burst into tears.

Under the bandages, Emily's face went white. "No. I don't believe it." She started to get out of the bed, but the nurse was at her side in a moment and carefully eased her back onto the pillows.

Between sobs, Joan said. "I didn't want to tell you. Not with you being in hospital and everything and having such an awful experience. But I don't know what else to do."

Emily closed her eyes and felt herself slipping into unconsciousness. She vaguely heard the nurse talking and her mother sobbing.

Then there was nothing.

CHAPTER Nineteen

The charge room at Hartwood Police Station was a dingy affair. Dominating the large room was a solid wooden desk with metal legs, bolted to the concrete floor. This was the "charge desk" standing on a raised platform, so enabling the custody sergeant to look down on prisoners when dealing with them. It not only gave him a psychological advantage, but also allowed him to observe them carefully.

Behind the desk, rows of pink custody sheets—a record of every prisoner in police detention—hung on bulldog clips. Details of any property in their possession when arrested was carefully entered and signed for, especially money.

Money was potentially the biggest cause of strife. That and women. When Jack had joined the police as a young man, his sergeant, Sid Rawlings, had given him a valuable piece of advice. Advice that Jack had passed on to the young recruits when he was a shift sergeant.

"Be absolutely scrupulous in respect of any dealings with money," Sid had said, "and keep your hands off of the women. If you just remember that, you will enjoy a trouble-free career."

Very importantly, there were spaces on the sheet for details of visits by the custody officer, solicitor or other police officers. Every prisoner had to be visited on an hourly basis to ensure his well-being. If the prisoner was drunk, then he would be visited every fifteen minutes. That was in theory. In practice because there was invariably only one custody officer assisted by a gaoler, it was rarely done, and the records were made up retrospectively at the end of a shift to comply with the Police and Criminal Evidence Act.

A prisoner like Darrell Cooper, arrested for the serious crime of murder would be put on "suicide watch." He would have a police officer sit outside his cell, watching him day and night.

Alongside the custody records, some wag had pinned a sheet of paper with the legend written in biro underneath,

"Please Do Not Ask For Bail As A Refusal Often Offends."

The charge room floor was painted in red brick non-slip paint, and the walls were finished in white glazed tiles. As there were no windows, the only light source came from the fluorescent tubes set high in the ceiling. In this place there was neither night nor day, and time was regulated by visits from solicitors, food, and lights out.

A wooden bench with room for four prisoners to sit down at one time was bolted to the floor in front of the desk. Towards the rear were three metal barred gates. One led in from the outside world—the route the prisoners were brought in by. One led to the cell block. The last of the three was the secure tunnel leading to the magistrates court.

Sometimes a detained person walked in of their own accord, hand-cuffed and under the watchful eye of the arresting officer. They would be brought before the custody sergeant and informed of the reasons for their arrest.

If the arrest was valid they would be searched, any personal property entered on the custody record and their rights explained. They would have the opportunity to speak to a legal representative and make a telephone call before being lodged in a cell.

At other times the prisoner, especially if violent, drunk, or both, would be carried in by four or five officers, struggling and fighting, shouting and swearing all the way. At these times they would be taken straight to the "drunk tank." On these journeys, it was quite common for the prisoner's head to come into contact with every metal door post between the egress point and the final destination. There were six posts in total to the nearest cell, so the journey could be quite painful.

After being unceremoniously relieved of anything that could be used either to injure themselves or a police officer, the door would be slammed shut.

These drunk cells did not even have a mattress, and the bare wooden pallet that was the bed was raised a mere two inches from the ground. Just sufficient to prevent him from laying on the cold, tiled floor, but low enough so that if he fell he wouldn't crack his head open.

And the noise from the cell block was deafening, a cross between Bedlam and Dante's inferno. Prisoners in pursuit of their rights were hammering on the metal doors relentlessly, requesting everything from a cup of tea to a smoke, or a meeting with their "brief." They all had call-buttons in their cells to alert the custody officer that they required attention, but invariably these was overridden and silenced by a master switch, because it was impossible to accede to all the many needs.

So shouts of "guv!" echoed up and down the block as prisoners endeavoured to catch the attention of the gaoler vocally; each convinced that their request was paramount.

On top of all that, the inmates shouted at each other incessantly, occasionally just passing the time, but at other times trying to fix up an alibi and get their story straight with an accomplice before interview.

Common sense dictated that if two or more prisoners were arrested for the same crime, they should be separated so that they didn't have the chance to fabricate their story. But so often there just wasn't the space, and the only thing to do was to shut the metal hatches to try and prevent collusion.

All this did was to encourage them to shout even louder.

Visits to prisoners by solicitors usually took place in one of half-a-dozen interview rooms, although occasionally when things were really hectic a solicitor would go to the cell in order to speak to his client. When this happened, it was often the solicitor who ended up banging the hardest on the door, because the custody officer sometimes forgot he was there.

It was into this underworld that Jack and Lewis descended in order to interview Darrell Cooper, arrested for the murder of Nelson Riley.

"All right, Ginger?"

"Ginger" Steve Fennell was the custody sergeant, short of stature and short of temper. He hated criminals with a passion, and was only happy when they were locked up tight. Like Jack, he was a bit of a martial artist and enjoyed using his skills at every opportunity. Everyone knew when he had "lost it" with a prisoner by examining the custody sheets. The angrier he got, the shakier his writing was. Sometimes it was totally undecipherable.

"I will be when I finish this early shift. What's it like outside? Night or day, wet or dry?"

"You're not missing anything today. It's bucketing down so you're best off in here." He turned as Lewis came into the room. "This here's Lewis."

Lewis smiled. "Hello, Ginger. You're a bit balder than when I last saw you. Are you managing to keep your fists in your pockets nowadays?"

"Well, well, you old sod, haven't seen you since training school. Chucked you off the squad at last?" There was a bit more banter, before Jack cut in.

"Break up the reunion ladies, please! We've only got a short time in which to interview Cooper. At this rate we'll all be drawing our pensions before I get a chance to speak to him." He glanced towards the custody record hanging on the wall. "Has he got a 'brief' and is he fed and watered and fit to be interviewed?"

"He refused breakfast. Can't say I blame him. I wouldn't feed it to my dog if I had one. He's been seen by the police surgeon and is fit to be detained, although he's had a bit of a whack over the head." He rapped Lewis over the knuckles with his biro as he saw the look on his face. "Not by me, you mong. He had a head wound when he was brought in. And his brief is waiting outside. I'll get him in for you. It's Chalky White, from Harper's."

Sergeant Fennell unclipped the custody record and quickly scrawled on it. "Sign here Sherlock; I'm handing custody over to you for interview."

Jack ignored the nickname, usually used only behind his back, signed it silently and headed for the interview room with the heavy metal cell keys on a ring. He also had a set of cassette tapes. He paused in the doorway.

"What cell number?" he growled.

"Three, and don't forget to bring the keys back."

Having lain hidden all night, Auriel was now struggling slowly and painfully along a woodland path, moving his body forward by sheer force of will. Day was well advanced, and he stumbled often, crying out to the Lord to give him strength. And the Lord answered. Because despite his terrible wounds he managed, contrary to all reason, to limp onwards mile after mile. Performing a seemingly endless, painful and futile cycle; force air past heaving chest and into lungs, keep legs moving. Force air past heaving chest into lungs, keep legs moving . . .

He clutched his soiled tunic over his torn and bleeding back, and willed himself to go on. He had to warn Talial and Captain Aanfial.

After Barbas and the other demons had finished their sport with him, they had left him for dead, lying broken and unconscious on the hard ground. But that was their error, and one that they would regret.

They were so full of themselves, so caught up in back-slapping and self-congratulations on defeating one of their hated enemy that they failed to notice the damaged angel crawling into the trees under the cover of darkness.

Once out of sight, he put as much distance as he could between them, before becoming too exhausted to move any further. He had to retain a vestige of strength to do what he had to do next.

Scraping desperately at the frozen, frost covered ground with his bare hands, he began to scoop out a shallow trench in the forest floor in which he could lie. It was slow work. At first it seemed impossible, but by utilising a piece of jagged rock as a tool, he was able to make some progress. He was forced to stop often by the excruciating pain tearing regularly through his protesting body. But he compelled his reluctant muscles to work. It was that, or die. He didn't have long. It was only a matter of time before they would notice him gone.

He knew he had neither the time nor the energy to dig deep. The most he could hope for was a shallow scrape that would disguise his outline sufficiently when covered with debris and leaves.

By this time, night was over and the first rays of day were beginning to filter across the sky. It seemed no time at all before he heard the cry go up, and he knew that he had finally been missed. He wished he had more time. Even a minute or two could make all the difference between success or failure. But he had done all he could. He prayed that God would protect him, and surrendered himself into his hands.

Laying face down in the hollow he had formed, he dragged leaves and bracken, dead twigs and forest debris over him, praying that none of him was exposed to view, for he had no way of knowing what kind of job he had made of his camouflage.

For some time there were sounds of furious activity. Coarse words were shouted, interspersed with shrieks as Barbas brutalised those he considered at fault for losing the angel. But although they flew in angry sorties over the area and searched on foot, poking into the undergrowth with swords and sharpened sticks, they found no trace of Auriel and eventually gave up in foul-humour.

Lying perfectly still under his shroud of leaves, the angel had time to think about what had happened, and what had been said. And what concerned him greatly, was a conversation he had overheard whilst coming back to consciousness. They'd been talking about a high-demon. And what they had carelessly said had caused him to shudder. They had spoken of "He whose name dare not be spoken."

He had heard of this ones reputation. A demon lord of great strength and power, accountable to Lucifer personally. All demons without exception feared him, and rightly so. Because he was a rarity in the world of evil and treachery that he ruled.

The majority of the demon lords had thoughts only for themselves; for their reputations, their power and wealth, for their own advancement. But this one was different.

He gave total and unswerving loyalty to his master whom he loved and served with fanatical devotion. Once appointed to a task, nothing and no-one other than death itself could stop him. He felt neither heat nor cold and he did not grow tired. Neither did he weary of his task until it was accomplished. And he had never failed!

His unshakable dedication to Lucifer, Prince of the Power of the Air was matched only by his implacable hatred of the enemy.

The God known as Adonai. The God who had created the world *ex nihlo*. The God of the Christians who had formed his greatest creation—Adam—from the dust of that earth.

The malevolent demon lord could not fathom why Adonai had created weak and pathetic humans to be his people. All that puerile talk of love and sacrifice. Strength and power was all that mattered, and that is why the enemy and his puny "saints" would lose and his master, Lucifer, the Morning Star, would win.

And if he hated God, his hatred for mankind and the self-abasing angels came a close second.

Auriel had heard tales of the ferocious battle between this formidable demon lord and one of Adoni's most powerful angels at the beginning of time when Satan was cast down to earth. But what the young angel was unaware of, what no-one knew not even Lucifer himself, was that this apparently invincible dark angel had come close to a defeat. Something he had never forgotten.

It was then that he had bound himself with a blood oath; a promise sealed with a terrible vow in the blood-red coals of the earth. A promise of such power, hatred and iniquitous evil, that its consequences would be with him for all eternity.

Because of his resolute obedience, Lucifer had given him authority in all things; given him the name above every demonic name. His was the supremacy and his was the power over high and low. Only the master had greater dominion.

Jewels and honour were lavished upon him. He was elevated above Benoth of Babylon, Nergal of Cuth, Ashima of Hamath, Bibhaz and Tartak of the Avites and Adrammelech and Anammelech of the Sepharvites.

His dominion was global encompassing cities, regions, nations and continents. He wielded his terrible and destructive supremacy relentlessly in the service of his god, sweeping before him anything and anyone that stood in the way of his dark lord's will. The oath he had sworn was that he would not, could not rest either day or night until he had overcome all of Lucifer's enemies and hurled them in chains at his feet. Especially the one who had come closer than any other to defeating him in single combat at the great rising.

A lowly angel named Talial.

She sat up in bed, shivering in the aftermath of the nightmare. The nightmare of the trees that played over and over every time she went to sleep.

Although there was a subtle difference this time. Because it had become so familiar to her she found it hard to analyse. She played it across her mind in rapid, fast-forward mode. The trees, the forest, the rain and the smell of earth. Then the laughter, the diabolical, maniacal laughter.

It came to her suddenly. This time someone had been there. There was a definite presence. In the past, the dream had been abstract. The trees had always been central, filling her mind, fuelling her fear. Irrationally of course and in her waking moments, she knew it made no sense.

And the laughter. In the past it had seemed to emanate from somewhere beyond. Out of sight, beyond her perception. And the smell of corruption that assailed her senses, however frightening, however distressing was always, "out there."

This time it was closer. Much closer. No longer "out there." Now it was *here*. Because someone was present this time. And she was certain that it had been a *someone*, and not a *something*. Just beyond the periphery of her vision. Lurking tantalisingly out of view. But present nevertheless.

How she knew she could not explain. Nothing about it made any sense. But someone was definitely there. And they were watching her . . .

CHAPTER TWENTY

Auriel continued on through the trees, heading towards town. Several times he came across bands of noisy demons winging their way North through the morning air. So full of bravado were they now, that they had abandoned their usual mode of operating mostly at night and now strutted their evil openly. Much to his dismay, because it slowed him down, he had to hide at these times in dank ditches and hedgerows to ensure he remained unseen by the myriad of pin-prick demonic eyes.

He was defenceless, his sword having fallen from his grasp during his fight with Barbas, and he had been unable to retrieve it as he escaped.

Lurching out of the woodland and into the residential area, he kept to the alleyways, staying close to the walls to avoid being seen. And that was going to be a problem. Because the area was awash with the black forms of imps, demons and other evil entities of various shapes and sizes, all of them on the move.

He was amazed at the numbers strutting carelessly along the streets as if they owned the place. They were all clothed in similar black shapeless smocks. Some were small, darting imps, others huge lumbering monstrosities. All had filthy talons extending from the tips of their fingers and tough, leathery skin. And they all had one thing in common. They reeked of evil, a real, physical smell of corruption. They were like flies, feasting on the corruption of mankind.

He shrank back against the wall, pressing himself into the shadows as a demon voice spoke nearby.

"Amduscias, can you smell something revolting?"

The noise of heavy sniffing sounded clearly in the still air. "Nah, nothing. Only your filthy hide Mantus!"

There was the sound of laughter and another voice chimed in. "You stink of angel, Mantus. You've been getting too close I think."

Then came the sound of a blade being drawn, followed by a rasping voice. "See this sword Amduscias, and you Rahu? This is the one I stabbed the angel with!"

It required all of Auriel's willpower not to launch himself around the corner at that point. His desire to exact vengeance on the craven, boastful demon knew no bounds. But the Holy Spirit was restraining him, and obediently he did not move.

"Amduscias the betrayer, you have dishonoured me for the last time," said Mantus. "If you dare so much as to even look in my direction again, I will run you through!"

"Okay, okay leave it out, Mantus."

"And you, Rahu, do you have more to say?"

The voice of Rahu sounded stunned. "Hey, we was just joking a bit!"

"Listen up," said Mantus. "Usually I'd like nothing better than to cut both your throats, but in case you've forgotten we've been called to an important meeting and I would think that every demon is going to be required. Even you two."

"Okay," responded Rahu shakily, "we'd better get a move on. It's the top man. I've heard that it's . . ."

There came the sound of a heavy blow, followed by an angry squeal.

"Shut your fool trap, Rahu." Mantus sounded alarmed. "Don't you ever, ever mention his name. Do you hear?"

The demon sounded cowed for the second time that night. "All right, all right. No need for violence."

The voices faded as they started to move off and Auriel breathed a sigh of relief as once more he continued his slow, painful progress in search of his comrades. His warning was even more pertinent now. It was obvious that the meeting taking place was with the arch-demon himself. The mighty Bal-Lgura. So feared that most demons—those that wanted to live anyway—could not even bring themselves to speak his name. His captain had to know about this at all costs, because perhaps this was a chance to inflict some serious damage on the enemies of God.

He had taken no more than half-a-dozen paces, before a familiar rasping voice spoke again. Mantus, acting on a hunch, had slipped back and was lurking in the shadows.

"My, what have we here then?" There was the sound of sniffing. "I knew I could smell something filthy," he said. "And I was right. It's angel stink."

Auriel glared at the demon. But he had no weapon with which to defend himself, and his gaping wounds were such that he could hardly stand let alone fight. But if he lacked strength, he certainly didn't lack courage. Leaning back against the wall for support, he stared steadfastly at his enemy.

Mantus was boastful. Speaking slowly and menacingly he threatened; "There are just the two of us. Soon, there will be just one. Now we will see who is the strongest and who is the weakest. The strong will live. The weak will die." He laughed at his own cleverness. "Angel of the Lord, prepare to meet your death."

For just a moment, Mantus wondered at the lack of fear on the defeated angel's face. But only for a moment. Looking at the crippled form in front of him gave him courage and he guffawed loudly, drawing his short sword and ambling confidently forward. "See you in hell," he said mockingly.

In the interview room, Jack sat with his back to the door, in the chair facing Cooper and his solicitor. Between them was a wooden desk, and like all the other furniture in this pit of darkness, it was screwed to the ground for safety reasons. Lewis sprawled easily in a grey plastic chair in the corner, observing the prisoner carefully.

Jack stretched his aching fingers and attempted to break open the cellophane wrapping around the twin tapes. He fumbled for a moment, but the arthritis in his hand made the fine motor skills needed impossible. He threw them to the Dc, who unwrapped them before inserting them into the recording machine.

"For the benefit of the tape, I am Ds Jack Somerville. With me in the interview room is detective constable Peter Lewis. I am interviewing Darrell Cooper who has with him his solicitor, Mr. Charles White."

Jack turned to Cooper. "Mr. Cooper, would you give your full name, date of birth and address?"

The prisoner reluctantly did so, glancing often at his solicitor.

"Mr. Cooper—may I call you Darrell? I want to put some questions to you about the murder of Nelson Riley on the night of Monday the 22nd of December. You do not have to say anything. But it may harm your defence if you do not mention when questioned something which you later rely on in court. Anything you do say may be given in evidence. Do you understand?"

Cooper glanced at his solicitor for reassurance and nodded. He looked pale and frightened.

Jack added, "For the benefit of the tape, Mr. Cooper is nodding. Darrell, may I ask you to reply either 'yes' or 'no'?"

"Yeah, I . . . I understand," he stuttered quietly.

Jack began to ask pertinent questions about the night the Cooper was arrested. Charles White interrupted only occasionally, once inviting his client to state "no comment," which he duly did. Every now and then, Lewis too put questions.

"Tell me again," said Jack, "why you went to your office at that time of night."

"It's my office. I often work there until late. That's not that unusual is it?"

"So you were working late last night?"

"No, I was out on a job until just after 7pm. I've already said. I got a message from Riley telling me to meet him. So obviously I went."

"And that was normal?"

"What, meeting with Riley?"

"Yes."

The prisoner thought for a moment. "Now you mention it, I suppose no. We didn't get on that well so he didn't usually contact me. Whenever we met, it was always on business and always at the church."

"And the same would go for you?"

"What do you mean?"

"Come on Darrell, it's an easy question. Do you—did you—contact Riley often?"

"No, never."

"How did Riley contact you?"

"When?"

Jack let his exasperation show. "When he arranged the bloody meeting, when else?"

Chalky interrupted then. "Ds Somerville. There is no need to browbeat my client."

"Okay, Darrell." Jack took a deep breath before speaking as gently as he knew how. "When inviting you to the Monday night meeting, how did Riley contact you?"

"He rang me at home."

"What time?"

"I think it was around 6:30pm."

"Didn't you say that you were out on business at that time?"

"Yeah. My wife took the call."

"What was the exact message?"

He was flustered. "I can't remember *that*. All I know is that he called to tell me the time of the meeting. 8pm at the office. I was out so she took the call."

Jack made a mental note to speak to Mrs. Cooper.

Lewis interrupted. "When was the last time you saw him alive?"

Cooper switched his attention to Lewis, and then dropped his gaze as the bright piggy eyes stared unblinkingly at him. "The day before. Benedict had called a meeting at his office."

"Benedict?"

"The apostle of the First Church of God. In Hartwood."

"Apostle?"

"He's the leader—a Bishop I suppose you would call him."

Jack sounded surprised. "What, like the Bishop of London?"

Lewis cut in, directing his question to Cooper. "Isn't he part of a non-denominational church?"

"Yeah—he's not mainstream church. More of a cult."

"What was the meeting about?" enquired Jack.

"Church business."

"Can you be more explicit?"

"He was worried about people haemorrhaging out of the church. A lot had left and he wanted us to come up with some solutions."

"What solutions *did* you come up with?" asked Lewis.

"None. There wasn't time. I thought that was what the late meeting was about. Benedict had been rattled at our meeting the previous day. I've never seen him like that before. He's a cold bit of work usually."

"Is that not unusual for a church leader? Being cold I mean?" responded Lewis.

Cooper laughed, but it sounded false. "He calls it a church. But it's a church of Satan more than anything else."

Jack thought the church thing had gone far enough. "So far we've established that you got this message. What exactly did it say?"

"Not a lot. It just said to meet him at my office at 8pm."

"That was it?"

"That was it."

"Why did you meet at your office? Or to put in another way, why did Riley ask to meet at your office and not at, say his house, or the church office?"

"I said we didn't get on too well. I've never been to Riley's house. We liked to keep work separate."

"Did Riley have a key to your office?"

"Of course not."

"Then how was he meant to get in?"

"Well obviously he would have waited outside for me to arrive and I would have let him in."

"But someone let him in. Who else has a key?"

"No-one that I know of."

Jack produced the brass rim-lock key from his pocket. It was in its plastic exhibit bag and securely labelled with a number. "For the benefit of the tape, I am showing the defendant exhibit PL/3," said Jack. "Mr. Cooper, is this your key?"

He leaned forward. "Can I see it?"

Jack passed over the bag.

"Doesn't look like mine. I have an enormous great bunch of keys on a ring. It's one of the necessities in the security business."

"It was found by detective constable Lewis here, on the floor of your office."

Cooper shrugged. "As I said, I don't recognise it. Are you sure it's my office key?"

Lewis interrupted. "It is. I tried it out."

Jack said. "Do you have any spare keys? One for the cleaner for instance?"

Lewis spluttered, tried to turn it into a cough, and ended up almost choking.

Darrell Cooper paid no attention to him, but Jack gave him a hard stare.

"There are no spares so far as I know. I began renting the office over eighteen months ago. The previous tenant may have kept a key back. I don't know," he said, clearly irritated. He was getting tired of the questioning and glanced desperately at his solicitor.

Jack picked up the signals. "We are going to finish now. Just one last thing." He regarded the prisoner closely, judging his facial expression. "Tell me again, what happened when you got to your office following the message?"

"As I said earlier. The place was in darkness. I unlocked the door and went to turn the light on. But the fuses must have blown. I went to get a torch, and the next thing I know I was laying on the floor surrounded by your lot with guns."

"That's strange," said Lewis.

Cooper looked up. "It doesn't get any stranger. How often have you woken up on the floor surrounded by coppers?"

Lewis shook his head. "I meant about the place in darkness." He checked his pocket book. "When our guys got there, you were lying across your desk unconscious, but the light was blazing away! That's how they found you in the first place. The whole block was in total darkness except for your office."

"You don't have to answer that," said Chalky.

"I've got nothing to hide. I really can't remember what happened. I think someone attacked me." He sat silent for a moment, screwing up his face as he tried to recall an elusive memory. He held up his fist, where the knuckles were cut and swollen. "I think I hit someone. Just a wild swing." His face suddenly filled with pain, and he put a hand to his bandaged head. "I really can't remember. It's all a bit of a muddle."

"Are you sure that the 'wild swing' you took wasn't at Mr. Riley?" asked Jack bluntly.

"You don't have to answer that," said Chalky mechanically.

"It's okay. Look, Riley was scum. It's common knowledge that we detested each other. But as for killing him? No way. Look somewhere else."

"Scum?" asked Jack. "What makes you say that?"

Cooper shrugged. "He was a nonce. Everyone hates nonces."

Jack leant back in his chair, digesting the new information. "He liked little girls?"

"I said he was scum. But it wasn't girls. Riley liked boys."

Jack was silent for a moment, taken aback by the unexpected revelation. Then he threw another plastic package onto the desk between them. He nodded. "You can look at it." Almost as an aside he said, "For the benefit of the tape I am showing Darrell exhibit PL/5."

Cooper picked it up and examined the piece of red cord. "What is it?"

"I was going to ask you the same thing. Have you ever seen this before?"

He appeared puzzled. "It's just a bit of cord . . ." Then the truth hit him with sudden clarity, and the package dropped from his hands. His voice was squeaky when he spoke. "My God, is this what was used to murder Riley?"

Jack didn't answer, but stared silently at him. Then he said, "Let's not pussy foot around any longer, Darrell. One last question. Did you kill Nelson Riley?"

The prisoner rose to his feet, his face flushed with anger. "No, I did not. You can't pin that on me." He turned to his solicitor. "*Now* I am finished. I have nothing more to say."

"Are you sure there is nothing more you need to tell me?"

Cooper thought for a moment about the briefcase he had set up in the office. Had that recorded anything? If it had, it might prove his innocence. On the other hand, it might incriminate him. "No, that's it," he said firmly.

Jack decided that they all needed a break. The interview had lasted two-and-a-half hours by the time he terminated it, and he didn't want the defence solicitor making allegations that he'd abused the prisoner by interviewing him at such an early hour without sufficient sleep.

As Chalky had other prisoners whom he was also representing, Jack left him sitting in the charge room for custody officer Steve to deal with.

He nodded, almost sympathetic for the young uniformed officer sitting outside cell three. He was the unfortunate who had been assigned to suicide watch for the eight hours of his shift. His unenviable task was to put up with the jeering and catcalling, the wall to wall noise from the other prisoners in the block while he carried out the mind-numbing task of watching Darrell Cooper, ensuring that he didn't top himself.

Jack slammed the heavy metal door shut with a bang that echoed down the corridor, provoking a barrage of abuse from the incumbents of neighbouring cells, some of whom were sleeping. The automatic lock engaged. Then he double-locked with the key before gratefully making his way back to the outside world.

His last memory of Cooper was of a forlorn figure, framed within the open viewing hatch in the door, sitting with his head in his hands. A man lost and alone.

The almost subterranean darkness of the cell block accentuated the feeling of depravity in the place, and Jack felt hugely relieved as he got out. He had the same feeling he'd felt earlier in the week in his office.

Which wasn't surprising because sitting alongside Cooper was a black shapeless creature with eyes like red coals, staring hatefully at his captive.

Along the white-glazed tile corridor, in every cell, similar entities swarmed like flies, whispering darkness and evil mischief into the minds of the desperate, hopeless men that they embodied and controlled.

Mantus was so close that Auriel could smell the foulness that exuded from his breath.

The demon knew that the angel was helpless, and so took his time, enjoying the weakness of the despised servant of the enemy. Enjoying a rare moment of power.

"You are too late—all of you," he grated, slowly and precisely. "We have been in this town for too long for you to take it back. You are weak, look at you! A guardian angel? How do you think you can guard anyone, eh?"

He placed the tip of his sword against the stricken angel's throat. "Don't you get it? These people don't want you and your sort. They don't want your God or his church."

Auriel remained silent, his eyes fixed unwaveringly on the demon.

The point of the sword was pushed harder against his throat. There was nothing he could do. Nowhere he could go. The wall pressed hard into his back, exacerbating the pain from the raw, open wounds. He knew as well as Mantus, that he was helpless.

"Where is your God now? Where is Adonai?" Mantus looked around as if searching for someone. "He will loose the fight my angel friend and we will win. Shall I tell you why?"

Auriel did not reply, but the demon continued anyway.

"As you die, consider this; Because of *your* ineffectiveness—you and all your angel kind—and due to *his* weakness in loving such poor specimens as the sons and daughters of Adam, the world will not be saved according to his plan."

Mantus spat on the ground, then wiped his mouth with the back of his leathery hand.

"His plan is flawed. How could it work when he allows the weak and feeble creation that he calls his 'children,' to make their own decisions? He could so easily have forced them to obey him, but no, he lets them decide! He gives them free will. And why? Because he wants them to love him!"

The demon broke into peals of laughter. "Love? How amusing. How pathetic. All that matters is power. Love is for the weak. Power is for the strong. So the world and all that is in it belongs to my Lord Lucifer. And do you know what the best part is?"

Mantus paused to savour the moment, his thin lips curled back in an unholy smile. "Mankind could have had Adonai and his heaven, but in their pride they have rejected him. He might love them, but they don't love him. Because people want to remain in their filth and their evil; they have no real desire to be transformed or to be any different. And if they do—well, we introduce them to religion. To church going and dead tradition. Anything that will keep their minds away from a relationship with *him*. And they won't even suspect until they draw their last breath and their souls are given up. Then as you and I know, it will be too late and they will be ours for all eternity."

Auriel's eyes blazed at the affront to the living God from the foul entity. "I will not grace your blasphemous words with the dignity of any argument, demon. As it is written, 'Do not give dogs what is sacred; do not throw your pearls to pigs. If you do, they may trample them under their feet.'"

Mantus drew back his sword. "It is mankind that my Lord Lucifer will trample under his feet. Now, no more talk. For you it is finished!"

And he brought his sword down in a swinging arc.

CHAPTER Twenty-One

"Right you lot, listen in." Jack addressed the gathering of detectives in the briefing room. "Sit down and shut up, I want to get this briefing under way."

There was a flurry of activity as the assembled officers found chairs, collected pads of paper and one or two picked up mugs of tea.

"In a nutshell this is what we have got at the moment." He pointed to a whiteboard on an easel at his side. "The deceased Nelson Riley, found dead in the offices of Ecoguard, a security company owned by Darrell Cooper shortly after 8pm on the 21st December. I've got the initial doctor's report here."

He picked up a folder and read from a sheet of paper tucked inside it. "Time of death between 6:30pm and 8pm according to the police surgeon, but the Post Mortem will confirm that later. Cause of death was strangulation with a length of cord which was still in-situ." He held up the article sealed in a plastic exhibit bag. "So much force was used that Cooper's head was almost severed from his body. The police 'quack' says he had never seen anything quite like it. Whoever did it must have had superhuman strength."

He checked his notes before moving on. "HQIR received a '9' call at 8:15pm from an as yet unidentified female stating that a fight was taking place in the upstairs office of a block in Garland Street, Hartwood. There's a transcript of the tape being sent down for me to listen to. The caller thought someone was being murdered, judging from the screams that she could hear. An ARV armed response vehicle was dispatched. Fortunately it was close by and on the scene within minutes. Two armed officers entered the building and found the door to the Ecoguard Security Office open. The defendant Cooper was found collapsed on his desk with head injuries. On the floor next to him was the dead body of Nelson Riley."

He glanced around the room. "Questions?"

A thin young man sitting at the back raised his hand.

"No need to put your hand up Dc Walker, you're not in school now. What is it?"

Detective Walker blushed. "I was wondering whether there have been any similar deaths over the past years?"

"Good question. The answer is, none that we know of. But it's worth checking. You get on with it. Next question?"

Walker was not deterred. "Does Cooper have cause to hate him? To hate him enough to kill him I mean? What is the motive here?"

"It could have been any of a number of people that hated him. He was a paedophile according to Cooper, who made no secret of the fact that he detested him as a nonce. Whether that is true or not is still being checked. I would say that that was a good enough reason for *someone* to want him dead."

There was silence for a moment after that revelation, so Jack continued.

"I've received the lab report on the mobile phone we took from Riley's body. The service provider confirms that it in fact his." In front of him he held a printout of all the calls made and received by the mobile over the past year. It ran to many pages. "This is important. On the night of the murder, a text message was sent from Cooper's mobile to Riley's, saying that he had received the message and would meet him at the office at 8pm. What do you think of that?"

"What exactly did it say?" Another detective, Dc Richards was sat at the back.

Jack read from the sheet in front of him. The message had been deleted from the memory, but it had still been available from the archives of the service provider.

"It just said 'Riley: Received message. Will meet you at office 8pm Cooper.' So, give me a motive for Cooper having killed him. When I interviewed him he seemed genuinely surprised that his mobile had been used to text Riley. How do we know that Cooper sent the message?"

"Well, you said the report . . ."

"I said the text was sent from Cooper's phone, Mr. Richards. That doesn't necessarily mean he sent it. That's elementary." There was a snigger and a muffled cry of 'Sherlock.'

Dc Richards wasn't going to give up that easily. "They were both in the office though, weren't they? I mean, Riley was lying dead and half-decapitated on the floor and Cooper was found next to the body. And what about Riley's phone? What does that tell us?"

"Good question," responded Jack. "There is still a lot of analysing to be done on both phones, but what is indisputable is that a text was sent from Cooper's mobile to Riley. But there is no sign of Riley having used his phone to either call or text Cooper."

"That seems to confirm things then, doesn't it?" Dc Richards raised an eyebrow questioningly.

Jack laughed, but without a trace of humour. "If only things were that simple my friend." He glanced back at his notes. "A telephone call was made by Riley to Cooper's home address. We have checked the BT records and they confirm that the call was actually made from Cooper's office at around 6.50pm. Now this is interesting. According to the analyst, the confirmation text was sent from Cooper's phone at 8:10pm."

There was a low whistle from the assembled officers.

"That's right. It seems that Cooper didn't reply until after Riley was dead!"

Jack held up Riley's mobile in its exhibit bag. "And there is something else that is puzzling me. Riley wasn't the neatest, cleanest man. In fact he was a mess." He surveyed the watching officers intently. "But strangely, his mobile was clean. And I mean *totally* clean. The soco boys have been all over it, and there isn't a single fingerprint on it. Not even his own! And the same goes for the office desk, the telephone, the briefcase found at the scene and also a tray and one of the drinking glasses. The other had Riley's prints on it, but they're the only ones we've found on any of the exhibits!"

There was rumble of noise from the assembled police officers, and another detective volunteered his opinion. "Sounds like someone did some housekeeping after the killing. What if someone else was there at the meeting? They killed Riley and left before the ARV's got there?"

Jack shrugged. "It's plausible, but we don't know enough yet. The soco boys have gone all over the place for prints and DNA. As you would expect in an office, they have a lot of samples. But it's too soon yet for them to have come up with anything of interest."

Dc Walker put another question. "What injuries did Cooper have?"

Jack picked up another folder and leafed through it until he found the photocopies of the custody record with the police surgeon's report attached. "Here we are. Cooper arrived at the station at 8:35pm, having been arrested at the scene shortly before. He had suffered a head injury which was bleeding profusely. Looks like he had sustained a couple of blows to the dome. He also had a minor hand injury. That fits both with his claim that he struck out at someone who attacked him, and also the scenario that he had a fight with Riley before strangling him. The police surgeon examined him around 9pm, sent him to the hospital to be stitched up and gave him a box of pain killers. Other than that he was fit to be detained."

A heavy set, middle-aged man wearing a brown corduroy jacket asked the next question. "You've interviewed Cooper, Jack. What's he say?"

"Not a lot, Mike. Says he went to a pre-arranged meeting at the office to see Riley. The next thing he remembers is that he was being escorted off the premises by the armed 'tops.'"

"Did he say anything about anyone else being present? Are there any lines of enquiry we can follow up?"

"He says doesn't remember much about anyone being there. He thinks he *may* have hit someone who *may* have attacked him, and he does have swollen knuckles. But he's very hazy and I wouldn't be surprised if he suffered from concussion. We probably shouldn't be interviewing him . . ."

"So does his explanation, such as it is, seem plausible?"

"Yes it does," said Jack. "I'm inclined to believe his account of what happened. He looked pretty shook up, and seemed genuinely surprised that Riley was killed." He consulted his notes once more. "Hmm, there is one thing that you can do, Mike." He gestured at the detective who had asked the question. "Find out what you can about a bloke named Benedict Ademola. He's some kind of apostle or something in a big church around here somewhere. Apparently he was one of the people that Cooper and Riley met up with the day before the murder. He might be able to shed some light on their state of mind."

"I've heard of him. Is there any apparent motive?"

"Murder like matrimony, generally has a motive."

Detective constable Mike Grosvenor pulled a face. "Quote me no quotes, Sherlock Holmes," he whispered under his breath, making a note in his pocket book. "Righto, leave it with me."

"Right," said Jack, "that's all for now. Dc Lewis here will co-ordinate things. Speak to him and he will allocate you your enquiries. When you have completed them, let him know so he can tick them off the list. I don't want anything overlooked, not even the smallest, seemingly unimportant thing."

Just then the telephone at the back of the room rang harshly. Lewis was nearest and picked it up, listening for a moment. "It's for you sarge," he said. "It's Radigan and it's urgent."

Jack muttered seditiously under his breath as he picked up the phone. Then his face took on a startled expression. The meeting had started to break up, and Jack put his hand over the mouthpiece. "Wait up you lot," he shouted, before turning his attention back to the phone.

He walked thoughtfully to the front of the meeting room, strangely quiet. "We're going to have our work cut out here," he said. "That was the DCI. They've just found Cooper hanging in his cell."

There was a gasp, followed by an outbreak of startled conversation.

"Come on guys, can it," said Jack. "Get on with your job so that we get this sorted out soon eh? I retire in just under a week and I don't want an unsolved murder on my record when I go!"

The death of Cooper momentarily forgotten, a stifled cheer went around the room, accompanied by muted exclamations of "Happy Christmas!"

Auriel waited for the sword to descend. He didn't fear it. But he was angry that his service to God should end in such a manner, and at the hands of such a fetid demon. Without his dreadful wounds, and with an even half-decent sword in his hand he would have dispatched this cocky imp without pausing to draw breath. But as it was, he was unarmed, weak and helpless. He would have liked to die with his sword in his hand.

It was then, when all hope had gone, that he heard a sound that caused his heart to soar. And the joy of recognition lit up in his golden eyes at the very moment the sword of Mantus began its downward arc. It was the familiar twang of a powerful bowstring.

Faster than the eye could follow, swifter even than the scything descent of the killing blade, sped the arrow of holy judgement and divine retribution.

Mantus looked up in fear as the very air was rent before him, and a golden arrow sliced a path to his heart with its message of death. The look of triumph in his blood-red eyes faded and a strange, contorted look came over him. For the briefest time there was the stench of fear, before the demon vanished with a high-pitched scream into the abyss. In the air there lingered for a time the distinctive odour of sulphur, and a black scorch-mark disfigured the ground.

Auriel saw Talial plummet out of the sky in free-fall, his wings flaring in a majestic display as he slowed his descent seconds before his feet touched down.

Dear Talial. He could see him running towards him, bow in hand, and even at a distance he could see the look of concern on his captain's face.

"Bar Lgura has come. Bar Lgura has come," he whispered urgently. Then his heart could hold on no longer, and he slumped to the ground in a tattered heap.

Talial was stricken with sorrow as he gazed upon the broken angel crumpled at his feet. Tenderly he cradled him in his arms, and as the full extent of the mutilation became apparent, his rage was terrifying to see. And in his face was death.

He called his name, Auriel, and he was gratified that there was the light of recognition in his eyes. Perhaps it was not too late. Here was one of the youngest and swiftest of the angelic host, a warrior whose prowess in the air was legendary. He turned his face away, lest his sorrow should be seen.

So many wounds and cuts scarred the body that it was difficult to see where one injury ended and another began. The warrior of God had been through a terrible ordeal, and he was fading fast. But what caused his heart to break, was the raw stumps projecting grotesquely from the back of Auriel's torn and soiled tunic, where his wings had been brutally hacked away.

As the phone was answered, the police officer intoned the usual mantra. "Do what thou wilt shall be the whole of the law."

"So mote it be."

"Cooper is dead. But there is a complication."

"That's your job. Deal with it."

"Mahoney has been talking."

"Then make him go away."

And the phone was abruptly put down.

Jack was not in a good mood. After the briefing he had returned to his office to find that it had been ransacked. His usually neat and tidy desk was now replete with the contents of its three drawers, which appeared to have been unceremoniously emptied onto it. The bookcase in the corner had also been emptied, the leather bound books strewn in an undignified heap across the carpeted floor.

Picking up his chair which was lying on its side, he sat for a long time in thoughtful silence. The pain in his hand was playing up, a sure sign that he was suffering from stress. What on earth was this all about? In his ten years at Hartwood police station he had never experienced anything like it. Surely it couldn't be a practical joke—no one in their right mind would want to do that to him.

Had someone searched his office? If that was it, it wasn't a very professional job. Everything had just been dumped, on his desk and on his floor and that would have made it difficult if someone was looking for something.

A theft? That sounded quite ludicrous in a police station. Anyway, what was there to steal? He sat back, pondering the matter, before poking at the pile of papers and personal effects that littered the top of his desk. Someone had been looking for something, but what? And had they found what they'd been looking for?

That was putting the cart before the horse somewhat. Until he discovered the object of the untidy search he couldn't possibly begin to deduce whether it had been successful or not. He began to sort out the mess, putting paperwork back in its appropriate suspended files, re-arranging statements, and returning the books to their home under the window. By the time he'd finished he felt a lot better. Just to have his office back in a neat order was major therapy to him. But he was none the wiser as to why, or who.

He emailed a quick report of the incident to his line manager DCI Radigan, knowing even as he did it that the response from her would be absolutely nil, and settled down to work.

He opened his briefcase, and it was then that he realised. The buff files that he'd left on his desk—the ones concerning the RTA victims— they had gone. Every last one of them! He sat back slowly, allowing his breath to escape from between his pursed lips with a whistle. So that was it.

He had the "what" of the situation, but the question now was why? Why had the files been taken? They weren't of any importance. Certainly no-one had needed to ransack his office. The files had been left clearly on his desk. There hadn't been any need to search his whole office.

The shrill ring of the telephone interrupted his thoughts.

"Jack?" It was DCI Radigan.

"Yup."

"Come up to my office. I want to talk to you."

"That's fine, because I sure need to talk to you. But I'm up to my eyes here. Can it wait a bit?"

"Just get up here will you," said Radigan, "*Now* would be a good time."

As he tried to think of an appropriate response, she replaced the receiver, and the conversation was over.

It was as he was leaving, that he spied something bright and shining just under the corner of his keyboard. He fished it out with a pencil. It was a gold cuff-link with the police insignia on it.

Not many people wore cuff-links. In fact he only knew one person off-hand who did. He held it in the open palm of his hand for a few moments, looking at it carefully. What was it doing there? At first sight, it meant that someone had been using his desk whilst he was out. Or perhaps something more sinister? Like reading his files? Or perhaps taking his files? Or ransacking his office?

Jack didn't know, and none of it made sense anyway. He knew what Sherlock Holmes had said. *One should always look for a possible alternative and provide against it.*

He scooped it into an envelope, stuck down the flap, and put it into his pocket. He needed more time to work this out.

DCI Radigan called out curtly, "Come," as Jack knocked. "Won't keep you a moment," she said, busying herself with some paperwork on her desk.

He sat with a sigh. They both understood what game she was playing, making the point that she was the DCI and he was just the detective sergeant. So he would have to wait until she was ready. Mind games, he thought cynically.

After a few minutes, she put the cap back on her silver Waterman pen and sat back, folding her hands on the table in front of her. "Update me with the present state of the investigation."

"Everything?"

"That would be useful."

Jack spent the next hour imparting all the information that he had. It wasn't a great deal admittedly, but he was making some progress. Radigan asked questions here and there until she was satisfied that she had debriefed him as much as she could. "Very well, Jack, now that we've got that out of the way I want to speak with you confidentially, because we've known each other for a long time."

Yeah, he thought, and we hate each other's guts. But he said, "If I can help?" and smiled what he hoped was a helpful smile. It didn't look particularly pleasant.

"What do you think of Lewis?"

"Ugly?"

"That's not helpful, Jack. You know what I mean."

He wasn't going to make it easy for her, especially after being kept waiting. "Suppose you tell me exactly what you do mean?"

"Would you trust him?"

"That's an odd question."

"Is that a 'Yes' or a 'No?'"

"Neither."

Radigan got exasperated then. "For God's sake Jack, can't you ever answer a simple question? Just say if you trust him or not, what is your gut instinct, that's all I want to know."

Jack wasn't going to give in just yet. "Do *you* trust him?"

She shook her head in frustration. "It doesn't matter what I think. Are you going to answer the question or carry on being evasive?"

Jack sighed heavily. "Look Michelle, I have only just met the guy. I don't like him and I don't particularly want to work with him. He asks too many questions about my private life for my liking. I think he has a screw loose. But I would hesitate to make any judgement on his honesty. Where are you going with this?"

"I'm not at liberty to discuss—" She stopped. "Never mind Jack, forget it. It doesn't matter anyway, it will all be sorted out soon."

Jack was now curious. "Sorted out?"

And it was now Radigan's turn now to be awkward. "Don't worry. But keep an eye on him will you?" She stood up to show that the meeting was over.

He walked back to his office, baffled. That had to be one of the most bizarre conversations he had ever had with Radigan. *One should always look for a possible alternative and provide against it.* Why had that phrase stuck in his mind, he wondered?

CHAPTER TWENTY-TWO

Several people had begun to arrive in response to the prayer call. They filed quietly in, not quite knowing what to expect but each had an air of anticipation and expectation.

First through was Marie Barrington. Marcus met her inside the foyer, warmly kissing her on the cheek. "So glad you could make it. We really need you, Marie."

"I wouldn't miss this for anything," she responded gleefully, disappearing inside.

Close behind came Lissie. Marcus hadn't really had time to sit down with her and explain all that had happened fully. He'd gone through the facts. And she had been so excited.

"Oh Marcus. This is all we had hoped for. To be in the centre of God's will. To see him at work."

And they hugged each other, the recriminations now forgotten. God was not only calling his church to new life. He was calling his people to new life too. As she sat down facing her husband, she smiled a huge smile. And this time the hidden worry was gone, erased in the warmth of the anticipation of all that the Holy Spirit would do.

Phil Sellars and his wife Jenny arrived, both smiling warmly too, a look of excitement in their eyes. Jenny touched Marcus lightly on the arm. "He's on the move," she said.

Then came Billy Southgate, unusually quiet and caught up in the seriousness of the occasion, and James with his guitar, a puzzled look still etched on his face.

Quiet a few of the new folk from the previous Sunday morning also began to arrive, but after waiting another ten minutes, it was obvious that the church had not responded as Marcus had hoped.

He went to the platform and surveyed the scene dismally. Out of a church membership of over two hundred, only thirty or so had seen fit to attend the prayer meeting. Adjusting the microphone disconsolately, he paused whilst Henry sat down in the front row.

"Friends, first of all thank you for turning out at such short notice and at such a late hour. I am really disappointed that so few have felt the call of God to pray for our community." He shook his head dismally. "Perhaps those of you at the back would shuffle forward a bit, so at least we will all be together?"

He waited while several people changed location, before continuing. "I expect that you are all wondering what on earth is going on?" Several people nodded in the affirmative. "Most importantly there is a serious need for prayer. We aren't very good as a church at corporate prayer. Perhaps that's why things are the way they are."

He could see the puzzled faces in the congregation, and smiled. "There are some things that I have to explain first, and it may take a little time, but I ask you to be patient and hopefully it will make sense soon enough."

He indicated to Henry. "You all know dear old Henry, and I'm really indebted to him for the way that he handled a situation here today." Henry met his eyes, smiling in encouragement.

"What I am going to say will shock you, and to be honest I don't know how you will react." He paused. "First of all we need to commit this to the Lord." The group bowed their heads and closed their eyes as the pastor led them in a short, simple prayer asking God to give them all wisdom and protection against the power of the evil one.

When he opened his eyes, his heart sank. Steve Coleman had slipped into the meeting, and was now sitting alone at the back glaring frostily at him.

Glancing briefly at Lissie for moral support, he nervously cleared his throat and began to recount the events of the evening. He stumbled over his words frequently, and when he mentioned his drink problem, there was a whisper of surprise from most of those present, but also one or two nods of support. He dared not look at Steve Coleman. He could only imagine what he was thinking.

He explained about the strange paralysis that had come over him, and how Henry had burst into the office and taken a stand against the demon. He provoked muted laughter as he described Henry with his stick raised above his head like a sword, and the old man blushed.

He stopped speaking. "I think this is where I hand over to Henry. He knows a bit more about this than I do, although I am learning pretty fast," he admitted with a wry grin.

The elderly saint of God made his way slowly to the front, and Marcus assisted him up the few steps onto the platform. He took his place at the microphone, while the pastor sat down, relieved at not having to see Steve's glaring eyes for a while.

Unused to speaking publicly, Henry began, his voice trembling slightly. "Some of you will know that I believe in the gifts of the spirit. All of them!"

There was a rustle and more whispering from the congregation.

"I believe that Satan is a very live foe and extremely active in the world today." He paused to let the effect of what he had said sink in. He continued, his voice gaining strength as he did so. "God has given us the weapons to use, but we often don't deploy them, for one very good reason. A reason that the devil is delighted with." He gazed around the hall, and the silence was total. "Most of us don't believe in his existence! What better camouflage could he possibly have?" The old man leant forward, and for a moment the years seemed to fall away and his eyes sparkled with excitement. "We have been given such a power by God," he said, "to have authority over the evil that plagues so many lives. Let's respond to the challenge that has been thrown down. The evil one has had his own way for too long in this place. He's controlled our town, messed up our youth with drink and drugs, ruined marriages, split families and spoilt the lives of so many people, including church families. Let's take our town back and send the darkness packing!"

There was a rumbling of approval from some, but several remained stonily silent. Steve Coleman was one of them.

"You probably don't know it, but I served the Lord for many years as a missionary in some very remote places. I went out, determined to convert hundreds! But I had a crisis." Henry leant on his stick, the effort of standing beginning to show on the old man's face. Billy Southgate went forward with a chair, settled Henry in it and lowered the microphone.

"Well done Henry," he mouthed encouragingly, before slipping back into his seat.

The old man continued; "I had a crisis. I had read the 'Word' for more years than I care to remember. In fact I could quote large passages from memory. And I still can, despite my age!" There was a muted laugh at that.

"But I had a very Western view. I doubted the supernatural aspects of Scripture. And that caused problems in my preaching. You see, the native population were used to displays of power. Many of them were totally under the control of spiritual witch doctors, and they knew very well the power of curses and oaths. If they crossed one of these spiritual doctors, they would fall ill, or die. Sometimes their cattle would die. I preached for month after month, and many were captivated by the stories of Jesus. They loved to hear of his goodness and love. Because in the past all they had heard was condemnation. All they knew was fear. The witch doctors demanded a share of their crops, or money if they ever got any. They demanded total allegiance and ruled by power and force. If they saw a woman that they found desirable, they just took her from her village, even if she was already married. I became increasingly frustrated because as attractive as they found Jesus, they would not commit themselves because they saw the witch doctor as being stronger."

Henry shifted in his chair until he was comfortable again. "A glass of water would be helpful. I haven't spoken so much in ages and I'm starting to dry up."

There was a break of several minutes, and a gentle murmur of conversation broke out while a plastic beaker of cold water was fetched from the kitchen.

Henry sipped it, before continuing. "I asked God over and over what I should do. I fasted, I prayed. Then one day I heard God's voice. I heard him as clear as you hear me now."

He glanced around the hall at the doubtful, but curious faces. "I realise that many of you will find this hard to accept. In society in general, and even in most churches, hearing God speak is the first step to the asylum." There was a titter of laughter around the room. "Don't most of us pray that God will let us know his will? Don't we constantly ask in our prayers that he will reveal himself to us? I guess that what we often mean is for God to lead us to a verse of scripture, or bring about a solution to a problem without intruding into our personal space. We want to know him, but only in the abstract."

Marcus was listening attentively. He was still struggling to come to terms with the recent dramatic "U" turn in his theology and was hearing things that still challenged him. He glanced at the people. Their faces were a mixture of expressions, but they were listening intently, that was for sure!

"Anyway, when God spoke I was both exhilarated and terrified. I wanted to run and hide. But a verse of scripture, from Psalms, came to mind. 'Where can I hide from your Spirit, where can I flee from your gaze?' And this is what God said."

There was a total hush in the room, as if the entire gathering were collectively holding their breath. People leaned forward in their chairs, riveting their attention on the elderly Henry Carson.

"God gave me words from the book of Job. This is what he said: 'I will teach you about the power of God; the ways of the Almighty I will not conceal.'"

There was a collective releasing of breath around the room.

"So I turned back to the Word of God, and I read it like I had never read it before. I have always loved it, but now it came alive. I couldn't put it down, and read day after day, late into the night. Sometimes I felt great joy filling my soul. At other times I just wept brokenly before God. But the Lord was true to his word. I began to understand, really understand for the first time about the power of God."

His voice was husky. "It was when I reached the book of Luke that I found the key to the problem. I couldn't believe that I hadn't understood before. How many times I had read it, and yet my anti-supernatural bias had so affected my thinking that I just dismissed it."

Henry painfully stood up, leaning once more on his stick. "I am going to pay for this tomorrow," he said, and there was a mutter of sympathy. "Where's my Bible?"

Marcus went forward, handed it to him, and then remained standing alongside him for moral support.

Henry found the passage in Luke that he was looking for, holding the book close so that his old eyes could make out the words, reading in a strong voice.

"'What is this teaching? With authority and power he gives orders to evil spirits and they come out!'" Henry shook a finger at his audience. "I suddenly realised what I had to do to win these people for Christ. The next time someone was ill because of a curse from the witch doctor, I confronted the evil spirit that was affecting the person. I called on the evil in the name of Jesus to depart. And do you know what? It did! Sometimes I could spiritually 'see' something dark and evil. I could see the moment it fled from a person it had been holding in bondage. And soon, people began to be converted as they saw the power of Jesus operating in their lives."

Henry sipped his water. "One of the names of the Devil in the Bible is Beelzebub, which means 'lord of the flies.' I always think of unclean spirits as dirty flies. They swarm all over any filth that they can find. They look for a wound in the body, and then they swarm in and infect us." He pointed a finger at his audience. "Let me warn you. If you have unrepented sin in your lives, even as Christians, the flies will swarm all over you and feed off your filth! And remember that the body is composed of all us believers collectively, and that the sin of one member can infect everyone else."

Henry's eyes blazed. "What I experienced this afternoon in Marcus' office, something dark and sinister, took me back to my old missionary days. I felt the presence of evil, and I sent it packing in the name and the power of Jesus!"

There was a stunned silence from the congregation for a long time after Henry had finished speaking, and Marcus felt his heart sink. It was too much for them to take in. They were overwhelmed. Hartwood had always been a conservative church, and it was obviously asking too much of them to take all this new theology on board.

He went up to the platform and began to help Henry down, and then stopped as something amazing happened. People began to stand, and applaud. They were clapping, smiling and shouting encouragement. Several "hallelujahs" could be heard above the noise, and one or two people got excited enough to shout, "Praise the Lord," something unheard of in that Church.

As the clapping went on, Henry tried to stop them, but that only encouraged them more. Finally he gave up, and pointed a finger to the heavens, indicating that the glory should go to God and not to him.

Billy held Henry's arm and helped him from the platform. "Thank you William," he said gratefully.

"No. Thank you. What you said just now was mind boggling. I believe it will have the most dramatic impact on this church and this town. And in people's lives."

Henry brushed off the compliments, but as he sat down, his face was shining.

Marcus stood up again at the front. "That was really great from Henry. Now I just want to read a couple of passages from God's word, and then we need to get into some serious prayer."

He turned the pages of his Bible, and began reading from Ephesians;

"For our struggle is not against flesh and blood, but against the rulers, against the authorities, against the powers of this dark world and against the spiritual forces of evil in the heavenly realms."

Then he turned to Corinthians, and began to read. "The weapons we fight with are not the weapons of the world. On the contrary, they have divine power to demolish strongholds."

Turning his gaze upwards towards the people, he continued; "The weapons that we fight with my friends are not the weapons of the world. We fight with the sword of the spirit, which is the word of God. We pray. Prayer is the most powerful weapon we have in the armoury. It demolishes spiritual strongholds. And the enemy is the devil, the spiritual power of evil in this dark world. I have told you what happened to me today, and how Henry prayed in the Spirit against something quite evil. This isn't something that my theology prepared me for. I have preached many times from this very spot, that the gifts are not for today." He looked wryly at his audience for a moment. "Fortunately, Henry and some others in this church I suspect, know better."

He scanned the group gathered in the church building. "Any questions before we pray? It's better you know what's in store if you decide to enter the fight."

He immediately wished he hadn't asked, as Steve Coleman stood up to speak.

Lorna Brooks loped easily up the worn stone steps of the late Victorian house. She glanced again at the yellow post-it note in her hand for reassurance. Yes, this was the address that Nick had given her. She glanced at her wristwatch. Fine, she was in good time.

She lifted the wrought iron knocker in the centre of the door. It was one of those really heavy pieces of engineering, sculptured in the form of a gargoyle pivoting from a hinge at the top. She knocked with what she'd hoped would be an appropriately gentle tap, but it came crashing down, causing a deep echoing boom.

"Lorna, you made it!" Nick allowed his eye to remain on her for just too long, noting the casual jeans and cashmere sweater. She was one of those women who looked good no matter how she dressed. "Come on in and meet the others. I think you are going to enjoy this evening."

She obediently followed him along the hallway, noting the original looking black and white tiled flooring and the immaculate decor. Whoever owned this place had spared no expense in renovating it, and to a high standard. Inside, the house was even larger than she had imagined it would be.

Nick beckoned her into a large, comfortable room with high ceilings. One wall was dominated by a beautifully tiled fireplace and hearth, with dried flower arrangements displayed in polished brass containers set around it. Parquet tiling covered the floor. The middle of the room was adorned by an exquisite Indian rug of maroon and cream. Positioned strategically on the outside of it were several leather settees and armchairs, arranged facing each other in a loose circle, presumably so that those present could see each other as they sat.

There were three other people present in the room, two men and a woman, all of whom stood in welcome as she entered. She immediately had her worst fears realised. Both the men were wearing lounge suits, and the woman was dressed in a grey skirt with matching jacket and pale blue blouse.

"Lorna, this is the man you've been waiting to meet," said Nick with more than a touch of sycophancy, "Dr. Benedict Ademola."

"Please, please. Call me Benedict. We're all friends here." The large man held out his hand, a heavy gold watch glinting expensively on his wrist as he grasped her small hand firmly.

For one awful, inexplicable moment she felt repulsed by him. That took her aback. She certainly hadn't expected that! There was certainly no reason for feeling that way. He wasn't a good looking man, in fact quite the opposite, but he was obviously very wealthy. He had that sort of "rich look" about him that excessively wealthy people often did. But the moment she heard his voice, the feelings vanished.

Benedict stared deep into her eyes and said soothingly, "Lorna, you are very welcome to my home. I hope that you find what you are looking for?" His slate grey eyes were strangely persuasive, his voice smooth and hypnotic.

She felt something touch her heart, and an indescribable feeling of helplessness washed over her, amazing in its depth and power. "Thank you," she managed to whisper, sitting down heavily in the only empty armchair available, which happened to be set between Carla Lippincott and Paul Riemann.

Carla, a woman in her early forties with short, cropped black hair and thick black-rimmed spectacles, leant over, introduced herself and shook hands. When she spoke, her voice was precise and clipped, and fitted perfectly with the first impressions that Lorna had of her. A no-nonsense woman with a plethora of opinions on society which she was only too ready to impart to others. A liberal teacher perhaps? Or a trendy social worker?

"Welcome Ms. Brooks, to our circle."

The man followed suit from her left, forcing her to twist around so that her hand could meet his. Paul Riemann a large, florid man, probably in his late thirties and with a receding hair line, had a surprisingly high pitched voice.

"Delighted," he said stridently.

Tait sat down on the right of Lippincott, and Benedict sat next to Riemann so that he was positioned directly opposite Lorna.

"Thank you for coming this evening," said Benedict, "and I hope that we will all leave here enlightened and blessed."

"Blessed be," intoned Carla.

Benedict smiled. "Thank you Carla. Now for the benefit of Lorna for whom this is the first visit—the first of many I hope?" He paused and fixed Lorna again with his eyes, an action that made her both want to run and stay in equal proportions, before continuing. "This is an informal meeting in which we explore, discuss and experiment with religion and kindred philosophies. There is no right or wrong. Everyone has the right to their own opinion. There is only one rule really. No bigotry."

He glanced at Lorna to see if she had any questions, and discerning that she had none, he continued. "I have had to introduce the 'bigot rule' as I call it, because there are those individuals who insist that they alone possess the truth, that only they hold the key to knowing God. Such views are stunting to intellectual and metaphysical development alike. The reason—or at least one of the reasons—that we meet, is to explore all possibilities, to travel all roads in the greatest adventure of all. The search for deity."

"Amen," said Riemann shrilly.

"I am honoured to be the leader, not only of this little gathering, but of many others scattered around the world. Some of my acolytes out of their love for me are pleased to call me 'master,' a title I accept in all humility. But you may call me Benedict if this suits you better." He glanced across to Tait. "Nick, I don't want to do all the talking. Perhaps you would be so good as to explain a little more to our guest?"

"Of course, master." Tait turned to Lorna. "We are intentional in our spiritual quest. We recognise that there is more to life than most people suspect. There is a power that we may all tap into to aid us in our search. Entry to this select group is by invitation only. But although we extend the hand of friendship only to those we recognise as possessing the necessary qualifications, in truth those who are excluded, exclude themselves."

"People like Christians," interjected Riemann helpfully, "by their insistence in believing the mythical accounts of the Bible. They have closed minds and worship a long-dead carpenter." He chuckled at his own cleverness.

Benedict shot a warning glance at him. "Paul, it's too soon for Ms. Brooks," he said soothingly, but his eyes showed his deep displeasure. "Lorna, you've been a bit quiet so far, are you taking all this in?"

She smiled broadly. "You bet! This is really the most exciting thing!" Then she remembered and added shyly, "Master."

Benedict acknowledged the good judgment of the new member, and suddenly Lorna was happy to sit at the feet of this great but humble man.

Tait continued. "The master assigns us a *monograph* each week, outlining a spiritual exercise, an explanation of a timeless mystical truth, or a special piece of knowledge that he wishes to impart to us. There are teachings for new spiritual seekers—the 'neophytes,' as well as the advanced mystics—the 'adepts.' We study these during the week, and come prepared to share our new knowledge and experiences with the rest of the group every Wednesday evening."

The master turned to Carla, "You have been studying something new this week haven't you?"

"Yes, I've been studying astral projection." She turned to Lorna. "Do you have any knowledge of this?"

"Not much. Isn't it an out of the body experience? Where your spirit supposedly leaves your body and travels through space or something?"

"There's no suppose about it. If you join us, you will learn. We all possess hidden powers, natural universal forces within ourselves that have the potential to transform our lives. With the astral projection technique we can go anywhere, either in this world or to other worlds." She then addressed Benedict directly. "I am ready master. Do what thou wilt shall be the whole of the law."

Benedict placed the palms of his hands together as if in attitude of prayer and nodded benevolently. "So mote it be."

"I meditated on the teaching on astral projection contained in my *monograph* every night for five days. On the sixth night I tried the spiritual exercises as you set them out. As usual, I offered up my worship to . . ."

Benedict silenced her with an imperious wave of his hand. "Careful Carla. Remember that there are non-adepts amongst us this evening, and as I had to remind Paul, Ms. Brooks isn't yet ready for the deeper truths."

He turned to Lorna to explain. "Carla is my star pupil, and she sometimes forgets that she is ahead of most other people. No offence my dear, but your studies must be done in a strictly controlled and orderly manner so that your understanding grows in a way that you can handle. You start as a neophyte at the bottom of the ladder, and as your knowledge, powers and abilities grow you are enabled to move on to the next level. It can be positively dangerous to attempt the advanced things before you are ready . . ."

She nodded understandingly, eager to know what secrets these people possessed.

Carla, suitably corrected but nonetheless glowing from the unexpected praise, continued her account. "I lay back on my bed in a relaxed state. I did the breathing exercise, and soon had my first success. I slipped out of the shell of my body!"

Lorna leaned forward in her chair, her eyes bright, absolutely riveted on Carla Lippincott. This was exactly what she had been looking for all her life. Real power, real ability. Not physical power, but spiritual power. She couldn't help interrupting

"What did it feel like?" she asked breathlessly. "Did you feel liberated; did you feel that you had somehow escaped? Did you feel like—?" She stopped when she realised that she was gabbling. "Oh, I'm sorry . . . I didn't mean to butt in. It was the excitement of it all!"

"No, No. It's good to see someone so enthused," replied Benedict. "Please, carry on, with what were you about to say."

"I wanted to ask whether, like in John Gillespie Magee's writing, you felt you had thrown off the shackles of this earthbound life. You know, the poem;

Oh I have slipped the surly bonds of earth . . .
Put out my hand and touched the face of God.

Benedict pointed across the room to Carla. "Watch out, you have a successor at your heels! There may be another star in the ascendant."

Carla seemed less pleased then and scowled. "Shall I continue, master? she asked, with just a touch of defiance in her voice.

Benedict nodded, and she continued to share her experience.

"It was strange, and at first I didn't know what had happened. I could see my body in front of me. Then I realised that I was floating somewhere near the ceiling, looking down on myself as I lay on the bed. The body that I was now in, my astral body was bright and shining and I could somehow move just by thinking about it. I only had to think what I wanted to do, and my astral body responded immediately. I was worried at first that I wouldn't be able to go far, because there was a silver cord connecting me to my earthbound body. But as I started to move, I found that the silver cord stretched effortlessly and didn't impede my progress at all."

She stopped and looked around the room to gauge the effect her story was having on her audience, especially Lorna. She was gratified to see that she was bursting with excitement. Tait was nodding knowingly, remembering the first time he had done the same thing. Riemann who hadn't progressed as far was also excited, but spoiled it by being jealous. Benedict smiled encouragingly, although his face was paradoxically quite impassive at the same time.

"As I moved, I discovered that I could pass through the walls, and went outside into the night air. At first I was surprised that I didn't feel cold. Then I realised something else."

She removed her spectacles with a flourish. "As you can see, I usually have to wear these. But not in my astral body!" she said triumphantly. "I could see for miles, as clear as anything. I started to ascend upwards towards the stars, but as I did, a beautiful being clothed in shining white approached me and told me gently that I had to return to my body. She explained that I needed a guide before venturing out into the wide open expanses of space."

Carla grinned hugely at those around her. "This is the really exciting part. The being was an ascended female master. Her name is Alven and she promised that she would be my spiritual guide from now on. Whenever I need her all I have to do is meditate on her name, and she comes!"

There was a round of applause from the circle of mystics, and Carla beamed happily.

She stared at Lorna. "You are correct, neophyte Brooks. I did feel release. I now know that I am in charge of my own destiny. You shall know the truth, and the truth shall set you free. As for touching the face of god as you eloquently put it, why it was then that I realised that god by whatever name you may call that entity, was all and in all. I saw the stars—and there was god. I saw the planets and the darkness of space and realised that the life-force of the creator was in every tree and every living thing too."

Steve Coleman had just stood up to speak. Although he had been seated at the back, his voice was loud enough to carry to all those present, even without a microphone.

"I have never heard such unbiblical teaching in all my life," he said angrily. "This church has stood here for fifty years, and never before have we heard of such goings on. Never have we felt the need to encourage such teaching as this!" He glared around the room, daring anyone to contradict him. "Demons? Spiritual warfare? I don't blame Henry, he's an old man. But be warned. This pastor is leading us into serious error."

He waved his Bible above his head. "The scriptures clearly teach that these things, these evil spirits and other phenomena, ceased after the Bible was written. Is it plausible that today we should expect to see demon-possessed men? No! Is it believable that we should have such powers as the early church had, of casting out demons, of hearing God speak and other such things that were obviously temporary? No! God no longer creates women from the ribs of man. He no longer creates fish or birds or plants from nothing. Such manifestations of God's power had their time and place. But not now. No!"

Coleman checked to make sure that everyone was listening, before continuing.

"If we believe that demon possession continues today, then the person possessed will be so for their entire life, since it takes a miraculous gift to cast out a demon and such gifts have ceased to exist. St Paul said so in the book of Corinthians."

"Steve," said Marcus, "If you will let me . . ."

"You've had your turn," retorted Steve angrily, "now be good enough to let me have mine!" Turning to his Bible he read aloud. "For we know *in part* and we prophesy in part, but when *perfection* comes, the imperfect disappears." He checked to make sure that everyone was still with him.

"What was the 'perfection'? Clearly the Word of God. Now that the Word is confirmed, it does not need to be confirmed again and again, so the imperfect, the prophesy and miraculous gifts, have disappeared."

Coleman pointed directly at Marcus as he finished speaking. "Because the miraculous gifts are no more, demon possession is no more. You are being deceived if you believe otherwise. If you want to remain in error, then you stay here and listen. If you value God's word, then like me you should leave." He walked briskly out, leaving the congregation in stunned silence.

Mania, a black shapeless form that had been clinging tightly to him in the area of his heart as he spoke, now detached itself and fluttered cockily up to join its comrades high in the church roof.

Marcus was ashamed. Not because he was offended by what Steve Coleman was saying. But because to his sorrow, he recognised his own words—words from a sermon he had preached a year or so earlier. And now Coleman was using those very words, throwing them back at him in challenge.

He got to his feet, undecided what to do next. This was something he hadn't come across before—and conflict wasn't something he found easy to deal with. He prayed quietly under his breath, a quick "arrow" prayer. "Lord, I believe that this prayer meeting was your idea. You have work for us to do in this town, and somehow the decisions we come to tonight are crucial to your plan. Help us now we pray."

Mania, Chamos and Melchom sat on the high window-ledge of the church building, grinning with pleasure. Things were turning out exactly as they had planned.

Mania was an anti-Christ spirit. He was proud of his ability to lead unwary saints of God into displays of open unbelief. He had been working with Steve Coleman for some time, and had managed to open up a nice wedge between him and the pastor. He swung his skinny black legs back and forth as he regarded the other two demons critically.

"Chamos, how is it going on the strife front? Have you managed to proliferate your craft to any extent here?"

Chamos regarded him with barely-concealed hostility. "See for yourself. There is a clear split here tonight between those who are against and those who might side with the pastor."

Melchom, a demon of Indifference, leant back against the wall and grinned hideously. "I think you'll find that the winning strategy here is mine. Look how many have turned up tonight. Barely thirty of 'em. I've worked in churches all over the South, and take my word for it; indifference is the greatest threat of all to the enemy."

Mania waved a hand dismissively. "You're both two-a-penny."

Melchom retorted with what he considered an unbeatable reply. "You may not have heard, but because of my work Barbas himself has recommended me for advancement—"

Mania cut him off in mid sentence. "Barbas? Hah! You obviously don't know the latest then?"

"About Barbas?" Chamos' voice was tinged with curiosity. Barbas had treated him badly in the past. In fact contemptuously, and anything he heard to the detriment of that particular demon was a matter for rejoicing.

Melchom was not going to be taken in. "You know nothing."

Mania was enjoying his moment. "I wouldn't expect you two to have heard because you don't mix in the right circles. But as you may know, I report directly to master Bune himself." He paused to allow that fact to sink in. And he was not disappointed.

Chamos was reluctantly impressed. Melchom too gave the boastful Mania his full attention.

"Anyway, I was summoned to his presence earlier today, and I overheard something." He leaned forward conspiratorially, and lowered his voice as the other two drew closer. "There are two absolutely enormous guards that protect him night and day, and they prevent anyone from getting within any distance of the master unless they have special clearance. Usually they ensure that he is ready before ushering anyone into his presence, but today for some reason they messed up." He looked around carefully to make sure that he could not be overheard, for he was about to utter treasonable words, punishable by instant death.

"They say that people are praying in the Spirit!"

Chamos was leaning so far forward that he nearly fell from his window ledge, and flapped his stubby leather wings furiously in order to retain his balance, causing Melchom to laugh derisively. But he too was clearly entranced by what was being whispered.

"As I was being escorted along the corridor," continued Mania, "I heard Bune speaking to someone. It wasn't difficult, because you know how loud his voice is. I couldn't hear all he said, because the moment the guards heard him, they realised that he wasn't ready for me, and they quickly dragged me back out of the way. They were well frightened I can tell you. He would have dispatched them straight to the abyss if he'd found out what they'd done."

Chamos could hardly contain himself. "Well, what did you hear?"

Melchom was beginning to dislike the boastful talk. Not that he minded boasting, but he liked it to be from himself and not a competitor. "Nothing. It's all hot air. I don't suppose he heard anything."

Mania just gave a self-satisfied grin. "You'll find out that I speak the truth when you go to the meeting later. Because from what I heard, I know who the top demon is who'll be there." He smirked at Melchom. "Your patron Barbas may not have much longer for this world. He's stirred up a hornet's nest by his arrogance and disobedience, and the top man is going to sort him at the meeting. Publicly."

"What's he done?" asked Melchom. Not only could he see his long expected promotion flying out of the window, but also his personal security. If there was to be a cull, anyone suspected of misplaced loyalty would be joining Barbas under the sword of the master.

"Apparently," continued Mania, "in contravention of explicit instructions, he took one of the enemy's angels captive and did him some serious damage. Somehow he escaped after they'd cut him about, but he was so badly injured that they think he must be dead by now."

"I would have thought he'd get a medal for doing that! Who's worried about a filthy angel?"

"You fool. It's not that anyone is concerned with its death. But not at this time! Don't you pay attention to what's going on? We've had the run of this place for a long time, and part of the reason is that we've kept low, working quietly and in secret. What Barbas has gone and done will rouse the wrath of the entire Heavenly Host if they find out. There is a time coming when we will have plenty of them to kill, but not until the order is given." He stood up, and prepared to fly off. "The church here has been sleeping for so long. Why go and wake it up?"

Chamos let out his foul breath with a whistle. "It must have been bad. What Barbas did to the enemy I mean."

"Bad enough I would think. There's a huge search going on now for this angel, to finish him off before he can get back and inform his other stinking kind."

There was a few seconds silence as the information sank into the thick skulls of Chamos and Melchom.

"So, who is this top demon who is going to take on Barbas?" asked Melchom.

In spite of his boasting, Mania had to take a deep breath before he managed to whisper. "It's He whose name dare not be spoken."

CHAPTER TWENTY-THREE

Bune darted his blood-red eyes at the mystics sitting obliviously in their chairs, and laughed. A sound full of hatred and revulsion for the humans that the enemy loved so well. Carla indeed had a spirit guide! The being that this pathetic woman knew as Alven, was present in the room at that very moment. Only it was not the beautiful and shining guide that she had been deceived into seeing and trusting. Her "guide" was in reality the most hideous of demons; huge and muscular, terrifying and dark. The stuff of nightmares. Baphomet, demon of religion clung ever tighter to Carla's back, his taloned feet raking her body as though he were riding a horse.

Yes, Carla Lippincott as she was known to the group, did indeed have a guide from the spirit world . . .

"Sarge!" It was Lewis. He shuffled ponderously into the office and placed a black briefcase on the desk in front of him.

Jack swivelled round in his chair to face him. "What are you still doing here? You should be off-duty now."

"I brought this back from soco, and I though you would want to see it."

"What have you got?" he asked, begrudgingly interested.

Lewis slid the case across the desk. "Nothing from soco. No prints belonging to Cooper or Riley. Or anyone else for that matter."

Jack huffed. "I'm not impressed so far Lewis. Where are you going with this?"

"We had to bust the lock, but . . ." Lewis leant forward and clicked open the case with his paw-like hands, and then Jack *was* interested. On two counts.

Firstly because nestled inside the case was a pinhole camera and a recorder.

Secondly, as Lewis leaned across Jack could see that he wore cufflinks. Gold ones with the police crest on them. Just like the one he had found on his desk. His face impassive, he examined the case in front of him. "Is it safe to touch this little lot?"

"Yeah, fine. SOCO has dusted everything."

"Hmm, it's a pin-hole camera. Cooper obviously made a habit of spying on people. But then he was in the security business so I'm not too surprised. It's well-made. No-one would ever know what it was, even on close inspection."

"And a voice recorder. It uses a standard CD, a long way from the old tape recording devices our boys use. It has a sound detector fitted, so that the battery doesn't run down. It only needs someone to speak to activate both sound and vision."

"Anything recorded?"

"That's the interesting thing sarge." Lewis's piggy eyes were filled with what appeared to be pity. "It doesn't make pleasant viewing. There is a glitch with it so unfortunately the sound is intermittent. But what you can see is enough."

He removed a CD from its plastic jewel case. "This is a copy made by the lab boys." He put it in the tray of Jack's computer and waited for autoplay to engage.

On the screen they could see that the covert camera was running, activated by a sound that neither could hear. The view was of Cooper's office. Not a good view as the line of sight cut across the office at an angle. The kitchen, with the door ajar could clearly be seen in the background.

Just visible in the foreground was a small table, with a tray and two glasses on it.

The camera continued to silently record what seemed at first to be an empty office, then there was some movement at the edge of the shot, and a pair of legs could be seen, apparently belonging to someone who had just sat down. A pale pink blob suddenly covered half of the picture.

"It's a hand holding a pen," said Lewis helpfully.

"I can see that," responded Jack.

The hand suddenly disappeared from view, and the back of a man could be seen walking towards the legs. There seemed to be a struggle going on for a few moments, then the man began to turn and walk back towards the camera.

"Blast," said Jack, "I was hoping we'd be able to see his face, but the camera angle is all wrong. All we've got is a shot of his chest."

The shot showed that the man was of large build, wearing a waistcoat, jacket and tie. He walked back to the disembodied legs once again, carrying what looked like a sheaf of papers. There seemed to be a discussion going on, as the large man waved the papers about. He was clearly angry.

He turned, came back towards the camera and disappeared from view.

"This is the bit," said Lewis hoarsely, "poor guy."

The chair on which the man had been sitting suddenly came into view as it toppled forward. It was immediately apparent that the man secured in it was Nelson Riley. His eyes were wide open, and his mouth was moving soundlessly.

"Pause that," said Jack.

Lewis did so, and Jack peered closer. "Look at his neck. It's the murder weapon. The cord that killed him. Move it forward slowly. That's it. Stop now. Back just a bit. That's it."

Jack pointed at the computer screen with his pencil. "There, you can just see a pair of hands either side of his neck."

Lewis nodded. His voice was faint as he spoke. "He's being garrotted from behind."

The struggle went on for a few more seconds before Riley fell sideways onto the floor, thrashed around for a while and was still, his head turned to one side and his lifeless eyes looking vacantly upwards at the camera.

The two detectives were silent for a moment as the awful reality of witnessing a brutal murder—the cold-blooded termination of a fellow human being—sank in. Then Jack let out his breath in a rush. "We need this examined in minute detail for anything that might be of help. Lewis, get back to the lab boys and get them working."

"I left them doing just that," he responded.

"Re-run it again."

"All of it?"

"Bloody hell Lewis, what bit of 're-run it' are you finding it difficult to comprehend?"

Lewis sighed, and complied.

"Stop it there. Now go back a minute or so. That's it. Now play."

Lewis did as he was told.

"Did you hear that?"

"No, boss."

"Turn up the sound. A bit more. That's it, do you hear it now?"

Lewis listened. There was definitely something. A clicking, staccato noise. "Is it just some feedback or something?"

"No idea. As you seem to have no home to go to, tell the lab boys to isolate it if they can, then meet me in the yard." Jack got to his feet, picking up a set of car keys from his desk.

"Where to, sarge?"

"Cooper's house first, and then Riley's."

———————

The chairs had been moved to the far side of the room, the central rug rolled up, to reveal a large white circle painted onto the dark oak flooring. Within the circle, a white pentagram—a five-pointed star—emblazoned with strange writings and symbols.

Lorna Brooks was surprised, and turned to Nick Tait questioningly. "Isn't this stuff used in black magic?"

He laughed. "Don't be silly, Lorna. There is no such thing as *black* magic. And there is nothing sinister about the pentagram. You'll see," he said comfortingly.

Benedict was suddenly beside them, and Lorna jumped, startled.

"My, you are nervous." He placed a comforting hand around her, and immediately she felt soothed. "You were asking about the pentagram?"

Even Nick was amazed. How on earth did he know what they were discussing? He'd been nowhere near when he and Lorna were talking.

Benedict smiled. "The pentagram is one of the most powerful symbols in history. It is important to almost every ancient culture; India, China, Egypt. It has been found scratched on the walls of Neolithic caves, and in Babylonian drawings."

Paul Riemann and Carla Lippincott joined them.

Carla said, "It's the secret symbol of the goddess Kore, who is the deity that I worship. Kore's sacred fruit is the apple. That's because when an apple is cut through, both halves show a pentagram shape, with each point on the star containing a seed."

Benedict chuckled. "You see Lorna, we are well-schooled here. Isn't it sad that the symbol is always associated, at least in the minds of the ignorant, with evil?"

Lorna flushed at the word "ignorant." She'd hoped Benedict hadn't heard her earlier words. To cover her confusion she said, "Tell me more about Kore, Carla. Why is she so special?"

Benedict interrupted then. "It's too soon for you to know all at present. Some things are best left until a more opportune moment."

Carla went quiet and Riemann took the opportunity to chip in, and the question went out of Lorna's mind as she listened.

"According to Pythagoras, the five points of the pentagram represent the five elements that make up man: fire, water, air, earth, and psyche, or mind. The Pythagoreans believed that the pentacle was sacred to Hygeia, the goddess of healing. And she is one of *my* deities."

Benedict laughed. "Enough," he said, "let us get down to some practice."

He gestured to the little group around him. "Let's position ourselves inside the circle, shall we?"

The five of them stepped inside the pentagram and Benedict motioned Lorna to stand on one of the points, whilst the other three followed suit, each choosing a point for themselves. Benedict positioned himself on the last one.

"It is important that you do not step out of the circle once we begin," warned Benedict for Lorna's benefit. "The circle is our protection against disruptive forces. They cannot cross the sacred line, so as long as you remain inside you are quite safe." He closed his eyes, and the others followed suit.

"I call upon the deities of light, to come now to our aid," he intoned. "Guard us and protect us. I call upon Benoth of Babylon, Hamath and Adrammelech. Stand before us and guard us. Ensure our safety as we worship you."

He stretched out his arms towards his people and Paul, Nick and Carla intoned in unison, "Do what thou wilt shall be the whole of the law."

"So mote it be," responded their master.

He continued: "Bibhaz and Tartak of the Avites and Nergal of Cuth, we swear our allegiance to you. Kali, Hygeia, Kore, and all who reign in the great pantheon of divinity, we proclaim you gods and goddesses. As we worship you, accept our prayers." He knelt down ponderously, followed by his three acolytes. Nick tugged at Lorna's arm, indicating that she too should kneel.

When they were all on their knees, Benedict began to speak in a rhythmic monotone; a strange tongue that made no sense to Lorna's ears. But the words had a strange, hypnotic effect, and she found herself beginning to slip into a trance-like state.

She heard the voice first before she realised that someone was standing beside her. A soft and gentle voice, soothing, flowing, touching her mind in a gentle caress of sound.

"Welcome Lorna. We have been waiting for you."

Looking up, she saw the most beautiful creature standing before her. Not entirely male, nor entirely female, it seemed to possess the beauty of one gender and the strength of the other. Dressed in a flowing robe of silk-like substance that caught the light and reflected it into a glorious rainbow of colour, the being exuded love and gentleness.

"Who . . . who are you?" stuttered Lorna, not altogether sure that she was really seeing this.

"You wear my amulet," she said softly.

Lorna instinctively glanced at her wrist, and she suddenly knew. A single word escaped from her lips, and it came almost as a moan of ecstasy.

"Kali!"

The deity smiled, and it seemed as if light had dawned in the room. In person, she was entirely different to how she had been portrayed in her images. The statues representing her were ugly, fearful. But the goddess before her was beautiful.

"Come deeper. Come deeper into us. Come, know the spirit world and all the wonders it contains. Know the truth Lorna. That all men and women are as one. That God is all and is in all. As you are, I once was. As I am you may become."

Lorna struggled to understand. "How can I be like you? I am just human. I am not worthy even to stand in your presence."

Kali smiled. "Yes, you are worthy. Don't believe the lies of those who would hold you in bondage. Who would seek to hide the secret from you. The truth that we are all Gods." The she/he apparition gently stroked Lorna's hair in a soothing, calming motion.

The information staggered her. Here, finally, everything had become clear. She realised that with startling clarity. There was no God "up there" seated on a throne. No heavenly being far above her. She had been looking in all the wrong places. God had been here all along. Throughout the long reaches of her searching. In all her times of despair and hurt. During times of loneliness, God had been there. She had just been too blind to see it. But now she knew. God was inside her. Because she was God!

Inside the circle, Bune stroked Benedict's head gently; his thin lips stretched over his sharp teeth in a ghoulish grin, whispering evil and deception deep into a compliant, receptive brain.

Tait and Riemann too, had similar demons speaking into their hearts the seductive, lying words of death. Lies calculated to take them further and further from the reality of a loving Heavenly Father, and deeper and deeper into the catacombs of deceit and eternal separation from him.

Clamped tightly to Lorna, "Kali" licked the head of his deceived captive, his black tongue oozing mucus from the open abscesses and boils that covered its length. A demon of lies, Gresil was as ugly and hideous as the false image in the mind of Lorna was beautiful and delightful.

Had she but known. Could she have but seen the reality, the betrayed woman would have vomited violently, and ran shrieking hysterically from its clutches. But blissfully unaware, she willingly submitted to the ministrations of the foul thing from the pit, even as it toyed playfully with the amulet tied securely to her wrist.

Carla too, had her familiar. The muscular Baphomet, demon of religion was in his usual place on her back, his taloned feet tearing at her body in his hatred and contempt as he grinned hideously, whispered, caressed and embraced.

Her demon had been in place for so long that she wore him like a garment. So long in fact had they been joined, that she was beginning to assume his likeness. Her face was getting darker daily and her eyes were a pale shade of pink. Soon she would be totally assimilated into the being she knew as Alven, her spiritual guide. A guide who was directing her straight to hell.

Having roused Mrs. Cooper from her bed, the house search was disappointing and turned up nothing of interest. Speaking to her, it seemed that her husband had been a normal hard-working man. She and the daughter had already been spoken to and statements taken. Mr. Cooper had left the previous evening around 7:45pm. He often went out late and he seemed his usual self that evening. He'd told his wife that he shouldn't be too long. And that was the last time she saw him alive.

"Okay," said Jack, "I may want to talk with you again."

Mrs. Cooper nodded, holding a handkerchief to her eyes. "He wasn't a bad man," she said softly, "he didn't deserve this."

Jack nodded. "I'm sorry," he said. "We need to take his computer. It might give us some information."

"If it will help find whoever did this awful thing . . ."

Jack turned to Lewis. "Bring it," he said, and went back to the car to wait.

"What do we do sarge?" queried Lewis.

"Open it," said Jack.

They were outside Riley's house and the place was in total darkness. The curtains had not been drawn, and it was obvious that no-one was in.

"Perhaps he lived alone?" said Lewis.

"If you get the door open, we'll find out," replied Jack shortly.

The hulking Dc applied himself to the door, and it fell effortlessly inwards onto the floor, leaving shards of splinters where once the frame had been.

"Remind me not to invite you round to my place," said Jack as they went inside.

"Looks like a single man's pad," he observed, switching on all the lights as he went through, noting the thick layer of dust that coated every surface. "I should know. Or perhaps the daily hasn't been in this week." He laughed, but without humour. "Lewis, you take the back rooms. I'll do the bedrooms."

Lewis did as he was told. This was clearly the home of a man of limited means. Nothing opulent by way of furniture or electrical goods. The living room was as dirty as everywhere else. An unwashed cup and plate sat on a table next to a threadbare settee. He peered into the kitchen, and found that the draining board was in a similar state. Riley wasn't too worried about cleanliness and hygiene, that was for sure.

Against one wall was a bookcase crammed full of books. Examining one or two Lewis could see that they were mostly cheap paperbacks, but there were one or two good quality hardbacks distributed randomly across the shelves. There was even a leather bound Bible. Lewis sighed. The worlds best seller in terms of numbers. Most people had a Bible somewhere in the house. But very few people ever read it. He guessed Riley was no exception.

A shout came from the bedroom. "Lewis, get in here."

"What is it?"

In lieu of a reply, Jack threw him a stack of bank pay-in books.

"What do you make of these?"

Lewis flicked them open, leisurely casting his eyes over the entries. "Just the usual." He paused. "Wait a minute . . ." Sitting down on the edge of the dishevelled bed he turned over several pages. Then several more. He thumbed forwards and then backwards.

"Have you read these?"

Jack nodded. "Of course. There are payments from Riley's account on a monthly basis going back many years. Made out to a Mr. D. Cooper!"

A search of the second bedroom revealed nothing, other than it was tidy. That in itself was strange, it being the only straight room in the entire flat.

"Looks like a youngster's room," said Lewis, looking at the music CDs and the computer games laying around. "Did Riley have children?"

Jack shook his head. "No idea. No one's come forward to report him missing yet if he has." He opened the wardrobe, and was confronted by rails of casual shirts and jeans. "Modern stuff—looks like a young man's clothing. Perhaps he has a son?"

Further searching showed nothing of interest, and they left in disappointment. They had hoped that they might turn something up.

They were in the car heading back to the station, with Jack at the wheel. "I can't help thinking . . ." began Lewis, but Jack stopped him.

"Don't overdo the thinking Lewis, it might get to be a habit. You've had cobwebs on your brain too long to change now."

Lewis grinned good-naturedly, refusing to let Jack get to him. He'd only been giving Jack half his attention anyway, letting the insults fall on deaf ears. He was thinking about Riley's small flat and the sparse echoing loneliness of it. He couldn't begin to imagine what it must have been like to live there, forlorn and loveless.

But something that Jack had said caught Lewis's attention. "What was it you just said?" he queried.

Jack looked across curiously. "What's this about, Lewis?"

"It's important. You just said about cobwebs and not overdoing the thinking or something?"

"I was cautioning you about not doing too much thinking, having been on crime squad and all that. You must be a bit rusty, I suppose?"

Lewis ignored the insults. "That's it. Not rusty, but dusty. Stop the car, sarge."

Jack had rarely heard him speak so strongly, and found himself pulling over to the kerb, where he switched off the lights, and sat drumming his fingers impatiently on the steering wheel as Lewis pondered over something.

"That's it!" he exclaimed, "How could I be so stupid. We need to go back to the flat."

Jack looked quizzically at the usually docile Dc, but something in the urgency of his manner was compelling.

"I hope you're not wasting my time," he said dourly, turning the car without warning, to the accompaniment of aggressive tooting from irritated drivers having to brake hard to avoid a collision.

"Lights, sarge!" shouted Lewis.

Back at the flat, Lewis led the way into the lounge. "I was looking at the bookcase," he said. "It's mostly paperbacks, but there are one or two quality books."

Jack stared at it, with its rows of untidy volumes.

Lewis continued. "I was thinking that most people have a Bible, but very few actually read it."

"And your point is . . . ?"

"I didn't twig it at the time. It wasn't until after we'd left. It was what you said about my brain. About cobwebs?"

Jack may have been slow off the mark to start with, but now he saw the point of what Lewis was saying.

"Cobwebs," he whispered, walking swiftly over to the bookcase. The books had obviously been unread for some time, because the bookcase was no different from the rest of the flat, and a thick layer of dust enveloped everything.

Except for one shelf, which had been wiped clean.

"Why would he dust just one shelf?" asked Jack thoughtfully, more for the benefit of his own thought process, and less of a question to Lewis.

Nevertheless Lewis responded. "My guess is that he removed one of the books from the shelf for some reason, and then realised that the disturbed dust was showing very clearly what he had done."

"And having put it back," interjected Jack, "he saw that he was leaving a trail."

"That's it," affirmed Lewis. "So, if he had something to hide, he wouldn't want anyone to know what he was doing. So uncharacteristically he dusted the shelf to conceal that fact. Unfortunately he had lived in squalor for so long that he didn't realise how much one clean shelf would stand out in an otherwise filthy house."

"I didn't imagine that our Mr. Riley was a Bible basher," said Jack, removing it carefully from its place and peering into the cavity behind it. He expressed disappointment. "Nothing!"

In his frustration he removed the remaining books with a single sweep of his hand, letting them drop to the floor and sneezing as the dust hit his nostrils. The shelf was empty. There was nothing hidden, nothing concealed. He turned back to Lewis. "So much for that idea," he said. "Whatever he was doing we will never know." He threw the Bible dismissively back onto the shelf. "Let's get out of here."

He walked to the door with Lewis following reluctantly after him.

"Hang on a minute," he said, hurrying back. "What's the book *you'd* be the least interested in on a bookshelf, Jack?" he asked.

Jack didn't have to think for too long about that. "Definitely that one," he said, pointing to the Bible.

"That's what I thought. Which makes it the perfect place. Let me just check . . ." Lewis picked it up and began flicking through its pages, starting from the front. "Genesis, Exodus, Leviticus, Numbers, Deuteronomy," he read aloud, "Joshua, Judges, and bingo!"

Jack wasn't a Bible reader, but even he knew that bingo sounded a bit odd. "Bingo?"

Lewis turned the book towards him so that he could see. A section had been cut from the pages in the centre so as to leave a hollow. Inside that cavity was a CD in a plastic case. "Yup, bingo!" said Lewis.

The girl could see only light. Brilliant and blinding. It beckoned her, warm and welcoming, pure and clean. She had no idea where she was or what had happened. She couldn't remember clearly, other than that there was a painful memory that she didn't want to surface. She was floating in a cloud, moving effortlessly, light in body and mind.

Ahead was a shape. A person standing motionless in the radiance that was all around, and without thinking, she began to move towards him. She instinctively knew it was a "him." How she knew she was unaware. She just knew.

Drawing nearer, it was clear that he was big. Taller than any man, broad, and with a massive chest. His hair was pure golden flax, his eyes the colour of the sky. And he was clearly a warrior, because across his back, held in a leather scabbard was slung a great sword.

Then he spoke, and a distant memory of rushing waters filled her ears.

"Hello child of God, the Lord is with you."

She knew the voice. And in an instant the memories that had been repressed for so many years came flooding back.

"You are my big Jesus!" She felt herself blushing at her reversion to childhood terminology.

Then time seemed to cease; and earth and sky came to a standstill as the years fled before her. She cried tears of regret mingled with hope that surged in her barren heart. Suddenly she was a child once more, and running forward with a cry, she threw herself into the angel's arms, and he folded them around her.

He smiled; that strangely familiar, beautiful smile and his eyes gazed deep into hers.

"No," he responded, in exactly the same way as he had in the bedroom of a small child one Christmas Eve. "But I serve him." He appraised the teenaged girl fondly. "You've grown."

"I was only four," she said, stuttering in her excitement, her eyes wide. "I thought it had all been a dream. I told my mother, but she said I had imagined it all. And I thought I had, but here you are and . . ."

The angel smiled again. "Do you remember what I told you when we last met?"

She screwed up her eyes as she tried to remember. "You said not to forget."

The angel nodded. "God has a plan for your life. But you need to know him personally. Then you will be his, and he will use you in a way that you cannot begin to imagine."

"I don't understand." She was almost too embarrassed to continue. "Surely you know the awful things I do? I don't go to church, I don't pray." She screwed up her face. "Anyway, I don't know the God you speak about. And what use would someone like me be, when he has better people in the church?"

The angel said nothing, but looked kindly at her. And suddenly, she knew.

The girl felt tears welling up as for the first time she saw the reality and the emptiness of her life. Emptiness that she had tried to fill with every conceivable pleasure. And when that had not worked, she had turned her hatred—her self-hatred—and bewilderment on others. Despite being told that she was beautiful, whenever she looked in the mirror, all she saw was ugliness staring back. Every blemish, real or imagined, was highlighted in her eyes, magnified and reflected back in what she believed was indisputable truth.

She couldn't escape the image that she saw, and in her despair, she became the girl depicted there. But whatever she did, whatever she tried, she had been unable to satisfy the deepest longings of her heart. Nothing had even come close. And at that moment she knew why.

It was because there was a void in her soul that only God could fill. "Is it possible that he would he want *me*?" she asked, hardly daring to believe what the answer would be.

The angel laid his hand on her head, and her turmoil was instantly stilled, extinguished in a moment. "He is near to all who call on Him."

"I remember those words!"

The angel smiled. "You must go back now."

"But what am I supposed to do?"

She felt herself drifting back to consciousness, and fought against leaving the place where she had found the first real peace she had known.

"You have some things to put right, don't you?"

"Wait—I don't know what to do. I don't even know your name!"

He leant over her and whispered softly into her ear.

And as she awoke in her bed, his name was on her lips, and her tears were wet on her pillow. "Aanfial," whispered Ashley Coleman. "Aanfial."

Ashley had dozed off in front of the television set, and it was a moment before she could get her mind right. It hadn't been just a dream, that was for sure. It had been too real. And it had stirred up memories that had been dormant for so long. But for what purpose? Part of her rebelled against these new feelings. What was she worrying about others for? No-one worried about her. Especially her father. At the thought of him, she felt the influx of anger. Her old, familiar anger.

Why couldn't he understand how much she needed him? Why couldn't he see that when she swore and shouted at him, when she rebelled—it wasn't what she *really* wanted. It wasn't who she really was. She was crying out for his love. She needed him to show it. She wanted him to care enough to say *no*. But he hadn't. He had let her do exactly what she had wanted to do. And that meant he didn't care. He didn't value her enough to stop her from wrecking her life.

She struggled out of the chair, undecided as to what she should do, but somehow knowing that she had to get to Hartwood Community Church. And right away. And that was a daunting prospect, because it was getting late in the evening. And it was dark, and she was only too aware of the dangers in town. She didn't want to go anyway. In the cold light of her awakening, it all seemed ridiculous. Not cool at all.

"The Spirit will guide you," that's what the angel had said. And she knew he meant God. But who was God? He had never been a part of her life for as long as she could remember. And she wasn't too sure if she wanted that to change. There was the fear of rejection. What if *he* didn't want her?

The young girl knelt apprehensively in her living-room, feeling self-conscious and foolish "You don't know me, because I haven't spoken to you often," she began uncertainly, feeling quite ridiculous. If her friends could see her now, they would put her in the same category as that loser Emily Bowman.

Even as those thoughts entered her mind, remorse washed over her. And with dreadful clarity and certainty she knew that she was the one who was the loser. She was the one who was lost unless she did something about it. It was hard to change all at once the feelings and thought patterns that had been ingrained in her for some time. Selfishness and arrogance were difficult traits to negate. And she had had a lot of practice in that area.

But even as she acknowledged these things to herself, a transformation gently and invisibly started in her life. There was a long way to go and the change would not be complete this side of eternity. But she had made a start. She acknowledged that of all people, she had no right to look down on Emily. With absolute conviction she recognised the blackness of her soul. Her sins of pride, anger, selfishness, her rebellion. And other things, secret sins that she could barely acknowledge even in the hidden place of her heart.

And yet once it had started, she was unable to stop the awesome process, as each and every one of her sins flashed clearly into her mind as if at some unknown bidding. She flinched as they struck her almost forcibly. And she felt pain. And knew in those moments that God was the only answer. That Jesus, the Messiah, the Redeemer was the only way that she could escape an eternity of separation from God the Father.

And she knew desperately, that what she wanted more than anything in life was to know that God. To be his. To belong to him and be loved by him through all ages to come.

She wept as she called out to the God whom she still did not know, but who had known her before she was created. "God, if you are there I know my life has been pretty awful up to now, but I guess I really want to change. I want to believe in you, I want to know you but I don't know how. Help me to find you."

She opened her eyes and looked around. There was no bolt of lightening, no heavenly choir that she could hear. She didn't feel any different. For a moment, doubts assailed her, but Aanfial's words came to mind, and she strengthened her resolve to put her trust in the God that she was searching for.

In the heavens, a choir began to sing songs of praise. Beautiful songs of glory and majesty, power and might flew across the span of the heavens as the angels rejoiced that a new soul was seeking the true God. One of his wayward children, a prodigal, was seeking the way home.

But all that was lost on Ashley. For now, all she could concentrate on was getting to the church. Before she changed her mind.

Get moving Coleman, she told herself firmly, as she slipped out of the silent house and headed along the cold, dark streets. She presumed that her dad was out somewhere—and she was glad. She wasn't sure she could face him and explain what she was about to do. And if *anyone* she knew saw her going to church, she would just die. She really hoped that none of her friends would be around to see her.

On either side, invisible to her eyes, two angels guarded her. In the air above her flew two more. Before and behind her she was hemmed in by a whole battalion, and every angel had a sword drawn or a bow at the ready. It had been a long while since such a large army of the heavenly host had gathered to protect one solitary soul.

The angels themselves did not know why. All they knew was that the Spirit was directing them. Ashley Coleman was crucial to the Lord's plan for Hartwood Community Church. And for reasons that she did not comprehend, Ashley felt totally secure as she walked the deserted streets.

CHAPTER Twenty-Four

Jack was back at the office with Lewis. He slid the CD into the computer tray. "Let's have a look at what was so important to Riley that he hid it so carefully," he said.

At that moment, Jack's phone rang. "Blast," he said, irritated at being disturbed. He picked it up. "No calls for the next hour!" he shouted, and went to slam down the phone. But what was said caused him to stop. "Hello, Michelle. How come you are on duty so late? I thought you were a nine-to-fiver?" His voice suddenly grew terse. "When? Right. Thanks." He turned to Lewis. "We've had another garrotting," he said slowly.

Lewis raised his eyebrows. "Two in two days?"

"Yup, that's not a co-incidence. Come on Lewis." He got to his feet. "Does the name Ben Mahoney mean anything to you?"

Lewis paused, both shocked and embarrassed at the same time. "I paid him a visit earlier. It was his son Nathan who hung himself in the woods some years back."

"You what!" Jack rounded on the Dc, the anger sharp in his voice. "Why the hell didn't you tell me?"

"I didn't exactly have time, sarge. What with the interview and everything."

"We need to speak about this later, Lewis. I will not have you gallivanting off and making enquiries that I have not cleared." He stopped then. "And because of that, someone is dead." He angrily left the office, not looking back to see if the Dc was behind him.

After the short journey from the station, Lewis, suitably chastised, followed his sergeant through the door, the same one that Ben Mahoney had slammed behind him just a few hours previously. Only this time there was a uniformed police officer stationed outside to preserve the scene, and keep at bay the Press that had miraculously heard about the crime. Wrapped in thick coats and scarves and stamping their feet against the bitter cold, they were camped in the street, cameras everywhere, looking for a point of view, a throwaway sound-bite, anything in fact that they could put in their paper. And it didn't have to be much. In fact it didn't necessarily have to be true. A hoary old reporter had told him years back how it worked. "It doesn't have to be true," he'd said with a gleam in his eye, "after all, this *is* a newspaper!"

Jack shut the door, muffling the shouts of the reporters. To Lewis, it seemed strange returning under such circumstances. There was the same settee, the one he had sat on to drink coffee. The same furniture and stuff. It seemed unreal. Surreal in fact.

"Same technique it seems at first glance," said Jack, examining the body dispassionately. A length of red cord could be seen around the neck, and already the head was looking puffy and swollen. "It's only a matter of time now before the Press boys link this with Riley. Then we are going to have trouble. A serial killer on the loose. That's all we need in Hartwood."

Lewis knelt on the floor. "This is weird," he said.

Jack said nothing. He was still fuming, although trying to be professional about it.

"More sugar," he said. "Another bowl emptied onto the victim."

Jack imparted a final glare, and strode to the door, pausing just long enough to bark his final orders.

"Okay Lewis, I'm going to leave this one with you. SOCO will be here any moment." He fixed Lewis with hard eyes. "You seem to have the death touch, what with him being murdered so soon after seeing you. I want a *full* update this afternoon—do you understand? I want to know everything about your meeting with him and how all this relates to the suicide of a young boy. And try not to sod this one up, won't you?" He walked out without waiting for an answer, and the noise from the hoards of reporters gathered expectantly outside once again reached a crescendo.

Jack stood outside the house, both angry and confused by Lewis. Usually he had the ability to sum people up, but Lewis was somehow different. He didn't trust him, and he didn't know why. Was it because he was about the ugliest man he had ever met? He knew that was cruel, but nevertheless he believed it to be true.

And the DCI had asked him to keep an eye on him. What was that all about? He couldn't fault his work if he was honest. He was on-time, industrious, and had a good detective's mind. And it was Lewis' observation had led to the recovery of the CD from Riley's flat.

The problem was Lewis, of course. What can of worms had he opened by visiting Ben Mahoney? And what was the link between Mahoney, Nelson Riley and Darrell Cooper?

With all the unanswered questions, he resolved to find out a bit more about his detective constable, who kept his private life very quiet, and hardly mentioned his wife. On the rare occasions that he did, he used such glowing terms. Jack wondered what kind of woman would want to be married to someone like Lewis?

The thought jumped unwanted to his mind. What kind of woman would be want to be married to a man like Jack Somerville? He knocked at the door of Lewis's house and waited.

It was a real gloomy evening—typical late December—with the clouds sprawled across the sky, holding back the light in a suffocating embrace.

Even so, when the door was opened, he wasn't prepared for what he saw. The woman standing there in the half-light was stunningly beautiful with large eyes that stared disconcertingly at him.

"Sorry, I was looking for Jane Lewis. I think I've got the wrong house." He turned and started to go back down the steps.

"Please, I'm Jane Lewis. How can I help you?" Her voice was soft, as gentle as velvet and her smile was warm and open.

He stopped halfway down the steps, puzzled as to what he was seeing. "*You're* the wife of Peter Lewis?" he said, unable to keep the disbelief from his voice.

She stopped smiling then, and a shadow of hurt passed across her face. "Who are you," she said, and suddenly her voice was not quite so welcoming.

He held up his warrant card so that she could see it.

She gazed blankly at him, unmoving.

"Sorry." He realised he was standing in shadow. He moved nearer, holding the card so as to catch the hallway light. He saw then that she was blonde, with sparkling jade green eyes.

She responded. "You will have to say something. I'm blind you see."

Jack at first felt shock; then a twinge of pity. Such a beautiful woman, and yet only half a woman without her sight.

"Uhh, yes." He apologised, feeling awkward and foolish. "I was showing you my warrant card. I'm Detective Sergeant Somerville, Lewis's sergeant. I apologise for calling on you so late, but we've had a few problems." He put the useless means of identification away.

The smile was suddenly switched back on again and Jane held out her hand. "Then you are very welcome, Jack Somerville. Peter has told me so much about you. He likes you very much, and no-one is a better judge of character than he is."

Jack suddenly felt ashamed, knowing that he had done nothing to help him settle in. On the contrary he had done his best to give him a hard time. "Oh," he said gruffly. He shook the proffered hand and was not surprised at the firmness of her grip.

Inside the house, she unerringly manoeuvred along the passageway and into the lounge where she switched on the lights and directed Jack to a chair. She laughed, a pleasant girlish laugh.

"I don't usually bother with the lights when I'm alone. Saves money on the electric. Please sit down. Tea, coffee?"

"No I'm fine. I won't take up too much of your time. This might sound strange, but I just needed to see where Peter lives. I need to see *how* he lives if that's alright with you?"

Jane sat opposite him, staring at him with her sightless eyes, something he found quite disturbing. "You're right," she replied at last.

"Excuse me?"

"You said it was strange—wanting to know about Peter. Well it is." She seemed anxious for a moment. "He's not in any kind of trouble is he?"

Jack tried to be non-committal. How could he tell this woman that he suspected Lewis of ransacking his office? "He's working on a murder at the moment." There was an awkward silence whilst he wondered what to say next.

"Look," she said, "shall we deal with the elephant in the room?"

Jack wasn't sure what to say in reply to that.

"Oh, come on Jack. The elephant is something that everyone can see, but no-one talks about it. They pretend it's not there, but until it's acknowledged people can't be honest with each other."

"I feel kind of uncomfortable about this. Lewis, sorry, Peter, doesn't know I'm here." Jack suddenly realised that it was the first time he had thought of Lewis as having a first name.

Jane smiled that amazing smile again, and Jack suddenly thought how lucky her husband was.

"Don't be, Jack. Let me start. Perhaps it'll make things easier for you." She sat forward in her chair. "You're wondering how a woman like me could love a man like Peter?"

"No, that's not it." He felt crass and dirty, like something she had walked into the house on the sole of her shoe. He sat back in his chair, feeling contempt for his shallowness. Because he knew that that was exactly it.

"Don't feel bad, Jack. And don't pity me." She raised a hand as he started to deny it. "Let me finish." She took a deep breath. "You pity me because you think I can't see. But it's only my eyes that are blind. And I don't need them to see the kind of man Peter is. I love him because I can see him with my heart. And he's a good man Jack. A kind, loving, courageous and gentle man."

Jane's voice was full of love as she spoke and Jack wondered what it would be like to have someone love *him* like that.

"Scripture says that God doesn't look at the outside of people. He looks at the inside. Why is it that *we* only look at the external, Jack? Why are we so easily fooled by what someone looks like? Isn't it true that most confidence tricksters succeed because their victims trust them? Or rather trusts the person they think they are, that is their outward appearance." She sighed gently, as if she had been over this countless times before, championing her husband from the callous comments of a cruel and undiscerning world.

Jack scowled, knowing that he couldn't be seen. So she was a God botherer? And that would presumably make Lewis one too. Suddenly, a few odd things about his Dc began to make some sense.

"Do you know Jack, if you could see the beauty inside my Peter, you would love him as much as I do," continued Jane.

Jack wasn't sure what to say. He had started to like this woman, but now she was starting all that God talk and he didn't want to hear that stuff. She had seemed so sensible to start with. And as for loving Lewis! He couldn't even begin to contemplate that.

She went across to a drawer, removed something and handed it to him. It was a photograph. "Look at that Jack, what do you think?"

He saw a great hulking, handsome man, with dark chestnut hair and a beaming smile. Wearing a dark suit and tie, he was standing next to a stunning looking blonde with green eyes, dressed in a white wedding dress.

Before he could say anything, Jane spoke. "That's right, it's Peter and me on our wedding day. He wasn't always as he is now. We weren't always beauty and the beast." Her voice was strained. "You thought that I drew the short straw because I married an ugly man. That because I am blind and so couldn't see him, it somehow made it easier for me. But that's not true."

She ran her hand lovingly over the glass-framed picture. "Really it was Peter who had the worst of the deal. He was a good looking man. He had a choice of many girls. And yet he took me on with my blindness."

"How?" Jack whispered. He didn't trust himself to say more.

In answer, she handed him a folded, yellowing newspaper cutting. He read the headline slowly. *Detective Receives Royal Humane Award.*

Jane's voice swelled with both pain and pride. "There was a house fire. And a boy . . ." She paused, steadying her voice. "His parents managed to get out, but their son was trapped in his bedroom. A wardrobe had fallen against the door, and no-one could get it open. Peter was driving past, off duty at the time. He didn't hesitate. Despite the flames and the heat he managed to force his way through the door and drag the boy out."

Jack didn't feel surprised. He had seen Lewis open closed doors before.

"He saved the boy's life. The price Peter paid was the virtual loss of his face. He spent a long time in hospital, Jack. Eventually he was judged fit enough to return to work. But his face, his hands—they were irreparably scarred. You've probably noticed that he wears gloves all the time?" She leant forward and placed her hands on Jack's face, feeling the strong jaw and firm mouth.

"You've been feeling pity for me, but the truth is that I pity you. You might be able to see with your eyes, but your heart is closed. Inside, where it matters, you're as blind as I am, Jack."

He rose to his feet, backing away from the woman who was playing havoc with his mind. "I'm sorry, I must go," he said, painfully aware that his voice was hoarse. "Forgive me for intruding like this . . ." He rushed angrily outside into the fresh air, needing to put as much distance as he could between them. He had intended to find out a few things about Lewis. He hadn't intended for his own life to be scraped bare.

He walked for a while. The account of the fire was painful, evoking memories of his own sons' death. And he couldn't bear any more God talk. How could anyone believe in that stuff? It was almost as if he were being taunted. If there was a God, why wasn't someone like Peter bloody Lewis about when *his* boys needed him?

How anyone could believe in a divine being was beyond him. Didn't they read Darwin? Hadn't they read his *Origin of Species, The Descent of Man?* The works of an unbiased mind, whose theories had been proved true over and over again. Many scientists had said it clearly. *There is no need to bring a God into the picture in order to provide for a sensible theory of how the universe and its creatures came into being.*

He walked back to his car, where his demon was waiting. It had temporarily detached from him whilst he was in Jane's house. Evil had been prevented from entering by the angel who guarded Jane Lewis night and day.

And inside that fortress, Jane Lewis prayed for the soul of Jack Somerville.

Master Bune was addressing the mass of assembled demons, his black menace filling the space around him. Fixing his listeners with his cruel eyes, he enjoyed the satisfaction of seeing them brace up before him. There were several familiar faces gathered, such as Abigar the demon of alcohol, Rahu, Baphomet and Melchom. But it was overwhelmingly new demons that were now present.

They were gathered in their tens of thousands, crawling across the walls and the rock floor like the filthy carrion flies that they were, and the sounds of flapping wings, the scratching of leathery skin and the squeaks of anger as they jostled for position filled the air.

"He has come," said Bune.

The effect was dramatic and a collective gasp erupted from the mass of evil gathered in their hidden place just outside the town. One moment they had been brazen, ostensibly listening to their commander, but in reality more concerned with pushing to the front and exerting their own importance above that of their neighbour. The next moment, fear gripped them in an iron grasp that held them captive in its clutches. No name had been mentioned. But they knew.

"Now is the time," said Bune, "to see once and for all who is in charge of this place, this earth that the enemy calls his creation!" He paused, as there was a flurry of activity and a large demon entered. Innumerable pin-prick eyes glanced up fearfully, only to relax as they recognised the shape of Barbas. Melchom felt his heart surge. Forgetting in a moment the earlier warning from Mania, he began to push his way forward from the place he had been relegated to at the back of the crowd, much to the annoyance of the demons he displaced.

"Let me through," he hissed, pushing roughly through the crowds. "My Lord Barbas is my patron."

There was a snigger at the expression, "my lord." They at least recognised that Barbas was not entitled to such honour.

Meanwhile, Barbas strutted confidently towards Bune, his head held high. He was the angel destroyer after all. He had successfully encountered the enemy. And he had won. He knew that would count for something. Thoughts of advancement whirled in his head. Already he could see the red jewels of yet higher office embroidered onto his collar.

He glanced casually at the crowd. He was pleased that there were so many to see his moment of triumph. The moment when Bune would acknowledge him before all demons.

That attitude, that belief, lasted for moments only. Because in an instant, with a speed belying his great bulk, Bune grabbed the hapless demon by the throat and lifted him from his feet.

Melchom froze in his tracks. Waiting. Waiting to see what the outcome would be. Sick to his black heart, he knew that there could be only one. As big as he was, Barbas was no match for the mighty Master Bune. His mind reluctantly recalled the words of Mania. Surely he could not be right? Surely Barbas was not finished? Before he realised it, he had dropped the grand title. He was reluctantly aware that his dreams of advancement were over.

Barbas hung limply at the end of that powerful arm, his breath cut off and unable to speak. No longer proud and defiant, his eyes were now downcast. He dare not raise them to look in the face of the one who held him fast.

"My Lord Barbas?" asked Bune in his gravely voice, and a ripple of laughter flooded the assembly, replacing the pent-up tension that was now fit to burst. Melchom forced himself to laugh louder than most, but it sounded false and hollow.

Barbas gurgled an indecipherable reply. That was all he could do with the steely fingers clamped remorselessly around his windpipe.

"My explicit orders were that the enemy were not to be touched!" He shook the hapless demon like a piece of rag. "And yet you chose to disobey. And risked the whole plan."

With a look of utter contempt, Bune dropped the pathetic, sometime "lord" who fell in a crumpled heap before him. He grovelled pitifully at the feet of the powerful demon, and Bune immediately placed a black-booted foot on him, pinning him humiliatingly to the ground.

And that was where he lay, when total darkness descended. When winter came and slivers of ice plummeted to the ground in shards, as the very air around them froze. When fear, tangible and immense, like nothing they had experienced during the whole course of their evil lives fell like a blanket of corruption, smothering, dense and all-pervading. Then their minds, the totality of their being, every atom and fibre of their existence was filled with stark, unbearable terror.

For he had come.

The personal emissary of the Prince of Darkness himself. Of global dominion and of terrible, destructive supremacy. He who would relentlessly annihilate anything and anyone that stood in the way of his lord.

And now he had come.

To do his lord's will. To make all the earth and everything in it tremble for fear of the one he served. Lucifer. Prince of the powers of the air, lord of the flies. Satan.

The one whose name dare not be spoken stepped forward, disdaining even to acknowledge the minions, who fell reverently and fearfully to their knees, their heads bowed and pressed to the dank earth, their eyes screwed tightly shut.

Even Master Bune sank to his knees before the majesty of the great one. The one who was to be feared above all others, save only Satan himself.

For he was immense. Huge and all compelling, dwarfing all others. Reaching out a powerful, taloned hand, encrusted in jewels and precious stones, Lucifer's right-hand demon caught hold of Bune and lifted him from his feet as if he were nothing, holding him until his eyes were level with his own.

"You are?" he growled, and the stench of the vapour from his lips was as biting as acid.

"Bune, lord. Your loyal servant Bune."

The great demon stared for a long moment at his captive, with eyes that outmatched his underling in every way. Of deepest ruby, flashing with brimstone and evil, no demon could meet his gaze and live. As Bune closed his eyes to shut out the terrible sight, the mighty demon released his grip, letting him fall heavily to the ground, from where he nursed his pride, but grateful to be alive.

Then the supreme eminence focussed his attention on the trembling Barbas who was still cowering on the ground. Carelessly he lifted a gigantic, calloused foot, and brought it stomping down on the prostrate figure.

The assembly collectively sucked in its breath, certain that they were witnessing the destruction of Barbas. But the emissary stopped just short of killing. His foot continued downwards, but the fearsome power had gone. Then came the sound of Barbas shrieking in agony as his chest caved in and his spine bent at an impossible angle.

He would live to continue his work whilst it pleased his lord to spare him, but he would forever after be deformed, doomed to shuffle instead of walk, and to fly clumsily with much ineffectual flapping of his wings.

The mighty demon was pleased with his work. He did not kill for the sake of it. He did not even mutilate and deform without reason. Not that he had any scruples. Life, whether that of demon or human, meant nothing to him. The lives of demons certainly were his to take as he chose if it advanced the cause of his fealty-master, Lucifer.

If he could win a single soul, take one piece of territory, or destroy the witness of a single Christian, then he would labour night and day, neither sleeping nor eating until it was done. The warlords scattered across the world knew this, and so they feared him. That is why he had pre-eminence over them and was answerable to no-one but the dark lord himself.

His purpose was to instil terror and through it compliance and obedience. And he had done just that. By such small and insignificant displays of strength is great obedience bought. And now he was assured of the total loyalty of all who quaked and trembled before him. For a time at least. For he knew that even fear as great as he could impart would not last for ever. But he was fully able and willing to supplement that lesson in fear as and when necessary. But for now, Barbas would be a living example to remind them daily of just how much they should fear him.

"None of you are important," he growled, "you exist only to serve my Lord Lucifer." He glared around, daring anyone to suggest otherwise. But no-one was that stupid, and they nodded enthusiastically their agreement, studiously avoiding any eye contact. He was not deceived. But it would suffice. They would serve their purpose.

"It is time for 'The Plan' to be put into place," he said. "To usher in the end of days. The End-Times. And we begin by taking this town totally and forever to the glory and majesty of the morning star."

The hidden place erupted with cheers, and the emissary smiled within. He knew beyond doubt that for now at least, they were his. He raised his voice, and they quietened immediately, all eyes fixed intently on him.

He lifted his hand, and a shaft of red light flashed from the ruby ring he wore. "The Son of the great enemy, the Christ, has said that no-one knows the time or the hour when the end will come," he mocked, "but *my* lord disagrees!"

More shouts filled the night air.

"Now we begin. With the destruction of this insignificant place and its equally insignificant people, we begin a chain reaction that will spread across the Globe. We will put in place the beginning. The beginning of the end. The end of the world!"

The demons went wild when they heard this. At last, the overthrow of the enemy and the restoration of all the earth to their dark lord was about to come to pass. It had been a long time coming. It had been so many long centuries since they had been thrown down from heaven, and they yearned to be restored to their rightful place. As rulers, as princes, as kings.

"Those who have not sided with the enemy are already ours. They belong to us and they have no defence. We will start with them. Much good work is already going on, and the harvest of souls for our master will be beyond numbering."

He acknowledged their maniacal and delirious shouts, before gesturing once more for silence. "This is a significant time of year, fellow demons. It's Christmas!"

There was a universal feeling of pride that this great lord had called them "fellow demons," and there came a murmur of approval from all around.

"My Lord Lucifer particularly hates this season in the lives of those who love the enemy." He struggled over the word "love" forcing it out with difficulty.

"With the others he has no problem. In fact he encourages them in their Christmas gorging, debauchery and drunkenness. He wants them to stay filled with their empty, hopeless and false spirituality. As long as they continue to focus on the greed and the gluttony, they will not see the danger. Your job is to make sure they never do. Until it is too late for them to do anything about it."

Prolonged applause broke out, and continued unabated for several minutes. Some clapped their horny hands, whilst others rattled their leathery wings or stamped huge, misshapen feet until the noise was deafening.

"Now all of you. You have done well in spreading false hope wrapped in bright paper and coloured lights. You have excelled in encouraging dead religion devoid of any personal relationship with the enemy. Now is the time to use that. Now is the time to deal a fatal blow to the enemy's creation. Take them, because they have no defence. Probe deep into their minds; they have no discernment. Uncover secret sins, anger, filth, envy, striving, greed, violence and hatred. Stir them into action, free them from all restraint. Swarm over their defenceless souls and feed on the sin that emanates from within them. For they are yours. Now, demons of anger, greed and envy. Where are you? You have a particularly important work to do tonight."

A multitude of grotesque shapes shuffled forwards scattering those who stood in their way. They were grinning hideously, proud at being singled out by the great demon himself.

"Set their spirits free, unleash their innate selfishness and lust—let them destroy first their town, then their hope and finally their souls. Show the 'have-nots' what they are missing. Let them see the unfairness of those that 'have.' Engender greed in their hearts and hatred for others. Stir up their anger and violence like a flame, unleash all your powers. Take away all their restraint, fill them with envy and set them free to burn and to destroy!"

The emissary drew his sword, slashing calculatingly at those demons nearest to him.

"Fly, all of you, fly! Let the end begin! Make them captives and servants of our master for all eternity."

Then the air became thick and dark and the smell of foulness and corruption filled the chamber where they congregated. And the clamour of thousands upon thousands of leather wings became an avalanche of sound that rumbled and echoed across the fields, the streets and the villages. One of the largest armies of evil ever gathered in one place, descended upon the unsuspecting town and people of Hartwood.

Bar-Lgura, He whose name dare not be spoken, had finally come . . .

Jack's mind was still in turmoil as he returned to his computer. Both he and Lewis had left the station in a rush on hearing of the murder of Nathan Mahoney, and they hadn't had time to view the CD they'd taken from Riley's flat. In fact he had left it sitting in the tray of his computer.

But it wasn't there now. The tray was open—the CD gone. It seemed someone didn't want its contents known.

Lewis had nipped back. For the car keys he had said, after they had left the office together. He would have had the opportunity. But that didn't make sense.

Jack smiled quietly to himself, a curious look on his face. He spent some time on his computer, examining something intently. Then he picked up his coat, collected a set of car keys from the board and headed out. "Going out!" he shouted to the control room staff. "I'm on the radio if you want me."

CHAPTER TWENTY-FIVE

The demonic hordes flew across the darkening sky. A mighty outpouring of filth, unleashed at the express bidding of the demon-lord. Their certain conviction was that *now* the appointed time for the end of all things had come. They had cast aside the prophetic truth of the Word of God, assured that they could subvert His will and bring in the kingdom of darkness. With the overthrow of Adonai and his angels, the enslavement of all mankind, the so-called children of God that the Christ had given his life for, was assured.

So demons of all sizes and disciplines flew in obedience to the command. Some already had humans prepared. They had worked on them for some time, and their depravity was assured. It would not take much for the last barriers of restraint to come crashing down. And that would cause a chain reaction that would spread across Hartwood, the county, the United Kingdom and eventually the entire world.

Experimentation across the continents had already established that once a riot was stirred up, many would join in who had no interest or even knowledge of the reasons. For every activist with a cause there were ten who had no allegiance, no cause, and no aim. Just violence, hatred, fear and anarchy.

Demons of betrayal, division, lust and of alcohol and drugs whipped their people into insane frenzies. Drug dealers found themselves overwhelmed by sudden demand, and they struggled to fulfil their orders. But they managed somehow, pocketing their vast sums of money, mentally insulated by greed from the life destroying effects of their repulsive trade. Prostitutes had never seen anything like the trade that was now theirs, and they found themselves totally unable to cope with the overwhelming demand for their services.

Demons of argument, of destruction, hatred and murder tried to outdo the demons of rage and wrath to see who could provoke the bloodiest fight, the most terrifying killing or the most destructive outburst of senseless, violent aggression.

And when the pent up fury and unrighteousness of these souls could be contained no longer, they emerged onto the streets in their hundreds, and then their thousands. Each one possessed, indwelt and controlled by the satanic forces that they had unwittingly courted by their rejection of God. Every last one of them, by their acceptance of evil, had voluntarily opened a door in their lives, an entrance by which they permitted the lord of the flies to enter and take control.

Now they would vent their hatred on something, or someone tangible. On the town of Hartwood that had been their home. On the people who had been their neighbours. They would burn, and destroy and kill, and maim and rob and rape and terrorise. And in the front line of their vengeance would be the police. Many would look forward to that, having had dealings with them at one time or another. Most for just minor things. But under the evil influence of the demoniac uprising, these incidents were inflamed, embellished and exaggerated until they fired up an all consuming desire for bloody revenge.

A sixteen-year-old boy was one of those. He had been afraid for most of his life. A violent father had abused him ever since he could remember. And suddenly he remembered being beaten and humiliated by a police officer. All he had been doing was drinking with some friends. And a detective had pushed him off of a wall, before tearing into him ruthlessly. He had hurt him more mentally than physically. Disrespected him in the presence of his friends. And in his captive mind, that event had taken on magnificent proportions, eating away at him until only violence would assuage the memory. Now was his chance to get his own back. To address the balance of power in this place.

Do what thou wilt shall be the whole of the law . . .

_____

Returning to the police station, Jack leaped to one side as a group of uniformed officers came hurtling through the side door.

"Trouble at mill, sarge!" one of them shouted in a fake Yorkshire accent. Then seriously. "Sounds like a mini-riot to me."

"I'll come with you." Without waiting for a reply, he squeezed into the rear of the already over-full police car, holding on grimly as it accelerated out of the car park with a squeal of tyres. "What in tarnation is happening here?" he said, to no-one in particular.

Rob Costa, a chunky officer in his mid-twenties who was sandwiched next to him, ran a hand through his thick black hair as he responded. "Sounds like the balloon has well and truly gone up, sarge," he said. "HQ said there are people fighting in the High Street. They want an update ASAP."

Jack glanced at his watch. It was just 7pm, although the winter evening had long drawn in and it had been dark for some time. "It's a bit early for the Christmas crazies," he shouted, trying to make himself heard above the wail of the sirens and the screaming of the engine. "Surely people haven't had enough time yet to get that tanked up?" He held grimly onto the back of the passenger seat in front of him as the car lurched around a corner.

Rob turned to the officer next to him. "It's your beat Jeff, you know them—or at least you should."

Community officer Jeff Harding ignored the barbed comment. "We usually have a bit of grief at chucking out time. But nothing we can't handle. I wouldn't be surprised if it's another hoax call. We were plagued with them at this time last year."

"Well, if it is a hoax they are doing a good job," remarked Jack dryly. "Take a look up there." He pointed over to his left, to where the sky was tinged with red fire. Even as they stared in disbelief it was visibly spreading, smearing out across the skyline above the town. He leant across the seat in front of him and grabbed the radio handset from its cradle on the dashboard. "HQ, this is . . ." He nudged the tall, skinny officer in the front seat. "Pat, what's our call-sign?"

Having received the answer, he shouted it into the handset, above the din of the accelerating car and the shriek of the siren that the driver had just switched from "wail" to "yelp," the change of tone corresponding with the uplift in adrenalin.

"Foxtrot golf three, FG3," repeated Jack, "we're going ten three. You need to get more troops running and get 'Trumpton' out. Looks like there's a large fire in Hartwood Town Centre."

The clinically cool voice of the HQ operator came back. "Ten seven?"

"You heard me first time!" shouted Jack, "Get the fire brigade and any other bodies you can turf out of their offices. Sounds like there is a full-scale riot in progress."

"Sorry FG3, you are totally broken. Can you try another location and re-transmit?" He threw the handset at its holder. It missed and it fell into the footwell at the front of the car just as they turned the corner towards the High Street. "So much for that," he said. "Looks like we're on our own."

The police driver, Tony Evans, brought the car to a skidding halt, throwing the passengers forward violently. Unusually, there was no word of complaint. They were too busy surveying the scene that now confronted them.

Jeff, the local man, was the first to speak, his voice quavering with emotion.

"Oh my God," he cried, "they've torched the whole High Street!"

Grief was still clearly etched on his golden face as Talial faced the angels packed into the barn on the outskirts of town. They were positioned on the floor, the beams in the ceiling and the high window ledges. They were there in their hundreds. And they were ready to do war. There were rumblings of anger, and from all over the rude building came bursts of unbearable light as swords were drawn, and angels glorified.

"Auriel has gone home, but he conducted himself with valour," Talial was saying, "unlike the enemy who conducted himself with his usual cowardice."

Battle cries were shouted then; the angelic host were just itching to get into the fray and avenge the terrible injuries of their comrade.

Talial smiled then, despite his sorrow. "My brave angels," he said, "ready to jump in the thick of it as usual. But we must wait until the Spirit tells us to move." He held up his golden bow, and shook it above his head. "Auriel managed to pass on some vital Intel. And I have an arrow or two for the demon army and those that used him so despicably. They will pay dearly. But not yet my friends, not yet."

Sounds of disappointment floated up from the assembly.

"Soon enough, soon enough dear comrades. But the Spirit is not yet ready. We must remain hidden and out of sight for now."

A bulky angel carrying a spear over his shoulder was not too pleased. "We must hide? Skulk in dark corners like villains?"

Talial strode forward, placing his hand on the stalwart angel's muscular arm. "I can't imagine your corpulent physique skulking too well in any corners, my valiant Bathor," he said with a smile, and there was uproarious laughter from all around.

Bathor joined in the laughter, and lowered his spear point to the ground. He clasped the arm of Talial in a firm grip. "Yours in life and in death, my captain," he said.

Talial acknowledged the pledge of loyalty with a grin, and bounded back to his place at the front. "Until the trumpet sounds, my friends. Disperse, and keep low. The enemy believe that they have us on the run and that they must win. But our God reigns!"

There was a huge cheer, and praise to Almighty God erupted from all around. Then the assembly began to quietly file out, until one last time the voice of Talial sounded, causing them to stop in their tracks.

"This is for Auriel," he said, and there was a catch in his voice. He drew his sword, pointing it skywards. "To Him who sits upon the throne, and to the Lamb!"

And the response filled that place with heavenly cries and a wall of blinding light, as every angel drew his sword, glorifying in an instant and transforming the darkness of the barn into a ball of luminescent fire.

"To Him who sits upon the throne, and to the Lamb, Amen," they shouted into the heavenlies. "Amen and Amen and Amen . . ."

CHAPTER TWENTY-SIX

"Reverse! Tony, do it now! Get the hell out of here!"

Jack was shouting loudly at the driver, who seemed mesmerised by the scene unfolding in front of him. On one side of the High Street, a large department store was a blazing inferno. Flames had engulfed it; already the roof had gone and the walls were beginning to collapse under the fury of the furnace. Many of the other shops either side of the big store had thick, acrid smoke pouring from their blackened and broken windows. Every now and then a sheet of incandescent flame burst out, leaping skywards and causing the mob to howl with delight.

More smoke was beginning to build at the corner where the Magistrates Court was situated. An abandoned car, strangely out of place in the middle of the shopping mall was in the process of being torched. Flames were also licking out of the front windows of a public house where looters were going wild. They were running out carrying bottles of wine, packs of beer, cigarettes, bags of crisps—anything they could get their hands on. Some had driven their cars onto the forecourt so that they could fill them up with the stolen goods.

Bizarrely, a pair of Christmas trees had defied the flames, and stood, still decorated with their finery either side of another large store out of which a mass of shouting, yelling, violently angry men and women were exiting, screaming, pushing and tearing at each other as they ran, carrying plastic bins full of clothing, jewellery electrical and other goods.

On the pavement, a child's blue and white striped pushchair lay crushed and abandoned. Further along beside a fountain, which incongruously continued to spout water into the air, an elderly man lay in a crumpled heap, motionless.

Adding to the scene of mayhem and carnage was a black four by four

Mercedes full of enraged youths, forcing its way through the crowd, its horn sounding stridently in competition with the cries of the mob.

Even as the police officers watched in horror, they saw that the numbers of separate fires were growing exponentially, breaking out over a wider part of the High Street and filling the night air with the choking, pungent smell of destruction.

As the police vehicle began to turn, a Ford Transit became visible, lying on its side and looking curiously vulnerable with its underside exposed. A group of young males were busy smashing every piece of glass they could find on it, using metal bars, bricks—anything they could lay their hands on.

It was Jeff who saw the chequered decals along the side of the transit, identifying it as a police vehicle. "Wait," he shouted at the confused driver, simultaneously grabbing him by the shoulder and causing him to stand on the brakes. "It's one of ours. The transit—it's a Job vehicle."

"So what," screamed Tony, "we can't do anything, there's too many of them. If we go in without backup we'll all end up getting killed."

"The crew might have got away," suggested Rob half-heartedly, "I can't see any sign of movement over there."

"There won't be any movement from us either, if we don't get out pronto," shouted Pat.

"Someone make a decision for Christ's sake," cried Jeff, "they're coming our way!"

Ahead, a group of rioters had spotted them and were running furiously down the High Street towards them.

"It's the pigs. Get 'em."

"Kill the Bill! Kill the Bill! Kill the Bill!"

The chant was taken up by more and more of the insane mob, until it became a deafening roar. Then an avalanche of bricks hit the car with a sound like metallic thunder, shattering the windscreen and obliterating the drivers view to the front as the toughened glass crazed over.

Jack made the only decision possible. "Pat's right, get out of here," he shouted reluctantly. "Drive, and make it fast!"

Even as he spoke, the car door on his side was wrenched open, and the twisted, hate-filled face of a goatee-bearded man in his mid-twenties filled the space. He jabbed a long metal pole inside, stabbing Jack in his side, and despite his thick overcoat he cried out involuntarily in pain.

Shouting a string of expletives, he grabbed his assailant by his coat lapel, pulling him sharply forward whilst at the same time palm-striking him to the face with his other hand. He felt the satisfying crunch of breaking cartilage, followed by a piercing shriek as his attacker fell backwards and out of view, leaving Jack in possession of the metal pole.

He slammed the door shut, and Tony floored the accelerator. The car shot back at speed, colliding with a rioter attempting to climb onto the boot. He vanished underneath the rear wheels with a scream.

Quickly shifting into first, Tony deftly spun the wheel, accelerating away from the maddened mob, their cries gradually fading as he put distance between them.

Pressing his face close to the windscreen, he tried to see through the cracked glass that was now acting as a prism, but the street lights and the flickering of the fires in his eyes all but obliterated any view of the road ahead.

Pat picked up the handset, but the radio remained stubbornly silent with no response from their requests for assistance. The dratted equipment was duff. Whether HQ was aware of the seriousness of FG3's situation was not clear.

"Watch out!" shouted Tony.

Headlights loomed in the rear-view mirror, as the black four by four Mercedes they had seen earlier came alongside, striking the rear offside of their vehicle a glancing blow. Tony momentarily lost control, swerving as he struggled to correct the slide, the tyres screaming as they fought to grip the tarmac.

"Here he comes again, my side this time!" shouted Rob fearfully, seconds before they were struck once again with terrific force.

"He'll wreck us if this keeps up," complained Tony, "He's got bull-bars and they're making mincemeat out of this heap of tin."

He hit the accelerator again, and the car surged forward, for a short while creating a gap between the two vehicles.

"Can we out-run him?" said Jack.

"Not on this road," responded Tony, "he's too fast for us. If we had a winding road with a few sharp bends where some skill is needed instead of just speed, then I could really kick butt. But on the straight . . ." He left the sentence unfinished.

Pat got on the radio again. "HQ, this is foxtrot golf three," he shouted desperately, "this is a 10/9. Repeat 10/9. We need urgent assistance."

At that moment the pursuing Mercedes rear-ended them, causing the back end of their vehicle to break away, and almost forcing them off the carriageway.

"Not good news," said Tony, automatically correcting the sideways slide, "and we're running low on fuel."

"For Pete's sake give us some good news then," said Pat. "What with the ruddy radio being U/S. It must be the transmitter in the boot."

"That's it. The boot! Tony, do you know what equipment's in the boot?" asked Jeff.

"Usual traffic stuff I expect," he responded, "why?"

"If there's a 'Stinger' we could sort this twat out in no time."

"Stinger?" asked Jack.

"Don't you CID blokes know anything? It's a bit of kit to stop stolen vehicles. An expanding metal frame studded with hollow spikes. When a vehicle drives over it, their tyres deflate, and they come to an undignified stop!"

"What'll we do, chuck it out the window? Don't you have to lay the thing in the road?" said Rob.

"We can do that," said Jeff. "Sarge, can you rip the back parcel shelf out and see if there's one in the back. And can you try and be swift about it; I'm starting to flap a bit here."

Jack fumbled around and cursed as he struggled to remove the shelf. "Aren't you meant to open the bloody boot before taking stuff out?" he said, to no-one in particular. Then he cursed once more, only rather more loudly as they were struck again, causing their car to lurch violently onto two wheels.

He unclipped the fire extinguisher from its bracket under the rear seat, lifted it above his head as far as he could in the confined space, and brought it smashing down on the parcel shelf.

"Is this it?" he asked gruffly, reaching through the mangled wreckage of the shelf and pulling out what appeared to be a piece of metal trellis.

Jeff took hold of it and nodded. "That's the baby," he said, "now all we need to do is find somewhere to deploy it."

Jack wound down his window and peered at the Mercedes now racing alongside them. Shouting against the buffeting of the open window, he said, "Okay, I've got an idea. Can you do a handbrake turn Tony?"

"Yeah, is the Pope a Catholic or what?" he shouted back.

"Right, this is the plan for what it's worth. If you can keep alongside them for a few seconds, I think I can distract them long enough for Jeff to do his stuff." He hefted the metal pole that he had acquired earlier, grunting as pain from the injury in his side stabbed through him. "As soon as they overshoot us, do the turn and then blatt down the road as fast as you can 'till I tell you. When I shout stop, make sure you do exactly that. We won't have much time, and they are going to be pretty peed off with us by then. That's when you get out Jeff, lay out the stinger behind us, and make sure you know exactly where you put that baby, because we've got to come back this way again unless you want to try going through the town."

Jeff nodded in acknowledgement. "Roger that, sarge."

"You've done this before Jeff, right?" asked Pat.

There was silence for a moment. "Well, not exactly."

"What the hell is 'not exactly?' You've either done it or you haven't."

"I had a practice once in the back yard of the station."

"Great," said Pat, "we're relying on a hare-brained scheme, being carried out by an equally hare-brained amateur!"

"Right boys, shut the gab and stand by, here they come again."

"Hang on, there's another vehicle coming towards us," exclaimed Rob, as headlights appeared in front of them.

There was the strident, angry sound of a car horn, and the Mercedes swerved back onto its own side of the road as a breakdown truck roared furiously past. An upside down Micra swung wildly across the road on a length of tow chain, sparking as it scraped along the road on its roof.

"What *is* going on?" asked Tony, "it seems that the whole world has gone raving mad tonight." Just then the Mercedes sped up once more, and he had to accelerate hard just to keep alongside.

Jack wound down the window again, ignoring the buffeting of the slipstream that caused his eyes to water and almost blind him. Gripping the piece of metal pipe tightly in his hand, he waited for the right moment. A man's face was leering at him from out of the open passenger window, shouting inaudibly as the wind snatched away the words. He could see the lips moving, but there was no sound. However, the look of hatred on his face made it clear what the general tone of the message was.

The police car began to fall back, as the more powerful Mercedes forged ahead.

"Tony, get a bloody move on. We need to be right alongside for this to work."

"I'm doing my best. They've got a Merc remember, and I can hardly see out of my windscreen."

He dropped a gear, and the car leapt forward slightly, enough so that for just a second they were once more level and Jack could once more pick out the moving lips of the man screaming in a perverse rendition of a silent movie.

It was at those lips that Jack hurled the pipe, with all his strength, shouting in agony as the pain in his side erupted at the exertion.

The leering head snapped back as the metal hit him full on, his face taking on a soundless scream of pain as he fell sideways and out of view. The four by four swerved and veered away across the road, loosing speed and finally coming to a halt.

"Okay, turn now!" he gasped.

Tony yanked the handbrake hard, turning the steering full circle as he did so. The car rocked violently, but spun obediently around so that it was facing the direction it had just come from. Then accelerating at full throttle he headed back down the road to put as much distance between the two vehicles as he could.

"Stop!" yelled Jack, "hit the brakes!"

Tony stood on the pedal, and as the car slewed to a halt in a shower of gravel, Jeff leapt out, ran behind, and in a swift movement flicked the stinger across the road.

He cursed gruffly, and they could see him dragging it back towards him, closing it up ready to re-deploy it.

Pat shouted through the window, his voice quavering in panic. "Get on with it, we haven't got time for you to sod around!"

"Shut up!" screamed Jeff, "The ruddy thing turned upside down, and it won't work like that. I'm doing the best I can."

"You can do it Jeff," said Jack soothingly. "Try again."

He could see behind that the Mercedes was once again on the move. It had turned around, and was even now making its way back towards them, its engine screaming as the unknown driver gunned the engine, grating the gears as he changed up coarsely.

Under his breath he said, "For God's sake don't fanny around for too long."

Jeff flicked the stinger out once again and there was an unbearable pause as he checked its positioning, before he jumped back in with a look of satisfaction on his face.

"You were right, sarge, I think he's more than a bit peed off now," he said nervously.

"Get moving!" yelled Jack.

The police car leapt away as Tony once more hit the accelerator, the lights of the pursuing vehicle growing ever larger in the rear view mirror as it screamed towards them.

"He's holding nothing back this time," screamed Rob, "if he hits us at this speed we're toast."

No one replied, but they all held on even tighter.

"Where's that stinger?" yelled Pat. "They don't seem to be slowing any. Are you sure you laid the thing the right way up this time?"

"Shut up Pat," said Jeff, "I did the best I could with it."

"They're just about to find it now," said Jack. He paused for just a moment. "Yup, that's it," he added in satisfaction as the four by four careered across the road and came to a stop, broadside across the carriageway. "Get past Tony, and let's see what's going on. And don't hang around."

Tony responded, and once again the car screamed in a full circle. This time they did not stop, but raced onwards.

Passing the vehicle stranded across the road, keeping well out of the path of the stinger, they could see all its four doors hanging open. There was no sign of the driver or the occupants, but they were not about to stop and check them out just now.

"Well sarge, that seemed to go off rather well. What next?" asked Tony.

"Back to the station I think. We need to find out what on earth is happening, and with a duff radio set we aren't much use out here."

"We're going to run?" asked Rob, who up to then had been a bit subdued.

"Unless it's escaped your attention, that's precisely what we've been doing for the last ten minutes," responded Jack sarcastically. "If you have a plan as to how the four of us without any equipment can defeat a drunken, insane mob, then please tell me."

"Perhaps rather than think of it as running, we should look on it as success deferred," muttered Tony, pointing the car toward Hartwood police station.

Despite, or perhaps because of the tension, everyone laughed except Jack whose side was beginning to throb badly now that the adrenalin had started to disperse. Those that did laugh felt a bit better afterwards.

CHAPTER TWENTY-SEVEN

Undoubtedly God had called his people together. But for what reason? There didn't seem to be any answer as yet. If it was so important, and Marcus firmly believed that God had placed a burden on Hartwood Community Church for intercessory prayer, why was it that so few had turned up? Where was God in all this? He reluctantly acknowledged a sense of disappointment that his flock had failed to heed the rallying call to prayer. If he was honest with himself, he felt let down. He felt that somehow, he himself had failed.

So much had happened in such a short space of time and he felt a huge sense of responsibility towards his flock. He had led them into error in the past by denying the power of God, and he was now concerned that he might be tempted to get carried away on a tide of emotion and commit an equal, but opposite error.

He remembered reading somewhere that the devil uses two effective strategies against the church. He initially tries to convince them that he doesn't exist. If that doesn't work, he tries to encourage them to see demons under every bed. Either way, the saints of God can go off track. Denying the strategies of the evil one render them helpless in the face of demonic attack, and permit their communities to fall into captivity and bondage. Giving the devil too much credit encourages the church to concentrate more on the devil than on God. Which is exactly what his ego craves.

But it seemed that tonight, most of the church would not have the opportunity either way, as they had voted with their feet and stayed at home

At that very moment, the doors at the back of the church opened noisily, and a straggle of people began to flow through. One after another they came, filling the empty seats. For a moment he felt relief, but the feeling lasted for that moment only as he realised the incomers were staring hostilely towards their fellow church members as they filed in.

Not knowing how to respond, he remained silent. He wouldn't have trusted himself to speak anyway, as the seats began to fill until there was no room left. He wasn't sure that they even understood why they had come. But even if they didn't know it, he was convinced that they were acting under Holy Spirit compulsion, keeping a divine appointment that was part of their destiny, and that of their community.

And still they came, old and young, men and women, church members and people he had never seen before, all moving quietly to the back and sides of the room. As the seats filled, they stood with their backs against the walls whilst others sat on the floor in the aisle.

Something was wrong. He recognised it not just in his spirit, but in the exchange of glances between them. Many of them had fallen out with each other at some time or another over the years. Some had not spoken in a very long time. And they were studiously ignoring each other still.

The sense of God's peace that he had earlier felt was gone, dissipated in a moment of time. And despair flooded over him.

Across the room was Joan Bowman, looking pale and drawn. Clutching her arm was her daughter Emily. He couldn't believe that she had been discharged from hospital so soon, with her face visibly bruised and swollen, even under the bandages that she wore. The terrible battering that she had taken was now evident. She walked stiffly and slowly with the aid of a stick, but the determination and sheer anger was all too clear in her eyes. She sat down alongside her mother, staring straight ahead.

That Emily had come was yet another shock to him. She hadn't been for a long time.

Joan herself looked distraught. From where he stood, Marcus could see that her eyes were puffy and swollen from crying. That wasn't surprising, seeing as she had lost her husband and had had to come to terms with the savage assault on her daughter, all in a short space of time.

He knew that Joan wasn't a Christian, even though she had been attending the church for many years, and that her husband, Bob had been a major stumbling block. Perhaps in his death he could help her in a way that he never had in life, and that God would break through.

Marcus allowed his gaze to rove around the meeting place. He asked the question yet again. What was God doing? Why had he brought these warring factions together? It was clear that they were very unhappy, and he would have thought that the last place they'd wanted to be at such an hour was among people they so patently disliked.

And as if that wasn't enough, the door at the back once more flew noisily open and Steve Coleman stalked back inside. He was in a foul temper as he walked determinedly to the front. No one had taken him up on his invitation for them to leave the church with him, and so he had decided that something more needed to be done. One thing was for sure. He wasn't just going to leave things as they were to a relative new-comer like Pastor Bentley. He needed removing—by force if necessary.

Brushing past Marcus, he took the microphone and faced the con-gregation. He was surprised to see that there were so many people now present including many that he had personally fallen out with over the years. But he wasn't about to let that stop him.

"I think things have gone too far here," he shouted into the mike, "and I for one am not going to let it continue."

There were some catcalls from the back, notably from those who had left the church on account of Steve some time ago.

"Get off!" shouted someone, and at the back of the church a clique of disgruntled former worshippers began a slow handclap. Steve had to shout even louder to make himself heard above the row, but he was up to that.

"It's no use you trying to stop me speaking. I am still an elder in this church, and I have a right to address the congregation."

Some, seated either side of the hand clappers were speaking concil-iatory words, seeking to persuade them to stop, which eventually they did, although with bad grace. They were enjoying the spectacle of Steve's discomfort enormously.

There were others also getting pleasure from the open display of hostility. Mania, Chamos and Melchom, along with dozens of other demons were strolling cockily around the church, whispering their poison into ears that were willing to hear.

Mania, the anti-Christ demon, clung to Steve, feeding words for him to repeat to the church. Others whispered subversive rebellion to many who had unrepented sin in their lives. Especially those who were out of fellowship with God and who harboured resentment towards other church members. Sin had opened up a landing-strip in their lives, so enabling the demons to home-in and influence them in ways that would otherwise have been inviolate to them.

Melchom, the indifference-demon, had so blinkered the minds of many that they sat back wondering what was going on, but having no desire to do anything about it. They decided that it was best to keep quiet and hope it would all blow over.

Chamos wandered around spreading the strife that he loved so much. His evil was like a spark set to dry straw, and it spread throughout the church with alarming rapidity.

He paused to bait the handful of angels who were standing passively, yet on high alert. He insolently approached one large celestial being standing vigilantly in the church entrance. He pressed his face close, taunting, and laughing contemptuously when he refused to be drawn.

The captain, the angel singled out by Chamos for the swaggering display, placed a hand on the hilt of his sword and gazed steadily at the skinny demon with his disconcertingly sky-blue eyes. He said not a word, but his intentions were so clear that despite the overwhelming superiority of demonic forces, Chamos felt led to move hurriedly to the other side of the church. Here he hooked into Emily Bowman. He enjoyed whispering his evil into her ear very much. She had been lucky in escaping the clutches of Brandon Riley, but she was still of use. Her anger could really split this feeble church wide open.

The prayer cover had been so weak for so long, that the few angels that were in the church were hopelessly outnumbered. Despite this, several fingered their weapons longingly, itching to go on the offensive. But the Spirit was clearly restraining them. They knew that he would have his reasons, but the scene in the little church at that moment was one of chaos, anger, resentment, apathy and strife, combining together in a lethal sinful cocktail. Not at all like the usual church meeting. And the demons loved it!

Marcus felt misery flooding his soul. "Lord, where are you in all this? Have I heard you wrong, have I misunderstood your call? How could you, *why* did you bring these people here?" He took a deep breath. "So many of them hate each other, why can't they go somewhere else. There are plenty of other churches in the town, why are they in mine?"

Suddenly and unexpectedly, the awesome presence of God fell upon him like a blanket. His earlier experience with Henry seemed faint in comparison with this overwhelming display of power. His body became irresistibly weighty, and to his dismay he felt himself buckling at the knees as he began to sink inexorably to the ground.

"No, Lord," he cried out, "not in front of the people." His pride was still important to him. Perhaps that's why God acted the way he did, as Marcus made ineffectual efforts to remain standing, clutching at the lectern for support. "Please don't humiliate me in this way," he pleaded, but it was to no avail as the weight of his body caused the lectern to collapse with a resounding crash. He just had time to catch sight of the panic stricken face of Lissie staring at him, before his descent to the ground followed with absolute and uncontrollable certainty.

He lay on his back, hearing the sound and the fury continuing unabated, but it was as if from afar. Pastor Marcus Bentley was isolated in a bubble of time and space that the world was excluded from. The angry sounds faded into the background. And then he heard the voice. Whether with his ears or whether it was in his mind, he did not know. But it was real. An unmistakable voice of power and awe-inspiring majesty, rushing through his being with the cleansing flow of a mountain stream.

"Marcus!"

He tried to move, but his body was overwhelmingly heavy, held motionless by an incredible yet gentle power. "Lord," he whispered, suddenly afraid.

The voice was clear and cool. "Why do you question me?"

"Forgive me." His voice was as broken as his pride.

"Will you ever doubt me again?"

"Lord, no," he said, his voice quavering. "Forgive me for ever doubting your power."

"I want you to obey me."

"O God . . ." Marcus whispered, unable to say more.

Marcus was silent, as the persistent voice continued, filling every part of his being with its unrelenting authority.

"Holy fire will break out in this place. And it will be for the glory of my name."

The voice spoke of many things, and then there was silence. Then, just as Marcus thought it was over, there came a final word.

"I will bring my Jeremiah Man, with a passion in his heart for my Word, stored up in his bones like a fire."

Marcus held his breath then, as the voice quoted scripture. He could not believe that God was speaking his very own words, those that he had given to the prophet Jeremiah over two-and-a-half thousand years earlier.

> 'But if I say, "I will not mention him
> or speak any more in his name,"
> his word is in my heart like a fire,
> a fire shut up in my bones.
> I am weary of holding it in;
> indeed, I cannot."'

And as suddenly as it had fallen, the sense of power was gone, leaving Marcus broken and weeping on the floor.

In the spiritual realm there came a sound like the clap of thunder, and heaven touched earth in a momentous display of raw, uncontrollable power that shook the forces of evil to their very core.

And the demons that had been tormenting the congregation fled in fear as a legion of angels, their swords unsheathed, exploded through the building, their robes glorified white and incandescent. Demons that hesitated were immediately put to death, and those that fled pursued relentlessly.

Aanfial, the captain of the heavenly host, drew his sword, and his drab clothing too burst into radiant, shimmering white. A sheet of molten light blasted a handful of demons that had not the wit to fly, throwing them from their perches in the building and scattering them in disorder.

Chamos was the first that he dispatched. The insolent demon who only a short while earlier had taunted the mighty angel of God, never saw death approaching. One moment he was whimpering. The next, searing pain as hot as the noonday sun scythed through his evil form, as Aanfial's sword cleaved him apart.

Melchom had moved quickly, the dispatching of Chamos giving him a few vital seconds in which to gather his limited wits together. And he fled. Up into the sky as fast as he could, speeding his way to safety.

Mania was made of sterner stuff, and stayed to put up a fight. Drawing his sword, he launched himself at the captain of the Heavenly Host. He would have been no match for the angel, even if his eyes had not been burned by the searing light. As it was, he lasted mere seconds before Aanfial's sword sent him to join his comrade in the pit.

He was tempted for a moment, wanting to take off after Melchom. He knew he could easily overtake him and obliterate him, but the Spirit even now was speaking. It was clear that his duty was to protect the saints of God in Hartwood and not to chase fleeing demons for the moment. Anyway, there were plenty of other angels soaring above who were only too keen to undertake that duty.

There remained other bolder, displaced demons prowling around outside, absolutely furious at loosing their control. And they were looking to pick a fight. But only a handful was courageous enough to approach the door of the church.

However, one look at the huge angel standing guard with the golden bow slung across his shoulders was enough to keep them at a distance. It was clear by the look on his face that he was more than ready for a fight.

Talial was more than ready to take on any demon—*all* of them if necessary—that dared to approach him. Were it not for the Spirit's leading, he would already have been unleashing his arrows into their black and evil hearts.

The Spirit was speaking to the assembled angels, in words that were strong and sure. They were being called out. Their duty now lay elsewhere, and the sense of anticipation for a great battle was strong in their hearts. Now they were close to doing what they did best. Doing what they were called to do. Protecting the children of earth. And upholding the glorious name of God and his Christ. Riding into battle with the trumpet sound in their ears. Destroying the enemies of the Lord of heaven and earth.

Habriel and Diniel along with Captain Aanfial were the only angels who were to stay behind, and their duty was simple. To stand guard over Emily Bowman and Ashley Coleman, preventing the evil from working in their minds. And they would do that. To the death if that was required of them.

In the human realm, the church had no knowledge of the crucial skirmish that had just taken place. But the people knew that *something* had happened. Because the noise had stopped. The shouting had ceased. Animosity suddenly seemed obscene. Now they stood around, bemused and unsure of what was happening. Or what they should do.

It was into that scene of hushed confusion that Ashley Coleman walked, nervous and dishevelled. Looking hesitatingly around, she withdrew to a place against the side wall, trying unsuccessfully to blend in with her surroundings. Had she come in five minutes earlier, no-one would have been any the wiser. As it was, every eye was on her.

Even taking into account the bizarre scenes earlier, it still came as a shock for most people to see her. Including Marcus. Steve's daughter had never come to church as far as he could recall. The stories of her wild ways were legendary, and had been a source of discomfiture to him. As an elder he had a biblical responsibility to keep his children in check, and he considered that he had failed in every respect in Ashley's case.

From the platform where he had earlier been conducting his diatribe against the pastor, Steve Coleman was as stunned, if not more so than everyone else to see his daughter. He stood silently, the microphone hanging lifeless in his hand as he watched her enter.

Being a small town, and a gossiping community, people already knew about her part in the attack on Emily. So they held their breath. And waited.

And they didn't have long to wait. Emily Bowman was already climbing unsteadily to her feet; squeezing awkwardly past the row of curious people. Leaving her stick behind, she made her slow and painful way towards Ashley Coleman.

Knowing the reputation of the spiteful daughter of their church elder, the church family guessed it was time for her to get what she deserved. Not before time, either.

Without support from anyone, Emily paused often, holding onto the backs of chairs as she covered the short distance. Those who wondered if they should help held back, instinctively aware that some divine scenario was playing out. One in which they should not interfere.

Her face set like flint, painful step by painful step she made her way onwards. Towards Ashley, standing against the wall, her face pale, her whole body trembling.

For a moment it seemed that the confrontation would be too much, and that she would run. But she held her ground, her blue eyes anxiously searching the battered face of Emily Bowman, the girl whose life she had ruined.

It was almost unbearable as the gap between the two young girls closed. One blue eyed, blonde and beautiful. The other puffy faced, bandaged and bruised. One unsure, afraid. The other steely and determined.

Marcus wondered whether he should intervene in case things got out of hand, but loathe to return once more to the floor, and conscious of the words that God had spoken, he remained obediently where he was, trusting that God was in control.

Ashley was mentally rehearsing her defiance. But it wasn't working. Somehow she couldn't summon up the feelings of superiority. The truth was, she felt distinctly inferior. She felt humble and contrite, one of the very few times in her whole life she had ever felt that way.

She was the first to speak, her face full of the bitterness of remorse. Her voice strained, she spoke falteringly just above a whisper. Even so, her words carried with acoustic clarity. And they were not the defiant ones that she had planned.

"I'm so sorry that I hurt you Emily, that I ruined your life. I'm sorry I hated you. Please forgive me."

Her shoulders slumped as she turned towards the door, to take her worthless self away from these people of God. She didn't fit in here—she never had and she knew she never would. These were good people, not like her, full of darkness and sin.

"Wait!" The voice was weak, but nevertheless it carried authoritatively. It filled the four corners of the meeting hall. It reached the ears of every person there. "Wait."

Agonisingly slowly Emily shuffled forward, reaching out a trembling hand to take hold of her enemy. She had run through this moment many times in her mind, over and over. She relished the prospect of revenge. Of satisfying her feelings of hurt and anger, her need to get back, even though it would be just a small gesture compared to the enormity what she had been through. She wanted to inflict hurt because she had been hurt. To humiliate because she had been humiliated.

Ashley froze. But the hand that reached out was not the one of enmity that she expected and deserved. Instead of striking her, it touched her gently on the shoulder.

With difficulty, her voice rasping dryly through swollen lips, Emily began to speak. What she wanted to say, what she had purposed in her heart to say was, "I hate you with every fibre of my being. Why . . . how could you do this to me? You selfish, vain bitch, you have destroyed my life."

But to her surprise she heard herself saying, "I . . . I forgive you."

And Ashley fell to her knees and sobbed.

The angels looking on, praised God, their robes shining white as they glorified. Their voices rang exultantly through the heavens whilst Aanfial laid a hand on the kneeling girl's head and prayed vehemently to the Lord for her peace, and the transformation of her heart.

Perhaps it was the tension, perhaps something more. Whatever the cause, a collective sigh escaped from the assembled church family. A sweet, gentle sigh. A sound like the whispering of the wind across a field of summer corn.

The two demons were frantic. They had wandered nonchalantly in, unaware that their fellows had been severely routed. They had ruled the territory for so long that they had become blasé and careless. Now they saw that two of their subjects were in danger of escaping their control, and they were in no mind to explain that to Master Bune. Or even worse, to He whose name dare not be spoken.

A fat, squat demon named Merihim moved forward to retrieve the situation, to whisper his hatred into Emily's ear. His compatriot Botis, a thin, wrinkled demon with short wings folded flat against his back, descended on Ashley.

But they had not gone far before three angels appeared, seemingly out of nowhere, and blocked their way, drawing their swords and glorifying in a blaze of light. They had judged that now was as good a time as any to get involved. They knew the Spirit's prompting in their hearts.

"No you don't demon spawn," said Aanfial, "they are the Lord's."

Merihim glanced nervously at Botis. He hadn't expected angels to be present—certainly not to intervene—their sudden appearance with drawn swords unnerved him. And he didn't much care for the light that filled the place where they stood. He much preferred the dark.

Botis was bolder. He drew his own sword, pointing it menacingly in the direction of the holy guardians. "I don't think so. They have been ours for a long time. We won't relinquish ownership that easily."

The captain laughed derisively. "You cannot own that which belongs to another, satanic imp," he said.

Botis regarded all three scornfully. "Possession is nine tenths of the law! Anyway, you don't have any proof of ownership that I know of," he stated emphatically. "Show me your entitlement to ownership, and I will *consider* releasing them."

The angel Diniel leapt forward, his sword flashing, but was restrained from cutting down the insolent demon by Habriel taking hold of him by the arm. "Good Diniel," he said, "time for that later."

Merihim, emboldened by his companion's boastful attitude, joined in the debate. But whereas Botis had had the sense not to make any irrevocable promise, in his arrogance this demon made a statement that he would regret.

Smiling smugly at the other fiend, he said confidently, "Do so, and they are *yours!*"

"You fool," rasped Botis, immediately seeing the situation they had been placed in. "Why don't you keep your mouth shut?"

"I trust not your words, for *your* lord is the father of lies," said the captain.

Botis tried to retrieve the situation. "Then we will just take them," he said. "How can either of them belong to your God? You have seen the way they live as clearly as we have. The Bowman girl has no knowledge of Adonai. She rejected his church long ago. She has sinful thoughts and is full of anger and hatred."

"And the Coleman girl! Hah!" Merihim laughed loudly, spittle showing on his thin black lips as he did so. "She is even more rebellious than the other. And didn't she do a good job with the Riley boy? You show me one act of godliness from either of them. Otherwise, we take them."

"They have no godliness in them," admitted Captain Aanfial sadly. "You are correct in what you say. They are sinful, and they have rejected God's salvation. If they were to die in their sins, then truly they would be your father's for all eternity."

Both demons hissed approvingly at this. "Then you concede?" asked Botis, with a sly look on his face. "They are ours?" He flexed his wings excitedly. He was looking forward to working again with the Coleman girl especially.

"I concede all that I have conceded," responded the angel, and the demons triumphantly shuffled forward to claim their human prizes.

"Not so fast," said the huge captain of the heavenly host. "I agree with all you have said about these girls. But that doesn't make them yours." He pointed to the painted banner hanging on the wall of the church. "Look up. What do you see?"

The demons followed his outstretched finger—then averted their gaze with a cry of pain. Because their eyes had alighted on the beautifully coloured embroidery of the Lord Jesus Christ nailed to the cross. And such is the power of that cross, that even to look upon the representation caused them agony.

"No tricks," shrieked Botis. "You know that we cannot look upon the Christ and his cross!"

"Then I rest my case," responded Aanfial. "I have admitted that these two do not glorify my Lord in their lives. But let me read the scripture which is written underneath that which you dare not gaze upon."

The demons were suddenly afraid. What would they say to Bune if they lost these two?

"It says this," continued the angel, reading aloud as the demons cringed under the word of God. "'And they sang a new song: You are worthy to take the scroll and to open its seals, because you were slain, and with your blood you purchased men for God from every tribe and language and people and nation.'"

"Hallelujah!" shouted Diniel and Habriel. "You see? Christ owns them. He bought them, and paid the price in blood. *His* blood. They are *his!*" And all three angels glorified and worshipped God where they stood.

The demons shrank back from the effect of the praise, shielding their slitted eyes from the blinding light that danced around the church. Backing towards the door, Botis spat with contempt as he began to exit the hated place of the enemy. "Your time is short, angels," he said. "Enjoy your victory while you are able."

Before Botis could stop him, Merihim, embittered by their defeat, found it impossible once again to control his tongue. He said things that he should not have even thought, let alone vocalised. Things that he would not have dared to say, had he not been incensed with rage and indignation at the humiliation they had just suffered.

"We have a mighty army gathered here," he rasped, "more than you have ever seen, more than any of you will ever have experienced. Now is the time of the end of days. Now is the time that our lord will inherit the earth. For he has sent Bar . . ."

He never finished the sentence. Botis, unable to prevent the frantically gabbling Merihim from disclosing the plans that their demon lords had made, stopped him in the only way he could. He ran him through with his sword, before fleeing into the night.

CHAPTER TWENTY-EIGHT

Ashley was still kneeling as her father made his way down from the platform, the microphone slipping carelessly from his hand, falling to the ground and causing a protesting whine of feedback from the speakers.

He hadn't got on well with his daughter for a long time, not since the death of Janet. When that had happened he had withdrawn into self-pity, and he and Ashley had spoken less and less. They seemed to clash every time they met, and eventually it was just too painful for the both of them. Although at first he had tried to talk to her adult to adult, she obviously despised him and would flounce off in a huff whenever he tried to discuss things. So eventually he had given up.

Eventually she had gone totally out of control, coming and going at all times of the day and night without a word of explanation. Her rebellion had been a source of deep disappointment and hurt to him, and he had responded in the only way he felt able, by withdrawing totally from her life and having as little to do with her as possible.

On the surface he had coped. But inside his heart had been broken at losing first his wife and then his daughter. The daughter who was the image of his wife, and who had been the joy of his life when she had been born into the world.

He remembered it clearly, and had never forgotten the miracle of her birth. She had meant everything to him, and he had loved her so. And as she grew, he knew that she had loved him in return. When he was working late, she would leave him a note on his pillow, filled with childish expressions of love. And he had replied with one for her to find when she awoke.

She had been the joy of his life. Until that awful day when Janet had died, and Ashley had turned totally away from him.

He had discovered that she was seeing a boy, under circumstances that were totally at odds with his Christian principles. And she had been taking drugs. He knew he hadn't acted very well in the situation. But he had been unable to prevent his terrible, destructive anger from exploding, leaving Ashley terrified and in tears.

They had gone their separate ways ever since, and their hearts had hardened towards each other, to such an extent that they had become irreconcilable. He had really believed that she hated him.

Until now.

Because at that instant, seeing him coming towards her, something inside Ashley broke. Chains fell from her imprisoned heart, and she felt again the freedom to love. Scrambling to her feet she ran to him, throwing her arms around his neck.

"Daddy, I'm so sorry." The tears coursed unchecked down her cheeks, her shoulders shaking uncontrollably as she sobbed in sorrow and despair. "I've been so hateful to you, so disobedient."

The father put his arms around his daughter and hugged her tightly. His voice was thick when he spoke. "It's all right, Ashley, it's all right." He kissed the top of her head. "Don't you know that I love you?" he whispered in a trembling voice. "Ashley, I've loved you all of your life."

And then he could pretend no longer. He didn't care about pride. He didn't care who knew, or who saw him fall apart. And so he wept, holding Ashley close to him. His own shoulders shook, as he forced broken words out through the torrent of tears.

"Forgive me for not showing you how much I love you. For being judgemental, when I should have been there to help you. I'm sorry that I never thought about the hurt in your life, only my own. And I missed your mum so much . . ." His speech dried up then, and he was unable to go on.

Sometimes, words get in the way, and this was such an occasion. So they clung together in a world of their own, oblivious to everything but the joy of filial love rekindled. Two hearts reconciled by the grace of God. A wayward and errant daughter reaching out to her father, seeking his love and forgiveness. And an absent and selfish father reaching out to his daughter, seeking her love and acceptance.

At last, reluctantly, almost as if she was afraid of loosing him now that she had found him again, she pulled gently away.

"There's something I need to do," she said, and she walked determinedly to the front of the church where Marcus stood amidst the wreck of the lectern, his mouth slack in disbelief.

"Pastor, how do I find God?" she asked desperately, but with a spark of hope in her tearful eyes. She sank to her knees at the front of the church, clasping her hands together and bowing her head.

Marcus felt such joy surge through him, as he went to the weeping young girl, kneeling alongside her and placing an arm protectively around her shoulders.

"Do you believe that Jesus is Lord?" he asked gently, "And that he died for you?"

She nodded, her head still bowed. "If . . . if he will have me," she cried brokenly.

Marcus hugged her tightly. "He loves you, Ashley. He wants you, if you will have him."

"What about me?" A contrite Steve Coleman, an altogether different Steve Coleman from the one who had been so angry just a few minutes earlier, was making his way down the aisle, to kneel alongside his daughter.

"I need the Lord too, Marcus," he said. "I've been in church all these years, but I have never made a personal confession of faith." He looked up, with a plea in his voice. "Forgive me, my friend. I've been living under the law, not under the grace of God. I've been trying to do things my own way, believing that my own efforts would be enough to get me into Heaven." He gestured helplessly with his hands. "My life has proved that trying to follow the rules doesn't work. There's nothing I can do to save myself, is there?" he concluded despairingly. Closing his eyes, he bowed his head alongside Ashley.

Then came the sound of the shuffling of many feet, and looking up, Marcus saw a large number of people moving forward, convicted of the emptiness and sinfulness of their own lives. Some had suddenly seen, that just like Steve and Ashley, they needed to make a personal confession of faith in Christ Jesus. Others saw with awful clarity that they had backslidden, and that their lives were a travesty. And they desperately wanted to get right with the God who loved them.

There was insufficient room for them all to come forward, so many stood right where they were, making their public confession of need.

But there *was* room for one more person at the front, and Emily shuffled her painful way forwards to fill the space alongside Ashley. "I don't want to live any more if this hateful world is all there is." She was unable to kneel, but she bowed her head, placing one hand on Ashley's shoulder. "I don't know this God you speak of, but if he is even half what you say he is, I know I want him. I know I need him, in my life."

Marcus deliriously praised God in his heart. Could there be anything more wonderful, he thought?

"Do you believe that Jesus is the Son of God, that he was crucified for your sins, raised from the dead and that he now rules and reigns in the heavens?" he asked gently.

The Coleman's simultaneously said they did, and Emily too whispered her agreement. There was a corresponding rumble of assent from those standing in the body of the church.

"If you confess with your mouth that Jesus is Lord, and believe in your heart that he was raised from the dead, then you will be saved."

Then a great song of joy arose from the angels packing the church. A hymn of praise, winging its way to the throne of God and filling that place of worship with the fragrance of Jesus.

Because many dearly loved and precious souls had come home at last. For all eternity.

The church family sat silently in their seats, their hearts strangely warmed by the most amazing act of reconciliation and salvation they had ever experienced in their lives. There was not a dry eye in that place as they saw the salvation of their God. And they worshiped in awe and praise.

God had promised in Holy Scripture. "I will change your hearts. I will give you a heart of flesh instead of a heart of stone." In a most amazing way he had done just that with Emily, and Ashley and Steve Coleman in full view of his assembled people. And now it was the turn of that congregation to have their hearts changed.

En-masse they began to turn one to another, hesitatingly at first, but then with increasing confidence as they found their advances, far from being rebuffed as they had feared, were welcomed with equal openness. Soon, they were hugging and shaking hands. Those who had not spoken for many years chatted quietly together. Differences were resolved, forgotten and considered of no-account as bitterness was dissolved. Broken relationships were dramatically mended. Old arguments and dissension was swept away on the wings of the Spirit as he reclaimed his church.

A sense of the peace of God swept quietly through them. There was no shouting. No overt exclamations of joy. No exultations. Just a deep and overwhelming knowledge that Hartwood Community Church was once again a community. The once riven body of Christ in that place was healed and restored, every member re-united in the knowledge that each one of them was an essential and needed part of the whole. And for that moment at least, sin was conquered. Love had won!

Magnificent horses were ready, snorting and tramping at the ground in their impatience to do battle, their breath white and vaporous in the crystal clear air. The armies of heaven dressed in fine linen, white and clean were massed and waiting. And all were glorified and shining bright as the sun, their weapons sparkling in the light of God's presence. There were swords and spears, longbows of gold slung across broad angel backs. Arrows gleamed in their quivers, and shields emblazoned with the sign of the Lamb, were slung across their arms.

Their numbers were as the stars in the sky. They stretched across the heavens, row upon row, battalion upon battalion. Waiting for the trumpet call of God.

And then an angel, who appeared to be standing in the sun shouted out. Loud and clear, his voice reaching to the ends of the earth.

"Hallelujah!
For our Lord God Almighty reigns.
Let us rejoice and be glad
and give him glory!"

As the power of God rippled around the church, Billy put a hand to his jacket pocket, suddenly overwhelmed with the conflicting emotions of guilt and astonishment. Astonishment at what God was doing. Things that he had never seen in his life, and as far as he knew, neither had anyone else. Guilt when he remembered the note from Marie that she had given him during the Sunday morning service. He had totally forgotten about it. Not that he had intended to do anything with it. He didn't really believe in such things as a word from God. Or at least he hadn't up to now. But recent events had changed his theological position somewhat. Having witnessed for himself the remarkable reality of God's power, he was prepared, in principle at least, to believe that the Lord could do anything.

As he read the note again, he felt a strange emotion welling up in him. One that he was not used to. He prided himself that he was essentially a pragmatic man, not given to outbursts of emotionalism. He was the one who kept cool, who kept logical whilst others got all hot and excited about things. It was that tendency to remain detached from unhelpful feelings that had helped him make rational choices over the many years that he had been in business.

But as he re-read the message that Marie believed was from God, he felt a love for her that he had never before experienced. He felt strangely gratified that she should share that precious word with him.

"Jeremiah 20:9" the note said. Billy picked up his Bible and checked the verse, before walking over to Marcus, who was sitting silently at the front, his head buried in his hands.

He shuffled his feet for a moment, not sure whether he should be intruding into what was obviously a reverent moment.

But Marcus raised his head, and smiled. "Sit down old friend," he said. "What a time. What a time." And he shook his head in wonderment, looking on the verge of tears once again.

Billy grinned hugely in return. "You can say that again. Look, I don't know how relevant this is, but Marie gave it to me on Sunday morning. She said it was a word from the Lord, but . . ." He trailed off, embarrassed. Then, these things had seemed so far fetched. Mere deceptions for the gullible. Today—well today was different . . .

"What is God saying?" Marcus didn't question that God had spoken. That much at least he had learned from his time spent on the carpet.

"I'll read the verse," said Billy, picking up his Bible and doing exactly that.

"It's from Jeremiah twenty, verse nine." He cleared his throat.

> "But if I say, 'I will not mention him
> or speak any more in his name,'
> his word is in my heart like a fire,
> a fire shut up in my bones . . ."

He finished reading, and saw that Marcus was shaking. "Are you okay?" He was concerned that perhaps he had done the wrong thing in bringing the reading.

Marcus pulled himself together with an effort. Billy had just confirmed the word that God had placed in his heart. That *he* was calling someone to be his Jeremiah Man. He didn't yet know who it was. But God had a man in mind. Someone who would be revealed when the time was right. A man with fire in his bones! And by his grace, God had given that very reading to Marie to authenticate, if indeed he needed to, his word.

"I'm fine, Billy. Thanks for that word. You really have no idea. But it has confirmed beyond any doubt, something that God has spoken to me."

Billy was ecstatic. Never had he imagined that God would demonstrate his love and power in such a dramatic way. He had seen a father and a daughter reconciled. He had witnessed God use that to open the hearts of his people. A seemingly inconsequential act between Emily and Ashley Coleman, and then Ashley and her father had been used by an omnipotent God to melt the hard hearts of his church. And now God had brought a word via Marie, to confirm something that God had laid on Marcus' heart.

It was heady stuff, and Billy sat down, beaming brightly at all around him. At any other time, people would have wondered what on earth had happened to him. But there were so many people with glows that no one noticed. He was just one among many, swallowed up in the crowd of God's blessed people.

CHAPTER TWENTY-NINE

The rear yard of the police station was jam packed with vehicles. Fourteen seater riot vans with wire mesh covering their windows vied for space with dog vans, their occupants already sensing the mood and barking excitedly. The plain, dark coloured four by fours of the tactical firearms unit were also in evidence, along with traffic cars in their Battenberg cake livery and a myriad of other vehicles of uncertain pedigree.

"Looks like the cavalry has arrived at last," said Jack.

"Better late than never," opined Pat, trying to sound strong but in reality still very much rattled.

"We'd better park outside," said Tony practically, "else we'll get trapped in."

Rob was unusually quiet.

They parked a short distance away on the main road, and entered the police station, met by the overpowering smell of hot dogs and coffee.

"At least MILDU is efficient," said Jack, referring to the Major Incident and Logistics Unit responsible for organisation at all major incidents. Their job was to sort out food, vehicles and equipment, arrange sufficient units to be deployed, as well as standing down officers for a rest during long running incidents and providing others to take their place.

They snatched a hot-dog and coffee, and Jack joined the ranking police officers in the briefing room whilst the other three wandered off to find out what information they could.

The briefing officer, a Support-Unit Inspector wearing a black hood-over scrunched around his neck, matching overalls and high-sided, steel toe-capped boots, looked up and acknowledged Jack as he slipped quietly into the room. He continued with his briefing;

"We don't know what the trigger was for tonight's disturbances, but someone is behind it. It does not *seem* to be a random, sporadic event. More a planned occasion I would say." The SU Inspector continued. "We have no idea what this is in aid of, or what group is involved. But what we do know is that the place is fast becoming a heap of burning rubble, and the crazies who did it are still out there. Early estimates are that there are well over a thousand people on the rampage. We have mutual aid on the way from neighbouring Forces, but 'till they arrive it's all down to us."

There was a rumble of apprehension from the assembled officers.

The SU Inspector nodded grimly. "It's time we sorted this out. If you report to the MILDU Commander, you will get your orders as to where and when to deploy. Remember, we need to contain it as much as we can until help arrives. No heroics. Keep in radio contact at all times, those boys out there are not messing around."

There came the deafening sound of the scraping of a hundred chairs as the officers stood en-masse.

"Before you go . . ." The Inspector raised his hand. "Let me remind you that three of our men are in hospital, one on life-support. Their van was overturned and they were dragged out and set upon by a whole bunch of these thugs. They were lucky to escape with their lives. We don't want any more casualties. Take care!"

―――――――――――――――――――――

When the police went in, they went in hard. Support-Units were deployed at either end of the High Street, spreading across its entire width with their long shields interlocked, effectively blocking it to any-one entering or trying to exit. Behind them were the snatch squads, equipped with small, circular shields and "ASP" extending metal batons. Their protective helmets were firmly strapped on, visors down. Three foot "Arnold" batons were in the hands of the front line of shield bearers and they meant business.

Crunching broken glass and rubble underfoot, they trudged deter-minedly towards each other in a pincer movement, trapping the rioters between them.

Every now and then the line would stop; the snatch squad would dart through, take hold of rioters and drag them back behind the wall of shields. And they were none too gentle as they did it, mindful of their colleagues who were presently undergoing surgery in the hospital.

Captives were handcuffed and quickly bundled into waiting vans under the watchful eyes of officers detailed as gaolers. Not all were arrested. Some managed to flee in the melee, but they would have several lumps and bruises to remind them that they had been in a fight.

But it seemed a hopeless task. For every person arrested, two more seemed to fill the vacant gap. And of course the police lines were depleting in exact proportion to the number of officers who were dragging arrested rioters away.

Under normal circumstances, they could have been left in the prison busses, but there were just too many, and the vehicles were quickly overflowing with their human cargo. And on top of that, rioters were now mounting a determined assault on those prison busses, threatening to rescue the prisoners that had been won at such a cost.

It was a long, weary night of battle. Rocks, bricks and glass, metal and other ammunition was flung relentlessly at the advancing ranks of police. Most of the projectiles bounced off the shields, but even so the impact was substantial, and injuries invariably resulted. Officers were carried at regular intervals from the battle-lines, with injuries to head or limb.

A shield splintered in the front line ahead. Another became a wall of fire as a flaming bottle filled with petrol was flung from the crowd. And always, in the background was the glare and the heat of the burning buildings, and the acridness of the smoke that filled the eyes and stung the throat with choking pain.

Behind the serried ranks of shields came the fire-fighters, attacking the fires as soon as space had been cleared of fighting, screaming rioters. Water under pressure jetted high into the night sky, as they struggled with hoses in the impossible conditions.

Visibility reduced drastically as the water hit the fire, causing white hot steam to rise, hissing angrily into the air. But it was a never ending task. As soon as one fire was quenched, the flames of another leapt upwards into the darkness, stoked by the seemingly tireless mob.

Marcus knew that something big was about to happen. He could sense it in his Spirit. And he knew that the church had its part to play in God's scenario. He now knew what God wanted them to do. He was sure of it. He wasn't really surprised. Nothing he felt, could surprise him now.

He sought out Billy. "Billy, get a dozen or so people together—include James and his guitar. We're going to take God's presence out onto the High Street." He held up a hand as he saw a question forming on Billy's lips. "Don't even ask. I know it's late, I know it sounds irresponsible and crazy. But I also know that it is God's leading, so just do it. Speak to Marie. She's the organiser. We need the rest of the church praying back here, and if she can work miracles, get some of the local churches to join in if she can raise anyone at this unearthly hour!"

It was all very well believing in God's leading in the safety of the church. But neither Marcus nor any of his worship group was ready for what confronted them as they left the building and headed into town.

Inside, they had been protected. Wrapped up in the wonder of what God had been doing, they were totally unaware of the fury that was raging outside. The smell and taste of burning was sharp and bitter in the nose and on the tongue as they walked in the night air. A pall of black smoke, illuminated by the full moon and looking to all appearances like a huge night cloud, could clearly be seen covering the sky above Hartwood. Centring in an elongated shape directly above the High Street, it was lazily drifting out in a rolling plume towards the east, assisted on its course by the wind that drove behind.

It was the noise that was the most frightening. At least until they saw the maddened mob, who were hidden from view at that moment by the buildings separating them from the scene of the riot. None of them had ever heard such screams and shrieks. There was a roar in the air, a roar of anger and demonic destruction and their hearts grew fearful within them.

"Marcus, do you think this is wise?" queried James, his voice wavering as he spoke. He glanced at the two young girls walking alongside them. "Look at Emily, she can only just walk. And Ashley. Aren't we putting them in danger here?"

Marcus was undecided then. He had thought he knew what he was doing. But what if he were wrong? Surely God was not asking them all to walk into such danger? The more he thought about it, the more idiotic it seemed. More than idiotic—it was irresponsible. He knew he would be severely criticised by the authorities, and worst of all by the parents if things went wrong. Without realising it he began to slow his pace until the group was at a standstill, his faith in the calling of God and the rationalistic call of his mind fighting against each other.

A band of angels with drawn swords surrounded them, holding back the demons seeking to whisper doubt and fear into their minds.

The angel Serafina spoke comfort into the heart of the pastor. Reminding him of the promises of God. Encouraging the mustard seed of faith that burned in his breast, and yet which so easily wavered in the face of adversity.

He quoted sacred Scripture, the living Word of God that had a power all of its own. "Marcus," he said, "remember the promise." And he quoted. "'For no matter how many promises God has made, they are 'yes' in Christ.'"

At those words, the fearful pastor felt the surge of the Holy Spirit once more within him. "Yes!" he shouted, causing the others to look at him with startled eyes. "The promises of God," he explained. "They are all 'yes' in Jesus!" He began to pick up speed, his faltering a thing of the past. The prayers of the angels and the implanting of the Word into his heart had stirred him to his very depths.

"Come on," he said encouragingly, "God is with us. He won't let us down. James—get strumming. Guys—get singing. Ashley, help Emily. Let's show the inhabitants of hell that Jesus reigns in this place!"

It was Jack who saw, or rather heard them first. A group of respectable looking men and women standing in a group on the pavement. And two young teenaged girls, one of them with a walking stick. A bearded man was playing a guitar. And they were bloody singing!

He stared unbelievingly. How had they got through the police lines? And what did these fruit cakes think they were doing? Here they were in the middle of the worst riot ever seen in the UK, and they were holding a sing-along.

He strained his ears. It was even worse than he thought. They seemed to be holding a church service.

"Sir!" He shouted at the SU Inspector above the roar of the fighting and the shouting of the officers as they fought to control the situation that was rapidly getting out of control. There was no immediate response. "Sir!" He screamed at the top of his voice and waved his hands wildly to attract attention. The Inspector looked across, then followed the direction in which Jack was pointing. His face contorted in disbelief as he too spotted the religious maniacs singing on the street corner.

He came jogging across, holding his shield by his side. "What on earth, Jack?"

"Don't ask me. But we have to get them out of here or they will be toast as soon as the mob spots them." He scanned the vicinity urgently. Large groups of apparently drunken men were still hurling rocks at the police lines, smashing shop front windows, overturning any cars that hadn't already been trashed, setting fresh fires and shouting vitriolic abuse with all their might.

"I'm surprised that they haven't seen them yet."

"We'll take a deployment of men in with the large shields, box them in and get them out. Irresponsible I call it. Not only are they putting themselves at risk, but my officers too."

"Amen to that," said Jack, unaware of the irony of the remark, and the Inspector who did, frowned.

"I think we should provide a distraction first," continued Jack. "If you send in a group of your men to the other end of the High Street ostensibly to make some arrests, that should lure the crazies to you and we can get in quick and get the holy rollers out before they realise what's happening."

The Inspector nodded, and ran off to talk to a squad of heavily protected support-unit officers. There was a flurry of activity—then they disappeared down a side street, emerging several minutes later at the far end of the road.

When they went in, they made sure everyone knew they were coming. Whooping and banging their shields in Zulu fashion with their "Arnold" batons, they were a terrifying sight as they ran down the street. And as predicted, the mob turned on them with shouts of hatred, more and more of them pouring from every direction, heading for the enemy in blue.

At the opposite end of the street, twelve support-unit officers darted out from behind a protective row of shields, running towards the group of singers, and Jack went out with them, oblivious to the fact that he had no shield and no protective helmet.

There were around a dozen in all, and as the officers approached they could clearly hear the words of the song. Against his will, Jack found himself listening.

> In the armour of God we stand,
> The battle not ours, but the Lord's.
> We fight not against flesh and blood,
> And the battle belongs to our God.

He shouted, not so much to be heard, but to drown out the words that were having a peculiar effect on him. They were haunting, powerful even, in a strangely compelling way. Not that he would admit that for one minute, especially to himself.

"Listen you lot, your heavenly armour won't protect you one little bit if this mob gets their hands on you," shouted Jack above the sound of their singing. "You should be ashamed of yourselves too, bringing youngsters out into a desperate situation like this. Whatever were you thinking?"

The group smiled benignly, infuriatingly at him. The large guitar player continued to strum, and the rest continued to sing.

When the enemy comes in like a flood,
The Lord will raise up a standard,
And by his blood,
The battle belongs to our God.

Jack turned to the officers behind him. "Get around this lot with the shields boys, then let's get out of here before we all end up in either the nut house or the hospital."

The support-unit moved into position, surrounding the saints of God with their shields. And at that very moment a lump of paving stone crashed into their wall of defence, hurled from the other side of the street with amazing force and strength.

The front row of officers fell back, as further missiles began to rain down on them, some going over the top of the shields and narrowly missing the still singing Christians huddled inside.

"Cover," shouted the sergeant, and immediately the back row of officers ran into the centre, lifting their shields to form a roof, sliding them into place against those at the front to provide a defence against the airborne missiles.

Jesus, we worship and adore you,
we lift up your name in all the earth,
our hearts burn with passion for you, Son of God
we pray that you would fan the flame.
You are the power and the glory,
 wonderful Lord, Majesty.
Celestial fire eternal,
you rule and reign eternally.

Jack rounded on them furiously. "Can't you shut up for just a moment?" He glared at them, and for the first time actually *looked* at them. At their faces, at them as people, not just as a group of odd people.

Church-goers had always seemed to him to be elderly, the women usually with funny hats. And they were invariably odd. Not like normal people at all. Different, but in a weird way.

And this lot were different all right. There were two young girls; goodness knows what their parents had for brains allowing them to be in a danger zone at this time of night. They couldn't have been more than sixteen. And yet one of them was gazing unflinchingly at him with the most piercing blue eyes he had ever seen. He tried to hold her gaze, but couldn't, and he eventually turned his head away angrily.

Straight into the compassionate face of an elderly man leaning on a walking stick.

"Don't be afraid son," he said.

Jack rounded on the old saint, who had the glint of fire dancing in his eyes. Whether it was a reflection from the blaze that surrounded them on all sides, or whether it was something altogether supernatural was unclear. He was strangely challenged, but resisted the implications of Henry's words. "Listen you old fool," he began, but was interrupted by the rumble of falling masonry and the warning shout from the Fire Chief, who had darted out from behind the police lines.

"Get out from there you guys, some of these building are about to go. The fires have weakened them so that there's not much holding them up right now."

The PSU sergeant took over. "Right, move *now*." He pushed them roughly forward, and the officers surrounding them broke into a jog, forcing everyone to move with them at a fast pace.

In the melee and unnoticed by the group, the old man fell, rolling outside the protective ring of shields, his stick flying from his hand as he went down heavily.

At that precise moment, a brick thrown from the crowd struck his head with a dull thudding sound, and he rolled over once and lay still, a rivulet of blood running from his forehead and soaking into the dry ground.

The momentum of the shield protected group carried them onwards, oblivious to what had happened.

Hearing a shout, Jack stepped nimbly outside the moving cordon of shields and checked behind him, from where the shout had come.

"Henry!" A huge man in civilian clothing, totally devoid of protective kit, ignored the fast moving bodies and the hail of missiles that were immediately launched at his unprotected figure, and ran through the police lines towards a fallen man. It was the old religious man, and he was laying unmoving in the road.

Jack instinctively flinched as a large rock stuck the man's chest, and another hail of smaller missiles enveloped him. He must surely have been hurt, but he didn't even break his stride as he stooped, caught hold of the old man around the waist as though he weighed nothing at all, and cradled him protectively in his arms as he carried him to safety.

Jack recognised the looming bear like figure, though the combination of smoke and darkness had reduced visibility to virtually nil. It was Peter Lewis.

Then Jack too, dashed for safety, increasing his pace as further hails of rock and concrete fell on him. Looking ahead, he breathed a sigh of relief as he saw that the church group had almost made it back. For a moment, it seemed as though they would crash into the wall of police shields stretched across the street, but at the last second a row at the front pivoted open like a double-doorway, and they fell through, stumbling and panting to safety.

Back behind the police lines, Jack made his way to the command point, where the Fire Chief was deep in conversation with the PSU Inspector.

"We aren't making a dent on this fire," he said. "We can't get water close enough with these loonies chucking rocks and burning everything in sight. We're going to have to withdraw unless you can do something. But if we do, soon there will be nothing left of the town to worry about."

"What do you suggest?" asked the Inspector with deep sarcasm, "We've got every available officer from across the county here, and it's hard going just trying to contain this lot, let alone arrest sufficient numbers to clear the area for you."

"Can we help?" It was the slim man with glasses from the religious group, still looking out of breath from the unaccustomed exertion.

The Fire Chief looked away in embarrassment, whilst the Inspector spoke in a manner he hoped was both firm, and diplomatic.

"Mr . . . ?"

"Call me Marcus. I'm the pastor of Hartwood Community Church just on the edge of the town." He held out his hand, but the Inspector ignored it.

"Thank you for your offer and I respect your belief, but singing won't get us very far in this situation. We're having to call up support from neighbouring police forces, because we are fast running out of men. Quite a few have been injured and have had to withdraw. Some have been hospitalised. So you will understand if I don't share your little groups' enthusiasm for hymns at this time."

He turned to walk away.

"I wasn't thinking of songs, sergeant."

"Inspector. I'm an Inspector," he retorted impatiently, pointing at the pips on his shoulder. He immediately regretted it, wondering why on earth he felt he had to justify his position to a crank.

"Sorry, Inspector. But we can help. Or at least God can. We are the visible presence of God's people on these streets. I'm sure he can sort all this out. And of course he made fire. In fact he *is* fire according to the scriptures so I'm confident that he can deal with that too."

The Inspector shook his head despairingly and walked away to confer with his unit, muttering bad temperedly under his breath.

Marcus called the group over. "Ashley, Emily, Henry, Phil." He checked around him for the others. "Steve, Michael, James—all of you. We need God in this situation. If ever there was a time for spiritual warfare, this is it."

"Michael—get on your mobile and alert the prayer warriors back at church. I believe that there are strong demonic powers manifesting here. We need all available believers to plead before God to deal with the evil controlling the rioters or there will be nothing left of our town."

Michael flipped open his phone. "Are you sure?"

Marcus was. "God is going before us. We mustn't be afraid," he said encouragingly.

"Where's Henry?" It was Michael who noticed that the old man was missing, covering the mouthpiece of his mobile phone whilst he asked the question.

They looked around but there was no sign of him.

"Steve—go and track him down will you. He's probably cornered some young policemen and spreading the Word!"

Steve trotted off on his errand. Even amidst the fear he was amused at the prospect.

Michael closed his phone with a snap. "You won't believe this," he said, looking at the expectant faces flushed with faith. "Well, perhaps you will," he said. "I've just got through to Marie who is co-ordinating the prayer response back at church." He paused in wonder. "I don't know what's going on, but the whole of Hartwood is praying. Not just our lot. But every church!"

"All of them?" asked Marcus.

"All! There's more praying going on than you can shake a stick at!" said Michael triumphantly.

A cheer went up from the small prayer group, and thus encouraged they stood in a semi-circle, lifting their hearts to God, pleading with him to glorify his name in that place. They prayed fervently, powerfully, tearfully, and the anguish of the intercessor showed in each tired and dirty face.

Several prayed softly in tongues, the language of the Spirit that reached up into the spiritual realms. Into the throne room of the creator of heaven and earth.

One or two police officers regarded them curiously, but they had more than enough to do, keeping the maddened rioters at bay.

The trees that had surrounded her in all her dreams for so long suddenly gave way to a clearing. And she didn't want to see what was there. Because instinctively she knew that it was something terrible. The sum of all her fears.

There was a presence. She knew then that the corruption she had felt coming near had finally arrived. Something soulless. But more than that. Here was flesh and blood. Or at least the remnant of it in the form of a solitary figure standing under an old oak tree. A young man. She wept in fear as she saw that the figure was not standing. He was in fact hanging, a cord tight around his neck.

Then the screaming started in earnest as the figure turned towards her, and Brenda Marney saw that she was in the presence of Nathan Mahoney, her long dead son.

CHAPTER Thirty

Emily Bowman was reciting, leaning painfully against a wall as she did so. At first in a small, nervous voice that no-one noticed above the roar of the fire and the scream of the crowds. But as it grew stronger, forceful, powerful, as she was carried along by the Spirit of God, they heard her.

She was a young girl who had only just come to the Lord. And the goose bumps stood along the length of Marcus' arms and crawled across his scalp as he heard her speak directly from the scriptures that she had never learnt. A perfect rendition from the scriptures that she had never read. Words that could only have been placed into her heart by the direct implantation of a loving God.

"If my people, who are called by my name, will humble themselves and pray and seek my face and turn from their wicked ways, then will I hear from heaven and will forgive their sin and will heal their land."

And God's people were doing just that. Never was there such an outpouring of confession, of forgiveness and contrition, as borne along by the outpouring of a Pentecostal fire, their hearts burned within them with the fear of the knowledge of God.

Across Hartwood, in every magnificent church, church hall, gospel hall and lowly church building, hundreds upon hundreds of Christians prayed, empowered by the Holy Spirit. Crying out to God for their nation and their community. Overcome by the sheer emanation of the glory of God, many fell on their faces, weeping and calling on the Lord to heal their land and save the people.

Marcus was overwhelmed with amazement. Lord, he thought, only you could bring a young girl to salvation, inspire her to brave dangerous streets to bring your presence to the heart of a lost people, and then equip her to speak a prophetic word—all in a single night!

In the smoke filled High Street, Steve Coleman returned to the group. His face was drawn and anxious. "They've taken Henry," he said, his voice quivering. "The ambulance has taken Henry. He was hit by a rock, and he's not too good."

He placed his arm around Ashley and hugged her tightly. They stood in silence for a moment and wept, sending up silent prayers for the old warrior. No words were necessary. And they could not have vocalised their feelings anyway, their hearts were too full.

James began to strum on his guitar. His voice was faltering, his hair blowing in the breeze like smoke on the mountain top. And his eyes blazed with the power of God as he began to sing. And even the police nearby stopped, and stared, lifting their visors and wiping the sweat of conflict from their brows.

> "Jesus, be the centre of my life
> My hope, when all around me falls
> Jesus, be the fire in my heart
> Jesus, be the reason that I live."

As James came to the end of his song, there was a moment of silence. A deep, intense quiet. It was much more than just the absence of sound; it was the profound sense of the presence and the peace of God. The peace that is beyond all human understanding, as the beauty of the Lord came near and touched them. In the very centre, in the very midst of the sound and the fury, God stooped to bless and encourage his people.

And as they gloried reverently in that perfect moment of time, God answered the fervent prayers of his church.

In the heavenlies, the trumpets sounded, and the massed armies of the heavenly host responded to the call of the Spirit, reacting to the prayers of the saints. Before the throne room of God, four living creatures and twenty-four elders fell down in worship. Each one was holding golden bowls full of incense, and they were the prayers of the saints. And the bowls were full, overflowing!

A mighty angel lifted them above his head, and they were emptied, the prayers flowing in golden rivers of praise, the sweetness of the incense filling heaven. And everywhere was the sound of praise to the Most High. Angelic voice after angelic voice sang out in worship, until it seemed that even heaven itself could not contain the joyous sound that went up unceasingly.

Aanfial, the captain of God's army with Talial close behind, rode down on magnificent white horses, with legion upon legion of angels following in their wake, their robes white and glorified as they descended to the earth. Their swords flashed with Holy fire as they engaged the darkness that had taken root for so long.

And holy fear struck the demons as they heard the trumpet call of God.

Like a wave pounding against the shore, the legions of light came in like a flood, overwhelming the canker of evil with irresistible, magnificent glory, power and majesty.

Talial, huge and terrifying as he sat astride his horse, unleashed arrow after golden arrow from an inexhaustible supply, cutting down countless demons as they fled in fear.

Aanfial, not to be outdone swung his mighty sword with equal accuracy and precision, tearing boldly into the very centre of the massed hordes of darkness, scattering them before him like so much chaff on the wind in his unstoppable wrath.

No evil, no darkness could stand before the forces of the one true and mighty God, and they were routed from one end of the town to the other, falling in their tens of thousands under the relentless, remorseless, destructive power of the armies of the Lord.

The ripple of power swept across the United Kingdom, and men in the very act of committing heinous crimes stopped in their tracks, terrified as the might of God fell upon them. The awesome power, spreading out in concentric circles from the epicentre in insignificant Hartwood, caused the demons that possessed them to fall away in confusion and dread.

Freed from the demonic chains that bound them, fearful men ran unthinkingly, unknowingly, unaware of what was happening. Driven only by an inner, unacknowledged desire to escape the all-seeing gaze of the Creator of all heaven and earth. Confronted in their hearts by the King of kings and Lord of lords, evil men called aloud for the very rocks to fall upon them and hide them from the wrath of him who sits upon the throne.

Jack and his colleagues saw none of this. But what they saw and heard struck fear into their hearts. Because suddenly, the deluge started, and they ran for shelter. As the roar of wind, water and thunder assaulted their senses with mind numbing volume, shields were cast to one side, stretchers were dropped unceremoniously to the ground, and hoses were abandoned as the emergency services withdrew in great and undignified haste.

"Run to high ground," shouted the PSU Inspector to the silent group of prayer warriors, as he took his own advice, but they had either not heard him as the roaring wind snatched his words away, or they had chosen not to respond.

For now rain began to fall in earnest. No just the usual winter's rain. Not English drizzle, not sleet nor hail even. But a torrent, a mighty outpouring as the windows of heaven opened and gave up their waters. And those waters fell in a great Noahadic deluge. Filling the river Marr flowing alongside the ancient town, which finally burst its banks and mingled with the rain, whipped to foam by the fearsome wind driving it onwards in an almighty mass of liquid fury that crashed to the earth like the pounding of the great oceans against the rocks.

The fires that had ravaged in the shops and buildings were extinguished in an instant of time, as the tsunami of water flowed through the High Street, towering above the department stores and supermarkets, sweeping the terrified rioters from their feet and sucking them under its unfathomable depths before they had even time to scream.

Occasionally a hand would appear above the surface of the tidal wave, clutching at the air in vain as the repositories of satanic evil tried to save themselves. But it was too late.

And still it rolled on, a mighty breaker, roaring in its foam-flecked fury, hurtling through the streets and sweeping away everything in its path before dissipating outside Hartwood. Then, and only then did the outpouring of rain stop, and the river level stabilise. Suddenly, completely, as if it had been turned off at its source.

After the roaring of the elements, the silence that now descended was total and unnerving. Adding a poignant emphasis to the abrupt absence of sound, there came the warble of a bird that could be clearly heard against the backdrop of stillness. The grey clouds parted, and a ray of sun beamed down, touching the earth below in its enveloping warmth and light.

The police, fire and ambulance personnel just stood, confused both by what had just occurred, and the eerie silence that had fallen across the decimated ruin that had once been their town. There was no sign of the rioters. All had gone. Vanished without trace beneath the vengeful waves. The water too had gone. But strangely, so had the bodies. They were nowhere to be seen. And every fire was quenched

A conundrum that would exercise scientific minds for some time, would be the question as to how countless tons of water could fall in such a short moment of time, burst the river, and then flow away without the slightest damage, death or injury other than to the rioters and the property in the immediate location of the High Street. And where had all the bodies gone? For they were never found. It was as though they had not just been dragged beneath the torrent, but had totally ceased to exist.

But that was a conundrum to be pondered later. For now, that was not the uppermost thought of anyone.

Jack searched for the prayer group, fearing the worst. He looked around frantically, before he saw them. He should have been astonished he knew, but for some reason in a world that seemed to have tipped upside down and turned totally insane, it seemed perfectly logical to see them untouched by the flood. The fact that they were kneeling perfectly safe in the middle of the street on the only patch of dry ground within a mile of ground-zero devastation area, was just one more crazy thing in a world that increasingly resembled a lunatic asylum. As they knelt, their heads were bowed low to the ground as they worshipped their God. Lost in wonder, love and praise.

Jack had to will his feet to move forward, and it took every ounce of his strength. He was finding it hard to move, and his legs were refusing to cooperate. He staggered finally, like a drunken man alongside the small group of Christians who had now risen to their feet and were watching him.

As he got nearer, gentle hands reached out and held him, preventing him from falling headlong into the lake of mud that had once been a block-paved pedestrian walkway.

He had to force the broken words out, his voice thick and dry. He no longer felt anger. There was no trace of his earlier contempt. He no longer felt embarrassed at these church people who had dared to offer prayer in the midst of a war zone.

"I am afraid," he whispered. "Help me."

CHAPTER Thirty-One

CHRISTMAS EVE

Daylight was beginning to appear as the police helicopter flew above the ravaged town of Hartwood like a circling vulture, its propeller blades rhythmically thumping the air.

"Well I've never seen anything like it." Civvy pilot Julian Shew adjusted his headphones, and spoke into the mike attached to his helmet. He descended fifty metres, and in the light of the emerging dawn, the true extent of the devastation was unfolding. He eased further back into his seat, his burgeoning paunch thrusting forward petulantly as he did so. At fifty years of age, the veteran of numerous incidents both in the police and the army, he thought he had seen it all. But he clearly hadn't. He was shocked at what he saw below.

The town centre High Street had almost entirely disappeared. All that was left was rubble. A Beirut bombsite. The debris of what had once been the life, the hub of a community was now strewn across a water logged landscape as if flung carelessly aside by a giant hand.

Although Hartwood was very middle-class, it had its problems. There always had been a shortage of certain jobs, some homelessness. The usual group of embittered, aimless and disaffected humanity without structure or purpose in life.

But everything paled into insignificance when measured against the mass destruction displayed in panoramic view below. The flames had been quenched, but the stench of destruction still hung in the air. The grey carcasses of the few buildings that did remain were now just the relics of what once had been. Forlorn and broken like rows of rotten teeth waiting to be extracted.

Now there would be no jobs here, no shops to buy anything, no hope, no future. All because of the fires and the flood. For years to come, alongside the scientists who would desperately try to clarify it, would be sociologist's trying to give an explanation. Why had it happened? And what were the circumstances that had ignited this tragedy, this mindless rebellion?

The observer in the 'copter was Pc Lindsey Pittman, a woman in her early thirties.

"This is what comes of living in a liberal welfare country," she intoned acidly. "If we hung the murderers and perverts, locked up the scroats and the parasites and told the bleeding hearts to bugger off, we wouldn't have this problem."

Shew stared at her incredulously. "You're serious?"

"Too right. If I had my way I'd cut all social benefit for the work-shy scroungers and put them to work. Why should they sleep in bed all morning and drink themselves stupid all night at the tax payers' expense?"

"That kind of policy would have prevented this you think?" asked Shew thoughtfully.

"I reckon. They were probably all tanked up on booze and drugs courtesy of the dole!"

The pilot shook his head sadly and turned his attention back to the scene of destruction.

Below, the mass of police vehicles were beginning to move off, throwing up a wall of spray as they scythed through the remaining pools of water that had not yet drained away. They were followed by the fire engines and the ambulances, leaving behind the silent, water-logged acres of dirt. There was nothing else that they could do just now . . .

———————————————————

Across the far side of Hartwood in a secret place, there was pandemonium. Less than five-hundred demons were huddled together in the deep cave in the hillside where once there had been countless thousands, and they were all in shock. Devastated both by what they had just encountered at the hands of the army of the Lord and terrorised at the sight of the great Bar-Lgura who was incandescent with rage, their demoralisation and defeat was total.

The chief demon's eyes were maroon with anger; the depths of which were clearly indicated by the walls within the cave, which were deeply scarred where he had ravaged them in unrestrained fury with razor-sharp talons. Demons lurked as far out of reach as possible, fearing to venture near, less they too be subject to similar treatment.

"You wretched horde," he bellowed, "what did you do to arouse the enemy before we had accomplished our task? It was too soon, we were not yet ready. The church was sleeping, and all you had to do was steal away their souls from under their very noses."

He did not wait for an answer, but leapt forward, reaping the air with his merciless claws. In a single swipe, dozens of demons were sent prematurely to the pit as he cleaved them through, leaving a noxious smell of sulphur in the vacated space where once they had cowered.

The remnant cringed back, not daring to make a reply as he glared menacingly at them, his gaze tearing through the depths of their black hearts.

"How do I report this back to the master?" he hissed. "How?"

One pathetic demon was unable to stop from venturing a squeaked reply. Too late he regretted that he had done so, as he was plucked from his place by a scabrous hand that held him at arms length in a grip that slowly squeezed the life from him.

The great demon-lord gazed at the pitiful demon of betrayal with unblinking, baleful eyes, undecided whether to let the pathetic creature speak, or whether he should crush him like a withered leaf. Perhaps he would do both.

"Speak!" he commanded in a voice like the rattle of gravel against tin.

Amduscias whimpered, forcing out the words from a chest that was threatening to cave in under the force of pressure that encircled him. "I have heard that an angel named Talial is here. That he is . . ."

Those were his dying words.

For at the mention of his ancient enemy a spasm came over Bar Lgura's entire body, and he involuntarily closed his hand, crushing the sobbing imp in an instant of time. The demon who had been unable to resist a final act of betrayal, had betrayed his last.

His exterminator indifferently wiped the matter that had once been Amduscias from his horned hand, and roared his defiance with a bellow of hate and anger, his rasping words hanging like venomous barbs in the chill air. "When *he* is destroyed, I shall return for all of *you*. Of that you can be sure."

He took off, his mind exploding in a paroxysm of rage. His great wings flapped powerfully, and the veins stood out like cords across his colossal arms. In the might of his up-draught, demons were flung from their feet like so many rag-dolls, coming to rest in tangled, cursing heaps against the walls.

His scream echoed through the cloying underworld where evil lurked. "I *will* find you Talial. I *will* destroy you."

Then the darkness lightened perceptibly, the frost in the air dissipated. And he was gone.

After it was over, Jack sat silently in the office of Marcus Bentley. Lewis sat next to him with a large hand on his shoulder. It seemed a long time ago. The aftermath of the riot and the deluge of water coming seemingly from nowhere and washing everyone away.

A group of believers had accompanied him to the church. He knew some of their names. Steve, a young girl Ashley—the one with the piercing blue eyes who had stared him out—and James, a softly spoken man carrying a guitar. There were others, but he couldn't recall their names. Only that they had seemed concerned for him. But not half as much as he was for himself.

For in a short space of time, his carefully constructed defence mechanism had come crashing down almost as fast as the wall of water that had levelled the High Street. He had been challenged—seriously and terrifyingly challenged—about his view of God, and he wasn't happy.

"If this is what it feels like to know God, then I'd rather not, thank you very much."

Marcus had understood. "Jack, I don't know anything about you. But I can see that you are shocked. But there is a difference between knowing God and knowing about him."

"Shocked? I'm bloody terrified. What the hell was it that went on out there?" His fear expressed itself in anger and he shook his head uncomprehendingly. "Things like that just don't happen. They don't." He buried his face in his hands and Lewis gripped his shoulder in what he had hoped would be a comforting manner. A bit too tightly, and Jack winced. "Sorry . . ." He lifted his hand. "Jack, it's been scary for us too. I know you don't believe in God as I—as we do. But none of us have ever witnessed anything like this either. None of us. If it's any comfort to you, we're as terrified and bewildered as you are. Only a day or so ago we didn't even believe that God spoke today, let alone do all this stuff."

"Why didn't everyone see what we saw?" asked Jack plaintively. "They were rattling on about thunderstorms and freak weather conditions. Are they blind or something?"

Marcus nodded his head sadly. "Unfortunately, the answer is yes, Jack. Spiritually blind, and deaf as well. People hear what they want to hear sometimes and ignore the evidence of their own ears and eyes."

"But how can they ignore something like this? For God's sake, a bloody—sorry." He realised that he was swearing, and for the first time he felt bad about it—"A huge wall of water swept through the High Street, and washed everyone away." He shook his head again in despair. "I don't understand it."

"Two thousand years ago in New Testament times, God spoke from heaven. He actually spoke in the hearing of a crowd of people." Marcus reached for his Bible, turned to the verse, and began to read.

"The crowd that was there and heard it said it had thundered; others said an angel had spoken to him."

He laid down his Bible. "Can you believe that? God's voice came from heaven, and some said it thundered! It's no different today, Jack. It's part of the sound and the fury of a sinful world. When God speaks, some people hear only noise. All they hear is thunder."

Jack looked up, his face confused. "If God is powerful, and judging by what I've just seen there's no doubting that, why does he just let the world go its own way? Why does he let evil things happen and do nothing? Why doesn't he just sort it out?"

"What do you want him to sort out, Jack?" asked Marcus gently. "What is it that's eating you alive?"

Jack shook his head. This pastor guy was certainly perceptive. But he dare not open himself up or venture down the path that his mind was urging him to take. A major plank of his defence had already been demolished. That was the one that said there was no God. He knew that if he allowed himself the luxury of emotion, then he would turn something on that he would be unable to stop. He was petrified of what might spill out. Because he was scared witless that he would become religious. And he hated religion.

"It's your boys, isn't it, Jack?" said Lewis.

Marcus glanced questioningly at Lewis, who placed his hand sorrowfully around his sergeant's shoulders, ensuring that he was gentler this time. "He lost his young sons in a car accident," he explained.

"I'm so sorry. I understand."

Lewis winced then. He had said something very similar once, and Jack had threatened to put him out of the window!

And it did look as though Jack was about to give a similar retort. But something in the tone of Marcus's voice stopped him. The Ds was insensitive. He was usually rude, arrogant and downright mean. But he knew people. And he recognised authenticity. And that is what he was hearing right then in the pastor's voice.

"It's not the same I know, but I have lost a child too," said Marcus sadly.

Jack had never really considered the fact that other people could be aching just as much as he was. Self-pity had formed a protective enclosure around him, a shield that nothing and no-one had been able to penetrate. But the tragedy was that the self-imposed walls he had erected in order to protect his hurting soul, had also acted as a prison, rendering him unable to experience the outside world. And cut off from human contact of any meaningful kind, he had grown insular from the needs and feelings of others. So experiencing sorrow for another was something quite new to him.

"I haven't shared this with many people," said Marcus, "but my wife Lissie and I lost a baby two years ago." The grief was clear on his face. "It was a little boy. A beautiful little boy. We'd decorated his bedroom." Marcus smiled fondly at the memory. "It's a bit of an old fashioned thing to do, but we decorated it all in blue. The wallpaper had little teddy bears on it . . ." He had to stop then.

For the first time in years, Jack felt his heart go out to the man who was sharing from the very depths of his heart.

"Excuse me," said Marcus apologetically as he recovered his composure, "I didn't realise it was still so raw." He wiped his eyes. "Everything was ready for the birth and we were so excited. Lissie went into hospital the day before he was due and I left her there, expecting to be bringing my boy home quite soon." He stared at the floor. "We had named him Noah you know. But it was not to be. He died during delivery. There were complications . . ."

Jack instinctively reached out a hand and clasped Marcus's, and they both sat silently, sharing the grief of loss. Marcus wept for Noah, and Jack ached for Jamie and Andrew.

Lewis got up, and silently left the room.

Jack was with Marcus for some time. And during those moments he shared for the first time the experience of grief that had weighed him down and taken his life from him. He held nothing back, expressing his anger and rage, and the fear of loneliness. The wasting effect of hopelessness and helplessness on his life. He spoke of the loss of his wife and his implacable hatred for God. And his heartfelt contempt for those who leant on the crutch of religion.

"Marcus, I know that there is a God. I have seen his power. But I'm not sure if I want to know him. A lot of people died today."

Marcus gave him a sympathetic smile. "I guess he's God and we have to accept the way he does things. That doesn't make it any easier I know, but it helps me to live with it."

"And I have so many questions. What has Jesus got to do with it all? What does it mean that God send his son to die? Having lost my sons, that's one of the things I find impossible to understand. I wouldn't willingly give my sons up for anybody."

Marcus listened understandingly. "I know it's difficult. But let me tell you a story. If you have the time? It will help you to understand perhaps."

"This moment is probably the most important in my life. I have to make time. If I don't press on with this now, it will never happen again for me." He was sad for a moment. "Perhaps I will convince myself that it's all thunder anyway?"

Marcus just started his story.

"There was once a man who didn't believe in God, and he didn't hesitate to let others know how he felt about religion and things, like Christmas."

Jack recognised himself there.

"His wife, however," continued the pastor, "did believe, and she raised their children to have faith in Jesus, despite his antagonism. One snowy Christmas, his wife was taking their children to a Christmas Eve service in the farm community where they lived. She asked him to go with them but he refused. 'It's nonsense!' he said. 'Why would God lower himself to come to Earth as Jesus in the form of a man? That's stupid!' So she and the children left, and he stayed home.

A while later, the winds grew stronger and the snow turned into a blizzard. As the man looked out the window, all he saw was blinding snow.

He sat down in front of the fire for the evening and then he heard a loud thump. Something had hit the window. Then another thump. He looked out, but couldn't see more than a few feet. When the snow eased up a little, he ventured outside to see what it could have been.

In the field near his house he saw a flock of wild geese that had been flying south for the winter. They got caught in the snowstorm. They were lost and stranded on his farm, with no food or shelter. They just flapped their wings and flew around the field in low circles, blindly and aimlessly. A couple of them had flown into his window. The man felt sorry for the geese and wanted to help them."

Marcus paused. "Are you still with me?"

"So far. Geese, right?" responded Jack.

"There is a point," said Marcus as he continued.

"The barn would be a great place for them to stay, the man thought. It's warm and safe; surely they could spend the night until the storm is over?

So he went to the barn and opened the doors wide, then watched and waited, hoping they would notice the open barn and go inside. But the geese just fluttered around aimlessly and didn't seem to notice the barn or realise what it could mean for them.

He tried to get their attention, but that just seemed to scare them and they moved further away. He went into the house and came with some bread, broke it up, and made a breadcrumbs trail leading to the barn. They still didn't catch on.

Now he was getting frustrated. He got behind them and tried to shoo them toward the barn, but they only got more scared and scattered in every direction except toward the barn. Nothing he did could get them to go into the barn where they would be warm and safe.

'Why don't they follow me?' he asked himself. 'Can't they see this is the only place where they can survive the storm?' He thought for a moment and realized that they just wouldn't follow a human. 'If only I were a goose, then I could save them,' he said out loud.

Then he had an idea. He went into barn, got one of his own geese, and carried it in his arms as he circled around behind the flock of wild geese. He then released it.

His goose flew through the flock and straight into the barn—and one by one the other geese followed it to safety.

He stood silently for a moment as the words he had spoken a few minutes earlier replayed in his mind: 'If only I were a goose, then I could save them!'

Then he thought about what he had said to his wife earlier. 'Why would God want to be like us?'

Suddenly it all made sense. That is what God had done. We were like the geese—blind, lost, perishing. God had his Son become like us so he could show us the way and save us. That was the meaning of Christmas, he realised. As the winds and blinding snow died down, his soul became quiet and pondered this wonderful thought. Suddenly he understood what Christmas was all about, why Christ had come.

Years of doubt and disbelief vanished like the passing storm. He fell to his knees in the snow, and prayed his first prayer: 'Thank You, God, for coming in human form to get me out of the storm!'"

As Marcus finished, Jack knew that there could be only one answer for him. If he was to get out of the storm, he knew clearly what his response had to be. He had to trust in the one who came to show him the way.

Before he could change his mind, he knelt there and then to make his commitment to God. To trust Jesus Christ with his eternal soul. He realised that the tough kernel he had contrived around his life was just a façade. A hiding place. He knew beyond doubt that he was a man who needed saving.

So Jack Somerville surrendered his toughness and his anger. He let go of his hatred. He gave his life to Jesus. He acknowledged his Lordship in his life, his death on the cross, and the salvation that he alone could bring to a lost world. And as he made that commitment, God honoured it in a special way.

The floodgates of his sorrow burst open like the fountains of the deep, as for the first time in years he cried. And as the water of his tears soaked into the bareness of his dry and thirsty soul, so new life began to spring into being in the arid places of his heart. And once he'd started, he couldn't stop. He sobbed uncontrollably, and as he did so, kneeling in a crumpled heap on the carpet, all the pain and loneliness of the years flowed out of his body and soul. He prayed to a Father who, two thousand years ago had lost his own Son. Like the goose, he'd sent him into the world to show mankind the way, and they had killed him.

A strange sensation, like that of being enveloped in a warm blanket descended upon him, and he found that he was helpless on the floor. Whether he dreamed, or whether he saw visions, he never really understood. But one thing he knew. He knew that God was there. And that was all that mattered. And he never discussed what he experienced with anyone. Ever.

Marcus had some idea, because he heard him lovingly speak two names. He whispered the names of Jamie and Andrew. And there was delight on his lips as he did so.

And ever afterwards, he expressed his total, rock-solid, unshakeable conviction that his boys were with the Lord, and that he *knew* he would see them again one day.

They were interrupted by a knock on the door. It was Steve Coleman, and he came in without waiting to be asked.

His face was red, and he had obviously been weeping. "Sorry to intrude," he said, observing Jack kneeling on the floor, "but I thought you would want to know."

Marcus could see the distress on his face. "What's up Steve?"

Steve tried to speak, choked on the words and then tried again. "It's Henry," he said at last, "he's dead."

There was a stunned silence. Then Marcus spoke.

"How?" he whispered.

Steve motioned for them to follow him, and he led the way into the main meeting hall. Both Jack and the pastor were surprised to see that it was packed with people. Some were sitting silently, their heads in their hands. Others were kneeling, and praying. Some were holding hands together and speaking quietly.

"I was with him in the hospital when it happened," said Steve. "I rang James as soon as it happened and when I got back from the hospital, everyone was here."

Marcus gazed out at the congregation that had come to pray for their town, and had ended up praying for a departed brother. His heart swelled as he saw them love each other in a new way. They were inexorably drawn to share their sorrow and love for the old man as a church family.

Jack had a pretty good idea who Henry was. It had to be the old chap who had fallen when the shield bearers were clearing the riot area.

They retreated to a corner of the hall, but there was nowhere really private as the place was crammed full of people.

"I was at his bedside when he died," said Steve tearfully. "You remember that he was taken off by ambulance?"

They nodded silently.

"I couldn't believe it when I saw him. He was grinning broadly for all the world as if he was having the most exciting time of his life."

"Perhaps he was," said Marcus, mindful of the joy he had seen in Henry following his baptism in the Holy Spirit.

Steve agreed. "He said he was looking forward to seeing Ruby again."

"Ruby?" asked Jack.

"His wife," said Marcus and Steve simultaneously.

"She died some years ago," continued Marcus, "and he has missed her dreadfully."

"He wanted me to say goodbye to everyone," said Steve. "But he was looking forward to going home." He chuckled. "He said that he had never owned his own place, so was looking forward to moving into the home that God had built for him. He said he had held the title deeds to a piece of heaven for over seventy years, and was looking forward to making his claim!"

The three of them smiled fondly at the sentiments of their old friend.

"He's with the Lord now," said Marcus, "and his loneliness is over."

"I'm so sorry he's dead," said Jack.

"So am I," responded Marcus, "But I'm so glad that he lived."

As James strummed his guitar, the people of Hartwood Community Church sang. Their voices were as broken as their hearts, but still they offered songs of praise to a loving God. And then, wonder of all wonders, soaring above them, they heard the voice of an angel. Not a celestial being, but the voice of Ashley Coleman. The glorious sound rang through the meeting place, strong and loud. Borne along by the wings of the Holy Spirit, she was lifting her voice to her newly found saviour, singing from the very depths of her being. All the hatred and turmoil of her short, but troubled life had been transformed into a thing of beauty under the almighty hand of a loving heavenly Father.

It was not a song composed of human words. It was the crying and groaning of the Spirit in ways that words could never express. Ashley was singing in a language that none of them had ever heard before. Never had such a sound been heard there. Beautiful and clear. Clear as the tinkling of a crystal bell. Pure, holy and glorious it soared heavenwards in a great parabola of praise.

James began to strum his guitar, providing a background of gentle melody to the song of the Spirit that she sang. And Hartwood Community Church worshipped afresh.

CHAPTER Thirty-Two

It was Thursday evening by the time Jack returned to the station, having at long last caught up on some much-needed sleep. And he had slept well, for the first time in some years. Now there was something altogether different about him. He was lighter in mood and bearing. And the awful dullness of his office was gone too. The weak winter sunlight streaming in the window cast a golden glow across where he was sitting. He was changed, renewed by the Spirit of God. Not yet completely sorted out—that wouldn't happen this side of heaven. But Jack Somerville was on his way.

And no-one was more astounded than his colleagues. Sue in the control room had been treated to the "new" Jack as soon he came in.

"Happy Christmas, Sue," he said. "There will be a visitor asking for me this evening. Can you please show her up to the conference room if you have a moment?"

She was so shocked that she didn't respond, and sat there wondering if he had finally gone off his rocker as he ran lightly up the stairs to his office.

He'd been quite busy in the time since leaving Marcus's office. He'd managed to get hold of a large pack of Christmas Cards emblazoned with the message, "Peace on Earth and Goodwill to Men." That will cause a stir he thought, with a contented smile. Because he'd put them in the pigeon-holes of all his colleagues at the station.

Now he emptied the contents of his briefcase onto his desk. Putting to one side the files containing paperwork, he appraised the remaining items. There wasn't much. Just his notebook, a pair of handcuffs, a plastic bag containing a length of red cord and his police baton in its leather holster. He removed the baton, weighing it carefully in his hand. It was an "ASP," an extending metal weapon constructed of aircraft aluminium. When closed it fitted easily into the leather harness that could be worn undetected beneath a jacket. When racked, a feat that was accomplished by flicking the device skywards with a snap of the wrist, it opened with a satisfying metallic snicking sound, extending to just over eighteen inches in length.

He hadn't had reason to use it for some years. Nevertheless he removed his jacket and buckled it in place, before putting his jacket back on and ensuring that the weapon remained concealed.

Heading for the conference room on the top floor, he placed the bag containing the cord in the top drawer of his desk. Then he sat back to wait.

Michelle Radigan came through the door and regarded Jack curiously across the desk where he was sitting. "Sue said you were up here. What's this all about?"

He indicated the chair the other side of the long table. "Take a pew Michelle. Glass of water or something?"

She shook her head. "I don't have much time Jack, so I'm hoping here that you will get to the point," she said tersely.

"Absolutely. I've made a breakthrough in the murder of Nelson Riley and Ben Mahoney."

DCI Radigan leant forward, her eyes wide with interest. "Well?"

"There's someone else I want here before we start; he should be arriving at any moment."

Jack had no sooner spoken than Peter Lewis charged in. He was breathing heavily, and looked hot and flustered.

"I had to use the stairs," he explained. "The lift is out of order again. What's all this about, sarge?" he said, nodding in acknowledgement to Radigan.

"Sit down," said Jack pleasantly.

"Come on," responded Michelle edgily, "Get to the point Jack. Not the Poirot denouement *please.*"

Lewis glanced across at the DCI.

"Jack thinks he's made a breakthrough in the murder," she said by way of explanation.

Lewis sat heavily into the empty chair next to Jack and opposite DCI Radigan. "Then you'll probably find it more Holmes than Poirot," he muttered.

Ignoring the comments, Jack stood up and checked his wristwatch. "I don't *think* I've made a breakthrough. In fact, I now *know* who was responsible for the killing of Nelson Riley!"

There was a total hush in the room.

"Who?" demanded Michelle.

"In good time. Let me just go back over the scenario, to recap the events. That way, all will become clear."

Jack leant with his back to the window so that he could see both Michelle and Lewis. "We were called initially to the office of Mr. Cooper after receipt of an anonymous '9' call." He paused. "Incidentally, that informant has never been traced, which strikes me as a tad curious." He continued. "Anyway, upon police arrival, Mr. Riley was found dead on the floor, and Mr. Cooper unconscious nearby and bleeding heavily from a head wound."

Lewis fidgeted in his chair. "Jack, we all know that bit."

Michelle nodded. "We do," she said firmly, "I am going to have to ask you to get to the point, Jack."

Jack was determined to have his moment, and carried on regardless. "Riley had been garrotted with a length of cord. Someone with great strength must have done that, mustn't they Lewis?"

He stared hard at the Dc, before wheeling around to face Michelle.

"Whoever did this probably had a knowledge of Thugee. What do you think, Michelle?"

"Thugee?" she said.

"Correct," said Jack. "Wait." He rummaged in his desk and brought out the sealed bag containing the length of red cord. Tearing it open he threw it on the desk. Lewis regarded it with distaste.

"Jack," said Michelle, "this is all very interesting, but what evidence do you have to support anything you are saying? Thugee indeed, I've never heard of it."

"I'm getting there," he responded. "So, the investigation went on. But we got nowhere. It seemed that someone was against us. Someone was leaking information."

"Sarge, that sounds a bit paranoid to me," suggested Lewis. "Are you saying there was a spy in the camp?"

"More than that. I'm saying there was—is—a murderer in the camp!"

Lewis let out his breath in astonishment.

Radigan got to her feet and moved towards the door. "I've heard enough Jack. This is pure fantasy."

"What about the suicide of a young boy named Nathan Mahoney twelve years ago? The one you investigated? Was that also fantasy?"

Her face went white and she sat back down again abruptly. "What are you implying detective sergeant Somerville?" All of a sudden she was officious.

"You were a detective sergeant yourself at the time. You were in charge. You investigated the suicide after the boy was found hanging in the woods."

She was angry now. "And the inquest rightly found that he killed himself while suffering from depression. There was nothing fantastical about that. I did my job."

Lewis interrupted. "The detective chief inspector's right. What has this to do with Riley?"

"It has everything to do with him. Cooper was right when he said in interview that Riley was a nonce. Nathan killed himself because Riley was committing indecent acts against him," rasped Jack. "He turned to his 'church,' the evil outfit run by Benedict Ademola for help. He got none and eventually he could take no more and saw the only way out was to take his own life."

"Never!" exclaimed Michelle.

"And Cooper found out and blackmailed him," continued Jack.

"So . . ." said Lewis slowly, "Riley arranged to meet with Cooper to put an end to the blackmail? But Cooper overpowered him?"

"It seems possible," said Jack. "What really happened there we may never know. But as I said earlier, I have discovered who was ultimately responsible for the murder of Riley. That person and the one who actually carried out the act are entirely different people."

"Jack." The DCI spoke quietly. "We need evidence of this. It all sounds very interesting, but there *isn't* a shred of evidence."

Jack returned to his desk draw once again. "Yes there is." He held up a CD disc. "This is a copy of a short film clip found on Cooper's computer. It shows everything." He threw it on the desk in disgust.

There was silence for a while. Then Lewis said, "So, Jack, there's a link between the boy and Riley, and perhaps that was the reason for Riley's death. But I still don't understand. Why for instance was Mr. Mahoney killed?"

"Because he told you too much."

"Me?"

"You went to see him. And he indiscreetly mentioned Riley and Benedict Ademola. From the moment he mentioned Benedict, he was a dead man."

Michelle was impatient. "We are wandering away from the point here. I have heard of Mr. Ademola and I do not believe that he would be involved in anything criminal. Who are you suggesting would have killed an insignificant person like Ben Mahoney?"

"The same person who killed Nelson Riley."

Jack turned to Lewis. "Why did you do it, Peter?" he said sadly.

Lewis leaped to his feet, and stood opposite the Ds, his face flushed red. "Have you gone mad? Are you accusing me of killing? I'm a police officer for goodness sake. And after last night at the church, I thought . . ."

"I wanted to trust you Peter, even though you have been acting suspiciously. But you let your guard down. I didn't trust you the moment I saw you. And the DCI here confirmed that suspicion." Jack glanced at Michelle. She was sitting silently, just watching.

"I don't suppose the DCI will mind me telling you, Lewis, that she was so suspicious she asked me to keep an eye on you. Which I did. And it's just as well that I did."

Radigan nodded silently in affirmation.

Jack went on relentlessly. "As I said, it has been obvious for some time that information was leaking out of the office. And evidence going missing. For instance the CD we recovered from Riley's flat. You're the only one other than me who knew about it. Yet it went missing from my computer."

Lewis started to interrupt, but Jack stopped him. "Someone searched my office. It was obvious that they were looking for the Mahoney file." Jack fished in his pocket and brought out an envelope, emptying it into his palm. Out rolled a gold police insignia cuff-link. "I noticed that you wear these. I found this one under my computer where no doubt it fell during your hurried ransacking of my office."

"That's crazy," responded Lewis.

"Then you went to see Ben Mahoney. That had nothing to do with the murder investigation that we were supposed to be working on. Why did you do that?"

"Hey, you know why . . ."

"You're wasting your time. I don't think that it's a coincidence that he was found dead after you had visited him."

"You're nuts." He turned to Michelle for support. "For goodness sake, this is getting out of hand! Are you going to let him continue with this rubbish?"

It seemed that she was, because she sat there and made no attempt to intervene.

"And you are the perfect strong man to have garrotted both men. You saw the state of their bodies. Their necks were almost severed. It would have taken someone very powerful to do that. Someone like you Lewis." Jack looked disgustedly at the detective. "There's nothing as bad as a bent copper. You disgust me."

"I think you've finally gone off your rocker. Absolutely off your head. Probably something to do with those dead boys of yours that you won't let go of."

The insult about his sons was too much for Jack. and now he exploded into a fearsome rage. He had studied martial arts for many years, and although he'd not practiced for some considerable time now, there was still the residual of years of dedication. And combined with sheer anger he was a formidable aggressor. He literally threw himself at Lewis, his sudden charge catching the huge man off-guard, and almost toppling him to the floor. He followed up simultaneously with a back-hand strike to the jaw. A lesser man would have dropped like a stone. But Lewis soaked it up, the only indication that he was hurt was a quick shake of his head.

He quickly regained his wits and his balance, and struck back at Jack with a huge hand. There was no finesse. No technique. Just raw strength. And he felled him in an instant.

Although struggling, Jack was far from finished, staggering back to his feet and circling painfully around the hulking man in front of him. He raised his hands, palms open in a defensive attitude, ready to parry any blows but also prepared to strike as an opening appeared.

Lewis threw another punch. It was clumsy and unscientific. It was obvious that Lewis had never fought much in his life. But then he had never had to, even when at school. His size was daunting, and there were very few people who had ever summoned the nerve to fight with him.

Jack blocked the punch with his forearm, letting it slide along its length so as to dissipate its power. He knew from experience that to take the full impact of a powerful blow directly was just as likely to cause the limb to break. So he slipped the punch, twisted underneath Lewis' outstretched arm, and hit him with an open palm strike to the sternum. He was rewarded with a stifled grunt of pain.

Taking advantage of the momentary advantage he'd gained, he retreated to the far side of the desk so as to put it between him and the man mountain, who was now seriously irritated.

Glancing quickly to the side, he saw that Michelle had jumped to her feet and was now standing with her back against the door watching, her eyes wide.

"Give up, Lewis," puffed Jack, wiping a trickle of blood from his swollen mouth, "you can't go anywhere. There's nowhere you can hide." He flashed a glance at the DCI, not wanting to risk taking his concentration too much off of the angry giant. He packed a mean punch, and he didn't want to soak up too many of those. "Michelle," he shouted, "get some assistance in here."

But Radigan stayed where she was, making no attempt to move.

Lewis said nothing. Striding quickly forward, he flung the desk aside as though it were matchwood, scattering its contents across the office as he simultaneously caught Jack around the throat with a single hand. He took him straight to the ground where skill mattered least. Brute strength was now king. He leant over his prostrate victim, his body totally enveloping Jack, and began to choke him.

From the breathless gasps, it was sounded as though death would be soon for Jack unless someone rescued him. But that didn't seem likely. Radigan still stood frozen making no attempt to intervene.

Jack struggled ineffectually to pull Lewis' hand away from his throat, just so that he could suck in some air. He wormed his hand between Lewis' and his throat, and managed to relieve a little of the pressure. His legs were threshing wildly as he struggled, and a foot caught the waste basket, sending it spinning across the office, spreading its contents in an arc over the carpet. But even as he fought, his eyes were wildly looking around for a weapon of some sort. Jack had never given up in a fight. And he wasn't going to give up now. But Lewis was so much stronger than he.

Something brightly coloured caught his eye. Where the desk had been upturned, it had scattered its contents and he could see the red "Thugee" cord on the floor near his left hand. To reach it meant that he would have to take his hand off of Lewis' hand, the one that was around his throat. It was just out of reach of his outstretched arm, so he would have to manoeuvre nearer if he was to stand any chance of getting hold of it.

He took a deep breath, then shouted, "Michelle!" Simultaneously he snatched his hand away from Lewis, arched his back throwing his opponent off balance, and gained the necessary space required to move to one side.

His fingers scrabbled wildly on the carpet for a long moment before closing over the cord. Scooping it up he flung it in the direction of Radigan.

She moved quickly from her position at the door, her outstretched fingers scratching the cord up from the ground. Quickly she leapt on Lewis, looped the cord around his neck. And began to pull it tight.

Immediately the pressure on Jack's throat was gone. As big as Lewis was, the ferocity of Radigan's attack arched his neck backwards, as the cord began to bite into his windpipe. For such a slim woman, she was amazingly strong.

It was then that Jack crawled from underneath the big detective, quickly removing his "ASP" from its concealed holster and racking it open with a deft flick of his wrist. Raising it high above his head, he brought it down in a vicious sideways forty-five degree angle cutting blow.

It missed Lewis's head by inches, and impacted the shoulder blade of the DCI with a sickening thud. She fell backwards with a squeal of pain, and the cord fell from her hands. Even as she did so a look of comprehension filled her eyes, eyes that had taken on a red tinge.

"You set me up," she hissed, scrabbling desperately backwards and away from Jack, her arm dragging uselessly at her side. "And you've broken my arm."

"Well done, Lewis," said Jack, stooping to pick up the cord. "In fact a bit too well done. You almost choked the life out of me."

Lewis grinned hugely, rubbing his throat where the cord had started to bite. An angry red weal had already started to appear just above his collar line.

"Sorry boss," he said affably, seemingly unaffected by the attempt to garrotte him, "but you did say it had to look right. And I'm sorry I threw in the bit about your sons. I know we didn't plan for me to say anything like that, but I genuinely wanted you to be angry with me and that was the one sure way I knew would produce the right effect."

He nursed the area of his face where Jack had struck him. It would soon be a nice blue bruise. "I thought you were going to break my jaw."

Jack shrugged. "Operational necessity." He walked to the door and shouted down the corridor. "You can come in now."

The two uniformed officers who entered stared with disbelief at the wreckage in the office.

"Strewth," said Tony Lewis, "it sounded as if the whole building was being torn apart."

"Just as well you said not to come in under any circumstances until you called," said Lloyd, the other officer, "we were getting a bit worried about you." He looked at Lewis. "Not him though, he's big enough to look after himself."

Lewis winked good naturedly, although even that gesture appeared threatening coming from his scarred face.

"Thanks guys," responded Jack. "I owe you both one. How's the driving coming on by the way Tony? You were rubbish last time I was with you."

Tony sneered good humouredly. "Got you out of a scrape anyway, didn't I?" Then as an afterthought. "How's the injury to your side by the way? Didn't you get poked by some wuss with a stick?"

Jack grimaced. "It's nothing compared to the pasting I've just taken from the BFG here," he said nodding towards Lewis, and Tony nodded understandingly.

His demeanour changed abruptly as he walked slowly up to Michelle, who was still sitting on the floor with her back against the wall, muttering incomprehensibly to herself and nursing her limp arm. The good-natured banter vanished as, bending over, he grasped a handful of her hair in his hand.

"No, sarge." Lewis came quickly forward. "Remember, you are now a Christian. Don't revert to unnecessary violence. She'll get her just punishment for what she has done."

"Him a Christian?" exploded Tony with a laugh, and would have said more but for the warning glance from Lewis.

The word "Christian," had a dramatic effect on Michelle. Previously she had remained sitting quietly on the floor, her face impassive. But *that* word galvanised her into action.

Almost crab-like, she scuttled backwards, causing Jack to lose his grip on her. She continued to retreat until she was prevented from further movement by the wall underneath the window. She leaned against it, oblivious to her arm hanging down limply at her side. Her eyes were crimson points of hatred, her lips drawing back over her teeth in a startling manner, spittle flecking as she spat out her words. Her voice had taken on a deep, guttural sound that made everyone in the room instinctively recoil from her. "Christian? You think that changes anything?" she croaked. "You think you have won. But you haven't. They don't want him."

"What are you talking about?" said Jack impatiently.

She moved her head towards him slowly, before answering.

"He knows." She inclined her head towards Lewis, laughing in a most disconcerting manner.

Tony and the other officer stood in amazement while this was going on. Michelle had obviously gone off her head.

"They. The people out there." She waved a hand in the direction of the town. "They don't want your God. They don't want sweetness and light. They have rejected him!"

"Get her out of here," said Lewis.

"Wait." Jack went forward and grasped her hair again firmly in his hand.

CHAPTER THIRTY-THREE

In a wood at the edge of Hartwood, Aanfial had gathered his command of angels around him. Talial was there, and many of the brave warriors that had taken the Community Church from the grasp of evil. The countless legions released by God to cleanse Hartwood had long since departed back to heaven.

"Praise God," he intoned. "And now it's time for most of us to depart earth. Those of you who are remaining already know who you are. Take care of those that God has entrusted to you."

There were nods and smiles, the shaking of hands and warm goodbyes.

There was just one piece of unfinished business. Slumped by a tree in the corner of the field, bound fast by angelic cords, was the demon Barbas. He was a pitiful sight. His body broken and distorted as he lay, a twisted pathetic bundle of misery. His underlings had either fled, or were dead—banished to the abyss to be dealt with by Adonai. He was alone. And afraid. And dangerous.

"What do we do with this one?" exclaimed the captain.

There came the sound of a dozen swords being drawn, and incandescent light split the darkness as they were unsheathed. But the many offers to deal with him were suddenly interrupted by cries of delight.

Because every eye was suddenly on Auriel as he strode into the clearing. He had always been an awesome sight, but now there was something different. Talial felt his heart surge as he saw it. Auriel was wearing the insignia of a captain of the army of the Lord! He ran forward, and clasped his hand. "Auriel! You are indeed a sight for battle weary eyes."

Auriel hugged Talial and Aanfial in turn, pointed his sword to the heavens and shouted his battle cry; a sound that filled the air, scything through it with such power that the ground itself seemed to shake and the earth tremble.

"To Him who sits upon the Throne and to the Lamb!"

And the glory of God filled the place. It touched the small group of angels with power, and then something totally unexpected happened. The new captain spread his wings. Where once there had been bloody stumps, wings had re-appeared, larger and more majestic than ever—a huge canopy of white feathers. He saluted Talial with his sword, and as he did so both he and his weapon shimmered with the brilliance of purest light.

Barbas, not for the first time in his life, knew fear in his black heart. The first time it had been Bune. Then He whose name dare not be spoken. This time it was the piercing light that blinded him, causing him to throw up his arm in a futile attempt to block it out. But it was everywhere. Remorselessly it enveloped him, penetrating his body and his mind. It filled his eyes and his ears. It fell upon him, burning his leathery flesh as if it were corrosive. He cried out in agony, and shrank back, unable to lift his head before the mighty angel, as he came relentlessly onwards. His sword flashed, singing through the air as he swung it in blinding arcs before him.

And the cords that bound the demon fell at his feet.

Auriel acknowledged the cheers of his comrades. "Give this coward his sword," he whispered, "I don't fight in the same craven way that he does." His eyes were full of anger as he pierced the demon with a gaze of purest light. "Look to yourself Barbas; prepare to meet your death."

The servant of Satan feigned to ignore the sword that was flung at his feet, but he took good care to notice that it was his own. For the first time a look of hope came to his eyes. He was a good swordsman. He knew that. If he could but defeat this young, inexperienced angel, he had a chance at freedom.

He flung himself to the ground at the feet of the majestic warrior standing over him. "Have mercy," he cried in his most pitiful voice. "Does not your God require mercy?"

A roar of anger erupted from the on-looking angels. "Where was your mercy when you mutilated Captain Auriel?" cried one.

"But I have never claimed to show mercy," whined Barbas. "My lord does not demand that. But you claim that yours does. Unless Adonai is a hypocrite?"

The new Captain Auriel raised his sword. "Be careful in what you say. Do not defame the glory of the Lord of Hosts."

"Hold!" Aanfial stepped forward and placed a restraining hand on the angel's sword arm. "He speaks true, Auriel my friend. Our God is a God of infinite mercy. But you are the one who suffered at the hands of this piece of evil. The decision is for you and you alone to make."

For a long moment the new captain stood motionless, his eyes searching the dim red orbs of the broken demon at his feet. Then he sheathed his sword and turned away. "Leave, before I change my mind."

"You are indeed merciful, young angel," whined Barbas, as he began to rise clumsily from the ground. Almost it seemed by accident, his hand closed over his sword. His ragged smock hanging grotesquely around his deformed body covered the movement as he awkwardly attempted to regain his feet. Struck by pity, one of the angelic host began to move forward to assist, his heart moved by the obvious pain of even such contemptuous evil. And as the angel did so, Barbas leapt forward, a misshapen bundle of hatred and deception.

He slashed wildly at the proffered hand of help, causing the angel to fall back with a grunt of pain as the short sword cut across his forearm. Then holding his weapon straight before him, he hobbled towards Auriel with surprising speed, stabbing in a forward motion at his unprotected back.

Before the others could shout a warning, almost at the moment when the black sword of the demon looked sure to pierce Auriel in a fatal strike, the angel whirled away in a move so fast that the eye had difficulty following it.

In a flash of light the glorified angel unsheathed his sword, clashing against the razor sharp sword of the demon deformed in both mind and body, deflecting it from its murderous path in a shower of white hot sparks that exploded like the birth of a Super Nova as the two weapons touched.

Then he moved so fast that he was a blur of impossible speed, lifted his sword above his head and cleaved the demon in two, sending him with a scream of fear into the abyss. A smell like rotten eggs drifted on the air, and the others grimaced with distaste.

"Light has come into the world," intoned Aanfial reverently speaking the Word of the Lord God, "and the darkness has not overcome it!"

There was a moment of silence; Then Aanfial and Talial each placed an arm around Auriel's broad shoulders. "Nice wings my friend," said Talial.

Auriel smiled. "They that wait upon the Lord shall renew their strength. He will lift them as with eagle's wings," he said.

"Shall we get out of this foul smelling place?" suggested Captain Aanfial.

There was no more need for talk, as all three rushed forward together, spiralling up into the night sky. Over Hartwood town, now peacefully sleeping, incandescent light streaked across the heavens with the brilliance of the noonday sun.

Shaun O'Connor was sitting in his garden chair as usual at the rear of his house. His surroundings were covered in white frost. Fresh, crisp, clean.

In his hand was a glass of fresh orange. Earlier that evening he had telephoned his ex-wife, and had also spoken to his daughter. There were no simple answers. There wasn't going to be a quick fix. In fact his wife was very suspicious. But she had managed to talk to him. And for that he was grateful. There was a long way to go, but now there was hope. And while there was hope, as far as he was concerned, there was life.

He'd been thinking quite a lot about God. And angels. In fact he had resolved to go to church on Christmas morning. He raised his glass in salute as a brilliant light spectacular passed overhead, heading away from earth and orbiting up into the star studded sky.

"Thank you, God," he said. And he really meant it.

"Do what thou wilt shall be the whole of the law."

"So mote it be," replied the Bishop. He fingered his unaccustomed clerical collar uncomfortably as he did so.

"So we start again?"

"We do." He placed his hands across his corpulent stomach, straining against his purple shirt and smiled gently, as the demon Bune enveloped him in his familiar, cold embrace. "Our plans are delayed, but that is all. We are not defeated. Already I have this new church."

There came a thin smile. "Then you will need my services again, I expect?"

"I should think so." He reached out a puffy hand for the kneeling figure to kiss his ring of office. "I'll be in touch, *jakushou*," he said, as he closed the door.

Jack made sure that he had a firm grip on Michelle Radigan's hair. "I'm not sure if there is any punishment in this life that will adequately atone for her crimes," said Jack, "but don't worry. I haven't so quickly forgotten the promises I made."

Then he wrenched her hair with a powerful tug.

The faces of those in that office were a picture of shocked disbelief, as the blonde locks came away in his hand, revealing underneath a head of black, short cropped hair.

"Michelle Radigan, alias Carla Lippincott, I am arresting you for the murder of Nelson Riley and Ben Mahoney. You do not have to say anything unless you wish to do so, but it may harm your defence if you fail to mention something that you later rely on in your defence. Anything you say *will* be used in evidence."

She said nothing, but curled back her thin lips and spat forcefully in his direction.

He turned to the two uniformed officers. "Take her out of here." he said.

Lewis followed behind. "I'll brief the custody officer to get her seen by the police surgeon and banged up for the night. Then I think we should get together for tea. I feel we deserve that at least."

"I'm up for that."

"I also deserve an explanation. Who on earth is Carla Lippincott. What was all that about? And why on earth would Michelle want to kill

Riley and Mahoney? It doesn't make sense at all. This whole scenario seems so unlikely."

"Sherlock Holmes once said, that when you have eliminated all possible explanations, whatever is left, however unlikely, is the truth. Meet me for a cup of tea," said Jack, "and I'll reveal that truth to you."

Lewis couldn't resist a mumbled side-swipe at Jack's fictional hero as he left.

"I heard that," said Jack. But he was smiling. Picking up his notebook that had fallen to the floor in the fight he began to write;

9:45pm 24ᵗʰ December. On duty Hartwood Police Station. Arrested Michelle Radigan for murder . . .

The silence was suddenly shattered by a heart-rending scream, followed by the sound of breaking glass and running feet. Tony put his head round the door, his face white with shock.

"Sarge. There was nothing we could do. It was so unexpected." He was breathless with adrenalin rush and he panted out his words. "Why would she do that . . . ?"

Jack hurried out of the conference room and surveyed the scene in the corridor. He was annoyed with himself for not having taken more precautions. He should have expected something. And because of his lack of thought, she had cheated justice after all.

A large full-length window at the top of the landing was obliterated. A few fragments of glass lay on the stairway, but not that many. Most of them were out in the yard three stories down, alongside the broken body of Michelle Radigan which was lying at an impossible angle on the concrete below. Already, uniformed figures were exiting the building and running towards her.

Lewis took his arm. "Come on Jack. Perhaps it was for the best after all. It's not great in prison if you are a copper."

"She got away with it Lewis. After all she's done, she cheated justice."

"Don't you believe it," replied the Dc sorrowfully. "Right now she's facing the judge. And her sentence has already been decided."

"You mean God?"

"Yup. He's *the* judge."

"And he's already decided?"

"No. She decided herself, when she rejected him."

"And the sentence is death?"

"No. The sentence is life. But not the kind of life we would wish on anyone. Instead of eternity in the presence of a loving God, she has an eternity of separation from him."

Jack was stunned. "You mean hell?"

Lewis nodded sadly as he drew Jack away. "Come on sarge, you can't do anything more. It's someone else's job now."

Jack followed, quiet and subdued. The enormity of the judgement of a righteous God was only just beginning to dawn on him.

Jack was sipping tea when Lewis came back.

"Michelle's been taken to the morgue, and the Chief Constable's been informed. He's very concerned and wants the whole circus called out. So in a short space of time we won't be able to move with the HQ lot crawling all over the place. There will be an enquiry of course."

"Well it won't be my concern," said Jack.

"Sorry?"

"I'm retiring."

"Of course, I'd forgotten. When do you go?"

Jack checked his watch. "Five minutes ago," he said tiredly. "But if you still want that tea? Someone needs to have all the facts for the enquiry, don't they?"

CHAPTER Thirty-Four

"Something wasn't right at the start," said Jack. He was sat with Lewis in the otherwise empty police canteen. "I couldn't put my finger on it," he continued, "but things were going wrong."

Lewis nodded. "Yeah. Someone was interfering in the investigation."

Jack was embarrassed for a moment. "I really did think it was you at first."

The other man held his hands up as if to say, "me?"

"I didn't like you from the first."

"My good looks put you off, then?" Lewis laughed.

"I'm sorry. I allowed my dislike of you to colour my view of what was happening. Instead of being reasonable, I was prepared to believe almost anything if it pointed in your direction."

"Pretty impartial, then?"

"The first thing that caused me some problems was the ransacking of my office. Why would anyone do that? It wasn't until later that I found a file missing. It was the Mahoney one, the boy who killed himself."

Lewis nodded. "I read the file that day in your office. I remember it." He scratched his head and looked thoughtful for a moment. "I reckon it's okay to tell you now. I would have hesitated to tell the old Jack."

"Tell me what?"

"Your ransacked office. It wasn't Michelle. Or me."

"Then who was it? Who else is involved in this that I don't know about?"

Lewis reassured him. "Don't worry. It's not what you think. The person who wrecked your office wasn't looking for anything. Although I reckon Michelle did take advantage of the mess to retrieve the Mahoney file."

Jack was really curious. "Then what was it all about?"

Lewis chuckled delightedly. "It was Simon Green."

"What, the beat officer? The new boy?"

"The same."

"But why. .?"

"Didn't you meet him in the High Street when he was having an altercation with some youngsters being generally a pain?"

The light slowly dawned. "You mean because I put him straight about being too soft, he wrecked my office?" The look of incredulity on Jack's face was a picture.

Lewis laughed. He was enjoying this. "That's dead right. You made him look small, so he thought he would get even with you."

Jack sat silent for a moment. Then he too laughed loudly. "Good for him. He isn't as soft as I thought he was." He collected his thoughts before speaking again.

"Back to the crime. You went to see Ben Mahoney. Unfortunately, that visit led to his death."

"But no-one knew. Except you."

Jack sighed. "I have to take responsibility for that. If I hadn't been so pig-headed I would have taken note of what you were saying. As it was I went to see Michelle and told her everything."

"And so she murdered him?"

"I told her you'd asked Ben about the death of his son, Nathan. That was all it took for his death warrant to be signed. If only I had known. An innocent life would have been saved."

"It's not your fault. How could any of us have known that Michelle was a rogue cop and a murderer? But I still don't understand why she killed him. What had Ben Mahoney and the death of his son to do with anything? And why did she kill Riley in the first place? It doesn't make sense."

"It didn't at first," responded Jack, "But things began to fall into place after we had searched Cooper and Riley's homes. You remember the film clip I showed you and Michelle from Cooper's computer?"

Lewis nodded in distaste.

"Well that's not all that was on it. It tied up with the accounts that we removed from Riley's home, you remember?"

Lewis did. "You mean the payments?"

"Exactly. We traced the payments to Cooper's bank account. Putting two and two together, and actually making four for once, it was apparent that Cooper had been blackmailing Riley for some time. He'd filmed him in a compromising position with Nathan Mahoney, probably using the covert briefcase that ironically recorded his violent death."

"But where does the murder of Ben Mahoney come into all this. Why would Radigan involve herself with a small-time blackmailer?"

"We need to go back a bit, to make sense of this. You remember that originally I thought it was you who was up to no good?"

Lewis nodded woefully.

"I realised at long last that I was letting my emotions dictate my views when I called to see your wife."

Lewis raised his thin eyebrows. "She said you'd been to see her."

"There was something that didn't make sense. And after listening to Jane, I knew that you couldn't be the person I had you figured for."

Lewis clapped in mock appreciation. "So all it took for me to gain your trust was a visit to my wife?"

Jack was uncomfortable. "It was more than that, Lewis, but it did put things in perspective. She's an amazing woman isn't she? And I just knew that if she trusted you, then you had to be trustworthy."

Lewis smiled then. "I'll put in a good word for you when I see her later."

"Now, before you start to mock me, as I thought things through a phrase that Sherlock Holmes used kept coming to mind." He looked suspiciously at the Dc, to see if he was laughing.

Lewis's face was impassive.

"I said earlier on, that when you have eliminated all possible explanations, whatever is left, however unlikely, is the truth. Michelle had gone out of her way to make me distrust you. I guess it was her that left this on my desk?" Jack dipped into his pocket and threw the envelope containing the gold cuff-link at Lewis.

The other caught it, his face lighting up. "I had wondered where that had got to." Then it was his turn to look ashamed. "It was actually me, Jack. I was checking a file in your office while you were out. The one about the car accident involving your family?"

"So it wasn't Michelle? How interesting. Anyway, I assumed, wrongly it seems, that she had planted it. Then later she expressed her doubts about you and asked me to keep an eye on you. Which of course I did."

"And?"

"And I suspected you to start with. Especially when we got called out to the Ben Mahoney killing. I left a CD in the computer. You remember, we were about to view it when I got the call from Michelle about the Ben Mahoney murder. When we got back it was missing."

"Someone took the Riley evidence?"

"As it happens, no. I don't get caught out too often Lewis. I may have been a bit slow on the uptake to start with, and I may not have known who, but I knew that *something* was up. So I substituted the CD. And of course, as we were leaving, you went back for the car keys. That made me even more suspicious after I found it had gone."

"So what did you leave instead of the Riley CD?"

"Mozart's piano concertos!"

Lewis laughed loudly at that.

"So everything pointed at you. And of course, you having come off the squad made it seem reasonably likely." Before Lewis could protest at that, Jack went on quickly.

"But anyway, as I said, that was before I saw your wife. So, I had to rethink. Who would gain by the deaths of Riley and Mahoney? Who wanted to stop us viewing the Riley CD? Who was capable of killing by garrotting, and not just a crude strangulation, but a trained hand?"

Lewis nodded understandingly as Jack went on.

"Another thing I don't understand Lewis." He fixed the Dc with unblinking eyes. "I did a bit of door to door after Ben Mahoney was murdered. A neighbour reported an unusually large man—that had to be you—calling at the house during the morning."

The Dc nodded in agreement. "That was me."

"The witness said that after you left the house by the front door, you then went down the side of the house and around the back. You were gone for quite some time."

Lewis put up a gloved hand. "Stop. I need a tea refill. What about you?"

They paused for a while, and then, suitably refilled, Lewis continued where they had left off.

"Whilst talking to Ben Mahoney, I sensed that there was someone else in the house. There was a tray on the table with two cups on it. Mahoney had just got out of bed, so he couldn't have had visitors. So someone was in the house. Someone he didn't want me to know about. So after I left I went around the back to see if I could spot anyone."

"And?"

"I did. There was a woman there. Smart looking, in a suit. She seemed a bit out of place in that untidy hole."

Jack nodded, a smile on his face. "That woman was Brenda Marney. She is—or at least was—Ben's wife."

It was Lewis's turn to look amazed. "You said Brenda Marney. Wasn't Ben's name Mahoney?"

Jack corrected him contentedly. "That's a common mistake. You see 'Mahoney' should in fact be pronounced 'Marney,' although most people pronounce it to rhyme with 'phoney.' All Brenda did was to change the spelling."

"So she was Nathan's mother?"

Jack nodded and continued. "She and Ben split up after Nathan's suicide, and she went to work for Benedict. Seems a bit strange considering that he and the church had a part to play in her son's death. But perhaps we'll discover that when we speak to her. That's if we ever get the chance."

Lewis raised his eyebrows. "Why, is she on the run too?"

"No. She's locked up in a secure mental facility at the moment. Seems she has gone totally insane. The neighbours found her running down the street in her nightdress screaming her head off. They called out our boys and they immediately did a section 136 under the Mental Health Act. We don't know what happened yet."

"I can't understand why she would ever work for Benedict?" responded Lewis, "unless she was unaware about his covering up Riley's involvement in the suicide of Nathan?"

Jack shook his head. "I don't know. But she seems too smart to have been taken in by Benedict. Perhaps she was playing some devious game of her own, and it went wrong? Anyway, there are a lot of questions about this case that I don't know the answers to. And perhaps never will. We're having to make a lot of assumptions at the moment."

He was thoughtful for a moment before speaking again.

"And you had a bruise on your face, Lewis. Cooper said in interview that he managed to hit out at whoever attacked him that night in his office. That could have been you."

Lewis rubbed his cheek. "I see. Well, I really did walk into the door frame in the dark as I told you."

Jack nodded. "Of course I know that *now*. But at the time . . ."

Lewis looked aggrieved, and Jack continued.

"Then I thought about Michelle. She had called me to her office to sow the seed of doubt in my mind about you."

"As if she needed to do that!"

"Actually, it was as well that she did. Because she over did it. That made me suspicious too. Anyway, when I went to her office, something struck me about her as unusual. She was wearing make-up. And she never does that. It didn't make sense at the time, but after I began to suspect her, I realised that she was the attacker that Cooper had hit, and the make-up was to hide the bruising."

"Sherlock Holmes would have been impressed."

Jack stared suspiciously at Lewis for signs of a smirk. He didn't see one. "The garrotting intrigued me," he continued. "Sorry Lewis, but there you were again. It was obviously carried out by someone very powerful. The chips were stacking up against you. But I'm going back on myself here. As I said, I had taken you out of the frame. But having done that, I wasn't sure who to put in your place."

"Why did it have to be a police officer? That's a bit unusual, you must confess. And Michelle wasn't particularly strong, was she?"

"Well the strength bit threw me for a while. Michelle was a bit on the scrawny side. Then I remembered something that happened when I was getting the Incident Box off of the shelf in the store room. It was heavy, and it slipped. I thought I was going to fall off the chair and break my neck. Fortunately Michelle was there, and she helped me with the box. I didn't think anything of it at the time." He remembered what it was that had been occupying his mind at that moment. It was the thought of having to work with Lewis. Jack didn't think it wise to share that piece of information.

"It was when I saw the two police officers struggling with it at the murder scene that my brain tried to tell me something. The penny didn't drop at the time, but it did later. That box was *very* heavy, and yet Michelle swung it to the floor easy as anything."

He scratched his head thoughtfully. "So, when you have eliminated all possible explanations, whatever is left, however unlikely, is the truth. I had forgotten to apply that. So I never factored in the possibility of the DCI being the culprit all along! If I had, perhaps Ben Mahoney at least might have lived. Ironically, it was because of his murder and the missing CD, as well as the other things that didn't quite add up that made me think, no pun intended, outside the box."

"Such as?"

"Well . . ." He paused as the canteen telephone rang. Lewis answered it. "There's a young lady downstairs in the front office asking to see you. Says her name is Lorna Brooks."

Jack nodded. "Ask someone to bring her up, would you?"

"Sit down, Lorna," said Jack as she almost loped into the canteen area. "Your timing is perfect. This is Lewis."

Lewis smiled at the dark haired woman in front of him, and she smiled back, an easy, confident smile.

"Lewis, this is Lorna Brooks. Sergeant Lorna Brooks from the covert unit."

"Covert unit?"

"Do you want to explain," said Jack, turning to the young woman. "I've been talking non-stop for the last half-an-hour and I could do with a break."

"Of course." No longer the breathy young girl that she had earlier portrayed, her voice was now smooth and assured. She faced Lewis as she began to fill him in on the events that had been talking place.

"First of all Lewis . . . That can't possibly be your name can it?"

"It's actually Peter," he said, for some reason stammering as he did so.

"That's better. I don't know why Jack calls you Lewis. Peter is a much nicer name. So, Peter, once I've told you what I know, please forget that you've ever met me."

Lewis nodded. "Consider it done," he said, but he knew it would be a hard job to forget this self-assured young woman in a hurry.

"I work for the government, police, armed forces—in fact any of our agencies who require an undercover operative. I was tasked with infiltrating a sect called 'Awakening!' led by a man known as Apostle Benedict Ademola from a church in Hartwood."

Lewis was surprised. "I didn't know our paymasters were interested in sects?"

Lorna smiled sweetly. "It depends on what they are up to, Peter. In this case it was known that large sums of money were being diverted from the UK to various unstable regimes abroad. Benedict was behind it. He used his so-called church as a cover. His real aim was to fund anti-Christian organisations, and he in effect was propping up a whole ragbag of disillusioned groups, some of them with the potential to go nuclear over the next few years. Stability in one particular third-world country was severely threatened by his interference."

"May I just cut in a moment Lorna," said Jack. He held up a CD disc. "This is the CD you discovered in Riley's flat, hidden in a book."

"A Bible."

"Excuse me?"

"It wasn't just a book. It was the Holy Bible," said Lewis.

"You're right," said Jack. "Anyway, this CD showed all the accounts that Benedict had paid his money into over a period of years. And it was umpteen millions. It showed links to terrorist organisations and other disaffected groups around the world that he used in his quest."

"His quest?" asked Lewis.

"He wanted to usher in a new age," said Lorna. "An age of lawlessness and satanic evil. He believed that if only he could somehow discredit Christian organisations, and attract nominal Christians to his beliefs, he could somehow unleash the power of Satan and bring about a paradigm shift in world history. He wanted a world where people were unfettered by religion. He wanted everyone to be able to do whatever they wanted." She laughed. "That's anarchy of course and would never work. But I think he was right in so far as religion is concerned. We would all be a lot better off if the traditional concept of God was finally laid to rest. And as for Satan! Of course we know that that is all rubbish, but he believed it, and he became dangerous."

"So," said Lewis, "you don't actually believe in Satan?"

"Goodness, no," said Lorna, "nobody seriously believes in that stuff today, do they?"

Lewis did not respond, but made a mental note to speak to her about the reality of good and evil if he ever got the chance.

"Mind you, I did have a queer experience when I was in Benedict's house." She could picture how Benedict had succeeded in conjuring up the goddess Kali. She shuddered, and erased the memory from her mind. She had almost come to believe that it had been real. So she quickly moved on. "But that's another story."

Lewis took advantage of her pause to pick up on a point. "Jack, can you explain what led to you finally identifying Michelle?"

"It was the sugar."

Lewis was bemused. "That was weird. Whatever did the sugar have to do with murder?"

"Everything. I did some research and found out that the cords we removed from Riley and Mahoney's bodies were similar to those used by the Thugee cult in India. They worshipped Kali, the goddess of war and battle. The Thugee practitioners used sugar in a sacred ritual when they killed, pretty much I suppose as sumo wrestlers throw salt into the ring before they fight."

"But what has India got to do with these murders?"

"I discovered that Michelle had been brought up in India. And that got me thinking."

"So," said Lewis, "When you threw the cord to Michelle during our choreographed fight, what did you expect?"

"Precisely what happened. That was the final piece of the puzzle for me. If she was really trained in Thugee, then she would act instinctively. And of course, as far as she was concerned, you were the suspect. If she killed you in saving my life, then she would be a hero and her problem would go away."

Lewis shook his head slowly. "Hence the Rupee tied into the cords? A sentimental reminder of the old country. I can't believe all this was going on around me and I didn't see it."

"Don't be too hard on yourself Lewis," said Jack, "don't forget that I had Lorna here reporting back to me. That gave me a real head start."

"I think I've got most of it now," said Lewis. "But how did you know that Michelle was this other woman. This Carla you mentioned? And of course, who on earth was Carla anyway and where does she fit in with this?" Lewis was suddenly aware of how little he did know.

"Lorna passed me the names of all the people associated with Benedict Ademola. I just ran them through the system. When I put Carla Lippincott through, it came down to an address in Southend. I got it checked out discreetly, and found out that it was a house owned by Michelle. It didn't take much detective work then to discover that Michelle and Carla was one and the same person."

Lorna took the tale again. "You see Peter, Carla was Benedict's right hand woman. She was not only excellently placed to keep him in the loop of any police activity around his business, but she was also a willing and able killer. He couldn't have asked for a better follower."

"Where is Benedict now?" asked Lewis, "surely he has a few questions to answer?"

"Too true," said Jack. "You will remember what I said earlier? That I knew who was responsible for the murders? Well, I hold Benedict to blame for the murders as much as Carla, or Michelle. It was his directions that she followed, his orders that she carried out."

"Unfortunately, he has vanished," said Lorna. "Crime Squad launched a raid on his home shortly after Carla was arrested. But we were too late, and he'd fled. We have an 'All Ports' warning out, and we hope to intercept him soon. Someone like him will find it very difficult to remain hidden anywhere he goes in the world, and we will have people watching."

She stood up. "I must go now, gentlemen. My people want to debrief me on the operation." She shook hands with Lewis. And then Jack.

"Well," said Lewis, after she was gone, "she certainly plays a dangerous game."

Jack nodded. "Probably far more dangerous than she knows herself," he said.

Lewis looked blank and sat back, but Jack didn't elaborate.

"Whew, that's some story. And it's a good one to end your career on. I don't think I've come across such stuff in all my time in the Job."

"Yeah, you're right. It is a good one to go out on. You know, I never thought I'd be leaving on such a high. I've been dreading retirement for so long."

"Well, make sure that you don't keep to yourself too much. In fact, why don't you come round for Christmas lunch with my wife and me?"

Jack beamed delightedly. Now that he was getting the habit, it came easily to him. And his face looked a whole lot better when he did. "That would be good," he said gratefully.

For the first time since he had known him, Lewis removed his glove, and then Jack understood. He could see the angry red scars that covered his hand and the deformity in his fingers where the heat of fire had welded them together. He extended it towards Jack, who didn't hesitate but shook it warmly.

"Happy Christmas, Jack," he said softly. "Is 1pm all right for you?"

"It sure is. Thanks Lewis." He flexed his wrist. "Would you mind shaking hands again?"

Lewis was bemused. "If you insist." He enveloped Jack's hand in his and shook it. "How's that?"

"That's the strangest thing. I've suffered from arthritis in that hand for so many years. Ever since . . ."

"Ever since you broke your knuckles punching a prisoner in a charge room?"

Jack flushed. "How do you know . . . ? Oh, never mind. Perhaps another time. But the pain has gone, and I can move it properly. The blessed thing is healed!"

Lewis didn't look at all surprised. "There are a few more things in store for you now that you have turned to the Lord," he said. "Wait and see." And he grinned delightedly at the confusion on Jack's face.

Jack turned to leave. "Look," he began awkwardly, "the lunch invitation. I know . . . That's to say, are you sure I would be welcome?"

"Shut up Jack. Just be there."

Jack walked out of the station for the last time as a police officer. He didn't feel sad. He felt overwhelmingly excited, although he couldn't explain why.

As he walked towards home, the snow began to fall thickly, laying down a silent bed of white that covered the dirt and grime of the town, transforming it into a picture of cleanliness and purity. Oddly, it evoked an emotion that he hadn't experienced for a long time. Hope. It seemed an appropriate feeling for Christmas Day.